THE SET UP

Chief sighed. "What is it, Angie?" He gave a long inquisitive look to Billy's clothes spread out on the bed. "Aunt Della's worried. You hardly said a word all evening. That ain't the Angie she knows." His quizzical gaze turned in my direction. "What happened in Logan that's got you so upset?"

I knew I was going to have to break it to him sometime. So, exhaling in a mild sigh, I lifted the manila envelope and dumped my cousin's things on the bed. Then, rising to my knees, I laid them out like a blackjack dealer. My grandfather watched without comment.

"These were on Billy when that deputy found him. Notice anything strange?"

Chief shook his head slowly.

"According to the Highway Patrol, Billy was doing some logging in the Topanas. He was using a chainsaw when a heavy limb fell out of the top branches. It struck him on the back of the head. Fractured his skull. The sheriff up there says it was an accidental death."

"What are you getting at, Angie?"

"You remember that tobacco pouch we made for Billy when he came back from Panama?"

Chief's gaze darted to the bedspread, and his expression changed. Slight narrowing of the eyes. Sudden tightening of the mouth.

"This is everything that was at the scene, Chief."

"Could be the sheriff's men missed it." His voice was deceptively calm as he played the devil's advocate. "A red squirrel could have come along . . . dragged the pouch to its den."

"Bullshit!" I snapped. "They set it up nice and pretty, Chief. But Billy was Nuche, heart and soul, and he would never, ever touch a living tree without first making the offering. Never. Th-they killed him, Chief."

AN ANGELA BIWABAN MYSTERY

DYNAMITE PASS

J. F. TRAINOR

ZEBRA BOOKS
KENSINGTON PUBLISHING CORP.

For Mom, Dad, Maureen and Carolyn

"Necessity is the mother of taking chances."
Mark Twain

Chapter One

He was an old man, and he clubbed the big blue dance drum with a slender willow wand. He was *Nuche*, like my uncle Matt and cousin Bill, a huge, bull-shouldered fellow in a crisp white shirt and an eagle-bone choker. Many years at powwow had taught him precisely where the shade of our makeshift arbor would be at two o'clock, and there he sat in his foldout chair, cloaked in cool shadow, while the dancers—me included—sweltered under a torrid Utah sun.

Standing beneath the awning of brittle branches, I surveyed the crowd. Pretty good turnout for the annual Northern Ute powwow. Nuche people lined the inside of our sagebrush dance corral. Just beyond the fence stood a goodly number of the new people— those displaced Europeans who have been hanging around our continent for the past few centuries. Genus: tourist; species: out-of-state. Plenty of baseball caps and worn Levis and cotton T-shirts with silk-screened vistas of Operation Desert Storm.

The old man reached for the microphone. Nerve-tingling squeal from the loudspeakers. He waited for

7

it to subside, then began his song. The tune blended perfectly with the drumbeat, a haunting melody that was old when the Nuche first glimpsed the Great Salt Lake.

"Taw mana, taw mana, way-ha-ha!"

It was both a prayer song and an invitation to this visiting princess to come and dance. I would be honoring the ancestors, and in particular, Uncle Matt and Aunt Della, whose guest I was. Rising on tiptoes, I arched my back and readied myself to enter the dance circle.

And now, folks, for your afternoon entertainment, we present that oh-so-charming Anishinabe princess, that dancer extraordinaire and winner of the Miss Ni-Mi-Win title—the lovely and talented Angela Biwaban!

A tourist raised his camcorder, and I wondered how I'd look back there in Des Moines.

Well, if you took Crystal Gayle and painted her copper-brown, trimmed that long, sleek hair a bit, stretched those well-shaped legs, added a quarter-inch of meat to the shoulders and fanny, and upgraded that classy orthodonture into a truly dazzling four-hundred-watt smile, well, that's me, folks. Crystal and I even share the same contralto voice. Trouble is, whenever I sing, I sound like a sick buffalo calf—which is why I'm here in Utah and not in Nashville.

Couple of hours back, I had been properly dressed for powwow, wearing my ceremonial Anishinabe jingle dress. Unfortunately, black velveteen is not the best fabric for a sun-drenched July afternoon in the Wasatch, so I had switched to the garb most favored by young unmarried Nuche women. The Ute casual

8

look. Hair long and wavy. Big turquoise loop ear-rings. Sleeveless aqua V-neck tank and roll-cuff denim shorts.

As the others took up the prayer song, I gave my eight willow hoops a firm shake and toe-stepped into the circle's center. The step is called a *fancy,* and it's really not too hard—if you've been practicing since babyhood, that is. Bounce, bounce, sidewinding kick. Twirl to the right. Bounce, bounce, kick with the left. Twirl again.

To the drummer's left, three elderly Nuche men in ten-gallon hats played the *woni'thonkunaps.* What's that? Well, try to visualize a miniature hockey stick with serrated teeth. Now, place the stick on a rawhide-covered resonator and run a deer's shinbone up and down the teeth. A very strange and enchanting sound.

I guess the first white men who ever heard it were the friars Escalante and Dominguez, who were wan-dering these mountains the same month Thomas Jef-ferson was writing position papers for that committee in Philadelphia. Uncle Matt's people told them the name was *Nuche,* pronounced *Noo-chay,* but the fri-ars botched it. They pronounced it *Yoo-tah.* Which is a dandy name for a desert state but is not the name of the people Aunt Della married into.

Of course, it had been a while since I'd done the Hoop Dance at powwow. But I hadn't forgotten how. And I was very eager to show all those tourists how I'd won the Miss Ni-Mi-Win title back home in Du-luth, Minnesota.

Deep breath. Pick up the tempo a bit. Hold the hoops aloft. Crabwise step to the left. Slip through a hoop. Drop another one from my right hand over my

9

head. Bend at the waist, with my nose touching my kneecap. Sinuous leftward glide, bounce and kick and . . . *hey, how did she do that!?*

Smattering of applause. The Nuche really liked my quirky jackrabbit style. Grinning, I bowed and scooped more hoops from the ground, never missing a beat. As I held them aloft, I caught a glimpse of one of the Nuche chiefs. He was a heavyset man in a satiny lavender shirt and a white sportsjacket. A face like a Colorado cliffside. Thin lips curled in admiration.

Perspiration dampened my hair. Back and forth through the hoops I went, trying to ignore the warm ache in my biceps, shoulders and thighs. This was almost as rough as Ni-Mi-Win, and, believe me, that powwow is a marathon! I did some back-and-forth hops, like a little girl playing jumprope, and then it was back up to *fancy* speed for the grand finale. Bounce, bounce, kick and twirl. One, two, three, four—bow and smile.

Applause surged into the sagebrush corral. I played to the camcorders, posing in profile, flashing a bit of leg. Then I did a pert about-face and a jaunty fanny-shaking strut all the way back to the arbor.

Not bad for a maiden lady of twenty-eight summers, eh?

A familiar male voice sought me out. "You always have to put on a show, don't you?"

"I try."

Leaning against an aspen post, my cousin Bill Shavano handed me a threadbare towel. He was a year older and seven inches taller than me, A rugged, brawn-shouldered Nuche male with glossy black hair, good cheekbones, close-set eyebrows, and his father's Roman nose. "You about finished up here?"

"I'm always available for a curtain call."

"Not today, Angie." He hooked his thumb at the restless crowd. "Your public is going to have to do without you for a while. I need your help."

"Bill-leeeee!" I draped the damp towel over my shoulder. "Right this very minute?"

"Listen, I've got six, seven stray horses up sightseeing on Timpanogos. You and me, we could work our way over toward Stewart's Creek."

"We could," I nodded in agreement. "But then I'd miss the Grand Entry, wouldn't I? Besides, isn't this a man's job?"

"Ain't many that can ride as well as you, Angie."

"Flattery doesn't work on me, cousin."

"Whatever happened to Women's Lib?"

"Nor appeals to feminism, either."

Scratching the back of his neck, Bill added, "You know, there's a Princess Dance scheduled for right after the Flag Dance."

I blanched at the thought, then showed my cousin what an old cellmate had called a "fussbudget face." Eyes narrowed angrily. Two vertical ridges just above the bridge of my nose. Tightly compressed lips.

"You're a damned liar, Billy."

"Of course, I can see why you'd want to participate, being a visiting Anishinabe princess and all. Still, it takes a lot of nerve getting up there with all those other aging princesses, letting everybody know you're not married yet—"

"Enough!" I lifted my hand for silence. "Give me a minute to change?"

11

"You've got it. I'll bring the horses over to the rec vee."

Okay, so I'm a coward. I love being an Anishinabe princess, but I'd really rather not advertise my marital status. You see, once those Nuche women find out you're single, you spend the rest of powwow being introduced to eligible sons, cousins, nephews and grandsons. I'll find my own boyfriend, thank you very much.

So I trotted down the well-kept trails of Cascade Springs. The tribal council had gotten Forest Service permission to use the campground for our powwow. I strolled past the cascade's rocky face, luxuriating in the fine chilled spray. Then it was over the little wooden bridge and down along the riverbank, descending into a moist grove of red cedar and box elder maples.

As I emerged from the woods, I saw the food vendors lined up in the parking lot, their vans partially obscuring the huge Forest Service sign. Behind them, the gray granite rockpile of Mount Timpanogos punched its way into a cloudless azure sky. I made my way over to a lengthy Winnebago with Utah plates, pulled open the screen door, and found myself facing a human posterior, definitely female, measuring perhaps five axe handles across. It was wrapped in an Anishinabe jingle dress that had been modified to suit the climate.

"Hey!" I said, "You're blocking traffic."

"You can get by." Tin tinkled as Aunt Della stood erect. She was an inch over my five-foot-four, truly a daughter of the Blackbear family, with the same broad, high forehead, prominent cheekbones and slender aquiline nose. She wore her graying hair parted in the middle, with two ceremonial braids brushing her collarbone.

"Sure," I said, "but I may need a shoehorn."

Aunt Della wrinkled her nose. "Let's see how you look when you're fifty-eight."

I gave that ample waist a loving hug. "You're too heavy, Aunt Della. You've got to lay off the frybread."

"More eating advice from my anorexic niece?"

I hugged tighter. "Health advice. We want you around for a long, long time."

She gave me a one-armed squeeze. "Don't worry—I plan to be. After all, somebody has to ride herd on you."

After ducking into a closet-sized bedroom, I flung my suitcase on the bunk and hastily unzipped it.

"If you're looking for your dance dress, I hung it outside," came Aunt Della's voice.

Frantically I rummaged through the contents. "I'm looking for some jeans."

"What for?" Her puzzled face peered into the doorway.

"Your son just drafted me into a horse-hunting expedition," I said, shucking down my denim shorts.

"Angie! You'll miss Grand Entry."

"Can't be helped," I answered. I pulled a pair of sturdy Levis out of the suitcase froth. Sitting down on the bunk, I slithered my way into them, then, holding my breath, zipped them up. The zipper rose with ease, leaving me very proud of my twenty-three-inch waistline.

Posing before the mirror, I gave my slender figure

a critical look and wondered if the main man in my life—my parole officer, Paul Holbrook—had ever noticed it.

You see, a few years back I had some trouble with the law, and I wound up slinging laundry at the state women's prison in Springfield, South Dakota. When I finally made parole, Paul was assigned to shepherd me back into civilian life. I was ordered by the Parole Board to "participate willingly and with diligence" in Paul's Work Experience program.

Trouble is, even though your Angie is a Dean's List graduate of Montana State University Business School with a Master's in accounting, no way is she ever going to get another good-paying job again. Not after doing three years in the slam for embezzlement. So the best Paul can come up with is a lousy waitress job—and he's spent the last six months laying those on me, one after the other after the other.

I emerged from the bedroom and watched my aunt ladle simmering wild rice stew into a quintet of Styrofoam bowls. She glanced at me over her shoulder. "You haven't told me much about him."

I blinked. "About who?"

"Paul Holbrook."

Honestly, sometimes I think that woman really is a mind-reader! Smoothing my hair, I replied, "He's a royal pain in the ass. That says it all."

"What does he look like?" Aunt Della asked, twisting a piece of dough into the familiar frybread spiral.

"Oh, kind of tall." I preened before the kitchen mirror, seeking the proper tilt for my white straw

14

Stetson. "Brown hair. Good strong chin. Kind of good-looking, I guess."

I listened to twelve seconds of Aunt Della's nonchalant humming before the inevitable question.

"Is he married?"

"Of course not. No woman would have him." I glared at my aunt's spine. "Is there some *significance* to this line of questioning?"

"Angie, when a man is single, reasonably good-looking, and has a steady, well-paying job, I'd say he's worth a second look."

"Paul Holbrook!? No way!" I slipped on a pair of Polaroid sunglasses. "Besides, I think I can do much, much better."

"Well, you and Paul are seeing a lot of each other—"

"That's not my idea. If I don't report every weekend, the Department of Corrections will put me back on the laundry detail."

"Sounds to me like he's interested."

"Then I commend him for his good taste—but I'm not setting my cap for my parole officer. I'm not *that* desperate."

Levelling her wooden spoon, Aunt Della said, "There's no such thing as the perfect man, Angie. If you keep turning up your nose at this one and that one, you won't be getting married at all."

I steeled myself for another one of Aunt Della's famous lectures on the necessity of settling down. Fortunately, before she could add to the comment, a pair of horses whinnied just outside the window.

"Raincheck!" I said, then pecked her cheek. "We'll be back around dark."

"Both of you be careful, now," she admonished.

"We will. Always!"

By four o'clock, I was sitting astride a lively Appaloosa mare named Paquita, lowering my hatbrim against the afternoon sun glare and listening to the grasshoppers in the trailside junegrass. Paquita responded well to a light touch. We went clip-clopping along, taking the lead, with my denim-clad derrière comfortably pressed against the saddle's flared cantle.

Just up the trail was Bishop's Hat Pass, really just a broad notch in the rugged Wasatch skyline. I'd been up here once before on a geology field trip during my coed days. The pass had once been a glacial cirque. Ten thousand years of Wasatch weather had scoured it, battered it, widened it into a lush mountain meadow bristling with bluebell and columbine and Indian paintbrush.

My cousin brought up the rear, a stolid fellow in a broadbrimmed gray Stetson and Foster Grants, content to let his roan Morgan set her own pace. The mare's nostrils were flaring, and a dollop of grayish-white foam clung to her withers.

I smiled at Billy over my shoulder. "I think she'd rather chase strays down on the flat."

He gestured at a boulder-strewn slope fronted by a grove of mountain cedar. "Just a few minutes more, and we can stop and rub them down."

As Bill and I dismounted, I heard the spattering sound of a mountain creek. A moist breeze soothed my parched face. Paquita smelled the water, whinnied, and stamped her forehooves. She chewed the bit as I led her around the meadow, sort of like trying

16

to bring an eight-hundred-pound Saint Bernard to heel.

Minutes later I removed the hot saddle, gave Paquita a honey of a rubdown with currycomb and brush, and then turned her over to Bill. He hobbled both horses near the creek, letting them sip the cool water and crop the overripe grass.

Leaning against an aspen trunk, I remarked, "So what are these big plans I've been hearing about?"

"You'll have to be a little bit more specific there, Angie."

"Uncle Matt told me you're thinking of running for the Northern Ute Tribal Council."

"True enough. I've been out gathering signatures. I've got till August tenth to get my name on the ballot."

"What about your job with the Forest Service?"

Bill raised his hatbrim slightly. "What about it?"

"You can't afford to lose this job, Billygoat. You're getting married next month. And I don't think Cindy's willing to support you."

"Look, I've already checked it out with Washington, and I don't have to quit if I get elected. There's no conflict of interest."

Tilting my head to one side, I asked, "So why the sudden interest in tribal politics, Billyum?"

Bill was silent for almost a minute. Then he jutted his chin in the direction of our horses. "Saddle up. I'll show you."

Twenty minutes later, we were riding north, rounding the aspen-clad flank of Cumorah Peak, cantering through narrow meadows studded with lupine. Bill reined up at the woods's edge, dismounted, and then looped his trailing rein around a slim white trunk. I did the same, affectionately rubbed Paquita's ear, and followed my cousin down a mushy woodland trail.

We halted at a broad balcony of granite. The land fell away abruptly, plummeting two hundred feet into a downward-sloping alpine valley. The brink offered a marvelous view of distant Ephraim Lake, but I wasn't interested in that view. No, I was too busy gaping at the scene of utter carnage at my feet.

Regiments of splintering stumps marched uphill from the creek, assaulting the valley's talus slopes. Amputated crowns and limbs littered the valley floor, drowning the terrain in a sea of highly flammable slash. The creek itself, once a torrent of fast-running meltwater, had become a series of turbid ponds, awash in aspen leaves and dead saplings.

Complete and utter desolation. Acre after acre after acre. A mountain forest reduced to a moonscape. Caterpillar tread marks added to the battlefield imagery, making it look as if the valley had been overrun by an armored division. My mind couldn't quite cope with the totality of such destruction. I could only deal with it as a series of small, personal, searing images. The delicate sapling smothered in aspen slash. The creekbed sundered by deep bulldozer tracks. The dead beaver rotting in the ooze, its dainty forepaws at rest on brown belly fur.

I was suddenly conscious of a hot, angry cluster behind my collarbone. I have no idea what my expression was, but it sure scared the hell out of my cousin. "Take it easy, Angie."

I glared at him, my mouth tense and ugly. "Clearcut?"

Bill nodded. "In the Forest Service, we call it *nuked*."

"They didn't leave anything."

"They never do."

I gave a quick, despairing glance at the ravaged valley. "Tell me this isn't federal land, Billy. Please tell me it isn't."

"You really want me to lie to you?"

I felt like sobbing. "Why?"

Putting his hands in his back pockets, Bill rested one boot on a limestone outcrop. "Haven't you heard? Timber is America's best export. Japan won't let us into their markets unless we sell them what they want. And what they want is our timber."

"Congress lets them get away with this?"

"Angie, who do you think sets the timber harvest goals? The Wood Fairy?" Bill shook his head sadly. "It's like my boss, Mr. Longhurst, says. 'We must do as the Congress directs us.' Every year, the word comes down from Washington—increase sawtimber production. We're shipping out maybe seventy million boardfeet per year, nationwide." His mouth tightened in disgust. "That's one hell of a lot of chopsticks."

I couldn't believe what I was hearing. Back in college I'd spent a few summers with the Student Conservation Association, working in national parks as a coed rangerette. If there was one thing the Park Service drummed into me, it was the terms of the Land Policy and Management Act of 1976.

"Whatever happened to the concept of multiple use?" I asked, stepping back from the rim. "National forests are supposed to be used by everyone—hunters, backpackers, not just by loggers.''

"No, but there's a lot of wiggle room within that multiple-use mandate,'' Bill explained. ''Congress sets the priorities, and the lion's share goes to the lumber industry. Funds set aside for trail maintenance, recreation and improvement of wildlife habitat take up a big whole whopping three percent of the Forest Service budget. Would you like to guess the size of the lumber industry's share?''

I took a stab. "Twelve percent?''

"Try thirty-six.''

"Corporate welfare for the lumber industry, eh?''

"Bite your tongue, Shorty.'' Sarcasm colored Bill's tone. ''This is what's known as wise use of natural resources.''

"Wise use?'' I took a final glance at those clearcut slopes. ''Billy, there won't be a forest in that valley again until Captain Kirk takes command of the *Enterprise*.''

Leading me back down the trail, he added, ''You and I know that. But the only thing the boys in the boardroom know—or care about—is the fact that lumber fetches eight hundred dollars per boardfoot on the market. If you cut that timber on Uncle Sam's land and hold down your operating costs, you can clear seventy, eighty percent profit on every cut.''

"Pretty knowledgeable about the system, William.''

"I've been a timber sales officer for three years. I've seen just about every kind of timber scam there is.'' He smiled at me as we strolled along. ''That's why I want to get on the tribal council. I can put a stop to that shit. At least up in Saguache County."

"What do you have in mind?"

"There's a place north of here, up on the state line. Lodestone Canyon. It's the biggest aspen ecosystem in northern Utah. It's federal land, too. Bureau of Land Management. The talk over at BLM is that Lodestone's scheduled for *grove enhancement* this winter."

"Grove enhancement?" I echoed.

"That's what the industry calls clearcutting." Grim smile. "I've figured out a way to save it. But first I've got to get elected to the tribal council."

"You're going to make enemies, Billy."

"Already got 'em, Shorty."

He said it with such quiet conviction that I knew he wasn't joking. When I didn't josh right back, he glanced my way, saw my worried expression, and said, "Hey, don't look at me like that. It comes with the territory, Angie. The big loggers—guys like Karl Eames and Cue Broward—they like their timber sales officers sweet and reasonable. Me, I come on too hard-ass, I guess. Not that old man Longhurst ever backed me up or anything."

"Loggers ever give you a hard time?" I asked as we remounted.

"Once or twice. Couple of Eames's boys hassled me at a diner." As we trotted along, Bill took the canteen from his saddle horn and twisted the cap off. "Enough of my troubles. Let's talk about yours. You on good terms with that guy Holbrook?"

"Reasonable, I suppose. Why do you ask?"

"Well, it's like this." He handed me the canteen.

21

"There's a clerk-typist job open at the BLM in Salt Lake. You know how to type. I can pull a few strings and get you in. All we have to do is convince Paul Holbrook to turn your case over to our state corrections people. You can finish your parole here in Utah."

I had a long cooling sip. "That's very sweet of you, Billy. But that's not the way the system works."

"Bullshit. I work in government. You can always finagle something."

I sighed. "Billy, can you really see me and Aunt Della under the same roof?"

"Sure I can. You know, when you went out to Montana, Mom used to stand in the doorway of your room. Used to stand there and just look around. She said we wouldn't understand, being men and all, but maybe I do understand. She really misses you, Angie. You're the daughter she never had."

"Billy, I've got my own life now."

"Be honest with me. Are you doing anything up there in Pierre, South Dakota that you couldn't be doing just as well here at home?"

Subtle emphasis on "here at home". Damn that cousin of mine. He was making the offer too darned attractive.

"You're awfully interested in my personal welfare all of a sudden," I said. Capping the canteen, I showed him a fussbudget face. "How come?"

"I took Cindy up to Duluth last month. I wanted her to meet Grandfather before the wedding." Sidelong glance at me. "Cindy ain't much for fishing, so I let Grandfather show her around Tettegouche while I went up to the Gunflint. The walleyes were biting, and I had a mushroom head jig I wanted to try out. Stopped for gas at Nordlund's in Grand Marais, and got talking to him and Tootie. You know how Tootie is—chews your ear clean off. She told me, 'I seen that squirrelheaded cousin of yours.' Naturally, I just knew she was talking about you. And then she told me about some big mess over in the U.P. Said there was one of them police sketches in the paper, and damn if it didn't look just like Angie Biwaban.''

In spite of the summer sunshine, I experienced a momentary chill.

''I wouldn't have given it any more thought if I hadn't picked you up at the airport,'' he continued. ''That was one classy suit you were wearing, cousin. Those three Northwest pilots couldn't keep their eyes off it—and didn't that young one let out a whistle!'' He lowered his hatbrim slightly. ''That's when I got to wondering how a girl working as a waitress can afford a two-hundred-dollar linen suit.''

Vague and hopeful smile. ''Green Stamps?''

''I don't think so.'' He shook his head. ''You want to talk about it, Angie?''

''Not particularly.'' I licked dry lips. ''Have you talked about this with Aunt Della?''

''No, I haven't. I wanted to talk to you first. I'm offering you an escape hatch, Angie. If you're smart, you'll take it.''

Sour smile. ''Uh-huh. And if I'm back in Heber City with the family, I'm less likely to go out and wind up in jail again. Right?''

''That is the theory.''

My cousin was right, of course. If I persisted in these illicit adventures, sooner or later I would be back running a washing machine in a prison laundry. Perhaps a move to Utah would be in my best interest. I was much less likely to run into a familiar Michigan face out here. And yet . . .

I could feel my personal future slipping out of my grasp. Honest Angie. Long hours typing and filing at the BLM office. Pressure from Aunt Della to get married. A whirlwind romance, punctuated by a brisk march down the center aisle of some church. Next thing you know, I've got a casserole in the oven, a screaming infant in the playpen, and an irascible boss on the telephone.

The vision spooked me. Turning in the saddle, I said, "Look, Billy, I appreciate the offer. Really. But . . . I just don't think I'm ready for the rest of it, that's all. You know, getting married, having kids, being respectable, the whole nine yards. That's great for you and Cindy. That's what you two want. But me—I'm not so sure what I want."

Bill let out a long, hearty belly laugh. I endured it for just about thirty seconds, then reached over and swatted him.

"What's so funny!?" I snapped.

"Angie," he said, flashing that irritating grin. "Twenty years from now, when we're up here on the trail and you're complaining about Mom spoiling your kids, I'm going to quote that right back at you. Word for word!"

My face began steaming. "Never happen!"

"Oh, yes, it will. Mark your calendar. Twenty years. Your face will be fuller, and your seat will cover more of that saddle. You'll wince when I say it and wonder how you could have ever been so dumb.

But it'll happen. I'm so sure of that I'm willing to bet cash money on it.''

"You're full of shit, Billy. I've got fifty dollars says it won't.''

"You've got yourself a bet, Shorty.''

He held his palm upright. Wheeling Paquita about, I stood in the stirrups and smacked his hand loudly. Then I sent the mare cantering down the dusty trail, daring Billy to keep up.

That would be the easiest fifty dollars I ever won.

I would never collect it, though. Matter of fact, I never saw my cousin again.

Four days later, Bill Shavano was dead.

Chapter Two

The day it happened I was in Salt Lake with Aunt Della.

We'd spent the morning in the highrise Crossroads Mall, just across the street from Temple Square. It's impossible for my aunt to walk through Temple Square without being hailed by somebody she knows. She's lived out there better than thirty years now, and I think most of eastern Utah has passed through her classroom at Heber City High.

Our after-lunch destination was the Zion Cooperative Mercantile Institution—ZCMI, for short—the oldest department store in Utah. Of course, it's changed a bit since Uncle Matt's ancestors did their trading at the front counter. These days, the ZCMI is a galleria-style mall spread over three stories.

While I was looking over a delightful jade blazer, a twentyish salesgirl came along and hailed my aunt. She and Aunt Della had an animated twenty-minute chat. She looked vaguely familiar, so the minute she left, I fired my questions. Aunt Della informed me that the girl's name was Karen Sommer, that her older sister had gone to school with Billy and me, and that she had just become engaged.

"So who's she marrying?" I asked.

"Colorado boy. She met him skiing in Park City." Fingering the blazer's sleeve, my aunt nodded in approval. "Buy it. Jade looks good on you."

I thought of Karen's older sister. "Any word from Tina Marie?"

"As a matter of fact, yes—she's having a baby."

I detected a meaningful undertone in Aunt Della's voice. "That's nice," I answered.

"That's her second one, Angela."

"Well, the Saints are partial to large families."

Aunt Della was not so easily deterred. "Remember your cousin, Joy Washakie? Matthew's niece? She had hers a couple of months ago. A little girl."

"I haven't seen Joy since I was fourteen. I don't even remember what she looks like."

"She's three years *younger* than you."

"That's not a description, Aunt Della!" Folding the skirt with swift, brutal strokes, I muttered, "Why am I getting the Baby Report?"

Before she could reply, the ZCMI's loudspeaker system whined to life. "Mrs. Shavano, please report to the first floor courtesy desk. You have a phone call."

Aunt Della's expression shifted from surprise to confusion. I took immediate advantage of the diversion. Tugging at her forearm, I said, "Come on. We'll take the elevator downstairs."

When we arrived at the courtesy desk, a brown-haired teenager, visibly awed at holding her first job, flashed us both a megawatt smile and thrust the re-

ceiver at my aunt. I stood off to one side, very grateful for the reprieve, my purse dangling behind me,
absentmindedly grinding one spike heel into the
flooring.

I watched my aunt's face suddenly tremble. Her
full lips tensed in apprehension, and she listened
without making a sound. Then, mouth quivering, she
surrendered the receiver.

"What's wrong?" I asked.

"It-it's B-Bill." Her eyelids fluttered in alarm. "He
was injured on the job. Badly injured. They—they're
flying him into the city."

My glance zipped to the desk girl. "Phone us a
cab, would you?"

The helicopter beat us to the University of Utah
Hospital by a good forty minutes. By the time Aunt
Della and I rushed through the doors of the Emergency Room, Billy was in pre-op, his head shaved,
getting his first dose of sodium pentothal from the
anesthesiologist.

Buffeted by the pungent scent of blood and phar-
maceuticals, we confronted an earnest young intern
who expertly shepherded us into an antiseptic waiting
room and assured us both that Bill was getting the
best of care.

Ten minutes elapsed before the ER doctor appeared, and by that time I was not in a ladylike mood.
The doctor came plodding in, displaying a beard like
a wild lilac hedge. A California Forty-Niner in surgical green. "Mrs. Shavano? I'm Doctor Culhane."

Features haggard, Aunt Della rushed forward. "My son—will he be all right?"

"He's suffered severe head trauma." Doctor Culhane led us over to a gleaming conference table, then spread a handful of glossy angiograms across the black formica. "He's sustained an occipital fracture here." His pudgy forefinger tapped the photo, pinpointing the back of Billy's skull. "I didn't get a response when I illuminated the pupils, so I ordered an MRI—"

My patience snapped. "Save it for medical school, okay? Two questions, Doc. Where's Billy? What are you people doing to him?"

Aunt Della touched my shoulders. "Angela, please."

Taking my outburst in stride, Doctor Culhane gave me a long look and made a wrong, though understandable, guess about my relationship to the patient. "Your brother's in the operating theatre right now, Miss Shavano. He's bleeding internally. We don't have a choice. We have to stop it."

"What do you mean, you don't have a choice?"

Leaning over, he tapped the glossy printout. "This is an MRI. That stands for Magnetic Resonance Imaging. See the white line? That's the fracture. Now, down at the bottom here is the Circle of Willis. Those are the four blood vessels that feed oxygen and nutrients to the brain. The impact sent bone splinters flying into this area, damaging the arterial tissues. Pressure's building up in there—threatening Bill's brain stem. That's what controls his respiratory and cardiac functions. If we don't relieve that pressure, he'll die."

An aura of nightmare enveloped me. For a split second, I was back in Duluth again, listening to another middle-aged physician describe the cancer threatening my mother's life.

"You'll have to go through the brain to get at those blood vessels," I murmured.

Nodding swiftly, Doctor Culhane gathered up his pictures. Our eyes met. I sensed his unspoken reply:

That's right, Angela. And that means we may inadvertently damage Bill's optic and motor nerves. If he survives, he may live out the remainder of his life in darkness. Or in a wheelchair.

The ER doctor walked us to the door. "Your son is in good hands, Mrs. Shavano. Harry Payson is the finest neurosurgeon in Utah."

Aunt Della balked at the doorway. "When can I see him?"

"As soon as Bill gets to Intensive Care," Doctor Culhane added sympathetically. "Now, come with me. There's a private lounge for the immediate family on the seventh floor."

And so we waited.

The lounge was a small whitewalled stucco room with seven abstract paintings in soothing pastel shades, comfortable furniture, and a widescreen TV. Aunt Della found a corner of the plush sofa and gave way to quiet tears.

Bill's fiancée and Uncle Matt arrived about an hour later. Cindy Polenana was twenty-five, a slender Nuche woman with deepset dark eyes, lush brownish-black hair, and the delicate facial planes of a Mayan princess.

"H-how is he, Della?" she asked, brushing away the tears.

"I don't know." Aunt Della's mouth twisted in anguish. "We-we haven't seen him. The doctor said he could die!"

Uncle Matt turned my way. The day's events had aged him a whole decade. "How are you doing, Angie?"

"I can't stand it, Uncle Matt. It's like Mother all over again." And that's when I broke down. Uncle Matt cradled me in his embrace, easing me through the sudden weep. When I lifted my face from his shoulder, I sobbed and murmured, "H-How did it h-happen?"

"I don't rightly know. There was some kind of accident up there in the Topanas. The sheriff told me that much."

"Which sheriff?"

"Heber City. He got it off the radio from the Highway Patrol."

Cindy flashed me an anxious look. "Did you see him, Angie?"

I wiped away tears with the heel of my hand. Shook my head, no. "Just the ER doctor, Cin. He said they'll let us into Intensive Care as soon as the operation's over."

My uncle sighed. "We'll just have to sit tight and wait," he murmured.

Easier said than done, Uncle Matt.

The waiting is the hardest part of it all. You talk and you talk. Sometimes you talk for hours. You remember moments shared with the endangered one, savoring incidents, both happy and sad, ranging all

31

the way back to early childhood. And sometimes you need that moment apart from the rest of the family, even if it's only a few steps away in a quiet corner of the room, that spot where you can bow your head and shed your own personal tears.

I found my little sanctuary by the window. The glass showed me a seventh-story glimpse of Emigration Canyon, with its sharp brown ridges and its sparse woodlands, encircled by subdivisions. I folded my arms, frowned at my glassy reflection, told myself Bill was going to survive.

He had to, right? I mean, he was only twenty-nine years old. He was getting married, for Pete's sake. He and Cindy would contribute greatly to Aunt Della's quota of grandchildren. He was going to do great things on the tribal council. He had his whole goddamned life ahead of him. It couldn't be all over. It just couldn't.

Craniotomy. I tried to blot it out, but my mind insisted upon visualizing the procedure. The eye-dazzling white of the surgical arena. The beeping sound of the heart monitor and the gentle sigh of the respirator. The surgeon takes his scalpel and carefully slices the scalp, the muscle tissue, and the galea, that delicate membrane shielding the ivory white of the skull. The electric saw whirrs, and there is a fine misty spray of miniscule bone fragments . . .

Touching my lips, I blinked tearfully at my window reflection.

Okay, God, let's get down to some serious horse-trading here. I'm not asking for much, you understand. Just let my cousin live. Please.

What am I offering in return? Simply this. Let him

live, and I will walk the straight and narrow for the rest of my days. No more clever scouts. No more Angie scams. I'll move back to Utah and work that dull office job at the BLM and get married and have children and pay Billy his goddamned fifty dollars. But you must let him live . . .

I heard Aunt Della's soft murmur. "Angie."

Heavy thunderclouds cluttered the Wasatch ridgeline. Greenish-white lightning lashed the eastern side. Putting my fingertips to the glass, I could feel the vibrations of those distant thunderclaps. I knew it would be raining in Heber.

Aunt Della patted the sofa cushion beside her. "Come and sit with me, Angie."

Holding back the sniffles, I joined her on the couch. She gave me a hug, then offered a box of tissues. "You'd better wipe your face, dear."

Dabbing at my cheekbones, I aimed a resentful glance at the door. "What's taking them so damned long?"

"Angie, there's nothing we can do. We simply have to be patient—"

She looked up suddenly, her voice fading. A man in a light green surgeon's smock had just come in. Doctor Payson. He was about sixty, I think. A slim man with a bold military stride. Bristling moustache, pouting underlip, and neatly combed iron-gray hair. The front of his smock was unwrinkled and clean.

A shudder of alarm ran through me. In a successful operation, the surgeon goes straight to the immediate family to share the good news. If Doctor Payson had paused to shed his bloodstained operating smock, then that meant—

33

The surgeon's somber gaze found Aunt Della. His mouth softened in sympathy. "Mrs. Shavano, I'm sorry . . ."

And my aunt collapsed into the circle of my embrace.

Don't ask me how I got through the next few days. I don't really know, myself.

The nightmare that began in the hospital lounge seemed to broaden and lengthen as time went on. My memories of that period are a kaleidoscope of grief, a tumbling chaos of tears and anguish and numbing loss. Claiming my cousin's body. Making the burial arrangements. And, most frequently of all, trying to comfort Aunt Della.

Needless to say, my aunt took it the worst. The day before Billy's funeral, we were in the kitchen, Aunt Della and I. And she told me I ought to get in touch with my parole officer, to let Paul know what had happened. Even as she spoke, her voice took on a stilted, faintly shrill note. Then all at once she thought of Bill, and sudden grief shattered her composure. Letting out a keening wail, she nearly fell but caught herself on the table's edge. She stood there, her head bowed, yielding to the surge of tears, and then I hugged her gently and steered her into the bedroom.

So now I had a new role. Lady of the house. Somber Anishinabe woman in her black mourning dress. Finishing the funeral arrangements. Caring for her grief-stricken aunt. Accepting the condolences of neighbors and friends.

The family needed a few days to gather. My grandfather, Charlie Blackbear, flew down from Duluth. The news had aged him as much as it had Uncle Matt. The Marine Corps granted compassionate leave to Billy's brothers. Wayne showed up on Tuesday, with his Apache wife Lucinda and their two-year-old son. Wyatt came all the way from Saudi Arabia.

We buried my cousin on a sunny Thursday morning, in the tiny Nuche cemetery overlooking the Provo River. The Native American Church conducted the ceremony. Billy's pastor held an eagle feather aloft and sang the Nuche death song. At the center of the circle, two men thumped the dance drum.

In time, I would honor Bill's memory in the manner of my own people. But on this day I mourned with the Nuche. Taking a pair of scissors, I lopped a half-inch from the end of my ponytail, then I blackened my face with charcoal. Wearing my mourning dress and a long fringed shawl, I took my place with the women, and together we danced a slow, measured lament.

Afterwards, the family formed a reception line, with Aunt Della in the center and Cindy Polenana at her side. Mourners trooped past, each one offering whispered condolences. There was one wizened Nuche lady, perilously close to ninety, who hobbled along with the aid of her trusty walker, oblivious to the noonday heat. Nuzzling my cheek, she told me, "It's a good thing you're here, Geraldine."

I guess she had me confused with Mother.

I was feeling pretty low after the funeral, so while my aunt dozed in the bedroom, I sought distraction in my duties as lady of the house.

I found three pieces of mail in the aluminum box

and glanced at the envelope corners. Two looked like bills—one from Mountain Bell, the other from the Heber Valley Sewer District. The third bore the logo of the Utah Highway Patrol.

Shuffling the envelopes, I wandered into the living room. The broad Mexican veranda out front made this the coolest and shadiest room in the house. Aunt Della hadn't made many changes since my last visit four years ago. Same stucco walls in Indian brown and queen-sized sofa and matching chairs in a sub-dued watercolor print. One corner hosted my aunt's prizewinning cactus garden, another the TV and VCR. And then there was the long oak table proudly displaying the Shavano family photographs.

There was a portrait of my grandfather, whom I kiddingly call Chief, taken on a visit out here. He has a broad square head, with small, flat ears and thin white·hair meticulously combed back. With his deep-set obsidian eyes and flanking wrinkles, he looks a bit like old Rain-in-the-Face. And there was a picture of Aunt Della and Mother, taken on the dock of a Minnesota lake, back when they were known as the Blackbear sisters. A wedding photo of Aunt Della and Uncle Matt. School portraits of Billy, Wayne and Wy-att. And last but certainly not least, a shot of me with my fortyish and much, much slimmer Aunt Della.

My thumbnail tore open the Highway Patrol enve-lope. As I read the letter, I heard the soft slam of the back door, punctuated by the sound of slow footsteps.

"What have you got there, Angie?"

I showed my grandfather the cream-colored letter. "The Highway Patrol's holding Billy's personal effects at the barracks in Logan. They want Aunt Della to come and claim them.''

Chief tilted his broad head in the direction of the bedroom. "You'd better give it to her, then."

Folding the letter with care, I shook my head slowly. "I don't think so."

"And why not?"

"I don't think she could handle it, Chief."

"She's a lot stronger than you give her credit for."

"Look, they're going to be shoving Billy's things at her—the things he had on him when he died. I'm not even sure I could handle that." I stuffed the letter back in the torn envelope. "I have no idea how it'll affect her, and I am certainly not willing to experiment." Brushing strands of raven-black hair away from my cheek, I added, "So I'll go."

"All right. The hospital's already sent Billy's clothes. I put them in the attic. You can put his personal effects up there, too." Chief's obsidian eyes saddened. "When Della's ready, she'll look them over."

"Thanks, Chief." Hastily I undid my apron strings. "Listen, about supper—"

"Lucinda can handle it," he interrupted. "Don't break any speed records between here and Logan, eh?"

"I won't. Girl Scout promise."

Trying not to smile, he muttered, "I'll add that one to my collection."

The Highway Patrol barracks was a good distance north on Logan's lengthy Main Street, a hundred yards past the fast-food joints, car dealerships and venerable Mormon homes, situated across the street from the Cache Valley Mall.

After parking in the visitor's lot, I trotted up the front steps. With misgivings. After all, a police station—*any* police station—is not my favorite destination. From bitter personal experience, I know where you go from there.

My mourning dress had given way to a white sweater-knit top and a frosted denim miniskirt. Perched sunglasses served in lieu of barrettes. Mormon Angie.

The receptionist appeared very happy to see me—perhaps she was just enjoying a brief respite from that stack of pending court cases on her desktop. In any event, she pointed out an empty vinyl chair and informed me that Trooper McMurdie would be right out.

Five minutes later, Trooper Robert McMurdie came sauntering out of the dayroom, holster riding low on his hip, handcuffs a-jingle on his Sam Browne belt, clutching a bulky manila envelope. He resembled a Mountie in one of those old-time movie serials. Blond and forthright and steely-eyed. His Smokey Bear hat rode low on his forehead, and there were many, many fine blond hairs on his muscled forearms.

He gave me a long curious look. "You're a little young to be Shavano's mother."

Well, I didn't feel like getting bogged down in a lengthy explanation of the relationship, so I borrowed a misconception from Doctor Culhane.

"I'm Bill's sister. Angela Shavano. Mother isn't feeling well, so she asked me to come in her place."

McMurdie took a step to my left, and I knew he was looking out the window, grabbing a glimpse of Uncle Matt's pickup.

"Just a minute there, girl."

McMurdie reached beneath the horizon of the countertop. I heard the clackety-clack of a computer keyboard and guessed he was faxing the license number to the Department of Public Safety. Where, to his satisfaction, he would learn that the truck was indeed registered to a Matthew Shavano of 1405 Midway Lane, Heber City, Utah.

A very careful and competent cop, this Trooper McMurdie. I flinched at the squeal of a daisywheel printer. The trooper looked down. Then his grim mouth softened at the edges. Apparently, I was legit.

"Well, here you go." McMurdie slid the sealed envelope across the counter. "This is everything we got from the Saguache County sheriff. Please look over the manifest and let me know when you're ready to sign."

Nodding, I peeled away the flap and upended the manila envelope, scattering its contents across the counter. Loose change. Pocket comb. Swiss Army knife. The sight of that battered deerskin wallet made my eyes itch. Billy had bought it years ago on one of his many fishing trips to the Northland.

I steeled myself for a sudden rush of grief, but instead I experienced a strange sense of uncertainty. Once more I examined Billy's things, taking a few seconds to thoroughly study each one. I found nothing particularly sinister about them. Yet I couldn't quite shake the feeling that something was wrong.

McMurdie picked up on it. "Anything the matter, miss?"

My smile was flaccid. "Uhm . . . is this everything Bill had on his person?"

He consulted a clipboard. "Everything but the gloves."

"Gloves?" I echoed.

"Canvas gloves. The kind you'd wear to do work around the yard. They went back to the Forest Service with the chainsaw."

"What kind of chainsaw?"

"A McCulloch. Big model. Weighs about eighteen pounds."

"Bill was cutting down a tree?"

"That's the report we got from Saguache County. He was cutting down a lodgepole pine. The vibration shook loose a broken limb. Eight inches in diameter, it was. Dropped like a bomb. Struck him right smack on the back of the—" All at once, he remembered to whom he was talking. "Sorry, Miss Shavano. Way I heard it, your brother never had a chance."

"Where was Bill when they found him?"

"The Topanas National Forest. Place called Dynamite Pass."

"Who found him?"

"A county deputy. He found your brother pinned under the lodgepole limb. He's the one called it in. Sheriff sent in the helicopter."

"Bill was wearing gloves?"

McMurdie nodded.

"And the chainsaw?" I asked.

"The deputy found it on the ground a few feet

40

away. The bar was bent a little near the end. Must have gotten banged up when he dropped it.''

It all sounded perfectly plausible, of course. Falling branches are a routine hazard on a logging site. And yet, the more I heard, the more anxious and disbelieving I became. My gaze riveted onto Billy's pocket clutter. The items screamed that something was wrong.

Then my gaze shifted onto Billy's wallet, and I knew what it was.

''Trooper McMurdie, did my brother have a tobacco pouch on him? A beige deerhide sack about as big as a child's fist, with a beaded red thunderbird motif on the front?''

His broad hand swept over the bric-a-brac. ''This is everything we got.''

Sad, sweet smile. ''Would you please check the manifest? Maybe the sheriff forgot to include it.''

With a sigh, he flipped the page on his clipboard. He let his gaze roll down the page, then looked at me and shook his head slowly. ''Sorry. No tobacco pouch. Is it important?''

''Personal gift.''

My hand trembled with excitement as I reached for the pen. My voice sounded thick and alien. ''Where do I sign?''

He showed me. I signed on the dotted line, swept Billy's possessions back into the envelope, thanked the trooper for his time, and headed for the door.

I had much to think about. Beginning with that tobacco pouch.

I hadn't lied to Trooper McMurdie. The pouch had been a personal gift, a welcome-home present for

Billy after his combat tour overseas. Chief had shot the deer. I had done all the grunt work, fleshing and soaking and stretching and tanning and beading.

But the tobacco wasn't for smoking.

We Anishinabe are a forest people, and our lives are deeply rooted in our mother the Earth. The Nuche are much the same. We never take from the earth without giving something in return. And the most precious gift of all is a pinch of tobacco.

To us, tobacco is *ahsayma,* the sacred plant that cleanses the mind and the heart. Its smoke rises heavenward, bringing peace and harmony to the soul. To offer anything else would dishonor our mother the Earth.

I couldn't conceive of my cousin revving up that chainsaw without first kneeling at the foot of that lodgepole, digging a small hole with his fingers, taking tobacco from his pouch, and placing it in the hole.

Yet according to Trooper McMurdie, Billy had done just that. He had lugged the McCulloch chainsaw to the site, pulled hard on the lanyard, opened the throttle, and put the blade to the bark.

Just like any white man.

No, I didn't like the setup at all. Billy was the son of a Nuche father and an Anishinabe mother. He would never touch a living tree without first offering tobacco. Yet the tobacco pouch had been nowhere on his person.

Whoa, princess! Maybe you're reading too much into this. Maybe Billy lost the pouch when that bough hit him.

(But he didn't lose his pocket comb?)

Perhaps he left the pouch in his truck.

(He remembered to bring the chainsaw and not the tobacco!?)

The Dakota pickup's waxed surface showed a reflection of me with a fussbudget face. After pulling the door open, I tossed the bulky envelope onto the vacant passenger seat.

You know, had my cousin been felled by a lightning bolt, I wouldn't have been quite so bothered. But Bill hadn't been killed by lightning. His skull had been fractured by a massive blow. And a falling limb wasn't the only thing in nature capable of accomplishing that.

Questions, questions. It was high time I started looking for the answers. And I knew exactly where to begin.

Aunt Della's attic.

Chapter Three

Come the late evening, I was seated on my Navaho bedspread, propped against two pillows, frowning at the shadowy pieces of clothing spread before me. I heard a soft footstep just beyond my bedroom door. Click of doorknob. Muted squeak of brass hinges. A familiar masculine silhouette filled the rectangular doorway.

Chief sighed. "You're still up."

I shrugged. Scowling Anishinabe princess in her wrinkled sapphire camisole. I glanced at my cousin's clothes again. Short-sleeved khaki work shirt and cowpuncher Levis. Concho-studded belt and sturdy hiking boots.

"You weren't very talkative at supper."

"Nothing much to say."

Reaching my bedside, Chief flicked on the jug-handled lamp.

"What is it, Angie?" He gave Billy's clothes a long inquisitive look. "Della's worried. You hardly said a word all evening. That ain't the Angie she knows."

His quizzical gaze turned in my direction. "What happened in Logan that's got you so upset?"

I knew I was going to have to break it to him sometime. So, exhaling in a mild sigh, I lifted the manila envelope and dumped Billy's things on the bed. Then, rising to my knees, I laid them out like a blackjack dealer. My grandfather watched without comment.

"These were on Billy when that Saguache County deputy found him. Notice anything strange?"

Chief shook his head slowly.

"According to the Highway Patrol, Billy was doing some logging in the Topanas. He was using a chainsaw when a heavy limb fell out of the top branches. It struck him on the back of the head. Fractured his skull. The sheriff up there says accidental death."

"What are you getting at, Angie?"

"You remember that tobacco pouch we made for Billy when he came home from Panama?"

Chief's gaze darted to the bedspread, and his expression changed. Slight narrowing of the eyes. Sudden tightening of the mouth.

My hand swept over Billy's belongings. "This is everything that was at the scene, Chief."

"Could be the sheriff's men missed it." Chief's voice was deceptively calm as he played the devil's advocate. "A red squirrel could have come along . . . dragged the pouch to its den."

"Bullshit!" I snapped. "Billy was found at the foot of that lodgepole with his head split open and *these* on." I flipped the canvas work gloves. "They set it up nice and pretty, Chief. But it's bullshit, and you know it. Billy was Nuche, heart and soul, and he

45

would never, ever touch a living tree without first making the offering. Never!"

"Angie . . ."

"Oh, maybe he just forgot the pouch at home, huh?" My voice was turning shrill. "Maybe he was just getting forgetful in his old age. He remembered to bring the gloves. But he also forgot to bring along his helmet and steel-toed work boots—something *every* logger wears on a worksite!"

And that was it for me. I crumpled all at once, bursting into tears, pressing my fists to my forehead. Sitting beside me, my grandfather gathered me into his arms.

"I know," he murmured, rocking me gently back and forth. "Go ahead, Angie. Let it all out."

"Th-they killed him, Chief."

"Who killed him?"

"I don't know. Somebody," I wailed.

Chief handed me a box of tissues. Even as I blew my nose, I was thinking back to the powwow. In my mind, I was back on the trail with Bill, listening to him talk about his hassle with the loggers. Two names had come up that day. Cue Broward. Karl Eames. Not much to go on, I know, but at least it was a start.

Sobbing, I fumbled for another tissue, then wiped my eyes. Chief's broad hands came to rest on my shoulders.

"You're young, Angie, and you don't think it can happen like that. You think because a man dies before his time there has to be a reason. But it doesn't always happen that way. Life is the most fragile thing there is. And it can end suddenly—any time, any place. For anybody. You'll understand a little better when you're older.''

"What are you saying, Chief?"

"I'm saying there's a good chance it really was just an accident. That the tobacco pouch got lost in the shuffle. That maybe Billy buried the tobacco before he cut that lodgepole. I don't want you brooding about it, Angie. Billy wouldn't want that, either." He touched my face gently. "I think maybe you're reading into this some things that aren't really there."

"And what if they are there?"

Only his eyes moved. They looked up quickly—shrewd, defensive and fierce, all at the same time. "Do you know something you're not telling me?"

I ducked the question. "Do me a favor?"

He looked at me askance. "What kind?"

"Let me borrow your rental car?"

"What for?"

"A trip to Salt Lake."

"Are you going to answer my first question, young lady?"

Leaning against the propped pillows, I said, "I can answer it a whole lot better after I've been to Salt Lake."

My grandfather's face was unreadable. Lifting himself to his feet, he switched off the bedside lamp. "All right. I'll leave the keys on the kitchen table."

"Thanks, Chief."

Lingering in the doorway, he swiveled a blunt forefinger at me. "I'll talk to you when you get back," he said.

* * *

At eight o'clock the next morning, I was breezing down Interstate 15 in my grandfather's rented Toyota Tercel, playing *What's My Lane?* with platoons of irate Wasatch Front commuters and listening to some lively Tennessee violins on *Cat Country, Rowwwwwrr! KKAT Salt Lake City!*

I had zipped around Salt Lake a good deal during my coed days, so I had no trouble finding Cindy Polenana's place in Millcreek. Which may be leaving some of you with a question. Namely, how did I go from being the spoiled only daughter of a Duluth high school teacher to the unofficial sister of the Shavano boys?

Well, to make a long story short—when I was fourteen, my mother developed cervical cancer and was facing a lengthy convalescence. I wanted to stay at Tettegouche with Chief, but with Grandma Blackbear in poor health, my grandfather had troubles enough of his own. So Mother phoned Aunt Della, and they both agreed that I should finish the ninth grade at good old Heber City High.

I grew pretty close to Billy, Wayne and Wyatt. During the next few years, we spent our school vacations together, either on Lake Superior's north shore with Chief or at the Shavano house in Heber. With a little help and encouragement from Aunt Della, I enrolled at Utah State University in Logan and spent the ensuing four years as a genuine Wasatch rodeo princess, breaking the hearts of all those brawny Mormon boys.

Abandoning the commuter stream in Granite Park, I headed uphill on 3300 South, past the one-story furniture stores and cozy Forties bungalows with their Fort Apache picket fences. Lone Anishinabe princess in her blue-and-white striped yoke shirt and skintight indigo jeans. Raven hair brushed and ponytailed and fastened with a simple rawhide strand. Southwest Angie.

Cindy lived on the first floor of a fine old Victorian house on Twenty-seventh East. It had been built a century ago, when Millcreek was still a whistle stop on the rail line to Provo. It was a house fit for a Mormon bishop and his sprawling family, a Queen Anne double-decker with steep, overhanging gables and a wraparound colonnaded porch.

Parking out front, I was mildly surprised to see three cars in the driveway. A dark blue Oldsmobile Cutlass squatted closest to the two-door garage, obviously the property of the elderly couple living upstairs. Cindy's maroon Pontiac Sunbird sat right behind the Cutlass. Partially blocking the sidewalk was a brand-new Dodge Cummins Turbo Diesel pickup in midnight blue, Utah license plate SG7-498.

Curiosity lured me over to the pickup. I wondered who was doing the early morning visiting. That Dodge was right out of the showroom. The Utah sun hadn't been up long enough to dull that dazzling wax job.

Quick peek through the driver's side window. How about that? Less than four hundred miles on the gauge. Three empty Coors cans littered the floor on the passenger side. Pinned to the sun visor was a bright blue button from the Nuche powwow in Towaoc, Colorado. Behind the driver's seat was a varnished cedar gunrack sporting a bolt-action .340 Weatherby Magnum. Which, if memory serves, carries a 250-grain bullet called the Speer Grand Slam— very expensive ammo priced at fifty dollars per box.

So, princess, what do we know about the driver? Well, he's male. He's Native American. He likes Coors beer and shiny macho toys. And he takes awfully good care of his firearms. The Weatherby's slide was well-lubricated, and there wasn't a fleck of dust on that Tasco scope. I wondered if he would show the Dodge the same respect and affection.

I laid my palm on the truck's polished hood. The metal was warm. I felt a little better. Cindy was still being faithful to Billy's memory.

Climbing the back stairs, I heard Cindy's lovely alto voice rising in indignation.

"Just forget it, Jack. Just forget the whole thing, okay? I want you out of here—now!"

Deep baritone chuckle. "Come on, Cin. What's the big deal, eh?"

"Oh, don't put on that innocent face. I know you a damned sight better than that."

I noticed that the back door was slightly ajar. I folded my fist to knock, then thought the better of it.

"Look, Cin, I just came by to pay my respects. That's all."

"Will you *please* get out of here?"

My fingertips prodded the door. The widened aperture offered a much better view of Cindy's kitchen. Long counter with a stainless steel sink, a cozy two-person dining table, a tall and slender refrigerator. And the lady herself, tall and slender, looking quite fetching in an antique rose blazer and matching slim skirt.

Then Cindy's visitor entered my field of vision, his long legs sheathed in blue denim. That first glimpse startled me. Close-cropped raven hair, narrow nose, taut lips and eyes as hard and as tough as the che pebbles in a canyon wash. His frame was lean, panth-erish, with long, cable-like muscles on his tattooed arms. He wore a black fringed leather vest over a T-shirt. He was leaning against the dining table, vis-ibly amused by Cindy's alarm and discomfort.

He picked crooked teeth with a thumbnail. "Can't mourn forever, Cin."

"For Christ's sake, Jack! He hasn't even been dead a week!"

"No shit. Maybe I ought to visit the cemetery and help the flowers grow." He reached for his fly. "Might help if I had a few beers first, eh?"

"You wouldn't *dare* show your face around here if he was still alive!"

"But he ain't, is he? And here we are. Together again. Just like old times, sugar, don't you think?"

"Get out of here, Jack! I want you out of my house—this instant!" Lifting her hand, she waggled impatient fingers. "And I'll trouble you for that key, if you don't mind!"

Jack's vest fringe jiggled as he laughed. He fished around in his back pocket for a few seconds, then dangled a small brass-plated key.

"This key, Cin?" He dangled it in mocking pan-tomime. "This little key right here?"

Had I been thinking, I would have quietly closed the door, retreated to the convenience store across the street, and dialed 911. But no, not me. That crack about Billy's grave really stung. And I lunged at the opportunity to stick it to this asshole.

On tiptoe, I sidled up behind Jack, and then, quick as a weasel, I made the snatch. In profile, his face as if it had been chiseled from basalt. The furious blaze in his eyes had me seriously rethinking the whole maneuver.

No way to call it off, though. So I did a graceful pirouette away from Jack's flailing grasp and wound up at Cindy's side. She stared in amazement as I placed the key in her palm.

"Your property, Cindy."

"Angie!" she gasped.

Facing the unwelcome guest, I snapped, "You know the song, pal."

Comedy was wasted on him. "What!?"

I tilted my thumb toward the door. "Hit the road, Jack, and don't you come back no more."

His mirthless chuckle raised the fine hairs on the back of my neck. "Ooooooh! Gonna pay for that one, dolly!"

The threat, I knew, was in deadly earnest, and I had a pretty good idea of what kind of payment old Jack had in mind. So I sent my panicky gaze scurrying around the kitchen in search of a weapon. I found a hefty eight-inch skillet hanging from the side of a cupboard.

Well, if I learned anything from my three-year stay at the South Dakota women's prison, it's this—hitting an opponent with a utensil is a whole lot more effective than doing it with your dainty little hand.

I snatched the skillet off the hook, then held it aloft like a Wimbledon champ. Jack took a menacing step forward. I cocked my good right arm.

"Don't!" I shouted. "Don't even *think* about it!"

Scowling, Jack studied the polished metal bottom of the skillet. Angry tension radiated out of him like a soaked hound shedding water. "Some other time . . ." It took him a second to remember the name. ". . . *Angie.*"

Somehow Cindy found her voice. "Get out of my house!" she shouted.

"I'm going, I'm going." Hands upraised, Jack backpedaled to the door. "Be seeing you, Cin." One final fire-eyed glance at me. "And I'll be seeing you, too, Angie. Bet on it!"

The second the door closed, I dashed across the kitchen and slammed home the deadbolt. Moments later, I heard the reassuring roar of Jack's Dodge pickup. Only then did my trembling hand set down the skillet.

I glanced at Cindy. "Are you all right?"

My cousin's fiancée had tumbled into a dining chair. Her shaking hands moved about awkwardly, as if she were groping for an explanation. Her voice bordered on the shrill. "Thank you! Thank you. Angie, you have n-no idea . . . I came out of my bedroom, and he was right *there!*"

Taking a seat at her side, I squeezed Cindy's delicate, long-fingered hands and spoke to her in a soothing tone. She was teetering on the brink of hysteria, realizing the narrowness of her recent escape. Her mind was still too full of harrowing imagery.

So we talked about it, woman to woman. Cindy did most of the talking. From what I could gather, Jack Sunawavi was an old boyfriend. She had met him shortly after moving to the city from her hometown of Price. They had dated for a little over a year, and then she'd dumped him in favor of Billy.

". . . still can't believe it almost happened. He was

going to—'' Cindy couldn't quite say it. Gripping my hands, she babbled, ''I—I haven't seen Jack in nearly two years. It . . . it . . . Angie, it was like some sort of weird n-nightmare. I came into the kitchen, and he was sitting there, grinning at me! Sitting right there! Jack Sunawavi!'' She leaped from her chair. ''Oh, my God! Look at the time. I'm supposed to be at work.''

''Sit,'' I ordered. ''You're not going anywhere, Cindy dear. First thing you're going to do is call a competent locksmith and get that lock changed. Then we'll sip some tea and sit here and consign Jack to the oblivion he deserves.''

''But my job—!''

''You think Jack doesn't know where you work?'' I sauntered over to the stove. ''Give your boss a call and tell him you're taking a sick day.'' I flipped open the lid of the cardboard Lipton box. ''If I were you, I wouldn't leave the premises until there was a new lock on that door.''

''Good idea. That's just what I'll do. Oh, Angie, I'm so glad you dropped by. I—'' Her gaze reflected mild curiosity. ''Say, what are you doing in Salt Lake? I thought you were staying in Heber with Matt and Della.''

Flashing a disarming smile, I answered, ''I got a call from the Forest Service yesterday. They've collected Billy's personal things, and they're holding them at the regional office in Ogden. I'm on my way to pick them up. Figured I'd swing by Millcreek and say hi.''

''Boy, am I glad you did.'' Rubbing her arms, Cindy stood erect. ''Then this is a social call, eh?''

''Actually, it's a little more than that, Cin. Bill's

supervisor said he was working on some kind of project. Something he took home from the office. The Forest Service asked me to return it."

"Did you try Bill's trailer in Clover Creek?"

"Not yet. I thought maybe Bill left it here."

"What is it you're looking for?"

I drew an invisible rectangle with my index fingers. "Topographic maps. Maps of Lodestone Canyon." On to the jackpot question. "Did Bill ever talk to you about Lodestone Canyon?"

She shook her head slowly. "No. Not that I recall. Bill never brought any work here. I'm sorry, but I can't think of anything more unromantic than a site survey." Feeble smile. "I'm sorry, Angie. I wish I could be of more help."

"Do you know of any friends of Bill's who might be able to help me?"

Cindy tapped her lower lip with her thumbnail. "Hmmmmm. Mickey Grantz, perhaps."

"Is he with the Forest Service?"

"Lord, no. Mickey's a lawyer."

"With a law firm here in Salt Lake?"

"No, no, not exactly. Mickey's an environmentalist. He runs a small private, non-profit group. The Tribe of Something. Honestly, where is my memory going?" Smiling impishly, she rubbed her forehead. "Sorry, Angie. I wish I could remember. I've only met him two or three times. Like I said, Bill never brought his work here."

"Don't give it another thought." I handed her the empty kettle, disappointed at not getting the answers I needed but grateful nonetheless for the slim lead.

"I'll happily settle for some tea. What say, Cin? Fill her up?"

I didn't get out of Cindy's until well after lunch. I left my cousin's fiancee reasonably secure behind a shiny new deadbolt and a little anxious about her job with the investment firm of Hayball, Nibley and Thatcher. I assured her that conscientious administrative assistants do not get canned after losing one day to illness, and I should know. I'm an expert on getting canned. Ask Paul Holbrook.

Talk about coincidence. I drove right by Hayball, Nibley and Thatcher's glassine office building on my way to the Pioneer Museum. I needed a quiet spot where I could make some phone calls, and the museum fit the bill quite nicely.

So there I was, in the museum's well-lit lobby, standing at the public telephone, with all these framed photographs of the Mormon pioneers of 1847 peering down at me. I dialed the local chapter of the Sierra Club, bounced Mickey Grantz's name off them, and came up with the name Cindy had been unable to remember. The Tribe of DAN. That's DAN as in *Deseret Au Naturel,* "Deseret" being the original Mormon name for Utah. They had an office of their own on Second South Street, bordering the university campus.

I phoned the tribe next, only to learn that the Mick was testifying downstate. Some environmental impact hearing involving the San Rafael Swell. He would be back in the morning.

I made one last call before heading back to Heber.

A long-distance call. If I was ever going to clear up the mystery surrounding Billy's death, I would need a whole lot more time. So I put through a call to the man who holds the key to the captive moments of my life . . . well, at least until my parole expires.

The voice was just as I remembered it—deep, guileless and baritone. "Department of Corrections. Holbrook speaking."

"Hiiiiiyaaaa, Kemo Sabe." I dragged it out most cattily. "I'm here at poolside, drinking margaritas and wearing a swimsuit that'd have your boss, the dishonorable Randolph T. Langston, dragging his tongue on the floor."

"How very nice to hear from you, Angela." Paul's voice remained irritatingly unruffled. "And on the appointed day, too. See? I knew you could obey the rules if you really put your mind to it. By the way, I looked it up. Kemo Sabe . . . that means 'trusted friend,' right?"

Actually, it's Paiute for "horse's ass." But I wasn't telling my parole officer that.

"So where are you calling from, princess? And please don't feel that you have to entertain me. I prefer straight answers over the telephone."

"Paul, you have the sense of humor of an ocotillo." Troubled sigh. "I'm in Salt Lake City."

"How's the trip?"

"Rotten so far."

I tried to keep it light, but there must have been some undertone of sadness in my voice. Paul picked right up on it. Sudden concern softened his tone. "Angie, what is it? What's wrong?"

"It's my cousin—Billy, the oldest one . . . he's dead, Paul."

The surge of tears overwhelmed me. I'd phoned Paul with the intention of conning another week or two of furlough out of him. Instead, I ended up telling him just about everything. Billy's death. The funeral. Reclaiming Billy's pocket possessions in Logan. The only thing I held back on was the tobacco pouch.

Paul gave me his shoulder to cry on, and, from a thousand miles away, that's exactly what I did. He listened, and I talked. Paul did for me what I had done for Cindy.

". . . and I don't know what I'm going to do about Aunt Della," I said, pausing for a brief sniffle. "Losing Billy . . . it-it's just cut the heart right out of her, Paul. It's like she's become an old woman overnight. I—I can't stand to see her like this. I want my aunt back."

"It's never easy for anybody, Angie," he murmured. "Grief will change all of you. You, Della, your uncle, your grandfather. She isn't the same woman any more, and neither are you. Grieving is a process, and it's going to take some time."

"What am I going to do, Paul?" I thought of Bill's suggestion and blurted it out. "Couldn't I stay here? Couldn't you swing something with the Utah corrections system? Turn my case over to them?"

"Angie, that's just not possible—"

"It's not fair, Paul!" I sniffled repeatedly. "I can't turn my back on Aunt Della. You—you don't know what Billy meant to her."

"Listen, Angie, I know what you're going through, and I sympathize. We're just going to have to make compromises all around. There's no way I can let you stay permanently in Utah. But I can extend your furlough.'' I heard papers rustling at the other end. ''I'm putting you in for both a bereavement leave and a family emergency furlough, effective next Monday. They'll run consecutively, so that'll give you four weeks with your family.''

I knuckled my eyes dry. ''Thank you, Paul.''

''Now I want you to do something for me. Type up two formal letters of request and mail them to Pierre. I'll bounce them past the Parole Board. Oh, and I want you to phone in now and then. Stay in touch. Let me know how you're doing.''

''*Hol*-brook!''

''We do this by the book, Angie, or we don't do it at all.''

Very demure. ''Yes, Paul.''

''I'm going to need backup documentation, so make sure I get those letters. And don't worry about your job. I'll put a temp in that Work Experience slot until you get back.''

To be perfectly honest, I hadn't even thought about my crummy waitress job at Chang's Corral since leaving Pierre. But I didn't mention that to Paul. Might as well leave him with the illusion of diligence.

''Angie . . . is everything going to be all right?''

''I guess so. I'll keep an eye on Aunt Della and—''

''I'm not talking about your aunt. I mean *you.*'' The concern in Paul's voice was mildly startling. I didn't know the fella even cared. ''Listen, if you need someone to talk to, you know where to reach me.''

''Thanks, Paul. I'll keep that in mind.''

Funny thing. I meant it—every word.

* * *

I got back to Heber just after four o'clock. I stopped at the little red brick library on Main Street and used the reference room's battered old Royal to type out those two letters for Paul.

The route home took me right past the Hy Lander Motel, Chick's Cafe (''Where people eat by choice, not by chance''), and my one-time alma mater, Heber City High, home of the Wasatch Wasps, a long brick building four shades darker than the library. I slowed Chief's Toyota as I approached the familiar white cupola of the Heber Tabernacle, then hung a left onto Midway Lane.

The Shavano place is about a mile down the lane, just over the irrigation canal. It's a whitewalled Mexican ranch house with a broad veranda, bracketed by a pair of venerable cottonwoods. It's right out there at the edge of farm country, with an undulating ridgeline of gray-green Wasatch peaks on the horizon.

Chief stepped off the veranda as I pulled into the gravelly driveway. He looked as if he'd been playing handyman around the house. Yellow T-shirt and denim bib overalls and a dark blue baseball cap with a John Deere patch.

''Got something to show you, Angie.''

So I followed him into the backyard, wondering what it was all about. Chief led me into the small, tomato-colored, gambrel-roofed barn. I wrinkled my nose at the hot, stale manure smell, and flashed my grandfather a curious look. ''Well?''

Chief gestured at Uncle Matt's tool bench. ''See for yourself.''

Atop the bench sat a McCulloch heavy-duty chain-saw, trade name *Wildcat*. Yellow casing, dual grips, and an eighteen-inch guide bar severely bent at the tip. The chain dangled loosely from the housing. I recognized it instantly from Trooper McMurdie's description.

"Chief! Where did you get *that!?*"

"Ogden." His obsidian eyes shot me a wry glance. "You weren't the only one out investigating today."

"That's—"

"The chainsaw they found on Billy. Right."

"You did a whole lot better than I did." Picking it up, I thoroughly examined the guide bar, and found some noticeable scratches near the metallic teeth at the tip. It would have taken something a little harder than lodgepole to have made those scratches. Granite, perhaps. Or basalt.

I had a sudden mental image of a shadowy figure swinging the chainsaw, dashing the guide bar against a rocky outcrop. Unknown hands placing the chainsaw in Billy's lifeless grip.

I put down the saw. "How did you get ahold of this?"

"Forest Service gave it to me."

"*Gave* it to you!?"

He nodded. "I went up to the regional office this morning. Introduced myself as Billy's grandad. Had a nice long talk with the head honcho—fella name of Weidig."

"Whoa! Start at the beginning, Chief. What was Billy's chainsaw doing in Ogden?"

"The Saguache County sheriff's office shipped it

there . . . oh, two, three days ago.'' Leaning forward, Chief drew my attention to the yellow housing. ''Pay attention, Angie, and you'll learn something about Uncle Sam's property. See any stickers on this here casing?''

I shook my head, no.

''Damn right. And that's because it ain't government property. That's what Mr. Weidig told me. Any item belonging to Uncle Sam has a magnetic sticker on it. It shows the agency to which the item belongs and its federal inventory number. Now, if this was a Forest Service chainsaw, it'd have a little sticker down here reading USDA—Department of Agriculture—and a whole slew of numbers.''

I guessed aloud. ''Their equipment officer found no sticker when the sheriff's department returned it.''

''That's right. And when he didn't find it, he jotted down the McCulloch serial number and cross-checked it against the Forest Service's computerized inventory. This particular chainsaw never was government property, and he reported that to Mr. Weidig.'' Chief stood erect again. ''Mr. Weidig seems to think that this here chainsaw belonged to Billy.''

''That's bullshit,'' I said. ''Billy lived in a trailer park. What need did he have for a chainsaw?''

''If he needed one at work, he could always draw down from the Forest Service supply shed.'' Chief turned his shrewd gaze on me. ''It's high time we talked, young lady. What do you know about all this that I don't?''

So I laid it all out for him. I mentioned my trailside chat with Billy, his opposition to the clearcutting of

Lodestone Canyon, the enmity of the local loggers, and finished up with a description of my recent unsuccessful trip to Salt Lake City.

"Whatever Billy had planned, he didn't discuss it with Cindy. Maybe Mickey Grantz can fill me in on the background."

"That's assuming Lodestone Canyon had anything to do with his death. You're reaching, Angie."

"Reaching for a motive, Chief. Right now, that planned cut seems like the strongest one."

"You know, there are officers of the law who are paid good cash money to do this kind of work." Chief ran his thumb down the chainsaw's yellow housing. "What say we pay that Saguache County sheriff a visit?"

Minor fussbudget face. "Chief, who was first at the scene? That Saguache County deputy, right? He saw the evidence."

"Sheriff's office didn't know about Lodestone Canyon."

"Ah, but what if they did?"

Obsidian eyes flickered in comprehension. "What are you saying? Local law was in on it?"

"I'm saying, all we've got right now are some disquieting facts and some vague suspicions. None of this would stand up as evidence in a court of law."

"So what do you have in mind, Angie?"

"Nandobani," I said quietly.

His eyes widened. *Nandobani.* An old word among our Anishinabe people, evocative of bloodied stone tomahawks and flint-tipped arrows whizzing through dark Minnesota woods. Go on the scout. Infiltrate enemy territory. Find and target your foe.

I would assume that Billy's death was indeed foul play, and I would go hunting for his murderers. I would find out exactly why my cousin had been in the Topanas that day, and who had known he would be up there, and who had benefited the most from his death.

"I'm going to dig it all up, Chief, and turn it over to you and let you take it to the law. And I don't mean the distinguished sheriff of Saguache County. Billy was a federal employee killed on Uncle Sam's land. It's a natural for the FBI. If it was some bigshot logger who killed him, not all his clout in Salt Lake City is going to save him."

Chief cocked his head to one side. "Kind of dangerous for you, ain't it? That sheriff—if he ain't on the square—he can get rid of you mighty easily. All he has to do is haul you in. Your parole board up in Pierre will do the rest."

Fleeting hug. "I'll be very, very careful, Chief. I'll phone every few days. I promise."

Holding me at arm's length, he flashed a grim smile. "No need."

"Come again?"

"You don't think I'd let you go alone to Clover Creek, do you?" Aged eyes gleamed in determination. "I've already lost one grandchild. I don't aim to make it two."

Hugging him once more, I added, "That leaves us with just one problem, Chief. What are we going to do about Aunt Della?"

Chief touched the tip of my nose. "Got me some ideas along those lines. You find Mickey Grantz. Leave Della to me."

Chapter Four

Aunt Della let out a quiet sigh. "Oh, Angie, I don't know. Maybe this isn't such a good idea after all."

"Sure it is! Why, you haven't been to the North-land in ages." Smiling, I ushered my aunt onto the escalator. "You wouldn't want to miss the Fergus Falls Goose Gallop, would you?"

We were at the Salt Lake airport, Aunt Della and I, riding the silvery escalator up to a sunwashed mezzanine. Huge slanted windows looked out onto black runways, salt desert, dwarf sagebrush and the dun-colored Oquirrh Mountains. The windows acted like a giant magnifying glass, rendering me sticky and uncomfortable in my apple-green, short-sleeved chemise. Aunt Della, dressed for travel in a navy blue double-breasted jacket and long, flared skirt, seemed not to notice.

"Angela, I have no desire to watch a gaggle of stampeding geese—"

"Then give it a skip," I interrupted, leaning against the gleaming aluminum rail. "There's no shortage of things to do, Aunt Della. Ni-Mi-Win's coming up in a couple of weeks. You've got the cabin and Chie-ah, Grandfather's pickup.'' My aunt doesn't like the nickname, thinks it's disrespectful. ''You're all set.''

''I don't know.'' Casting me a troubled look, she murmured, ''It doesn't *feel* right, Angie. It—it's as if I'm running away.''

''Listen, you need to be away.'' Touching her face, I flashed a sympathetic smile. ''You've been through the wringer since . . . well, with everything that's happened. You need some time away from here, just you and Uncle Matt. It's not like you don't have any friends in Silver Bay, you know.''

Aunt Della frowned. ''I doubt I'll be very good company.''

''Maybe not. But the grieving process has to start somewhere.'' I was beginning to sound like Paul Holbrook. ''I can't think of any place better than Tettegouche.''

My aunt opened her mouth, intent upon a dispute, but a hearty masculine voice beat her to it. ''Girl's got some sound advice, Del. I'd listen to her, if I were you.''

Looking over my shoulder, I saw Uncle Matt strolling down the corridor with Chief at his side. In his bead-brimmed Stetson and charcoal gray business suit, my Nuche uncle looked like a successful horse breeder.

''Luggage all squared away?'' I asked.

''All set, Angie.'' He slapped their ticket envelopes against his upraised palm. ''Charlie's turned in his rental. I just gave him the keys to my truck.''

My grandfather and I had found a valuable ally in Uncle Matt. Without his help, I don't think we ever would have persuaded Aunt Della to make the trip. Like us, Uncle Matt felt she needed a healing place, far away from Utah. When I had casually mentioned Chief's cabin at Tettegouche, my uncle's response had been most enthusiastic.

Turning to Chief, Aunt Della asked, "Are you sure you're going to be all right, Dad?"

"I can handle it." He crushed her in a two-armed bear hug. "Take good care of yourself, Della. You hear me?"

Nodding, she showed me a moist-eyed look of regret. "I wish you could have come with us, Angie."

"What can I say? I'm not a free woman. The Department of Corrections decides my itinerary."

"Take good care of her, Dad."

"Don't you have that backwards?" I inquired.

Laconic smile from Chief. "I don't think so."

Just then the public address system came on. "Northwest Flight Number Six-Seven-Two to Minneapolis now boarding at Gate Twelve."

Chief and I walked them as far as the airport security booth. There was one final round of hugs and handshakes, kisses and farewells, and then, following a last-moment embrace, we watched them pass beneath the metal detector.

By the time we returned to the mezzanine, their Northwest jetliner was warming up its turbofans. Leaning against the railing, we watched it crawl away from the extended jetway.

"There they go." Chief turned to me. "What now, missy?"

Taut grin. *"Nandobani."*

"You're about to do something illegal, aren't you?"

"Now, Chief, you know if I answer that, you automatically become an accessory."

Flashing me a disapproving look, he muttered, "I still think we ought to take it to the law."

"We will . . . eventually." I glanced at the array of TV monitors, seeking the exact time. 9:04 a.m. The Tribe of DAN should have opened by now.

Chief escorted me to the escalator. "Can I drop you anywhere?"

"Second South Street will do for a start."

When I first walked through the doorway of the Tribe of DAN's headquarters on Second South, I thought I had inadvertently wandered into some sort of collegiate health club. Perky, bright-eyed coeds in halter tops and bike shorts. Sun-bronzed Mormon boys who seemed to be majoring in weightlifting. Ohhhhhhh . . . where were these gorgeous hunks when I was going to college?

Spandex pants were the order of the day—for both genders. They came in bright lollipop colors and lengths ranging from clamdigger to Olympic swimmer. In my apple-green chemise and midheeled pumps, I was definitely overdressed.

The tribe's hangout had once been a walk-in pizzeria and the scent of mozzarella still seemed to linger. Twenty-two students bustled about its narrow length, oblivious to the scattered papers, open textbooks and lipsticked coffee mugs littering the card tables. Two smiling coeds with mushrooming hairstyles manned the fundraising desk, selling homemade pottery, hand-tooled leather belts, plastic cups, tribal T-shirts and rolled-up posters.

I liked their posters. Two of them adorned the rear wall. One was a black-and-white photo of naturalist Aldo Leopold with the quote: *"A thing is right when it tends to preserve the integrity, stability and beauty of the biotic community."* The other was a full-color shot of an achingly lovely mountain meadow, a Wasatch-rimmed field ablaze with yellow cinquefoil and sego lily. Across the top—*Worth Saving*, and at the bottom—*Deseret Au Naturel*.

No trouble finding Mickey Grantz. He was the only person in the room over the age of twenty-two, and he was the only one whose shirt had a collar. It was a knit evergreen short-sleeved golfer's shirt, and it went well with his clean, well-ironed blue jeans.

The Mick was talking on the telephone, a slight, animated man with curly black hair, thick eyebrows, a hawkish nose with the tip tilting slightly downward, small peekaboo ears and a neatly trimmed Van Dyke. He was fond of making elaborate gestures with his hands. His voice would have gotten him a tenor's job in any Italian opera.

Hanging up abruptly, he swiveled those deepset dark blue eyes in my direction. "Can you type?"

Startled, I blinked and nodded.

"Great!" Ripping the top sheet from his yellow legal pad, he pushed it across the blotter. "Type that." Then he flipped open a bulky *Federal Register* and tapped at a printed notice. "Make a dozen copies of this page. Then type up a dozen envelopes. I want to get this Notice of Realty Action to the board before next Monday's meeting. Got all that?"

Wry smile. "Mr. Grantz, I think there's been some mistake."

"Mistake?" Mickey's wistful gaze was doing a yoyo routine—up and down my legs. "What mistake?" Frowning, he pulled his avid gaze away from my calves. Fondness gave way to mild confusion. "Aren't you the temp Zarahemla sent over this morning?"

I shook my head slowly. "Afraid not."

"Then who are you?"

"My name's Angela Biwaban. I'd like to talk to you."

"I'd like to talk to you, too, Angela." He had a warm and appreciative smile. "Unfortunately, I've got a court appearance coming up at eleven. So if you're interested in a secretarial position that promises mountains of typing and the chance to ride herd on twenty exuberant college students, by all means, please sit down. Otherwise, I'm afraid that I simply can't spare the—"

"It's about Bill Shavano," I said.

Mickey's expression changed the moment I mentioned my cousin's name. Instantly forgotten was the pass he'd been inching his way toward. Rising at once, he gallantly cleared off the visitor's chair for me.

Once I was seated, he gave me a somber, speculative look. "So you're the cousin."

"He, uh, took my name in vain on occasion, eh?"

"Once or twice." Reaching across the desktop, Mickey tenderly squeezed my hand. "I'm sorry about what happened. We were all pretty broken up around here when we got the news. He was a good man."

Dark blue eyes radiated a look of condolence. "How's Bill's mother taking it?"

So I talked a little about Aunt Della and Uncle Matt and Cindy, and found out Mickey had missed the funeral because he'd been testifying before the House Forestry Subcommittee in Washington. The pleasantries didn't last long, however. Mickey wanted to know what I was doing there.

"What can we do for you, Angie?"

"Billy and I had a long talk at the powwow. We got to talking about Lodestone Canyon." Time for a little white lie. "That's when your name came up."

"Lodestone Canyon . . ." Leaning back in his swivel chair, Mickey absentmindedly stroked his beard. "You know, if it wasn't for Bill, we never would have found out about that in time."

"Billy told you about it?"

Nodding, he motioned for me to stand. "You bet. He came to us, oh, just about a year ago. He told us some loggers were trying to get a permit to cut in the Topanas. He said the whole process was as illegal as hell."

"How so?" I asked.

Mickey led me to a huge wall map. "The way Bill explained it, his job was to review all requests to log in the national forest. That means he got his share of paperwork at every stage of the planning process. One day your cousin opened his mail, and there was a receipt for a performance bond from the First National Bank of Saguache County."

"Performance bond?" I asked.

"Any private firm wanting to cut timber on federal land has to put down some bond money," he ex-

71

plained, folding his long arms. "If they do a good job, the money is returned after the cut. If they screw up the environment, they forfeit the amount, and it goes to pay for cleanup costs. In this case, Bill learned that a firm called High Timber Associates, Inc. had deposited a bond in the amount of twenty-five thousand dollars in an escrow account at First National. Bill couldn't understand it. He checked the Topanas District Resource Management Plan. It hadn't been amended to include a new timber cut, and there was no listing for a new environmental impact survey within the district. So Bill did some checking. He contacted the BLM office in Salt Lake. They told him a Clover Creek lawyer named Dennis Simms had requested permission to cut in Sections 26 through 39 in the Topanas National Forest."

"What happened then?"

"Bill visited Lodestone Canyon on horseback. And was he *bullshit!* He couldn't believe his supervisor had actually okayed that performance bond. The potential for environmental damage was tremendous."

I vividly remembered the fervor in Billy's voice when he spoke of saving Lodestone Canyon. "What kind of damage, Mick?"

"Here. Let me show you." He ran his index finger along the map. "Bill took us up there back in April. You see, it's all old-growth forest along the rim, Angie. Aspen, mostly, with some black spruce and subalpine fir. Very steep slopes up there. Sixty degree inclines or better, I'd say. There's a thin, fragile layer of loamy soil along the top."

"Bill told me it was the biggest aspen ecosystem in northern Utah."

72

Mickey's smile was grim. "The biggest, and the most delicate, too. You couldn't cut trees in there without destroying it."

"No one has ever logged there before?"

He shook his head. "Too expensive. Aspen is what the lumber industry calls a *weed tree*. It doesn't fetch enough on the market to justify the cost." Taking my elbow, he escorted me back to my chair. "To cut in Lodestone, you'd have to run a skyhook and cable line up to the rim, cut skid trails, build some haul roads and logging docks. Not worth it."

"Apparently, it was worth it to somebody."

"That's not surprising." Mickey relaxed in his swivel chair, resting one loafer on the desk's edge. "There are people in this state who'd cut anything. Their vision of Zion is a mall at every corner."

Resuming my seat, I remarked, "I don't understand, though. How could a cut permanently damage the ecosystem?"

"Those aspen roots are the only thing holding that layer of loamy soil in place. You spent a winter in Utah. You know how the wind blows up in the Wasatch. Cut that aspen, and the soil will be blown to Nebraska with the first December blizzard."

I nodded in understanding, then asked, "What did Billy do when he found out about the bond?"

"Took it up with Longhurst, he told me. And got nowhere. He wanted to know why the proposed cut had reached the bond stage without so much as a notice in the *Federal Register*. Longhurst fed him some song and dance about the BLM taking care of everything. A few weeks went by, and Bill had another go-round with Longhurst, who finally admitted that he'd issued a waiver. That's when Bill told Longhurst that there was no way—no way!—he would ever consent to a cut in Lodestone Canyon. Longhurst warned him he'd better go along with it."

"How did Billy react?"

Genuine admiration filled Mickey's voice. "Your cousin was one hell of a forest ranger, Angie. Sure wish we had more like him. He handled it right by the book. He did his homework on the potential damage, got backup information from the Bureau of Reclamation, wrote a detailed memo advising *against* the proposed cut. Old man Longhurst refused to accept it."

"That's when Billy came to you people," I added.

Fond smile from the Mick. "He came in one day, and we did some talking. We'd had our misgivings about Alfred J. Longhurst, of course. Required public notices were awfully slow coming out of his Clover Creek office. But Bill really opened our eyes. There are good and bad district supervisors. Longhurst is one of the bad ones."

Thoughtful frown. "Mick, did Billy ever talk to you about the Bureau of Indian Affairs?"

He stroked his beard momentarily, then shook his head. "No. Not that I recall. Why do you ask?"

"Billy told me that he'd figured out a way to save Lodestone. But it had something to do with the BIA."

Interest gleamed in those dark blue eyes. "Like what?"

Mild sigh. "I don't know. He never got around to explaining it. He just said he wanted to run for the tribal council. If he got on the council, he could save the canyon."

"Well, that cousin of yours always did play his hand pretty close to the vest." Mickey's features suddenly turned troubled. "Now, would you mind answering one of my questions?"

"Not at all."

"What's your interest in all this?"

Steely-eyed gaze from the princess. "Let's just say I don't believe the official verdict."

He flashed me a sharp quizzical look. "Any proof to the contrary?"

"No." Another white lie.

Mickey was silent for a long moment. Then, shifting forward in his chair, he rested his bony elbows on the desk. "I'm going to give you a piece of advice, Angie. If by chance you do come across something that might contradict the verdict, take it straight to the FBI. Understand me?"

"I'm not sure I do, Mr. Grantz."

"You're not going to get anywhere in Clover Creek. The sheriff up there—Stead Mortensen—he's a political animal just like Longhurst. If he wants a comfortable old age, he has to keep the big loggers happy. Guys like Karl Eames, Henry Broward and Truman Kimball Sager. Bill didn't make too many friends in that crowd. Those boys logged out their private lands years ago. To survive, they need to cut on federal land. Your cousin didn't make it easy for them."

Eames and Broward again. Those names were becoming downright familiar.

"So I shouldn't stop in for a friendly chat with the sheriff?"

He looked me straight in the eye. "Here's some more advice, Angie. *Don't!* Stay the hell out of Saguache County. If Mortensen ever finds out you're related to Bill, he'll give you ninety days that'll make your stay in that women's prison seem like Club Med."

"Frame job?"

"It's been known to happen." Sudden anger pinched Mickey's features. "Three of our kids went up to Clover Creek a month ago. They spent a day handing out save-the-canyon leaflets downtown. As they were driving back to the motel, one of Mortensen's good-old-boy deputies pulled them over right in front of the junior high school. Told them, 'I smell marijuana in that there car!' He forced open their trunk, and, sure enough, there's a brick of the notorious weed wedged under the tail light." His smile turned to stone. "The kids got charged with possession with intent to sell. It'll never stand up, of course. I'll sure as hell get it overturned in Salt Lake. But it was a rough forty-eight hours for our people."

My expression of anxiety was not wholly feigned. "He wouldn't even have to fabricate, Mick. All he has to do is bust me. My parole board will put me behind bars for the duration."

Alert gaze from the lawyer-turned-environmentalist. "Then you will have that talk with the FBI?"

"As soon as I get back to Pierre."

As he walked me out, Mickey explained a little about the Tribe of DAN. It was a private, non-profit corporation subsisting on federal grants and foundation money. Mickey had set it up four years earlier, following his move to Salt Lake, a move prodded by a particularly acrimonious divorce.

"Where are you originally from?" I asked.

"Trenton, New Jersey. My old man was a dentist. He came out to the Northwest for a convention and fell in love with Tacoma. We moved out there when I was eight." Pausing at the entryway, he held open the door for me. "Are you sure I can't interest you in that secretarial job?"

Slow shake of the head. "Sorry, Mick. I'm afraid my parole officer would never approve."

He flashed a broad Lothario smile. "You'd certainly dress up the office."

My own smile was a bit tart. "That's an incredibly sexist remark, Mr. Grantz."

"You're an incredibly lovely woman, Miss Biwaban."

"Flatterer!"

"Dinner the next time you're in Salt Lake?"

I took a moment to mull it over. "Mmmmmm . . . perhaps."

"Perhaps yes?"

Flirtatious Angie smile. "We'll find that out . . . *next time.*"

I suppose dinner with The Mick would have been interesting, but I had work to do—namely, cooking up an alternative identity for my upcoming scout.

Every major American city has its red-light district, and Brother Brigham's town is no exception. There's a section of Salt Lake where God-fearing Latter-Day Saints don't go—a short stretch of State Street, just beyond Liberty Park.

And that's where I spent my Saturday evening, resplendent in a grape-colored minidress and stiletto-heeled mules, wearing enough mascara to clearly signal my supposed profession. I struck out in three bars before I finally got my lead.

I struck paydirt at the Gearjammer, a hole-in-the-wall saloon on Eleventh South. When the bartender, a hard-eyed Swede, saw that I wasn't exactly there for the merry social life, he waggled a finger and summoned me over to the bar and informed me that this was an Outfit place and only selected girls get to work it, so finish your drink, honey, and take it out on the sidewalk. I told him I was buying, not selling, and definitely in the market for some flash.

Flash, for those of you who have never been defendants in a criminal action, is what we graduates of Springfield call *false identification*. Because you flash it at the police officer, and, hopefully, he lets you go.

The Swede referred me to a seedy photo store off Ninth East. I turned up their bright and early on Monday morning. It was run by an aging veteran of Woodstock named Magic Sam, a thin, sallow fellow with a scraggly graying beard and weary, red-rimmed eyes.

What Sam lacked in neatness he more than made up for with his expertise in forgery. Using his graphic arts training, he had concocted giant-sized mockups of Wyoming and Colorado driver's licenses. His customers stood in front of the desired mockup, with their faces filling the blank photo square. Sam photographed the whole thing in living color, reduced it to actual driver's license size, and then laminated the print in clear plastic.

He asked me for a name and address. I was momentarily stumped, and then I came up with the perfect alias, thanks to Aunt Della.

When I was four years old, the Shavanos spent the summer with us in Duluth. Once I joined Mother and Aunt Della for a stroll around Superior Street. I saw a toy that I simply had to have, and Mother said no, whereupon I cut loose with a mammoth tantrum. Lots of foot stomping and hair tugging and earsplitting yowls. Mother was on her knees, trying to negotiate a solution. Aunt Della's expression kept getting more and more exasperated. Finally, my aunt took two steps forward and planted a stiff-armed wallop where my shorts fit the tightest, an open-handed smack that put me on tiptoe and had me wailing for real. "That'll *do,* Sarah Bernhardt!" she said, and looking at my mother, added, "You're too polite to that girl, Geri."

Okay, so *Sarah* it would be. Hmmmmm, lose the H—let's make it *Sara.* Sara what? Ah, how about *Sara Soyazhe?* A pleasantly euphonious Native American name.

Thirty minutes later, I walked out of Sam's store with *Sara Soyazhe*'s Wyoming license in my purse, plus a handful of blank diplomas from the University of Wyoming in Laramie. Magic Sam runs them off on his printing press for the benefit of jobseekers unwilling to sit four years in a college lecture hall.

Chief and I met for lunch, and I explained that I was going undercover. We agreed to meet again in Clover Creek. In the meantime, he was heading back to Heber to button up Aunt Della's house.

Early on Tuesday afternoon, August eighteenth, I turned up in Ogden, arriving by bus, taking care not to be seen with Chief. I picked up a copy of the

Standard-Examiner at the bus station, diligently reviewed the classifieds, and found a rooming house on Harrison Boulevard catering to single young women.

The landlady listened with interest to my tale of just arriving from Rock Springs, Wyoming, graciously accepted cash for the first month's rent and security deposit, agreed to let me activate the telephone jack, and informed me that most of my neighbors were nurses employed at the hospitals nearby.

I spent the next two days obtaining shopper's courtesy cards at Newgate Mall, opening a checking account at Western Fidelity Bank, securing a Mountain Bell phone bill with my new address on it, and, most importantly, swapping Sara's phony Wyoming license for a genuine Utah one at the local office of the Department of Public Safety.

Thanks to the *Standard-Examiner* classifieds, I also picked up a serviceable blue 1983 Honda Accord for two thousand bucks. True, that put a bit of a dent in my war fund, but I needed wheels of my own if I was going to scoot around Saguache County.

If Sheriff Mortensen felt inclined to check, he would learn that Sara Soyazhe is indeed a licensed driver in the Beehive State and is the proud owner of a duly registered Honda Accord with the license plates M25-728. And if he extended his inquiry to Ogden, he would learn that Sara is indeed a resident of the Nephi Arms on Harrison Boulevard, that she is a customer of Mountain Bell with a telephone at the same address, that she has a checking account with a balance of three thousand dollars, and that she is enrolled in store credit accounts at no fewer than seven establishments at Newgate Mall.

To paraphrase a famous general . . . when dealing with sheriffs, there is no substitute for respectability.

So, Miss Sara Soyazhe, daughter of the Nuche and apparent long-time resident of Ogden, Utah, just what do you do for a living?

Well, it's all right here on Magic Sam's diplomas. I happen to be a Dean's List graduate of the University of Wyoming with a Master's in geology. I'm hoping to pick up an assistant professorship over at Weber State College. But the Board of Trustees hasn't made the final decision yet. So I thought I'd spend . . .

". . . a couple of weeks up north. I haven't hiked the Topanas since I was in junior high. I can't believe how big Clover Creek has gotten," I said, wide-eyed and smiling, my big nylon suitcases at my feet.

"Oh, it's changed, all right," said Mrs. Thornley, fanning herself with a copy of *Good Housekeeping*. She was a stolid Mormon grandmother, her fine hair bleached white by the sun, a slightly bulbous nose, skin as tough as saddle leather, and steel-rimmed bifocal glasses. "There must be pretty close to twenty-eight thousand folks living here now. A whole bunch came in about ten years ago when Mr. Broward opened the Reata meat plant south of town."

"You mean Cue Broward?"

Mrs. Thornley seemed surprised. "You've heard of him, Sara?"

"I guess just about everybody in Utah has heard of Cue Broward."

"Sure right about that." She lifted her chin to laugh, exposing a delicate and incongruous string of pearls. "Who'd've ever thought Cue Broward would've gotten where he is today? And him not even a Mormon. A Gentile! Can you believe it?''

"I didn't know Mr. Broward owned a meat plant." A mosquito whined at my earlobe. I shooed it away with a toss of my hair. "I heard he was into lumber."

"Lumber, meatpacking, real estate—anything he can squeeze a dime out of." Envy added a slight rasp to her voice. "Old Cue is his own supplier at the Reata plant. He owns the Circle B ranch up by Tenmile. Got fifteen thousand head, I hear. Then there's the Willow Valley Dairy. That's his, too—lock, stock and milking machines. 'Course, that Cue, he made most of his money in real estate. Used to buy up land after the loggers had cleared it, cut it up into subdivisions, sell lots through that Willow Valley Realty of his. He built quite a few houses, too, And I know he's partners with Gail's daddy in that construction company. You know, when he came to town, oh, forty years ago, the only thing he could call his own was his saddle. Now there's a whole lot of folks mighty anxious to keep him happy."

Mrs. Thornley and I were standing in the driveway of the Trail's End Trailer Park, founded two decades ago by her late husband, Isaiah. My cousin's final home on this earth. The night was hot and still and alive with the clickety song of the cicadas.

Flinching from the circling mosquitoes, the lady said, "I'm not sure I can help you, honey. Sure, I've got the vacancy. But Mr. Shavano's family hasn't cleared out the trailer yet. There are still a few of his things in there."

"Let me have a look at it. Please?" Demure Angie smile, evocative of the youngest daughter returning home from college. "And if there's any more packing to be done, I'd be willing to do it."

"I don't know. It's an awful lot of work, Sara."

"I don't mind." Stooping, I grabbed the handles of both suitcases. "I really need a place to stay, Mrs. Thornley. The Coronet downtown is a little too pricey for us grad students."

"Can't blame you there, Sara." She flourished her rolled-up magazine like a baton. "That Pete Welker! For what he charges, you'd think it was the dad-blamed MGM Grand. Come on."

Mrs. Thornley led me down a winding path smothered in pea stones. Lengthy aluminum trailers flanked either side. Flower gardens and knee-high white picket fences camouflaged their cinderblock foundations. Billy's trailer was at the end, long and low, with a corrugated metal awning above the bay window. Standing beside it was a western juniper forty feet high.

Once inside, I pronounced myself well-satisfied with the accommodations. I also made a point of asking the whereabouts of the nearest LDS tabernacle. From the way Mrs. Thornley's eyes lit up, I could see that the trailer was mine. She instructed me to leave my suitcases by the door, fretted aloud about the lack of fresh linen, and hurried back to the house to make the call to Heber.

I wasn't worried. The only person in Heber able to accept her call was Chief. And, once she gave him my description, he would certainly allow *Sara Soyazhe* to rent it for the rest of August.

Flicking on the overhead light, I had a look around. Chief and Uncle Matt had done a pretty thorough job of clearing out Billy's things. Wire hangers dangled in the narrow, shallow closets. Weighty cardboard boxes were lined up beside the door. My next stop was the chest of drawers, where I found a thick Navaho blanket and some neatly folded pillowcases.

Close inspection of the rug and floorboards. Not a spider web or a dust kitty in sight. I couldn't believe this was the same Billy Shavano I had lived with fourteen years ago. The Marine Corps had noticeably upgraded his housekeeping skills. The whole room had a barracks flavor, right down to the olive drab footlocker at the foot of his bed.

The desk had the same appearance of spartan neatness. Plastic cover on the home computer. Pens and pencils stabled in a Heber Creeper souvenir glass. Papers neatly stacked in the out tray. And then my gaze was drawn to the brown leather map case beside the dictionary. It was a good two feet long, with the logo *U.S. Forest Service* embossed in gold on the cover.

I flipped the case open and thumbed through all the predominantly green topographic maps from the U.S. Geologic Survey. Maps of Clover Creek and the lower Topanas National Forest near Tenmile. And now some beige and brown maps of low-lying salt desert. I spied a town in one of the grid squares. *Penrose*. Think a moment. Sure, the other side of the Wasatch—down in the basin.

I found a notation in the lower left corner of the Penrose map. Three numerals scribbled in Billy's blunt hand. 206.

What could it mean?

At first I thought it referred to a map section. I

backtracked a few pages and discovered that most of the sections listed had double-digit designations. I found something else, too—tiny tufts of map paper caught in the cleft of the case's metal binder.

The sight made me nervous. Hastily I closed the map case, then moseyed on casually across the room. Kneeling before the door, I examined the keyhole. Suspicions confirmed! Very faint scratches on the keyhole rim, the kind a lockpick might make.

So Billy's trailer had had a visitor. Some time in the past two weeks, between my cousin's death and my arrival, a person or persons unknown had sprung the door lock and given the trailer a surreptitious toss. No doubt when the alert Mrs. Thornley had been at the tabernacle. The intruder had been very careful, too, taking pains to leave no trace of his passage.

Except one—those tiny paper fragments in the binder.

I could pretty well guess what had happened. The intruder had pored through the maps—just like me—and had found whatever he'd come looking for. Rushed for time, and perhaps fearful of discovery, he had ripped the maps from the case, leaving behind those tiny telltale shreds.

So what did you have in that map case, Billy? And how badly did the intruder want it? Badly enough to kill you?

Rising from the bristly carpet, I lifted my hem, tugged the wrinkles out of my ultra-sheer pantyhose, brushed off my narrow skirt, and swept my raven hair away from my face. And that's when I heard it. The sudden skittering sound of loose pea stones.

"Mrs. Thornley?" I called.

There was no answer.

I eased the door open a crack. The air outside was just as stifling as the air inside the trailer. I took a quick peek at the walkway. A line of electric lamps led back to Mrs. Thornley's bungalow. Nobody was out for a stroll.

Well, it could have been a stray tomcat, but I was taking no chances. I wiggled my feet out of my brand-new skimmers and doused the overhead light. I counted to twenty, then opened the door another few inches and sidled outside.

In stocking feet, I padded to the corner, my eyes flicking right and left, as soundless and as wary as a jackrabbit. I was feeling bold and tricky. Anishinabe woman warrior on the prowl.

That sensation lasted just about one minute. And then a harsh, sinewy masculine hand snapped shut around my blouse collar.

Chapter Five

The grip tightened. I felt the warmth of my captor's breath on my ear. And then a familiar male voice whispered, *"Gego zegiziken."*

Loud sigh. It was my mischievous grandfather, telling me not to be frightened. I might have known. He's the only one who can sneak up on me like that.

Quick glance over my shoulder. "Too late, Chief. I already need a change of underwear."

My grandfather showed me his patented warpath scowl. *"Ikigo anishinabemowin!"*

So I made the switch to our people's language. In Anishinabemowin, we're no longer Chief and Angie. It's *Nimishoo* and *Noozis.* Grandfather and Granddaughter.

"I expected you yesterday, *Noozis.*"

"I spent a little extra time strengthening my false identity. Mickey Grantz said to expect hostility from the local law."

"I've heard the same."

"From whom, *Nimishoo?*"

"The Nuche. They talk of a deputy, *Noozis*. He is a big man, and he likes to use his fists."

"Hmmmm . . . find out anything else while I was down in Ogden?"

"My grandson spent some time at a roadhouse in Cottonwood. The Briar Patch, it's called. He was there a lot before he took up with Cindy."

"Did you hear anything about a fight between Billy and two loggers?"

A faint smile tugged at Chief's lips. "The fight you speak of, *Noozis*—it took place in Clover Creek. During *Ickigamisigegizis*. My grandson fought well. *Tayaa*, he fought them both and won."

"Did you get the names?"

He nodded. "Ed Kearns and Joe Nielsen."

Ickigamisigegizis . . . Maple-Syrup-Making Month, known as April to the new people. Very interesting. Billy had had his run-in with those loggers about the same time he'd taken Mick's tribe on that tour of Lodestone Canyon.

Chief brought me out of my reverie with a murmur. *"Baadaasamose ikwe gichimookoman."*

I turned, and, sure enough, there was Mrs. Thornley, returning from the house, her rotund face showing a blend of surprise and pleasure.

"Why, Mr. Pahvant, what are you doing up here this time of night?"

"Hello, Kate." Ever the gentleman, Chief doffed his Stetson. "I was headed up to a horse auction in Montpelier. Thought I'd drop by and pick up a few more of Bill's things."

"Well, I'm glad you're here. I called his parents in Heber, and there's no answer." Touching my arm, she added, "Honey, this is Mr. Charlton Pahvant. He's related to Bill. Charlton, this here is Sara Soyazhe. She'd like to rent the trailer."

I had to smile at Chief's selection of an alias. *Pahvant* is a Nuche expression meaning *By the Water*. And what could be more appropriate for a man who makes his home on the rockbound shore of Lake Superior?

"Sara and I have been talking." Deadpan, Chief turned to me. "Bill's folks are out of town just now, but I'm sure they wouldn't object. It's going to take a few more days to clean out the trailer, though."

"I'd be happy to give you any help you need, Mr. Pahvant," I said, tongue in cheek.

"That's right kindly of you . . . Sara." He couldn't resist the impulse to tease me. "Are you married?"

"No, sir."

"Well, I hope you're not going to give Mrs. Thornley any trouble with loud parties and boyfriends staying too late."

Tart Angie smile. "Oh, no, sir. I'm sure my *grandfather* would *never* approve of that."

"Now don't you fret, Charlton. There ain't going to be any monkey business." Kate Thornley gave me a motherly hug. "Sara's a good Mormon girl."

Seeing a possible opening, I remarked, "Did Bill do much entertaining, Mrs. T?"

"Oh, no, Sara. Bill was a very private person. Occasionally he brought his fiancée around. My, she was a pretty thing! And sometimes that friend of his dropped by."

"Friend?" I echoed.

Emphatic nod. "Skinny guy. A Ute." Pudgy features tensed in concentration. "I think I've seen him around town. Name escapes me, though. The two of them used to stand out in front here and palaver away in that Indian talk. My husband, God rest him, knew a phrase or two, but I never could get the hang of it."

"If Sara stays awhile, maybe she could teach you." Stepping forward, Chief laid a palm on my shoulder. "And now, young lady, I'd appreciate a hand with them boxes. I'd like to get to Idaho before first light."

The next morning, I awoke in Billy's bed to the *sput-sput-sputter* of a faltering lawnmower and a stream of sunshine bright enough to turn my cousin's heavy drapery into a curtain of neon green. It promised to be another August scorcher, so I toddled off to the phonebooth-sized shower, chilled my sweaty self in a fine spray of clear, cold mountain water, and broke out the summerweight casuals. Sporty oversized T-shirt with elbow-length sleeves and nipped-in waist. Bright orange Spandex bike pants and comfortable white doeskin moccasins.

After gassing up the Accord at the downtown Chevron station, I stopped for breakfast at the Lean 'n' Mean Restaurant on West Radford, then set out on my get-acquainted tour of Clover Creek and vicinity.

Clover Creek is basically a typical Mormon grid overlying the confluence of the creek and the slightly larger Willow River. The main axis is Center Street, which is also known as Utah Route 302. Running perpendicular to Center is the other main drag, Radford Avenue. Where the two come together, you'll find the original 1858 Mormon Tabernacle, a sturdy gabled pioneer crackerbox with an ornate central tower built right into the facade. Right across the street is the Saguache County courthouse, a white wooden structure that might have been mistaken for the summer villa of Pericles, if not for the Victorian cupola on top. Further down Center is the Clover Creek City Hall, a utilitarian yellow brick building of an architectural style best described as WPA wedding cake.

Most of the town's commercial establishments were on Center Street. After leaving my Accord in the municipal parking lot, I strolled past the Northern Farmers and Ranchers Credit Union, S & S Hardware, Russell Maughan High School, the Golden Trumpet Bookstore, Hannah's Hope Chest (saw some smart-looking skirts in that window) and the Daughters of the Utah Pioneers Museum. I finished my hike half a mile up the road at the Valley View Market.

If you want to get to know a town, the best place to start is the local supermarket, especially its bulletin board. Perusing the posted notices, I learned that the Fourth Ward had scheduled a Labor Day picnic in Bridger Park, that the Willow Valley Harmonettes would be the main entertainment at the Grange Hall next weekend, and, most importantly, that the Exaltation Printing Company published the *Saguache County Herald*, reputed to be "the only newspaper that works for and cares about the people of the Willow Valley area."

So I backtracked seven blocks, stopped at the Exaltation office, plunked down thirty-five cents, and stalked off with a week-old copy of the *Herald* under my arm.

Herald was a good name for the weekly. The entire back page was devoted to the Book of Mormon, complete with full-color illustrations and commentary by Dr. Eldon T. Budge. Me, I was more interested in the lead story on page one. I wanted to read the Clover Creek version of my cousin's death.

RANGER SLAIN IN LOGGING MISHAP

Forest ranger William M. Shavano was killed Tuesday in the Topanas National Forest when a limb fell from the lodgepole pine he was cutting.

Shavano, 29, was still alive when he was found by Deputy T.P. Braddock. The injured man was flown to Salt Lake City by medical evacuation helicopter. He expired while undergoing surgery.

Deputy Braddock was on routine patrol in the Dynamite Pass area when he saw Shavano's truck parked by the side of the road. He stopped to investigate. He climbed a steep ridge and saw the injured Shavano some distance away. He then went to his assistance.

I read through the rest of the article, including Billy's obit. But my gaze kept coming back to that third paragraph.

The phraseology bothered me, and not because the *Herald* reporter had lifted it right out of the police blotter.

He stopped to investigate.

Investigate what? He sees a light green Forest Service truck parked by the side of the road, which is where forest rangers usually park when they're out doing work in the field. Tell me, deputy, what's so suspicious about that?

He saw the injured Shavano some distance away.

Really? That must have been some trick. According to Trooper McMurdie, my cousin's body was pretty well covered by that lodgepole limb. From *some distance away,* it must have looked like any other deadfall. How could Mr. Braddock have seen my cousin beneath it?

So now I had a new name to add to those of Eames and Broward. And a whole new set of questions. I needed to flesh out the name of Deputy T.P. Braddock. To match it with a face and a personal history. And that would take some doing. An experienced deputy was unlikely to fall for the standard Angie-scam. I would need another—and much safer—approach.

I gave the matter a lot of thought on the way home.

"... so there I was," I said, fingertips stroking my half-empty glass of Lowenbrau. "Up on Lost Creek Road in my coed rangerette outfit, and along comes this Ford pickup. California plates, natch. They've got their long-eared trophy strapped across the hood. And there's still seven weeks to go till hunting season. Anyway, the truck stopped, and this fella jumped out and said, 'Excuse me, honey. Are you an Indian?' I said yes. Then he added, 'Well, maybe you could tell us what kind of deer this is.' So I took a good look at it and said, 'It must be one of those mule deers.' And the guy said, 'How do you know that?' And I replied, 'Because he's still got his horse-shoes on.' "

Mark and Donna burst into laughter. Especially Donna. The more bottles her newlywed husband opened, the funnier she found my anecdotes of ran-gerette life.

Pushing her empty glass away, the recent bride gig-gled. "Honestly, Sara, you must have met all kinds up there at Crater Lake."

Mark cracked a broad grin. "Sure wish I'd been there when those Californios tried to get that mule through the game check."

They were a smiling and personable couple, the Anteros. I'd met them two hours earlier in the parking lot of the Briar Patch. I had needed a sponsor to get into that private club, and my newfound newlywed friends had filled the bill quite nicely.

You see, Utah has a number of dry counties, and Saguache is one of them. Cocktail lounges cannot operate openly in these counties, so the savvy saloon-keeper declares his establishment a "private club," which is able to serve liquor, and then sells one-dollar *memberships* to all comers.

For the past two hours, I had been regaling Mark and Donna with tales of my brief career as a rangere-ette. Carefully and casually, I had steered the conver-sation onto this topic. Because I had wanted to ask them about . . .

"Will? Bill? Yeah, that's it. Bill Shavano." I took a teensy sip from my room-temperature beer. "I met him in the Topanas—oh, two years ago, I guess. He told me about an old Bannock trail on the north face of Cheney Peak.''

''If Bill told you about it, he's probably been up there,'' Mark said, with a note of admiration in his voice. ''He could walk around in there blindfolded. He knew it that well.''

''Did you know him?'' I asked.

Mark shrugged. ''Well enough to talk to.'' Slow grin. ''Did he tell you about the Patch, Sara?''

Putting down my glass, I grinned. ''Well, he did offer to buy me a drink the next time I was up north.''

''That must have been before he met Cindy,'' added Donna sagely.

''Oh?'' I fondled my glass again. ''Bill had an active social life?''

Chuckling, Mark took another drink. ''Young guy—single, fresh out of the Marines—he don't exactly sign up for Sunday school.''

Trilling laughter from Donna.

''What's so funny?'' I asked.

''Oh, I was just thinking.'' She showed me a lopsided smile. ''Remembering Bill and Cindy. I guess he was kind of rough around the edges. Cindy was a civilizing influence.''

''How so?'' I asked.

''Well, before he met Cindy, he used to come in here from time to time with that fancy woman of his.'' Donna's eyes darted nervously to the left. ''I'm not mentioning names, you understand.''

Mark flashed a warning look. ''Honey—!''

''Let me finish, lover.'' Querulous glance at me. ''Honestly, that man steps on everything I say. Anyway, ol' Fancy Gal would come on to some cowpoke.

Sure enough, poor Bill would end up throwing knuckles before the night was through.'' Donna was really feeling the effect of all those Löwenbräus. "Funny thing . . . that's how Cindy met him. She had a spat with her boyfriend and came in here all upset. She ordered a drink, but she was so upset she'd forgotten her purse. So Bill offered to pay for it. They got to talking. Then that son of a bitch Sunawavi came in and—'' A brisk shudder terminated her tipsy narrative. "Four boys in my family, Sara, so I've seen plenty of fights. But I don't think I've ever seen a go-round like that one between Bill and Jack Sunawavi!''

Fatalistic shrug from Mark. "My old man said it was inevitable. Those two slugging it out. Had to happen, he said. Sorta like two bull elks during the rut.''

"I wonder how *she* feels.'' Donna's gaze had a dreamy, faraway gleam. "Miss Fancy Gal. I wonder how she feels now that he's dead.'' Her small hand wavered as it reached for the bottle. "Probably doesn't feel a thing. The only person *she* ever cared for was her own self!''

An expression of sudden alarm crossed Mark's face. Rising quickly, he guided her hand away from the bottle. "That'll do for you, honeybunch.'' He gave me a nod and a smile. "Excuse us, Sara. My better half needs a breath of fresh air.'' With consummate gentleness, he guided his bride to her feet. "Come on, now.''

"Mark, you *never* let me finish.''

"Listen, three beers and you turn into a motor-mouth.''

"I am *not* a motormouth!''

"We have to live in this town, Donna, and I *need* that job."

The burgeoning newlywed squabble vanished into the musical background of Texas swing. I took the opportunity to visit the ladies' room.

Ten minutes later, I stood in front of the long mirror, reviewing the status of the lipstick and the makeup, touching up my raven-black mane with a small plastic brush and complimenting myself on my fashion selection of the evening—a cotton floral summer dress in tropical green, with a halter top, a flared skirt, and two soft bows at the base of the halter straps.

I put the brush away and reflected on my cousin's intriguing social life. I was intensely curious about the woman Billy had dated before Cindy. Who was she? And why did idle chatter about the lady make Donna's young husband so nervous?

On my way out, I stopped at the bar, deciding to order one last beer. I would nurse it for the remainder of the evening, drifting in and out of group conversations, dropping Billy's name and watching for the results.

Now it was my turn to be nervous. No mistake about it—the Briar Patch was bristling with thorns, and most of them were at the bar. Nuche men, mostly. Sweaty T-shirts and concho belts and every style of cowboy hat from Texas flat crowns to Montana sugarloafs. Eagle feathers adorned most of the hatbands.

I heard a deep baritone voice right behind me. "Buy you a drink, dolly?"

I started to turn. "Not very likely—!"

I had something else to say, something very witty, too. But I never got it out. It vaporized the instant I looked into the grinning features of Jack Sunawavi.

My eyes fluttered wide, and there was a strange sickish sensation in the pit of my stomach. Oh, it was him, all right. Bright pebbly eyes and tight, thin lips and pantherish stance. He was wearing the same black fringed leather vest, too, over a black T-shirt. Silk-screened onto his shirtfront was a rippling American flag and a message in white. *Try burning this one . . . Asshole!*

Jack spun me around forcibly, practically pinning me to the bar. Snapping his fingers, he let out a jolly, "Hey, Neil!" The bartender's Irish head swiveled our way. "Another one for my little friend Sara here. On me!"

I could feel ice crystals forming in my bloodstream. He must have come in while I was chatting with the Anteros. He had drifted in close enough to overhear our conversation—had heard them call me *Sara.*

"Sara . . . ," he breathed, playfully fondling my chin. I recoiled instantly from his touch, my features tensing in disgust. "Pretty name." In a loathsome whisper, he added, " 'Course, it was something else the last time we met, wasn't it?"

Unable to stop trembling, I took a ragged breath. "Sunawavi . . . I'm going to walk away from this bar. And unless you're very, very stupid, you won't try to stop me."

Jack made a great show of trying to remember some elusive fact. "Now, what was that name again? That name you were calling yourself down in Salt Lake?

Why, it's on the tip of my tongue . . ." He let out a predatory chuckle. ". . . *Angie!*"

Taking a panicky look around, I discovered a notable lack of allies. The dance crowd was stomping to an overly loud Garth Brooks tune. A few men at the bar looked up, intrigued by the confrontation. A hard-eyed stare from Jack soon had them looking elsewhere for entertainment. After all, it was Saturday night at the Briar Patch, and good ol' Jack was putting the moves on some out-of-town honey. Nothing to get worked up about, right?

Bold stare. "Pretty certain about the name, Jack."

"That's what Cindy called you, dolly." He gave the seat of my skirt a patronizing slap. "What are you doing in here, anyway?"

"Watch the hand, Sunawavi!"

"I asked you a question, gal."

I gave my nose a spoiled adolescent tilt. And said nothing.

"And what's with you and that asshole Shavano?" Jack needled. "I mention the name to Cindy, and you come barging in. Now, here you are in Cottonwood holding a wake for the shit. What gives? Are you president of the Bill Shavano Fan Club or something?"

I watched him out of the corner of my eye. His flinty gaze suddenly lit up in comprehension. *"Now* I get it. He's an old boyfriend, right?"

Trying to keep my voice level, I pushed Jack's restraining arm aside. "Cancel that beer, Neil. I'm driving."

"Not so fast, dolly!" Jack's hard-muscled forearm, studded with faint bluish tattoos, circled my waist.

His ferocious smile exposed two crooked teeth. "Shit, what does it matter? You're going to tell me—sooner or later. We've got plenty of time, Angie."

I felt a sinewy grip on my left wrist, and then he yanked my arm behind me, exerting incredible pressure on my knuckles. Small bones collided, triggering a searing shock wave of pain. The surge of anguish danced up my arm, leaving me teary-eyed and weak-kneed. My breath exploded in a hushed supersonic gasp.

"Not so brave without that frying pan handy, are we?" Jack's hateful chuckle sounded in my ear. "You know, I couldn't believe my eyes when I walked in here and saw you sitting there. Well, looky there, I says, if it ain't little Angie . . . the same little Angie I've been looking all over Salt Lake for."

Tearful gasp. "Let me go!"

"All in good time, dolly. All in good time," he crooned, tightening his grip on my throbbing hand. "You and me are going to walk out of here nice and easy. Right out through that there door. And you're going to give everybody a smile and show them how happy you are to be with me."

I dug in my spike heels. "No!"

"Step lively, bitch." He prodded me forward with a good-humored chuckle. "Because if you don't, I'm going to break every bone in that cute little hand of yours."

"Let go of me this instant, or I'll—!"

My threat turned into a pained gasp. My hand felt like it was caught in a winepress.

"Angie doll, you can go easy, or you can go hard. But you're *going!*"

"Bastard!"

Jack clucked his tongue in mock sympathy. "You shouldn't have dropped in on Cindy like that. I had a mighty fine weekend planned for that gal." Hearty and sinister chuckle. "Well, since you spoiled it, Angie, I guess it's only fair that you take her place."

Shaking my head vigorously, I hissed, "No! No! I *won't!*"

Again the hateful chuckle. "Tell you what. If you're real nice to me, I won't keep you more than three days. How's that?"

And then we were on our way out, my tall heels clicking on the dance floor, with smiling Jack just a step or two behind. The exit loomed larger and larger with each and every stride. I was living a nightmare—every woman's nightmare—that brisk march toward the unthinkable, with the jovial rapist making his intentions clear in no uncertain terms. I wanted to faint, scream and vomit, all at the same time. The thought of Sunawavi looming over me in the darkness, of his brutal hands forcing my knees apart, brought a shrill gasp of despair to my lips.

And then the room fell silent. Garth's song faded in mid-chord. My gasp lingered in the quiet, and then it was joined by a new sound—the jingling of handcuffs against belt leather. I glanced at the doorway, and my mouth fell open in astonishment.

It was as if someone had taken a Douglas fir and dressed it in a khaki uniform and crowned it with a white felt Stetson. I mean, this guy was *big!* Six foot four or five, unless I missed my eagle-eyed Anishinabe glance. Loaded down with all his law enforcement paraphnalia—mahogany nightstick, belt-clipped walkie-talkie, handcuffs, polished black leather holster with its well-oiled .357 Magnum Colt Python, steel-toed para-trooper boots—he must have tipped the scales at well over three hundred.

He surged forward without a word. Patrons suddenly found something of interest at the bottom of their beer steins. I felt as if I were standing in front of a steep-sided butte. Massive chest and Olympian thighs. An impression of broadness and durability. The only hint of fat was the loose jowls on either side of his outthrust chin. Mirrored sunglasses and a lowered hatbrim concealed the upper face. The lower half resembled a cherub on steroids. Apple-tinted cheeks, uptilted nose, noticeable underlip, and a tight, petulant mouth.

Once the initial impression sank in, I picked out the fine details. Round silvery badge on the left shirt pocket. A hint of dirty underwear at the shirt's open neck. Wrinkled twill trousers. Colorful patches on each short sleeve—American flag on the left, Saguache County Sheriff's Department on the right.

Mammoth surge of relief. Never had I been so glad to see a cop.

He had a basso profundo voice. "Goin' somewhere, Jack?"

The vision gave me renewed strength. I gave Jack's shin a solid rap with my right heel. Twisted my hand out of his loosening grip. Took refuge at the lawman's side.

Ignoring me, the newcomer levelled a sausage-shaped forefinger at Sunawavi. "I've been lookin' for you. We have to talk."

Jack scowled mightily. "You've got one hell of a sense of timing, Ty."

"And I don't like to be kept waiting, either."

Glaring at me, Jack snickered. "Come on, Ty. Be reasonable. I'm entertaining a young lady friend."

The deputy's pouty lips returned the smirk. "She don't look all that eager to me."

"Very observant, my friend," I added, keeping a wary eye on Jack.

"Pussy hunt's over, Jack." The deputy hooked another sizable digit—the thumb, this time—in the direction of the exit. "Outside!"

With pachydermian tread, the lawman departed. Jack hesitated a moment, looking at me with a wolfish expression, then thought the better of it. Giving his fringed vest a tug, he flashed me a naughty wink. "Keep it warm for me—*Sara.*"

I watched Jack follow the deputy through the doorway, and then the reaction set in. Violent tremors. Chilled skin. Sudden surge of nausea. You realize how close you came—how close you were to the hurt and the shame and the violation, to that degrading feeling of absolute helplessness, and you want to be sick.

I fled in the opposite direction. Mindless escape, powered by an overwhelming desire to put as much distance as possible between me and Jack Sunawavi. I wanted to rush out the back door, hop into my Accord, drive pell mell back to Clover Creek, and stand in my cramped shower stall, under a streaming cascade of hot water, washing away the vile memory of that man's touch.

My flight ended in a panelled cul-de-sac. Slumping

against the cigarette machine, I sobbed and gasped, and let out a prolonged whispery wail of dismay.

Okay, princess. Calm down. Calm down. The bastard's gone—at least for the moment. Think clearly, now. You don't want to rush out there and have him waiting for you. Make sure you leave with people. Find Mark and Donna. They'll walk you to your car . . .

I emerged from the cul-de-sac minutes later, fielding a mighty shaky composure. A few women gave me an interrogatory look, alert to my discomfiture. An irresistible anxiety propelled me over to the windows. I had to know where Jack Sunawavi was, what he was doing. I had to know if he was out there in that darkened parking lot, waiting for me.

I sidled up to the damascene drapery and peered through the screen mesh. There he was, Cindy's former boyfriend, down in the lot, right beside his brand-new Dodge pickup.

Jack and the deputy were talking, and from the look of things, Sunawavi wasn't all too happy. He paced back and forth, occasionally hammering the truck door with his fist. The big deputy stood there, one hand on the butt of his service pistol. He shook his head once or twice in a weary, paternalistic fashion.

I strained my ears, hoping to catch a fragment of their conversation, but at this distance, their voices were a meaningless mutter.

Finally, Jack flung the truck door open, clambered into the cab, and brought the Dodge engine to life. Touching the driver's-side windowsill, the deputy gave Jack some words of parting advice. Then he stepped back, and the Dodge, its tires spitting gravel, rumbled down the rutted country road back to Utah 302.

I stood in the window, trying to see which way Jack was headed. As I did so, the deputy turned his head suddenly and looked straight at me. In the darkness, I could see nothing of the man's expression, but his sudden movement frightened me. Hastily I backed away from the window.

Now, what was *that* all about?

Unable to fathom an answer, I turned and shuddered and made my way back to the dance floor in search of the Anteros.

Chapter Six

Come Tuesday, a cold front sneaked down from Puget Sound and gave Salt Lake City a much-needed soaking. On my side of the Wasatch, squadrons of low thick cumulus littered the sky, offering here and there a glimpse of cerulean heights, with an occasional shaft of sunshine bathing the mountain slopes.

I had a choice view of the whole show, standing at the window in Mr. Longhurst's waiting room. It was a sizable suite on the second floor of the Cowdery Building—white ceiling, mint-green walls and a large, prominently displayed emblem of the U.S. Forest Service.

I had spent Sunday in Kate Thornley's company. She had sensed that something was wrong the minute I emerged from the trailer that morning. Gratefully I had accepted her offer of breakfast and had treated her to an edited version of my encounter with Sunawavi.

The memory of Jack's rancid touch was still too vivid. I had needed to talk it out with another woman, and I felt a good deal better after that breakfast with Kate.

The landlady was most understanding. After all, she told me, young girls have to go out, no matter what, and any place with music and dancing is preferable to sitting home on Saturday night. She made it quite clear that the Briar Patch was no place for a good Mormon girl, but, she added, if I really wanted to meet people my own age, she was willing to bring me to the LDS supper on Wednesday night and introduce me around.

As a result, I spent the remainder of Sunday at the tabernacle with Mrs. Thornley and learned a number of interesting things. First, that Cue Broward wasn't the richest man in town. Not by a long shot. That honor went to Truman Kimball Sager, whose name was invoked in the same hushed tones of respect as Joseph Smith's. The gentleman was always referred to in solemn tones as *Mr. Sager* or *Gail's daddy*.

It turned out that Cue Broward wasn't all that popular with the Latter-Day Saints, having had the bad taste to sweep Truman's youngest daughter off her feet and marry the lass in a gaudy civil ceremony in Las Vegas. Mr. Sager had never quite gotten over the embarrassment of being presented with a son-in-law his own age.

On Monday, I became Bookworm Angie, spending many long hours at the Clover Creek library. I gave myself a mild headache reading all those back issues of the *Federal Register,* and I kept the photocopier pinging under a constant rain of quarters.

It was well worth it, though. When I showed up for my appointment on Tuesday morning, I was toting

107

a notebook crammed with detailed background information, to say nothing of a list of significant questions for the district supervisor.

So there I stood, looking very crisp and professional in a lilac half-sleeved cutaway jacket and black gabardine slim skirt. Black patent leather pumps with two-inch heels and a stylish quilted leather handbag to match. The doorknob rattled. I turned to my right. Longhurst's baby-faced secretary beckoned from the doorway. "He'll see you now, Miss Soyazhe."

Alfred J. Longhurst rose from his chair as I strolled into the office. He was a youthful forty-five, with a Teutonic nose and a ready back-country smile. Not too tall, maybe two inches under the six-foot mark, and sporting a volleyball-shaped belly which nestled against the big silver buckle of his belt. Alfie had an oblong face, with deepset gray-green eyes, a broad, bristling brown moustache, and very thick eyebrows. There was a permanent vertical crease between the hairy brows and crow's feet to match, reaching for his graying temples. His hair was dark brown, well-clipped, and baby-fine . . . and it was steadily retreating from his eyebrows.

Greeting me very warmly, he gestured at the visitor's chair. Very well-dressed for a district supervisor. Beige shirt and a trim Donegal tweed sportcoat. Neatly pressed heather slacks and a silken paisley tie. A tiny diamond sparkled in the eye of his gold-plated Kiwanis tieclip.

We spent a minute or two getting acquainted. He made his plush chair even more comfortable by snuggling his shoulders against the top cushion. And then, beaming at me, he asked, "Tell me, Miss Soyazhe, how can I be of assistance?"

Sweet Angie smile. "I'd like some information about certain tracts in the Topanas National Forest." Open the notebook and shuffle the Xerox sheets. "I'm curious about their status, Mr. Longhurst."

"Which tracts are you interested in?"

I knew the numbers by heart. "Sections 26 through 39."

He gave me a thoroughly earnest look. Perhaps a little too earnest.

"I believe it's called Lodestone Canyon," I added.

"That's correct." His voice was a shade cooler. "But I'm not exactly sure what you mean by *status.*" Sudden stab at intimacy. "Ah, do you mind if I call you Sara?"

"Not at all. You see, I'm curious. I'm wondering if there's any logging planned for that area."

"That's a distinct possibility, Sara." Before my very eyes, Alfie mutated into a career bureaucrat. "Silviculture is an important part of the district management plan."

I thought of Billy's lovely phrase. "Is the canyon scheduled for *grove enhancement* any time in the near future?"

Longhurst dodged my sally. "There is that possibility. You see, Sara, the Forest Service doesn't oversee large-scale cutting any more. We've put an end to high-grading, that is, letting private sector loggers cruise the forest in search of the best grade pine. We have a new approach now. It's called integrated stand management. We try to harvest smaller areas more

109

intensively. We let Mother Nature have her own way in the rest of the district."

I wrote *Bullshit!* on the blank page of my notebook. "I didn't see a copy of the management plan on file at the Clover Creek library, Al."

"It's being amended, Sara."

"Have there been hearings on the amended plan?"

"Not yet. The overall plan is still being written." Smug smile. "It's a sizable plan . . . well over a thousand pages."

Of course, I could understand Alfie's desire to stonewall on the hearings. At any time, a group like the Sierra Club or the Tribe of DAN could stop the proposed logging cut by filing a formal protest with the Forest Service. The project would then remain in limbo until the Forest Service had proven that no environmental damage would result. But if there was no formal announcement of a cut, then there was nothing Mickey's group could protest.

Feigning a confused look, I placed some photocopies on his desk. "Well, I don't understand it. I found these four notices in last week's *Federal Register.* Notices from your office. This one, see? Request for proposals. 'The following public lands have been determined eligible for grove enhancement . . . Saguache County, Utah . . . T-12, Sections 31 through 34.' "

That smug smile of his began to sag, turning into a sickly rictus. Reaching across the blotter, he gave my hand a reassuring pat.

"Well, that's nothing, Sara. We're just inviting past contractors to update the proposals we have on file."
That's Lie Number One, Mr. Longhurst.

"Five contractors responded to the RFP," I said.

"And they're all contractors who have bid before, Sara."

"Eames Lumber? Larkin Lumber? High Timber Associates?"

Longhurst nodded vigorously. "That's right. Private contractors of past demonstrated effectiveness."

Lie Number Two! Both Billy and Mickey Grantz had told me that High Timber was a new outfit.

I was Schoolgirl Angie. Innocence personified. "Then no one has taken out a performance bond in anticipation of being awarded a Forest Service contract?"

"To my knowledge, no."

Lie Number Three! When Billy had accidentally received that bank bond receipt, he'd taken it straight to Longhurst.

"Are you sure of that, Al?"

"Positive, Sara." Lounging in his chair, he let out a small laugh. "Why, Pop Larkin couldn't raise twenty-five thousand if he tried. You know what Larkin Lumber is? A Ford Ranger, a gasoline-powered winch, and three chainsaws. Pop has a little spread down near Scipio. He logs during the winter. Him and those three boys of his."

"What about High Timber Associates?"

Mention of that name expunged Alfie's smile completely. He shot me a cold, wary look. "I didn't quite catch your occupation, Sara."

"I'm a geologist."

"Really?" Momentary bafflement. He couldn't quite comprehend a geologist's interest in the canyon. "Are you with the Survey?"

111

Ladylike shake of the head. "No, I graduated from the University of Wyoming in June."

"Then how did you hear about Lodestone Canyon?"

No answer. Demurely crossing my legs, I showed my cousin's old boss a Mona Lisa smile. Angie the Mysterious.

My coy silence had Mr. Longhurst inwardly fuming. I was a vague threat, a yet-unspoken challenge to his authority, and he wished I would go away. To a career bureaucrat like Longhurst, those vague, amorphous threats are the worst kind.

I waited until the irritation began to show in his eyes, and then I answered his question with another question.

"I'm a little rusty on the terms of the Land Policy and Management Act. The proposals received by your office—aren't they supposed to be aired at a public hearing?"

"Not always." His gaze rigid, Longhurst picked a pencil off the blotter. "It depends on the size of the acreage. If there's a significant change in store for that area, I'd have to call the hearing. But there is no significant change."

"Mr. Longhurst, we're talking about cutting the entire canyon."

"No, Miss Soyazhe, we are not." Taut, patronizing smile. "We're talking about several distinct grove enhancement projects to be undertaken over an unspecified period of time. As I said before, it's all a matter of acreage. Plans have to be aired at public hearing if the target area exceeds 640 acres. None of the proposals covers an area that large. Therefore, there is no significant impact that would justify a hearing or . . ." he cleared his throat, ". . . amendment of the comprehensive land use plan."

"No need for a hearing?"

"None at all."

All at once, it dawned on me what Longhurst was doing. The death of a thousand cuts. That's what the Chinese called it. My cousin's old boss was too sharp for the standard insider scam. You'd never find Alfie accepting cash under the table and letting outlaw loggers trim whole sections of the Topanas. No, Alfie was too clever for that. He was very careful to stay within the limits set by the Management Act. Alfie had been queering forest management at the district level, taking care not to attract the attention of his supervisors in Ogden and Washington. Five hundred acres here. Six hundred there. Dozens of lucrative little logging projects for the boys in Clover Creek.

The death of a thousand cuts. It can kill a man in no time at all. And it can do the same to a canyon. Or an entire ecosystem.

Back when he was a forest ranger, like my cousin Bill, Mr. Longhurst must have considered the bribes being thrown his way by small-time operators and decided that the risk just wasn't worth it. Why risk prison time for three or four thousand in untraceable cash? Especially when you can ride the GS career wagon into the district supervisor's chair and generally make yourself indispensable to the lumber barons. Longhurst must have made the proper contacts through one of Clover Creek's many social clubs, done some canny negotiating, and found himself a berth on someone's payroll.

But *whose* payroll? Broward's? Eames's? Or the formidable Mr. Sager's?

Okay, so in Alfie I had my pipeline into the Clover Creek establishment. Now it was time to erase that superior smile, to shake up his bureaucratic complacency and send him running to his hidden patron.

Closing my notebook, I remarked, "I guess what you're telling me is that the canyon cut was planned right here at the district level."

"Miss Soyazhe." Annoyed glare from the supervisor. "There is no cut! My office has merely requested updated plans from past contractors. When the work is ready to go to bid, I will have it properly listed."

Sure you will, Alfie. And the day after it's listed, the aspen of Lodestone Canyon will be on its way to Salt Lake City aboard a fleet of flatbed trucks. No need for me to fake antipathy. "We don't seem to be connecting, Mr. Longhurst. My point is, the process has been pretty much confined to your office."

"And that's all in keeping with the terms of the Act, Miss Soyazhe."

"What about your timber sales officer?"

Seeing him flinch at Bill's title, I shuddered to think what might have happened if I'd said the name. "What about him?

"Didn't he review the RFP before it went out?"

"Yes, he did." I noticed a nearly imperceptible trembling in Alfie's hands. "Bill Shavano was an important part of the review team. As a matter of fact, I sent him up to Lodestone to survey the tracts myself."

Lie Number Four, Alfie!

"And Mr. Shavano concurred with your decision to issue the RFP?"

Licking dry lips, he nodded. "Yes, he did."

Skeptical Angie frown. "I didn't see any letters from Mr. Shavano in the file down in Ogden."

Of course, I hadn't been anywhere near the Forest Service regional office, but Longhurst didn't know that. His calm demeanor melted like ice cream in the midday Utah sun.

"Well, it could've—I mean, it's no surprise—ah, Bill was way behind on his paperwork. Eventually he would have gotten around to it . . . ah, if not for the accident."

"Then Mr. Shavano never submitted any written documentation pertaining to Lodestone Canyon."

"No, he did not."

Gosh, Alfie, whatever happened to Billy's detailed memo opposing the proposed cut? Lie Number Five!

"Let met get this straight, young lady." Badly off-balance, Longhurst struggled to regain the initiative. "You've been to Ogden? You've reviewed the correspondence file?"

Angie the Schoolgirl nodded very respectfully.

Flinty gaze from the supervisor. "May I ask why?"

Enough talk about Billy. It was time to throw the slippery Mr. Longhurst a curve. "I'm interested in the canyon's mineral rights."

Startled blink. "Mineral rights!?"

"Yes." Putting both feet on the floor, I smoothed my skirt. "I'm wondering if the federal government has ever assigned the mineral rights to Lodestone Canyon."

Longhurst gave me an uncertain stare. Sure, it

made sense. After all, what would interest a geologist more than the mineral rights? Yet at the same time my questions about the canyon had badly rattled him. My interest in Lodestone established me as a possible competitor, a distinct threat to Alfie's patron in the private sector. I knew he'd try to get in touch—pass on his uneasiness about me. And I hoped his patron would reel me in for a closer look.

Thumbing the edge of his moustache, he frowned. "I couldn't really say. That's primarily a BLM matter."

"Could you find out for me?"

"Of course." He reached for his intercom button, then hesitated. Aimed one last guarded glance at me. "Are you sure that's all you're interested in?"

Polite nod. "Yes. I'd just like to know the current status of those mineral rights."

Looking more than a bit perturbed, Longhurst tapped the intercom button. "Arlene, buzz Jayne Clark over in BLM, would you? Ask her to pull the file on Lodestone Canyon. I'm sending somebody over."

I took my time getting to the BLM office, figuring to avoid a wait. I needn't have bothered. Jayne Clark was not one to be rushed. She was forty, a no-nonsense administrator with a lean, vulpine face, a wedge of reddish-gold hair that looked almost like a cap, and a small, tense mouth. She gave me a grim looking over, phoned Arlene to doublecheck my identity, gestured at a vinyl chair, and marched briskly to the green filing cabinets. Standing there, ruffling through the files, she looked like an inverted lollipop—small, narrow shoulders, a wasp waist, and a round, meaty backside.

While she pored through the files, I left the chair and wandered the room, trying to think of some way of conning the payroll records out of Jayne or Arlene. It would be interesting to see if Mr. Longhurst had signed out of the office the Tuesday morning Billy was killed.

As I passed the bulletin board, I spied a U.S. Geological Survey map and gave it an idle scan. Just then, a strange feeling of familiarity swirled over me. Backstepping twice, I studied it more closely.

Sure enough, I'd seen that pattern of brown and beige before. The little town of Penrose winked at me. This map was identical to the one in Billy's map case.

Someone had marked the bulletin board's map with red ink, though, outlining several squares into an oblong shape that resembled a gila monster.

Stiletto heels beat out a brisk tune behind me. "Here you go, Miss Soyazhe. I made you a copy of the original."

"Thanks." Accepting the sheet, I folded it in half and tilted my head at the posted map. "Can I ask a quick question?"

"If you like." Judging from her tone, it was clear that Jayne much preferred to be getting back to that big paperback romance novel propped against her typing stand.

"Why is that area outlined in red?"

"Those sections are up for a 206."

"206?"

"A land transfer."

I decided to get Jayne talking about her job. That always stirs feelings of camaraderie. "Have you done many of those, Ms. Clark?"

"Dozens!" Her rose-lipsticked mouth puckered wryly. "I've become an expert on conveyance documents, believe me."

Daughterly Angie smile. "Sounds complicated. I guess you'd have to be really sharp to handle it."

Smiling self-consciously, Jayne smoothed the velvety tie of her sateen blouse. "Actually, it's really not that complicated, dear. You see, Section 206 of the Act allows Uncle Sam to transfer public lands out of federal ownership."

"How does it work?"

"Let's say there are five hundred acres classified as federal land. Now, let's suppose that Farmer Jones owns five hundred acres of woodland, and the Jones property is good habitat for wildlife. The BLM would then approach Farmer Jones and ask if he would be willing to swap his land for the federal land on an acre-for-acre basis. Section 206 gives the federal government the legal authority to make that transfer."

"What happens then, Jayne?"

"Well, Sara, first we'd have to check to make sure the proposed transfer was compatible with the goals of the district management plan . . ."

And Jayne went on from there. She walked me through every step in the land transfer process. Her manner warmed with the telling. As for me, I was more than a little glad that Billy had not gotten me that BLM job in Salt Lake.

"How about the USDA land?" I asked. "Can you transfer it into the BLM and vice versa?"

"Oh, yes, that's allowable under Section 206. You see, Sara, the Forest Service is part of the Department of Agriculture, and we're under the Department of the Interior. That's what we call an interdepartmental transfer—IDT for short."

"Jayne, what about this area?" My palm patted the mounted topographical map. "The red-lined area. Is that BLM land?"

"Oh, no. That area's under the Bureau of Indian Affairs."

I blinked suddenly, all at once remembering Billy's decision to run for the tribal council. I could sense strange tentative linkages out there. Billy's interest in that salt desert. His sudden decision to run for the tribal council. The Bureau of Indian Affairs . . .

I had guessed wrong back at the trailer. The numbers *206* hadn't referred to an afternoon rendezvous. Bill had known of the BLM's pending transfer of that salt desert near Penrose.

But why had he been so damned interested?

Engaging Angie smile. "Has the transfer gone through yet?"

"Lord, no. We only received the letter a little over two weeks ago."

"Do you remember who sent it?"

"No, dear. I'm afraid I'd have to look it up."

I winced. "Gosh, Jayne, you've done so much for me already, I almost hate to ask." Anticipatory glance at the wall clock. "Listen, it's almost twelve. Let me impose on you just this one last time, and I'll treat you to lunch at the Rimrock Cafe. What do you say?"

"Oh, Sara!" She made a go-on-with-you gesture with her right hand. "You don't have to do that."

"Hey, you'd be doing me a favor," I said. "I just moved to Clover Creek. I'd like to find out where all the handsome and eligible men are."

Tart laughter from the BLM lady. "That won't take me too long to tell!" She made a beeline to the filing cabinets. "Rest yourself, hon. I'll be right back."

Jayne was as good as her word. She recrossed the room less than five minutes later, thumbing through a nearly new manila folder.

"Now then, Sara, what would you like to know?"

"The name of the person who requested the transfer."

"People, you mean." She grinned at me over the folder's rim. "There's two signatures on the letter. Uhm, Ned Pahaka . . . and William M. Shavano."

Jayne and I had a pleasantly chatty luncheon at the Rimrock. She did most of the chatting. Nodding in sympathy, I nibbled the Rimrock's famous buffalo-on-a-bun while she lamented her fate as a recent divorcee in predominantly Mormon Clover Creek. I gathered from her narrative that it was a shade more enjoyable than her previous status as a sports widow.

After lunch, I breezed into the Clover Creek City Hall and had a peek at the incorporation records in the tax office. Kate Thornley hadn't been exaggerating about Cue Broward's economic reach. His bold signature adorned over one dozen incorporation papers.

I was mildly surprised to find Cue's signature side-by-side with that of his reluctant father-in-law, Truman Kimball Sager, on the charter of the Sager-

Broward Construction Company, Inc. I would have thought the circumstances of daughter Gail's wedding would have precluded any possible collaboration between the two. Shows you how wrong I was.

By the time I got out of City Hall, it was close to three o'clock, and there was a band of cool shadow on the south side of Center Street. So I did some casual windowshopping on that side and wound up in front of Garrett's Shoes. They had the most adorable pair of Worthington's on display, polished black leather dress pumps with three-inch heels and flowery black velvet bows on the vamp. I have a weakness for bows. It's almost as bad as my weakness for shoes. I clutched my handbag tightly, steeling myself against temptation.

Coming up behind me, Chief offered some moral support. "Don't! You can't afford it."

"Wrong about that, Mr. Pahvant."

"You won't have your money long if you keep blowing it on them fancy shoes."

"And while we're on the subject of shoes . . . ," I said, falling into step beside my grandfather. ". . . how's the horse business these days?"

"Productive." Chief lowered his voice. "I've been talking to a lot of Nuche folks up in Cottonwood."

"Any talk about our boy from Heber?"

"Quite a bit. But, you know, folks get a bit close-mouthed when the subject rolls around to Billy's first year up here. There's mention of a woman—"

"The one before Cindy," I interrupted.

His Stetson dipped in a quick nod. "That's her. Folks are mighty shy about mentioning the name."

I thought back to my conversation with Mark and

Donna. "I've heard about her, too." Briefly I described the chat at the Briar Patch. "Mark got a little anxious when Donna took Miss Fancy Gal's name in vain. Idle gossip about that family appears to be the express ticket to the unemployment line."

"Only one name I've heard draws that kind of reaction." Chief put out his broad brown hand, stopping me as the corner light turned green. "And that's Sager."

"The old boy has that much clout?"

Nodding, Chief said, "Most people I talked to either work for Mr. Sager or know somebody who does. That fella's shadow covers more of this here valley than Cheney Peak's."

The light blinked red, and we resumed our stroll to the municipal parking lot. "Anything else on Miss Fancy Gal?" I asked.

"Just this. She has a guardian angel. A great big deputy. You know what happens when you reach up onto a rock shelf and wake a sleeping rattler? Well, that rattler's Mother Teresa compared to this here deputy."

"Boyfriend?"

Chief shook his head. "More like an unofficial bodyguard. Stay the hell out of that man's way, child. The word is he don't brake for Indians."

I thought of the khaki-clad man-mountain who had summoned Jack Sunawavi into the parking lot. "Too late, Ch—Mr. Pahvant, I think I've already met him."

"Oh? Where?"

"The Briar Patch. But he seemed pretty chummy with at least one Nuche."

"That'd be Jack Sunawavi. I heard those two are

122

asshole buddies." Seeing my reaction to that name, my grandfather flashed a mild frown. "Don't tell me you've met *him,* too."

"I had an exciting Saturday night."

I decided not to discuss the fine details. Even at seventy-five, Chief was perfectly capable of hefting a bowie knife and going in search of the miscreant. He was just liable to perform some impromptu surgery— the kind that would leave Jack Sunawavi talking like Mickey Mouse.

As the tabernacle steeple came into view, Chief asked, "So what else have you been doing with your time, girl?"

I gave my grandfather a quick rundown of my adventures at the Forest Service office. I explained Longhurst's timber scam in great detail, then mentioned the map in Jayne Clark's office.

"Alfie's got the strongest motive," I said, sitting down on one of the white park benches in front of the tabernacle. "He's been parceling out choice woodland to the loggers, always careful to stay below the limits set in the management plan. How much of a slice is he getting out of each timber haul Eames or Broward takes out of the Topanas? You know, if Billy hadn't gotten that bond receipt, he wouldn't have found out about the proposed cut until it was too late."

Chief looked skeptical. "I don't know . . . I can't see Longhurst sticking his neck out like that."

"Why not?"

"I mean, the burden of proof was on Billy. He couldn't bring down Longhurst with some wild-ass talk about kickbacks. He would have had to prove that his boss was subverting the process. From what you tell me, that Longhurst fella is very slick. Seems to me he could cover his tracks pretty good. So why kill Billy?''

''But Billy was a direct threat to Longhurst's scam. Alfie would have lost all that money—''

''What money?'' Chief challenged. ''Aspen ain't worth that much on the open market. What did Mickey Grantz call it? Weed tree, right?'' Mild sigh. ''It just doesn't make sense. I can't see killing a man to cover up something you ain't going to make that much money on.''

Time for a major fussbudget face. That grandfather of mine! Every time I come up with a neat theory that explains everything, along he comes and demolishes it in two seconds!

''There's a whole lot we don't know yet.'' Chief aimed a thoughtful glance at me. ''For instance, why did Billy file that—what'd you call it?—Section 206 with the BLM? Why was he so interested in that desert land? Does it have anything to do with Lodestone Canyon? If so, what? And, most importantly, who the hell is Ned Pahaka?''

''He's Nuche, obviously,'' I replied, trying to redeem myself in my grandfather's eyes. *''Pahaka* is Nuche for *eagle.''*

''Well, now!'' He beamed at me. ''You got quite the education living at Della's, didn't you?''

''Uh-huh! Nuche and Shoshoni. She taught me.'' Grinning, I put both hands in my lap. ''Think you can find him?''

''I'll give it a try. Any other requests, missy?''

''See what you can dig up about Jack Sunawavi,''

124

I added, my tone somber. "I would certainly feel a whole lot better knowing that man's whereabouts."

"Any particular reason?" he asked.

I told him about Sunawavi turning up at Cindy's place. "Jack seems to have played a supporting role in Billy's life. He was Cindy's guy before she met Billy, and Jack doesn't take rejection too well. Also, Billy kicked his ass at the Briar Patch."

"I heard about that." Chief nodded wisely. "It raised a few eyebrows around Cottonwood. Nobody had ever done that before."

"I don't like the pattern. Sunawavi loses to Billy two years ago. Next thing you know, he's back on Cindy's doorstep, crowing about Billy's death."

"Think he may have had something to do with it?"

"It's a distinct possibility," I replied. "Right now, the way I see it, Longhurst is Suspect Number One, and Sunawavi is Suspect Number Two."

Chief scowled. "This is starting to sound like 'The Dating Game.'"

"The what?"

"It was before your time."

By the time I got to Trail's End, the cottonwoods were casting long cooling shadows over the trailers. I found an empty spot in the residents' lot, carefully inserted the Accord, got out and banged the car door shut with a fluid motion of my hip.

Three steps up the pathway, I heard another door slam and a terse baritone voice. "Miss Soyazhe?"

Turning, I watched a tall man climb out of a dark red Alfa Romeo, Utah license plate 683-74R. I pegged his height at six-one and the weight on that stalwart masculine frame at one-ninety, give or take a pound. I smiled, as I always do when I meet rugged, dark-haired men with good shoulders. Very snappy dresser, this guy. Tailored Western-cut suit jacket in light heather brown with peaked yokes and flapped pockets, trousers to match, crisp white shirt and a silky striped tie in brown ombre. He had large, blunt-fingered hands with noticeable veins, and he held his hat in them. A sand-colored Stetson with a cattleman's crease and mild rodeo flanges.

Broad welcoming Angie smile. "Yes?"

"My name is Simms. Dennis Simms." He approached slowly, giving me a little respectful nod. "I wonder if I could talk to you for a moment."

"Sure, Mr. Simms." The name sounded vaguely familiar, and then I remembered. Mickey had mentioned it. Simms was the Clover Creek lawyer who had first requested permission to *enhance* the canyon.

From a distance Dennis looked quite handsome, but as he drew closer, the angularity of his nose spoiled the matinee-idol illusion. He had the same eye-and-nose configuration as those stone idols on Easter Island. They both shared the same shelf of overhanging brow, the same plumb-bob nose, the same brooding, deepset, hard-to-read eyes.

"I understand you're a geologist," he said.

"That's right."

"And you're interested in Lodestone Canyon."

"Right again."

"Interested in the mineral rights."

"You're batting a thousand, Mr. Simms."

"Please . . . make it Dennis." That country-boy smile must have stimulated quite a few feminine heartbeats back at Russell Maughan High School years ago. "May I ask why?"

"May I ask you a question, Dennis?"

"Be my guest."

A hot afternoon breeze blew strands of raven hair into my eyelashes. I removed them with a two-fingered sweep. "Did you and Mr. Longhurst have a nice chat?"

Didn't faze him a bit. "It was interesting. He came to see me at lunch. Tell me, are you serious about acquisition of the mineral rights from the BLM?"

My smile turned bland. "Do you have an economic interest in the canyon, Mr. Simms?"

"Only indirectly." Oh, our Dennis was very smooth. "I'm an attorney. One of my clients is very much interested in that area."

So that was it. Longhurst's private-sector patron was too sharp to make contact with me on his own. He had sent his lawyer instead.

"Are you mentioning any names, Dennis?"

Cracking a subtle smile, he buttoned his suit jacket. "Now, Sara, I'm sure you've heard of client privilege. I'm afraid I'm not at liberty to say."

"Sounds serious. Am I by chance being sued?"

"Not at all, young lady." The sexy smile widened. "Just the opposite, in fact. I'm here with an invitation."

"Dennis, I'm sure you're a very nice guy, but if this is a request for a date, I'm afraid the answer is no."

"It's more in the line of business, Sara. There's a cookout tonight at the Circle B ranch. I thought we might have a bite to eat and then sit down for a cozy little chat." His eyes narrowed in anticipation. "Just the three of us, Sara. You, me and my client."

"The client who's interested in Lodestone Canyon?"

"That's the one, Sara."

"What time is the cookout?"

"Eight o'clock on." Lifting his wrist, he displayed a gold Rolex. "What time shall I pick you up?"

Adopting a touch-me-not stance, I responded, "No need to trouble yourself, Dennis. I can find my own way there."

"I'll see you at eight then." Flourishing the Stetson, he pivoted sharply and strode back out to the parking lot.

Dennis Simms hadn't told me who his client was. Then again, I had no need to ask. I already knew the name of the owner of the Circle B ranch.

Cue Broward.

Chapter Seven

Sundown found me on the Circle B, deep behind enemy lines. Anishinabe princess on the scout.

Had I been Clint Eastwood, no doubt I would have been slouching about in a dirty swallow-tailed raincoat, with a black flat-crowned hat shading my eyes, a smoldering cheroot thrust between my lips, and my right hand at rest on the walnut butt of my trusty .45 caliber Dragoon Colt. I would have reached into my raincoat, withdrawn the taped bundle of dynamite, ignited the fuse with the cheroot's glowing tip, and hurled the charge through the sparkling glass of Mr. Broward's lovely French doors.

But no, I was Angela Biwaban, also known as *Sara Soyazhe,* sociable and well-mannered dinner guest, daintily sipping Diet Pepsi and admiring the decorative arched transoms of the ranch house. The avenger game had changed during the past hundred years. Different techniques for a different century.

The Broward cookout was only slightly smaller than the Republican National Convention. Turn to the left, and there's a foot-stomping bluegrass band. A very talented violinist in that crew. Cries of "Saw that fiddle, son!" and an occasional Rebel yell. Turn to the right, and see the smiling ladies in their short-sleeved blouses with lacy stand-up collars heaping platters of culinary delights onto the picnic tables. Creamy potato salad and smoked Idaho salmon and cherry cobbler and deviled eggs. U-turn, Biwaban! Or else you'll have to run *fifteen* miles instead of your usual ten per day.

I watched the haggard young mothers in hot pursuit of their yelping offspring. And the ranchers in their sport shirts and straw Stetsons drinking cold Coors and talking about weather and livestock. A couple of leather-faced old punchers were tossing horseshoes. Nearby sat a large family of orthodox Latter-Day Saints from way back in the Wasatch. Papa in his Shady Brady and string tie. Mama in a white muslin dress dating from the days of Brigham, spoonfeeding the latest baby as he squirmed on her lap. Solemn-eyed kiddies sitting side by side, the smallest ones closest to Mama, the preteens out at the end.

At roundup tie, old Cue was going to come up a steer short, because one of his prize Herefords was turning on a cast-iron spit over a spread of whitening coals. A Mexican boy in a tall chef's hat dipped his brush and lathered the sizzling meat with a pungent sauce.

I felt the pressure of someone's stare, glanced over my shoulder, and spotted a pair of bright-smiling college boys. I knew I was winning points for my outfit. It was Cookout Casual but perhaps a shade too casual for Saguache County. Black abbreviated halter-style tank top with a belly band of lace trim, plus a pair of snug-fitting white twill shorts with a sizable black belt. I had my long hair back over my shoulders, exposing my concho earrings.

So I wandered the crowded yard, waiting for my host to arrive, and gave some thought to my cousin and his schemes. *Just what were you up to, Billy? Why did you and Ned Pahaka put up that salt desert for a Section 206 transfer? Did you know that your boss Longhurst was on Cue Broward's payroll? Was the proposed land transfer some kind of opening gambit in a campaign to unseat Longhurst?*

I suspected that something had started the big wheels turning—had lured my cousin up to Dynamite Pass. But what? Was it Billy's memo advising against a cut in Lodestone Canyon? Or was it the Section 206 transfer request?

Just then I sensed another fervid gaze, but it wasn't the collegiate males this time. It was a female trio, all of them superbly coiffed and dressed in trim designer jeans and filmy, ruffled-yoke Western blouses. Two slender lipsticked matrons permanently stuck on their thirty-ninth birthday and a breathtakingly lovely brunette a decade younger. The youngster did most of the talking. Many pinched frowns and glares of disapproval.

Somehow I must have inadvertently violated the Saguache County code of fashion approval. Big deal.

Walking over to the patio's edge, I listened to the bluegrass boys wind up their pre-meal show. The last glimmers of daylight had thrown the whole Wasatch range into silhouette, backlighting the rugged peaks, suffusing them with a dreamy golden glow. Finishing my Diet Pepsi, I crumpled the plastic cup and looked around for a handy trash receptacle.

Oh and here she comes. The disapproving trio's junior miss. Small uplifted chin and determined eyes the shade of Hershey's milk chocolate. She had what Vidal Sassoon would have called "a classic diamond-shaped face." Flawless cheekbones and slim, straight nose and a perfect Cupid's bow mouth. High fore-head, well-sculpted eyebrows and a delicately tapered chinline. Her wavy dark brown hair was parted on the right, cresting and curling like a foaming breaker, sweeping down to partially obscure the left eyebrow. Bouncy chocolate waves caressed the open collar of her yoked blouse. Her lush lips tightened in a demi-smile that was polite yet condescending at the same time.

"Excuse me . . ." That lady-of-the-manor tone made my Angie smile turn frigid. ". . . are you sup-posed to be here?"

"I'm afraid so."

Okay, so maybe I'm a little too fresh for my own good. But I don't respond well to that sorority presi-dent style. She reminded me of a girl I went to school with at USU. You know the type. Drops into your room on Friday night, lets you know how privileged you are to be her size, and then tries to walk off with two or three of your best outfits.

No reaction. I don't know where she went to fin-ishing school, but her parents had certainly gotten their money's worth.

"Have you an invitation?" she asked tartly.

"I do."

132

She extended a languid hand. "May I please see it?"

"Well, it's not going to be quite that easy."

Long fingers waggled impatiently. "The invitation, please."

"Aren't you a little overdressed to be the ticket-taker?"

Brown eyes blinked rapidly. "I asked if you had an invitation."

"And I do, honey. A verbal invitation."

"From whom?"

"Dennis Simms. He asked me to meet him here."

For the first time, I glimpsed genuine emotion in Madame Sorority President's dark eyes. A sparkle of anger. "Oh, really?"

Well, she was mad at somebody, but I wasn't quite sure if it was me or Dennis Simms. I tried a conciliatory Angie smile. "Look, Dennis will be here soon. He'll vouch for me."

Features rigid, she inhaled sharply and let out a high soprano shout. *"Ty!"*

And around the corner he came, the mammoth deputy from the Briar Patch. Jack Sunawavi's bosom pal. Same khaki uniform and white felt Stetson. The mirrored sunglasses dangled from his left breast pocket. I was seeing his eyes for the first time, and they were small, narrow, swinish, porcelain blue, and alive with astonishment.

Rumbling voice. "What are *you* doing here!?"

For a man of his size and bulk, the deputy was very quick on his feet. Mammoth features glared down at me. I was instantly reminded of TV nature shows—footage of the enraged rhino as he's about to charge the camera truck.

"You gonna answer my question, Miss Sara?"

Somehow I just couldn't resist the opportunity to sting Madame Sorority President.

"Same thing as you, Ty. I got tired of the highbrow social life at the Briar Patch, so I decided to come down here and run with the riffraff."

Finally a reaction from the Ice Queen. Flared nostrils and widening brown eyes. Then her lips compressed in a tart moue. "Ty!"

Respectfully he touched his brim. "Ma'am?"

"This woman is leaving. Would you please see that she gets to her car safely?"

"Yes, ma'am."

The deputy's meaty paw reached for the back of my neck, and I knew I would not be going gently into that parking lot. I tensed all over, ready to duck, but the very next second a booming voice enveloped us all.

"Ty! You horny son of a bitch! If you're gonna run off with one of my guests, hell, at least wait till she's emptied her plate!"

My gaze snapped to the left, and I saw two men approaching from the house. One was Dennis Simms, darkly handsome and Cowboy Casual in a light gray embroidered shirt and black jeans. He followed a step or two behind the speaker—a lanky, bow-legged six-footer who looked to be ready for Social Security but who sauntered along with a kingly stride. At first glance I mistook him for the foreman. He wore a simple black-and-white cotton plaid shirt, copper-riveted workaday jeans, and a silver Stetson with a rolled brim and buckaroo crease—a hat that had seen a good deal of weather up in the high country.

I was struck by the sheer force of personality in his seamed and weatherworn visage. He had a long, hollow-cheeked vulpine face, with a high, wrinkled forehead, bristly eyebrows, twin curving creases on either side of his thin, wide mouth, and a drooping gray pistolero moustache. His nose might have been aquiline—if somebody hadn't knocked it sixty degrees to the right with the flat of a shovel, then hammered it ninety degrees in the opposite direction a few years later. Now his nose was almost as flat as Kansas up by those hard, clear blue eyes. The hair fringing his jughandle ears was stiff, gray and sparse. And he had a funny lopsided smile, up at one end, down at the other, like an S lying on its side.

"Sara Soyazhe." He gave me an appreciative glance, and then, letting his hundred and eighty pounds rest easily on a pair of worn riding heels, he bellowed, "Don't be shy! Come on over here, gal, and let's have a look at you."

There was something in his voice, some innate note of authority, that compelled instant and unthinking obedience.

"Usually when Denny tells me there's a good-lookin' filly in town, I think he's full of horseshit. 'Cause they all look good to Denny." The voice was a vibrant bass, redolent of thunder in distant canyons. " 'Course, some gals always go for a man in uniform. Ain't that right, Denny?" He came right up to me, and his blunt thumb and forefinger gave my cheek dimple a mischievous tweak. "But you! You're cute as a button. Yes, you are! And let me be the first to

135

welcome you to the Circle B. I'm Cue Broward, and this here's my wife, Gail." His hand was large and calloused, toughened by decades of range work. The thumb knuckle was slightly misshapen, leaving the digit permanently arched. Sometime in the past, Cue had caught his thumb in a lariat loop, and it had broken and set before he could reach medical attention. "And you, Ty—you'd better check in with Stead before he starts wonderin' where you've run off to. Miss Sara, it's high time you met people. Come on!"

"Cue!" The smoldering young wife took an indignant step forward. "Just a moment, please." Turned to the lawyer. "Dennis, did you invite this woman?"

Instantly respectful, the attorney replied, "Sure, Mrs. Broward. Sara and I met this afternoon, and—"

Cue cut right in. "Now, don't you fret, my love." He pronounced it *muh-luv.* "One more guest sure as hell ain't gonna put a dent in the larder. There's more'n enough for everyone." Blue eyes narrowed impatiently. "Where the hell's the main course? You don't want 'em all fillin' up on horse doovers, do you?"

"Hors d'oeuvres." Gail refused to let her husband rattle her. "I'll have a talk with him, Cue."

"Don't bother your pretty little head, honeybiscuit."

A kind of unspoken communication passed between them. Gail extended her lovely face. Dry lips puckered beneath the pistolero moustache. I'm sure Cue was aiming for her mouth, but Gail shifted her stance at the last second. His kiss tagged her on the cheekbone, leaving her flawless lipstick un-

136

disturbed. A very prim and proper Mormon princess, our Gail.

"Pleasure meeting you, Sara," said Gail, in a frosty tone that indicated it wasn't. Then off she went toward the food tables, spine perfectly straight, trim denimed backside switching back and forth.

Cue spent several seconds staring lustfully at that shapely derrière. Then he seized our shoulders and hustled us away. "Come along, Denny—Sara. Let's see if the bar's still open. Hell, it better be. I'm payin' for it."

Within seconds, Cue took the lead. Dennis and I followed in his wake. Funny how the guests seemed to melt right out of his path. Cue had that effect on people. No one wanted to get in his way.

"Sara Soyazhe," he drawled, tasting the name. "That's Indian, ain't it? Ute, ain't it? What's that mean in English?"

"Sara Little Star." At a petite five-foot-four, I had trouble keeping up with Cue's bandy-legged stride. His sly sidelong glance collided with mine, and we both grinned. "Horse doovers, Cue?"

"Hell, Sara, I laughed the first time I ever heard it."

"Forty years ago?"

Dry-throated chuckle. " 'Bout that, I reckon. Damned if them pitty-platters don't look like 'em, too. That wife of mine has got to stop usin' her daddy's caterin' outfit, and that's all there is to it."

At this range, I pegged Cue's age at sixty, give or take two years. He had the lean frame of a puncher half his age, the only flaw being the slight flaccid paunch pressing his huge bronzed NRA belt buckle.

137

"I don't know 'bout you, Sara, but all this palaver 'bout food has got my mouth waterin'." Clapping his tanned, gnarled hands together, he veered off toward the barbecue pit. "Gonna have me some words with that there boy. Ain't no trouble at all if you know the lingo."

I swear, Cue made himself heard over the band!

"Hey, Pancho! *Traigame* el beefaroo and make it damn *pronto, comprende, por favor?*"

Hearing that garbled Spanish, I thought of my old Hispanic cellmates, visualized their reactions, and gave way to a sudden fit of giggles.

Dennis whispered, "I'm going to give you some free advice, Sara. Don't you ever let that man hear you laughing at him."

I smothered the momentary mirth with my fist. "Sorry. Just couldn't help it."

"Lots of folks have made the same mistake," he added, leaning toward me. "The ones from prominent valley families—they looked down on old Cue. They thought he was just another dumb old puncher just in off the range." Grim smile. "Clover Creek sort of lost its allure for them, if you catch my meaning."

"Cue have anything to do with that?"

"He skinned them like so many beavers, Sara, and he did it laughing all the while. Not a man to mess with, no, ma'am. Fact is, there's only two people who've ever stood up to him." He cracked a grin of admiration. "Gail's one. The other one's Linda."

"Linda?" I echoed.

"Linda Beckworth. His daughter. She'll be along soon, I expect."

Dennis fell silent suddenly. I tried my best to keep him talking.

"Am I catching you out of uniform, Mr. Simms?"

"This week you are. I've already put in my fourteen days with the Reserve."

"Which branch?"

"The Army."

"Are you with that—what do you call it?—Judge Advocate something?"

Slow shake of the head. "No, Sara, I prefer something a little more challenging. Legal affairs are not part of my military occupational specialty."

I was about to ask what was when Cue's bellow drew my attention to the barbecue pit. "Sara! Damn it, gal, quit battin' your eyelashes at Denny and haul that cute little ass down here. I want you to meet somebody."

Cue's companion was another stockman, a stolid puncher in his middle fifties. Cue introduced him as Karl F. Eames—business associate—and the two gentlemen began discreetly quizzing me on my background. I fed them the *Sara Soyazhe* biography . . . born in Wyoming, educated at an exclusive girls' school in South Dakota, Master's at Radcliffe, recently moved to Ogden to take advantage of a possible faculty opening. Cue and Eames listened with ill-disguised impatience. They both wanted to get to the meat of our three-way conversation—namely, my interest in Lodestone Canyon.

"It's no big deal, really," I said, suitably mysterious. "If no one has the mineral rights, I thought I might be able to pick them up."

Eames was the more impatient of the pair. "Yes,

Sara, but *what for?* I still don't understand why you want them."

"Sorry, Karl. Trade secret. Let's just say they have a certain value and leave it at that, okay?"

"What value?" Eames's graying eyebrows rose in a gesture of skepticism. "There's nothing up there except granite and limestone!"

"Bridal Veil limestone of the Oquirrh Formation," I corrected. Angie the Geologist.

"Worthless!" Mild frustration tightened Karl's features as he took a sip of Pabst.

Enigmatic Angie smile. "That depends." I cast an inquiring glance in Cue's direction. "You gentlemen seem awfully interested in Lodestone Canyon. Might I ask why?"

Listening to Cue's Montana drawl, you'd never have suspected that Mr. Broward was one of the largest employers in Saguache County.

"Well, Sara, me 'n' Karl here 'n' some o' the boys heard Uncle Sam's 'bout to open up a few groves in Lodestone. Figured to bid on the cuttin' contract. We just want to make sure valley people benefit from the work and not some fast-talkin' hustler from Salt Lake. We put together a little pot o' money, and now we're waitin' for the RFP to come down."

"It had better come down," Karl added, his anxiety genuine.

Slowly I nudged our conversation in the direction of Billy. "What makes you so sure the Forest Service will issue a permit?"

Triumph gleamed in Cue's eyes. "I hear tell the local office is in favor of it."

"Really?" I replied. "Mr. Longhurst told me his

140

office was merely updating the district management plan.''

Cue's shrewd gaze raked me from chin to hairline. ''You're mighty familiar with that there canyon, Miss Sara.''

''I did some background research in Ogden,'' I replied, nervously rubbing my bare arms. ''Frankly, I don't think an RFP will ever go out.''

''Why not?''

''Well, for one thing, there was internal opposition. Longhurst's timber sales officer recommended against a cut. What was that name again? Oh, yeah . . . Bill Shavano—''

Eames's mouth tightened angrily. ''Son of a bitch!''

Dennis Simms spoke up behind me, his voice cool and conciliatory. ''Come on, Karl, the man was just doing his job.''

''Yeah? Tell that to my buyers!'' Eames slammed his empty bottle onto the picnic table. ''Tell that to the men at the mill. Go on, Mister Smart-Ass Lawyer. Tell them there ain't going to be any work this winter because some goddam Indian—!''

''Karl . . .'' Cue's voice had a warning tone.

Too late, though. Eames was already too far gone. Glaring at us, he muttered, ''We never had any trouble before that Ute son of a bitch went to work for Longhurst. Who ever heard of a timber sales officer *discouraging* a sale? That damned Ute used to hang around my logging sites, just itching for a chance to write me up. Son of a bitch wrote me up for silt damage. Silt damage!? Dammit, you show me a stream in Utah that ain't got silt in it!''

My obsidian eyes narrowed furiously. I was rapidly developing a dislike of Mr. Karl F. Eames.

"Indian bastard!" he spat. "He cost me two of my best boys. Why, Joe Nielsen's still got his arm in a sling—"

Cue's smile was unsympathetic. "Those boys knew the score when they walked into the Rimrock. Shavano had four years in the Marines. What'd they think those D.I.s taught him? Embroidery?"

Still seething, Karl added, "Well, they were pretty upset about that fine we had to pay."

I cut right in. "Was that before or after you talked to them about it, Mr. Eames?"

"Before, Miss Sara," he snapped. "You see, a workin' man gets a mite upset when he loses his overtime." Contemptuous snarl. "Not that a college girl like you would know anything about it!"

Emitting a deep-throated chuckle, Cue added, "Now, Karl, you know you shouldn't say *workin' man* if you're talkin' 'bout Ed Kearns. I ain't seen him around the mill, have I?"

Eames's harsh expression softened a little. "Well, no—"

"And I ain't going to, either. I hear tell he signed up for that worker's comp right after he got out of the hospital. Claimed he hurt his back in the fight. It don't feel right no more." Giving way to a snort of laughter, he grinned. "That old boy's back don't feel right less'n he's got it a-swayin' in a hammock. I never yet seen a Kearns willin' to do a hard day's work. Well, ol' Ed's got it made now. With them government checks comin' in, it's gonna be cold beer

142

and steelhead fishin' from now on. I'm surprised he didn't send Shavano a little thank-you note."

"Maybe I should have sent the bastard a thank-you note, too." Karl's expression turned hard and bitter. "Thanks for ruining my business, Shavano. Damn it! How am I supposed to survive if I can't cut? What am I supposed to do? Go on the welfare like all them niggers in Los Angeles!?" His ferocious glare tagged all of us. "Dammit, we're the ones payin' them federal salaries. Our taxes! Did Shavano ever think of that? Or can't them blankethead Indians think that far ahead!?"

Gritting my teeth, I flashed the logger a fierce warpath scowl. *"Mis-*ter Eames—!"

Cue suddenly cleared his throat. Eames caught the look of reproof and clammed right up. Blatantly ignoring me, he turned his back and walked away. "No need to say it, Cue. Wife's right. I talk too damn much. Evenin'."

I suppressed an urge to bounce the empty Pabst bottle off the back of his Stetson. Dennis's hands touched my shoulders lightly.

"Easy, Sara. He's had a bad year, that's all. Construction industry's way down. There's not much demand for lumber. It's got him worried."

I aimed a heated glance at Cue. "Sounds as if they all had a little maypole dance down at the mill when Shavano got killed."

"Well, gal, he didn't have all that many friends down there."

"Do you people still celebrate Custer's birthday, too?"

Genuine hurt glimmered in Cue's eyes. "That ain't

fair, Sara. I wasn't against Shavano because he was an Indian. I got . . . oh, six, seven Utes workin' my spread. Top hands, too. And Dan Kaniache—he's a personal friend of mine. I take him with me up to Montana every fall soon's I get my elk permit. I got nothin' against your people."

"But you did have something against Shavano."

"Bet your ass!" Cue resumed his stroll to the outdoor bar, with me and Dennis on his flanks. "I just can't abide a man who ain't loyal to the brand. That Bill Shavano—now, he worked for the Forest Service. His boss told him there wasn't anythin' wrong with cuttin' in that canyon. That was Al Longhurst's decision, and Shavano should've abided by it. But he didn't! 'Stead he goes runnin' down to Salt Lake— gettin' them tree-huggin' pointy-heads all excited. He *disobeyed* orders!" Haughty glance at me. "How long do you think the Circle B'd last, Sara, if I gave orders and they weren't obeyed? If I told my men to bring the herd down to winter pasture, and one of 'em says, 'Oh, no, Mr. Broward, I don't agree. Them old brindle steers like the cold. I think I'll leave 'em up there.' I tell you, Sara, if one o' my hands ever said that to me, he'd be off this spread so fast he'd think he was comin' out of a rodeo chute!"

"Shavano might have had a valid reason for opposing the cut," I offered.

"Like what? Knockin' me and Karl Eames flat on our ass? We don't knock so easy, Sara. He found that out soon enough." Turning to Dennis, he winked, "Some o' them pointy-heads are gonna find that out, too. Right, boy?"

144

Small grin from the lawyer. "I believe they've learned their lesson, Cue."

Arriving at the outdoor bar, Cue put in an order for Jack Daniel's. "Tribe of DAN!" he snarled, accepting a shot glass from the bartender. *"Deseret Au Naturel!* Who thought that up? Some queer-assed French hairdresser, more'n likely. And he's goin' to tell me 'n' Karl 'n' old man Sager how to manage our land? Shit! I tell you what you should do with the Tribe of DAN. You take all them pointy-heads and stick 'em all up there on Cheney Peak, and you let 'em dig post-holes ten, eleven hours a day. Same way I did when I was their age. And *then* they'd sure as hell have somethin' to protest about!"

Upending the glass, he put down the whiskey in one fast swallow, swiveled his head, and flashed me a rueful smile. "Gettin' ornery in my old age. Seems to me I promised you a drink, Miss Sara." A nod to the bartender. "You be good to this young lady, Mike, hear?" And then he turned that courtly, old-fashioned smile on me. "I do hope you'll excuse me. I see Pancho wavin' that big old *cuchillo,* so I guess I got me some steak-carvin' to do. You just grab yourself a chair and set, Sara. We'll be eatin' presently."

Apprehension flared in Dennis's eyes. "Wait a minute, Cue. I thought you said you were going to—"

Slapping the lawyer's shoulder, Cue chuckled. "Ain't important what I said before, Denny. Don't you worry none. Everything's settled now 'tween Sara 'n' me."

The finality in his tone made me shiver. "Settled?'' Confused blink. ''Cue, what are you talking about?''

''Why, your continued presence here in Clover Creek, little gal.'' On came that celebrated wrangler grin. ''Way I figure it, you're a smart little filly, and you've figured out some way to make money on those Lodestone mineral rights. Whatever it is, I'd surely like to hear it. So here's what we're gonna do. You're gonna stay here in town and think on it some, and when you've got the details all worked out, you bring it to me, and we'll talk it over. And if'n I like it, I'll go partners with you, fifty-fifty, and we'll both rake in the cash. If I don't like it, you can go on back to Ogden, no hard feelin's, and I'll talk to a few ol' boys in Salt Lake 'n' make sure you get that professor's job.'' A feral gleam altered his grin. ''Now then, Miss Sara, ain't that a sight better'n havin' your pretty ass run out of the valley by that mean ol' deputy?''

I felt a cold, damp spot on the back of my neck. The tendons behind my knees began to quiver. I was beginning to feel like Dorothy in *The Wizard of Oz,* trapped in the tower chamber, watching those relentless sands pour through the hourglass.

Somehow this just wasn't the moment to tell Mr. Broward that my name wasn't really *Sara Soyazhe*. That I had no way to turn a profit on those mineral rights. And that I was actually Angela Biwaban, cousin of the late Bill Shavano, trespassing on his ranch in the hopes of doing a little freelance snooping. No doubt Gail's pet deputy would leap at the chance to bounce me down to the Saguache County jail.

So I watched Cue bustle back to the barbecue pit,

glad-handing all the well-wishers, with the ever-faithful Dennis trailing a step or two behind. Leaning toward me, Mike the bartender said, "Miss?"

"Make it a Morning Dawn, Mike." Nervous Angie smile. "Double, no ice."

Dinner did much to soothe my jangled nerves. My sampling of the Broward cuisine was strictly low-cal. I feasted on several slices of choice top round, done to a juicy medium rare, plus lettuce, celery and tomatoes. I tried not to think about the fact that, if he found out what I was up to, Cue Broward could engineer a pretty rough ninety days for me at the county jail.

So I thought about something else. Namely, Karl Eames's rather hostile feelings about Billy. I had the impression that Eames Lumber was having a little trouble this quarter—that maybe Karl Eames desperately needed the Lodestone cut to salvage a dismal fiscal year.

So let's flash back a few months, and there is Mr. Karl F. Eames, hater of minorities, getting told by the Forest Service that he's being fined for silt damage. And he knows it's because Billy's been monitoring his operation in the Topanas. So he calls in his men and tells them how *that Indian* just cost them their overtime for the next quarter. And he is as happy as a meadowlark when Ed Kearns and Joe Nielsen go gunning for Billy at the Rimrock Cafe.

I wondered if a little money had changed hands before the boys set out for the cafe. Ahhhhh, probably not. If murder was Eames's intent, then the assault on Billy would have been a whole lot deadlier. Eames wouldn't have trusted to luck. Besides, had Billy been killed, and had Kearns and Nielsen been charged, one or the other could have easily cut a deal with the D.A. by turning state's evidence and fingering Eames.

Okay, so our dim-witted, Indian-hating duo had acted on their own, figuring to give my cousin a thumping, and they'd lived to regret it when Billy showed them exactly how he'd won that Silver Star down in Panama. But suppose Karl Eames had decided to bushwack Billy up in the Topanas. Coming up with a chainsaw was no problem. There were plenty lying around the mill, I'll bet. And if the investigating officer saw through the deception, Eames had a couple of ready-made patsies to throw to the law—Ed Kearns and Joe Nielsen.

Memo to my grandfather: Got a couple of things for you to check out, Chief. First, how badly was Joe Nielsen hurt during that brawl with Billy? If there's a broken arm in that sling, we can eliminate him as a suspect. There's no way Nielsen could have lifted and swung that weighty McCulloch chainsaw one-handed.

Second, what has Ed Kearns been up to since he went out on worker's comp? Let's not take Cue Broward's word for it. How does Mr. Kearns feel about his run-in with Billy? And since Kearns hasn't been to the mill, where has he been? Where was he the morning Bill was killed?

After dinner, I struck up a conversation with the neighbor at my right elbow, Mrs. Darcy Kohler. She was a soft-voiced lady on the high side of thirty, with a glossy strawberry blond pageboy and noticeable cheekbones. In no time at all, we found an interest in common—horses—and spent a delightful hour swapping stable tales.

Darcy and her laconic hubby owned a horse ranch in Sanctuary, on the Idaho state line. And Darcy told me a funny story about the origin of the name.

Prior to 1896, the year the LDS Church formally renounced polygamy, a fellow named Fred T. Dubois (no relation to Blanche) became the U.S. marshal up in Montpelier, Idaho, and he definitely disapproved of the Saints' plural marriages. So the Mormons installed a powerful telescope in the cupola of the tabernacle in Paris, Idaho. Whenever they saw Marshal Fred ride out of Montpelier, they used to ring the tabernacle bell, and there'd be a mad stampede of Mormon husbands running for Utah.

The refugees camped out in a lush meadow on the shores of Bear Lake, just beyond the marshal's jurisdiction. It soon became known as The Bishops' Sanctuary, and when they laid out the townsite in the early 1900s, they kept the last half of that name.

". . . and that stretch of road, Sara, going from Sanctuary up to Paris. That's called the Hallelujah Trail,'' Darcy told me. '' 'Cause that's what our boys yelled when they crossed over into Utah. They were awful glad to get away from Marshal Dubois. He sent plenty of Saints to that prison up in Boise, you know.''

The sudden roar of a car engine punctuated Darcy's tale. Looking over my shoulder, I saw a brand-new silver-and-charcoal Corvette barrelling up the driveway. It came to a sand-spitting stop in front of the garage, and I caught a fleeting glimpse of its Utah vanity plate: FASTGAL.

Frowning, Darcy muttered, "Oh, Lord, here she comes."

She was a light ash blonde in her middle twenties, about two inches taller than me. Sheepdog bangs, dynamic curves, and long, well-sculpted legs. She had a blunt, full face, pretty in a kind of hard-edged way. Aquamarine eyes set somewhat apart, finely-trimmed light brown eyebrows, firm cheekbones, pugnacious jaw and a wide, sensuous mouth complete with an Elvis Presley lip curl.

And that *dress!* Honestly, I had to pinch myself. It was sleeveless, Spandex, and about two sizes too small for her. A curve-hugging minidress in alternating navy blue and white pinstripes, with V-necked cleavage reaching clear down to the navel. The only thing keeping her in that dress—and out of trouble with Sheriff Mortensen—was the slender rawhide string zipping back and forth across the ample physique, dipping in and out of eyeholes on either side of the divide.

Past the picnic tables she sauntered, oblivious to all the whispers. She had the exact same stride as Cue Broward, quick and aggressive, chin up, hands on the hips. She went straight to the head table, her smile widening as she caught Gail's reaction to her party frock.

"You owe me five dollars, honey," Darcy's husband said, putting out a long calloused palm. "I told you Linda'd show up."

She slapped his palm playfully. "You'll get your money, Roy." And she turned to me. "I didn't think that gal would ever show her face around here again. Especially after last time."

"What happened the last time?" I asked.

"Kathy Murdoch made eyes at Linda's man. So Linda hung a shiner on her." Roy flicked the ash from his cigarette. "Poor Kath looked like she went six rounds at the Briar Patch."

"Did you see what she's got on?" Darcy nudged her husband, then shook her head in disgust. "You know she's doing it just to aggravate Miss Gail."

I fired a quick glance at Cue's young wife. Gail's pert frown would have frozen Bear Lake. "Linda appears to be having some success," I noted wryly, then took a guess. "Cue's daughter?"

Darcy nodded, then shot her husband a worried look. "Do you think she'll make trouble tonight?"

"And ruin this here barbecue?" Roy shook his head. "Never happen! Miss Gail wouldn't stand for it. No, Linda ain't gonna try anything. Not with old Ty Braddock around."

The name hit me right between the eyes.

"Excuse me? *Who!?*"

"Ty Braddock. That big ol' deputy keepin' an eye on the cars." Roy sent me a curious glance. "You know him?"

Sure do, fella. Ty Braddock. Also know as Deputy T.P. Braddock. Bosom buddy of Jack Sunawavi. Pet watchdog for the lovely Gail Sager Broward. And the man who had found my cousin's dying body up there in Dynamite Pass.

Chapter Eight

Learning that good old Deputy Ty and T.P. Braddock were one and the same changed my immediate plans. Instead of tracking down Alfie Longhurst's whereabouts on that fateful Tuesday, I delegated that task to my grandfather and headed up into Lodestone Canyon. I wanted a personal view of the murder scene.

Chief promised to check out Ed Kearns and Joe Nielsen as well as Longhurst. He also suggested a roundabout route to Dynamite Pass. Hike, he said, don't drive. The wrong person might drive by and wonder what Sara Soyazhe's Honda Accord was doing parked by the side of the road.

So I left the Accord at the Forest Service trailhead, shouldered my daypack and trusty canteen, and set off into the Topanas. Lofty Ponderosa pines and spreading junipers. Sparse carpet of dusty dry pine needles. Clusters of red heather and serviceberry.

Up the meandering trail I went, serenaded by a squawking sharptailed grouse. Angie the Backpacker. Anishinabe princess in her white watercolor-print

T-shirt and lime-colored Spandex bike pants. I wore a long-billed ballcap in the same shade of lime, with my lengthy raven-black hair poking out the stern in a bouncy ponytail.

The backpack contained everything I might need for an overnight stay. Hooded sweatshirt, snug blue jeans, tarpaulin, mosquito net, nylon rope, poncho, quilted liner and inflatable pillow. Clipped to the pack's webbing was my favorite forest tool. An old friend, Bob Stonepipe, had first introduced me to it when I worked for him as a guide on the Gunflint Trail. It was a stainless steel survival knife, trade name *Commando*. The hollow handle contained a mini-survival kit consisting of a snare wire, nylon fishing line, fishhooks, sinkers, needles, tinder, life-boat matches and gauze pads.

The matches were a luxury, not a necessity. Long ago, when I was barely out of the cradleboard, my grandfather plunked me down on the shores of Tettegouche Lake and taught me how to make a fire.

Were I to run into Jack Sunawavi, he would undoubtedly think twice before embarking on any mischief. A glimpse of the Commando's gleaming six-inch bowie-style blade would prove daunting. And if it didn't . . . . well, I learned quite a bit about handling knives during my three-year stay in the Big Dollhouse.

I picked up Papoose Creek about two miles into the forest, then followed it northwest until I came to the mouth of Lodestone Canyon. The canyon itself was a huge "U" cut into the eastern side of Cheney Peak. Sheer walls rose in a layer-cake arrangement of shale and limestone soaring above the forested floor.

Back in the Pleistocene, a glacier had come creeping down from Cheney's snow line, carving this broad, zigzagged trench, and when the glacier finally melted, it left those perpendicular walls and many mounds of gravelly debris. Swift-running Papoose Creek darted between those mounds on its way downslope, creating many knee-high, spattering waterfalls. Up near the canyon walls lurked a handful of hideaway wetlands and ponds.

A boreal forest had taken root in Lodestone. Ruddy Ponderosa had yielded to lofty lodgepole and bristling tamarack and dark Douglas fir. The mounds' slopes were wreathed in wildflowers: Greenish-yellow glacier lily and coppery, bell-shaped pinedrops and stubby pink alpine laurel. Looking down from the rim, like so many guardian angels, were the silvery aspens.

Midway up the canyon I veered off the trail, heading for a good-sized pond, and did some food shopping. I mean, who needs a supermarket when Lodestone Canyon is awash in edibles? I spotted some arrowhead leaves in the pond, peeled off my trail boots, waded over there, got my toes around the stalks, and pulled out some juicy swamp potatoes. Then it was up onto dry land to harvest a half-dozen yampahs. See the serviceberry shrubs? Get out the canteen cup and collect some.

After pulling some Ziploc bags out of my pack, I tucked my wilderness groceries safely away, pulled on my boots, and resumed the trek. In no time at all I got caught up in the rhythm of the forest. I became aware of the silence and of each living sound that breaks it—the scrabbling of loose talus stones, the

154

whistling of a mountain breeze through the tamarack boughs, the sloshing of swift creek waters over broken limestone.

With this awareness comes a heightened sense of self. A feeling of acceptance and placidity, a feeling that you've become one with the forest. That this is where you belong, and that it is both right and natural for you to be there. My people have a word for this—*wanuskewin*. The only word in English that even comes close to it is *harmony*.

Unfortunately, the feeling didn't last. Looking up at those slender aspens along the canyon rim, I experienced no sense of harmony, just a growing disquiet bordering on anger. Watching Lodestone Canyon wend its way up the mountainside, I knew why Billy had resolved to save it. I studied those lush, one-of-a-kind aspen groves, and I cursed Cue Broward for his stupidity. To reach the aspen, Broward's men would have to bulldoze a logging road through those wooded moraines, choke the creek with slash, tear up the wetland wildflowers, scar the limestone walls with their skyhook pylons. A priceless remnant of ancient Utah would be destroyed forever, and for what? Proceeds from the timber sale would hardly justify the financial costs of the cut.

By the time I reached Dynamite Pass, I was eager to hunt. Wild rose and blue camas mingled with the lush alpine grass. The pass itself was another holdover from the early Pleistocene. Lodestone's glacier had been born in there and had broken out through an old runoff streambed.

No problem finding the spot where Billy died. There was only one lodgepole missing a wedge from its trunk. I noticed a trickle of sap a bit higher on the trunk, looked straight up, and saw a blunt stump disturbing the symmetry of the upper branches.

Kneeling, I examined the nearby ground. It hadn't rained up here since that fateful day, so the tracks were still pretty well preserved. I immediately recognized the tread pattern of Billy's hiking boots and the imprint of a pointy-toed size fifteen Tony Lama that could only belong to Deputy Ty Braddock. The remaining footprints were masculine, low-heeled, deep at the toes. Men running around. Sure, the helicopter paramedics. They'd been hustling to give Billy first aid and then scrambling to get him aboard the chopper.

Squatting on my heels, I studied the roots of that gashed lodgepole pine. Picked away pine needles. Probed the soil at the base of the trunk. The turf hadn't been disturbed in decades. Billy had never buried tobacco at the base of this tree.

It was so nice to have my original suspicion confirmed.

Widen the circle a bit, Biwaban. Let's go about twenty yards out. Yes, there's Billy coming straight into the meadow from the asphalt road. Heading straight for the fateful lodgepole, as a matter of fact.

Another forty yards, and . . . hello, Ty! What are you doing over here? There's only one ridge hereabouts—that lateral moraine at the far side of the meadow. So what are you doing in this area, Ty? And why are those fancy bootheels all pointing towards the road, as if you'd walked straight in here?

I followed Ty's footprints all the way to the scuffed-up ground in front of the lodgepole. Then, just to make sure, I jogged over to the moraine and walked its sandy summit from end to end.

You're a damned liar, Ty Braddock! According to the Saguache County Herald, you stood on top of this moraine and saw my cousin Billy pinned beneath that lodgepole limb. Now, a three-hundred-pounder like you is bound to leave prints in the soft, sandy loam of a moraine. I see red fox and marmot and jackrabbit tracks but no size fifteen cowboy boots. You weren't anywhere near this ridge.

On my way back to the lodgepole, I crossed another faint trail. A man's footprints, a tall man with a long stride. I squatted beside the sparse trail, elbows on my knees, peering with interest.

How about that? There are no clearly-defined sole or heel shapes, just vague oblong footprints. My tall friend is wearing either moccasins or soft-soled Army boots. The right-foot indentations are slightly deeper on the outside. He's walking slightly lopsided.

Fussbudget face. No, he has something in his right hand, something that throws his balance off. A weighty object that made him walk lopsided. A chainsaw, perhaps?

Following the intruder's tracks back to the road, I saw the tire marks where Billy had parked his Forest Service truck and the squiggly tread pattern of a right front tire. Ty's cruiser? No sign of a third vehicle, though. So I took a little stroll up the road. Took me forty minutes before I found what I was looking for.

Disturbed sand at the road's edge.

Very careful fellow, the intruder. He'd taken care to park a good distance away from Billy's truck, and to keep all four tires on the asphalt, thereby leaving no telltale tread marks on the shoulder. A man very keen about not advertising his presence.

About face, princess. Back to the intruder's trail. As I suspected, it ended in that jumbled spaghetti of footprints at the foot of the lodgepole. Those running paramedics had done an excellent job of obliterating any useful traces.

Okay, Angie, looks like you're going to have to do this the hard way.

Dropping to my hands and knees, I conducted a narrow-eyed search of the jumble's perimeter. Inch by inch, I scrutinized the disturbed ground. Oh, ho! Here's our tall friend again, leaving the scene with a rather nervous and hasty stride. His footprints are a little different this time. More weight on the heel. He's more interested in getting away than in leaving no traces. His soles are flat and level. He isn't carrying that heavy weight any more.

Standing erect once more, I rotated my shoulders in a lovely stretch, returned to my waiting backpack, and grabbed my canteen. I seated myself in the lodgepole's shade. The water tasted good on a parched tongue.

In my head, I reconstructed the intruder's movements. Park sixty yards down the road. Lift the chainsaw out of the vehicle. Approach Billy on foot.

I wonder what Billy said when he saw you. Or did he even see you? Damn! If only those paramedics hadn't been running around like a pack of demented field mice!

But when you left, my friend, you didn't have that chainsaw with you any more. You left it in my cousin's lifeless hands, and then you angled off into the forest, returning to your vehicle by a long roundabout route.

You came here with that chainsaw in your hand and murder in your heart and a reasonably clever plan to make it all look accidental. If not for your ignorance of our Native American ways, you might have even gotten away with it.

Those vague tracks bothered me. Whoever the intruder was, he really knew how to move through the backcountry. He instinctively avoided stepping on twigs and dry leaves and loose soil. I might have thought he was Native American. But no Nuche would have made that mistake with the tobacco. That was a white man's blunder.

So what was the intruder, anyway? A white man with the outdoor savvy of a Nuche? Someone who had spent years in the wild country and had learned all the tricks?

I could think of only one suspect who fit that description. Cue Broward, the one-time Montana cowpuncher.

Then again, what if the intruder had omitted the tobacco on purpose? What if he had *wanted* to make it look as if a white man had set the scene?

Jack Sunawavi sprang instantly to mind.

Sunawavi had two strong motives. He had lost his girl to Billy, and he'd been licked in the most celebrated fistfight of recent years. Jack could have learned of the loggers' enmity, killed my cousin, and set up the flawed accident scene, maliciously relishing the thought that the blame would eventually fall upon the county's most prominent residents, Karl Eames and Cue Broward.

Yeah, just the kind of prank that would appeal to dear old Jack.

My stomach began to rumble. It was time for lunch.

I did it just the way Grandma Blackbear taught me. Gather the deadwood and build a small fire. Get out the aluminum pan and fill it with canteen water. Then wash and peel and boil the swamp potatoes and yampah roots. To see if they're done, bite into a yampah. Yummmmm—nice carroty taste. Now, toss out the old water and refill from the canteen. In go the swamp potatoes and the yampah roots. Pour in the serviceberries for thickening. Stir slowly and let it come to a nice gradual boil.

Following a leisurely lunch featuring piping-hot Wasatch vegetable soup, I recapped my canteen and hung it on the pack's aluminum frame. Then I shouldered my rig and headed back down the canyon.

Mild fussbudget face. I was troubled by Ty Braddock's role here. Was he here with Billy and the mysterious tall man? Or had he come later? Had he helped the tall man cover it up, or had he genuinely been taken in by the deception?

I doubted the last option. The report Ty had turned in to the sheriff was sheer, unadulterated Grade A horseshit. He'd never been anywhere near that moraine. So, for now, we file the mammoth deputy under A—that's A for Accessory—and head back to town.

As I hiked along Papoose Creek, I thought about the tobacco pouch we'd made for Billy. What had happened to it? I'd found no sign of it in Billy's trailer. And during my scout of Dynamite Pass, I hadn't come

160

across it among the pine needles. So just where is our little deerskin pouch with the red beaded thunderbird on the front? Did the intruder take it from Billy's person after the murder? If so, why?

I couldn't quite shake the feeling that I'd overlooked something back there at the pass. Some vital clue. I halted, casting a quick troubled glance over my shoulder, and wondered if I ought to spend the night. Give it a little time and see if anything significant popped into my head.

Just then, I heard a chittering sound to my left. My gaze zipped in that direction, and I let out a soft chuckle of delight. A red squirrel perched on a flat limestone outcrop, whirling and grappling with an apple core. He reminded me of a drunk trying to play a bass fiddle. Moments later, the squirrel pinned the core to the stone, then slashed away at the moist white fruit with his buck teeth. He broke into the pod, scooped out the seeds with lightning-quick forepaws, and then, sitting upright, gobbled them one by one.

My gaze drifted from the squirrel to the apple core, and I stopped smiling. Quite abruptly. If you're an apple-eater, then you know how fast the core turns brown. Takes about an hour, right?

This apple core was still wet and white . . . *freshly eaten!*

Leaning over, I snatched it away from the squirrel. Uttering squealing protests, he leaped from the rock and bounded into the underbrush. Ignoring the chatter, I held up the core to the bright sunlight. Hmmmmm. Rather sizeable bite marks at the stem. A man's mouth. And he had finished it about five minutes ago.

The apple enthusiast had entered the canyon after I did. A backpacker? Maybe. But if so, then why didn't he continue all the way up to the pass? Why stop here?

Sobering thought. Because I was up there?

I tossed the core to my squirrel friend. Unforgiving, he kept right on scolding me. Turning my back on him, I surveyed the trail a lot more carefully—and found something that sent a nasty chill up my spine.

A vague, oblong masculine footprint . . . identical to the ones I'd seen up at Dynamite Pass!

I obeyed my first impulse, which was to hurry down the trail, hoping to reach the relative safety of my car. Forty yards down the canyon, however, I slowed my pace, noticing that all the intruder footprints were incoming.

He wasn't between me and the Accord.

So I obeyed my second impulse and followed his faint tracks back to the squirrel's rock and then veered off toward an undulating ridge.

Wouldn't it be fun to trail our phantom intruder and, without him noticing, get a really good look at his face?

Whoa, Angie! Don't get careless. For all you know, our tall friend is up on the ridgeline right now, admiring your impish smile through a rifle scope. And wondering where geologist Sara Soyazhe learned to read trail sign.

So, princess, do it the right way. Keep to the shade of the Douglas firs. Reach behind and loosen the strap on your survival knife. Stop frequently behind trees and boulders. Tense and listen.

I did all of the above and heard nothing more sinister than the squabbling of grouse. I kept low as I crossed the skyline. The going was much easier on the other side. The mountain forest thinned out into broad meadows brimming with multicolored wildflowers and dry, knee-high grass.

Just then, I heard the fading engine whine of a speeding truck. As I reached the summit of a low hill, I caught a glimpse of a dark blue Dodge pickup a half mile downcountry. Raising clouds of dust, it skidded around a grassy bend and disappeared.

I frowned mightily. Twice I'd seen that particular Dodge during the past two weeks. Once outside Cindy Polenana's house in Millcreek. The second time in the Briar Patch parking lot. Its owner was not among the more pleasant of my acquaintances.

"Jack Sunawavi," I muttered.

I felt a sudden fearful chill. Sunawavi had followed me up to Dynamite Pass. He knew my real name was Angie, and he knew I was very much interested in Bill Shavano.

This could mean *real* trouble for Chief's favorite granddaughter!

But why had Jack left the area so abruptly?

Pondering that man's motives merely worsened the chill. Maybe Jack needed a little time to think, eh? Maybe he needed some time to come up with a foolproof way of disposing of the Angie nuisance.

Knees trembling, I started back to the canyon's trail. I wondered if Jack Sunawavi had delivered the chainsaw to the murder scene.

Probably not! I put myself in my cousin's shoes. *Hey, looky there! Who's that coming across the meadow with a chainsaw in his hands? Why, if it isn't*

163

Jack Sunawavi, who hates my guts because of Cindy and whose ass I kicked at the Briar Patch. Wonder what he wants?

Yeah. Right. No way would Billy have stood around, pondering Sunawavi's intentions. There would have been a fight. Both my cousin and Sunawavi would have gotten scuffed a bit.

And there had been no scuff marks on Billy. Just that massive fracture at the back of the skull.

Which may mean Jack Sunawavi didn't strike the fatal blow.

So what was Jack's role? Delivery boy, perhaps? Did he bring the chainsaw up there to Dynamite Pass? Was Billy already dead when he arrived? And who summoned him up there? A lying deputy, perhaps?

I had plenty to think about during the long hike down to the trailhead.

Well, I got back to Clover Creek just after dark. Reasonably quiet at the Trail's End Trailer Park. Ghostly flicker of TV lights from several windows. Everybody secure in their metal cocoons, gaping at the same tired old sitcoms, hooting along with the laugh track, oblivious to the rustle of the juniper leaves and the stuttering chirp of the grasshoppers.

I had no interest in television. All I wanted at that moment was to stand in the shower, sluicing away the dust and grit and sweat of the canyon's trail. The lock rattled as I turned the key. Pushing the door open, I reached inside and flicked on the light. Stepping across the threshold, I grimaced at the hot mugginess

164

of the trailer and headed straight for the window-mounted air conditioner.

The shower's steamy cascade felt good after a long day upcountry. I vigorously shampooed my long mane, shoved my head under the spray, and let out a long sigh of relaxation. Heaven!

Twenty minutes later, I emerged from the bathroom, my damp hair in a terrycloth turban, winding a bath towel into a makeshift sarong. I giggled at my reflection in the dresser mirror.

What? Another evening spent washing your hair? Face it, Angela. You need a man in your life.

And then I thought of the most recent man in my life, and my conceited grin faded abruptly.

Are you still living in the Upper Peninsula, Donald? And do you ever think of me?

Well . . . actually, he wouldn't be thinking of Angie Biwaban. Donald knew me as *Andrea Porter,* the lady realtor who ran off with all that money. I had a perfectly valid explanation for that, and I knew he'd forgive me. Unfortunately, the state of Michigan did not quite see it my way. As a result, if I ever did return to Tilford, my life would become very exciting, indeed.

Yes, Donald, I'll happily marry you. But first, lover, I have to do this ten-year stretch for bank robbery. You won't mind waiting. Right?

Scowling, I reached for my plastic hairbrush. Donald Winston Pierce wasn't the only man in the world—there are plenty more. Why, in Clover Creek alone, I'd met two interesting men. So maybe Cue Broward is a little snowy up top. He has a roguish charm and

165

a fantastic *joie de vivre,* and if he were single, I wouldn't mind having him sweep me off my feet.

And then there's Dennis Simms. Mmmmmm, love that jawline. And those shoulders! Those strong, silent types can really give you a run for your money once you've gotten them all steamed up. I wonder how he feels about petite brunettes . . .

I halted brushing in mid-stroke, then scowled again at my reflection. My thoughts had followed a logical procession from Cue to Dennis to *Billy.* And a sudden surge of sorrow banished all thoughts of romance.

Instead, I thought about Billy and Cindy . . . the marriage that would never be . . . the grandchildren Aunt Della would never have. The eyes of my mirror reflection glistened with tears.

Was I crazy? Cue Broward, Dennis Simms, maybe the both of them were tied into Billy's murder. How could I have even entertained such notions? I was behind the lines. No more thoughts of fraternizing with the enemy.

My thoughts returned to Cindy. That poor woman! How can she possibly deal with it? Honestly, if I ever got word that something had happened to Donald, I don't know what I'd do.

Finishing my hundred-and-one strokes, I grabbed my T-shirt and lime bike pants and tossed them into a laundry sack. I was definitely looking forward to a slow crawl between crisp percale sheets. Then, as I turned toward the cedar chest of drawers, a cold shiver crawled across my middle, a chill that had absolutely nothing to do with the air conditioner.

I took a sudden deep breath, feeling terribly, terribly vulnerable.

And for a very good reason.

Someone had been in here today!

And how did I know that? Well, when I was the new fish at Springfield, I was always getting ripped off. I lost my watch, my comb, my tampons, my shampoo, the locket Rory McDaniel gave me, all within the first week.

Then my prison mom, Becky Reardon, took me under her wing and showed me how to stop the pilfering.

First, dust the chest of drawers with a whiff of hairspray. Then, before it dries, pull a single strand of hair and lay it across the narrow aperture between chest and drawer. The hair will stay in place until you open the drawer and dislodge it.

Back in Springfield, I got in the habit of glancing at the chest of drawers every time I entered my cell . . . excuse me, *personal area.* If the hair was missing, that meant I'd been boosted.

A strand of raven hair is a most inexpensive watchdog. *De rigeur* for the Anishinabe princess behind enemy lines.

Slowly I slid the top drawer open. Yeah, I'd had a visitor, all right. He did his best not to disturb my lingerie, but the wrinkled nylon panties gave him away.

No man—repeat, *no* man—knows how to properly fold women's underwear.

Okay, so let's strike a lifeboat match and have another look at that door lock.

Ahhhhh—interesting. Looks as if my friend the lockpick is back. There are two fresh scratches on the rim.

I performed a rushed but thorough search of the trailer. Nothing of mine was missing. Then I checked the lower cabinet. Billy's map book lay undisturbed. So what is going on here, anyway? This is the second time Billy's trailer has been the target of a smooth and professional break-in. An unlawful entry perpetrated by someone with a notable expertise in lock-picking.

I couldn't understand the intruder's rationale. I could see breaking in here after Billy's death to retrieve something from the map book. But why wait two weeks and then come back *again?*

Unless, of course, my cousin wasn't the target.

Now there's a chilling thought. Maybe he dropped by to do a discreet check on Sara Soyazhe, lady geologist. Could it have been one of Cue Broward's people, trying to learn more about Lodestone's mineral rights? Or Gail Sager Broward's favorite deputy? You'd be surprised how many lawmen have mastered the art of busting locks.

And then I thought of another possibility, one that set my stomach churning. Standing up at once, I turned the deadbolt and hung the small brass chain. Perhaps the target wasn't Sara, after all. Perhaps that man had come here looking for *Angie* . . .

Chapter Nine

Come the next morning, I appeared in my landlady's doorway and gave the screen frame a friendly rap. "Hi, Mrs. Thornley! Can I talk to you a minute?"

"Sara!" Genuine pleasure radiated from that fleshy face. "Come on in, honey. You're just in time for breakfast."

Kate Thornley hovered over a rosewood table festooned with cornbread muffins, bite-sized fruit slices and tart raspberry jam.

Opening the screen door, I hesitated. Awkward Angie smile. "Thanks, but I usually go with a lighter breakfast."

"Nonsense, Sara. Here—you must try my sourdough pancakes."

I blanched at the sight of those golden-brown disks. "Hey, I've got to go jogging—"

"Goodness, if you aren't the fidgetiest young lady I ever met!" Shaking her head, Kate planted her palms on the puffed shoulders of my lavender peasant top and forced me to sit. "When's the last time you had a decent breakfast?"

"Mrs. Thornley, if I eat those pancakes, you know where they're going to end up?" I patted the seat of my white stretch shorts. "Right here!"

"Oh, get on with you! I swear, Sara, if you get any skinnier, you're going to fall between the pickets of Mr. Wayborne's fence." Pushing the back of my chair, she added, "Now, stop looking at my preserves as if they got poison in them. A little raspberry jam ain't going to spoil your shape. Go on. Have some."

Well, no chance of rye toast and tomato juice at the Rimrock today. But it was worth it to find out if any of Mrs. Thornley's other tenants had seen yesterday's intruder. I spread a thin layer of raspberry jam across the top pancake, sawed away at it enthusiastically, nibbled at it sporadically, and listened in respectful silence as my landlady brought me up to date on the latest Clover Creek gossip.

I learned that the lovely Gail was still seething about stepdaughter Linda Beckworth's choice of evening wear at the recent Broward barbecue. That a man named Randy Powell had walked out on his wife and gone to Salt Lake, that final refuge of lapsed Mormons. And that Gail's daddy had just purchased controlling interest in Stateline Cable TV. Found out, too, that Mr. Truman Kimball Sager also owns KWVR Radio, 1620-AM on your dial, and the Exaltation Printing Company, which puts out the *Saguache County Herald*.

Mindful of the religious orientation of the newspaper and KWVR, I had a feeling that the learned Dr. Eldon T. Budge would soon be bumping Paula Abdul off cable. And said so.

"I sure hope so," said Mrs. Thornley, pushing the

jam jar across the tablecloth at me. "My sister Eloise gets Dr. Budge's show, 'The Prophecies of Moroni,' down there in Tremonton, and she loves it. You know, I heard Dr. Budge speak at the tabernacle once. When he started preaching the word of God, I got a little funny tingle run right up me from my toes. He has the voice of an angel. And so smart, too. An oak in the garden of Zion." She showed me a dreamy expression quite similar to the ecstasies of the medieval Catholic saints. "We are the true Israelites!" Deep sigh. And then a sharp look at me. "Young people today'd be a lot better off watching more of Dr. Budge and less of that Paula Abdul. I swear, that little Ayrab gal shakes her bootie almost as much as Cue's daughter. And that's saying something." Hasty survey of my breakfast plate. "Oh, Sara, you've hardly eaten a thing. You know, it's a shame you came during August. I've only just started on my preserves. Still, if you want some good homemade raspberry jam to take back to Ogden, drop in at the Hildt place down in Garden City. Ask for young Trish. Every bit as good as mine. You'll see."

"I think I'll take you up on that, Mrs. T. I've got a long drive this morning, anyway." Broad Angie smile. "I'll probably be gone all day. Do you mind taking messages?"

"Not at all." She carefully smoothed melting butter on half of a crumbly cornbread muffin. "As a matter of fact, Miss Sara Soyazhe, I've been doing that right along. Nobody's ever going to accuse you of being a little stay-at-home."

My ears perked. "I've had visitors?"

"A few." My landlady smiled fondly. "That nice

171

Mr. Longhurst stopped by yesterday morning. And that handsome lawyer, Dennis Simms.'' Pudgy cheeks turned a soft shade of salmon. ''He came by just after supper. Gave me his card. Oh, ain't he devilish handsome? If I was a quarter-century younger, I'd—'' She kept the delightful fantasy to herself. '' 'Cleft on the chin, devil within,' that's what my grandmama used to say. Oh, and there was somebody else, too. An Indian.''

''When was this, Mrs. T?''

''Sometime last night, I reckon.''

Jack Sunawavi's grinning face loomed in my mind's eye. ''What did he look like, Mrs. T? Was he tall—thin? Sharp features? Wearing a black fringed vest?''

Mrs. Thornley displayed an apologetic smile. ''I wasn't the one who saw him, Sara. Fay Hunsaker did. She told me about it when I came home from the tabernacle. It happened around seven or seven-thirty, I guess. Fay opened her trailer door to put Buster out. And there he was, that Indian fella, right smack dab on your doorstep. Buster commenced to barking at him. Then Fay asked him what he was doing over there, and he said he was looking for Bill. So Fay told him about Mr. Shavano, and he left.''

''Any other description?'' I asked.

''No, Fay just said he was an Indian man.''

So I artfully shifted the topic of conversation back to Dr. Budge's syndicated TV show. And while Mrs. Thornley waxed enthusiastic over the Mormon elder's encyclopedic knowledge of scripture, I gave some thought to my evening visitor.

Okay, so who was he? Sunawavi? No, that didn't

make sense. Jack knows perfectly well that Billy's dead.

On the other hand, Jack might have been playing dumb for Fay Hunsaker's benefit.

I frowned. None of it made sense. If Jack—or anyone else, for that matter—had just arrived at my trailer, he wouldn't have tried to spring the lock. Not with the vigilant Buster roaming the yard, ready to let out an excited bark.

And if the intruder had broken in *before* Buster's arrival, then why would he hang around, standing on my front step?

My uninvited guest had been here between seven and seven-thirty. In other words, twenty minutes before my arrival. Would that have given him enough time to spring the door lock and toss my room? Somehow I didn't think so.

If it *wasn't* Jack Sunawavi, then who . . . ?

Deeper frown. Another one of Billy's friends? A Nuche who doesn't know he's dead? All at once, I remembered Mrs. Thornley telling me and Chief about the slender, thirtyish Nuche man who used to drop by the trailer park and chat with Billy.

Was *he* my uninvited guest? And, if so, then why was he prowling around *inside* the trailer?

Terrific! Another Clover Creek mystery.

The Bureau of Indian Affairs land was just southwest of Penrose, about two miles beyond the intersection of Utah Routes 102 and 543. It was treaty land, awarded to the Nuche by the Department of the Interior as a result of the now-forgotten Black Hawk War of 1868.

So what do you get when you lose a war? How

about a nice flat desert plain, rimmed by the ochre ridgeline of the Promontory Mountains? Thigh-high silvery green sagebrush and browning greasswood and slim Spanish bayonet. Yellow-brown junegrass and sparse clusters of wildrye. The only water came from Salt Creek, once an embayment of the big saline lake, now a zigzagging, caliche-encrusted trickle crawling across the desert floor.

Not the place where Nuche parents would want to raise their family.

Lifeless? Far from it. No sooner had I emerged from the Accord than I spotted the madcap scattering of field mice tracks in the shade beneath the sagebrush. Poking about a bit more, I found the paw prints of a kit fox. No sign of the animals, though. They were all safely tucked away in their underground burrows, waiting for the relentless Utah sun to dip behind the Promontories.

They say only rabid dogs and Englishmen are loony enough to go strolling in the midday sun. To this distinguished company we add one determined Anishinabe princess, but I was well prepared for it. Floppy cotton boonie hat. Arms and legs lathered in sunblock. Large Polaroid sunglasses. Fully-loaded backpack in the Accord's trunk. And, leaning against the back seat, a pair of Army surplus two-gallon canteens. That gave me four gallons of cool, clear water, enough to keep me going on the odd chance I had to walk back to Penrose.

Behind the rusting wire fence stood the caretaker's shack, a beige sandstone building with a slightly pitched cedar roof. No sign of any vehicle. That was fine with me. I knew the caretaker might be suspicious if I turned up unannounced on his doorstep. It'd be a whole lot better if he came to me.

So put out the bait, Angie. Bend over and unlatch the hood. Lift it and brace it with the steel bar. Off comes the air filter. See the gassy-smelling contraption? That's the carburetor. I see that the butterfly valve up top is moving just fine. Well, I can fix that. Pinch off a thumbnail-sized sprig of greasewood. Wedge it in good and tight, and make it look as if the sprig got sucked into the vent.

Getting behind the driver's wheel, I pumped the gas pedal, turned the ignition key, and smiled as I listened to the *ruhruhruhruhruh* of the engine. The internal combustion engine cannot combust without a steady flow of air into the carburetor. And a jammed butterfly valve impedes the flow of air.

A noticeable gasoline stink tickled my nostrils.

Leaving the hood up, I broke off two dessicated Spanish bayonet stalks and lashed them to the driver's door. They stood out like a pair of flagpoles. Then I draped my poncho over them, creating a very effective awning. I crouched in the shade, resting my fanny on my ankles, careful not to overheat myself by making body contact with the torrid ground.

About an hour later, I was watching a pair of golden eagles riding the thermals above the Promontories when I suddenly heard the mutter of a pickup's engine. Turning to the right, I saw a dark green Ford Ranger up to its bumper in sage, partially obscured by the heat haze. The truck slowed to a crawl, then turned to the right and headed for the cattle gate about a hundred yards up the road.

Within minutes, the truck was rolling to a stop beside my Accord. The driver jumped down from the cab. Tall, lanky, narrow-shouldered Nuche man in a sand-colored workshirt and khaki chinos. A Mount Timpanogos ballcap shaded his high cheekbones, slim nose and vulpine chin. "Hi! What's the matter? Broke down?"

"You bet!" Crawling out from under my makeshift awning, I stood erect and manufactured a relieved smile. "A jackrabbit ran in front of me. I swerved to avoid him. Skidded off onto the shoulder." Many frantic hand motions from Angie the Helpless. "Now I can't get the damned thing *started!* I keep turning the key but *nothing!*"

Shaking his head wryly, the caretaker said, "You sure picked a dandy place to break down."

"I know. This is the BIA tract, isn't it?"

"Sure is." Leaning under the hood, he twisted the battery clamps. "From here on down to Box Elder Lake."

"Are you the caretaker?"

He made a humming noise of assent. "Six years now. Name's Ned Pahaka. What's yours?"

I didn't answer immediately. I was too busy blinking, unable to believe my luck. Of all the people to run into out here! Ned Pahaka, Billy's partner in that Section 206 request.

Catching my startled reaction, Ned frowned in mild puzzlement. "Do we know each other?"

I shook my head. "I'm Sara Soyazhe. I'm a geologist. I recognized your name. You and some other guy—you wanted to transfer this BIA land, didn't you?"

"That's right. How'd you hear about that?"

176

"I talked to Jayne Clark at the BLM office in Clover Creek." Truthful Angie. "She told me you sent in a letter requesting the transfer. You and . . . Mr. Shavano, wasn't it?"

"Bill Shavano." Ned's dark eyes filled with genuine sadness. "He passed away about three weeks ago. Logging accident up north. I didn't even hear about it till last night."

Giddy sense of excitement. "Last night?"

"Yeah. I drove up to Clover Creek to see Bill. See, I just got back from Alaska. Took my boys flyfishing up on the Susitna. Bill told me he was gonna keep in touch, but when I didn't hear anything, I figured to drive up north and see what was going on."

"And you arrived last night?"

"Right. Bill's trailer was dark when I got there. At first I figured he was down in Salt Lake with his girl. Then the neighbor's dog started barking, and the lady came out and told me Bill was dead." Grief made his voice brittle. "Hell of a way to get the news, eh?"

"I'm sorry," I said. And I meant it.

"Bill got buried over in Heber where he grew up. Neighbor lady said Mrs. Thornley's renting to some college girl now. It's hard to believe. One week he's there, and the next he's gone. I'm sure gonna miss him."

Well, after that guileless explanation, I knew Ned Pahaka couldn't possibly have been the intruder. Nobody responsible for a break-in would stand around confessing his presence at the scene to a total stranger. So it must have been somebody else.

For a moment there, I thought about telling Ned that I was the college girl. But then I decided against

177

it. That would be stretching the long arm of coincidence too far. I didn't want to put Ned Pahaka on his guard. I liked him just the way he was—open, upfront and talkative.

"Were you close friends?" I asked.

"Close enough. Fishing buddies." Fond memories kindled a smile. "Meaning we lied to each other every chance we got. Bill sure knew streams, though. He put me into a couple of really good spots on the Weber." Reminiscence yielded to curiosity. "Tell me, Sara, why are you so interested in this tract?"

Bright Angie smile. "I'm opening my own consulting business in Clover Creek. I'm hoping to steer my clients toward available tracts with unassigned mineral rights."

Laughing, Ned made an expansive gesture that covered most of the sagebrush and greasewood. *"Minerals!?* You're looking in the wrong place, Sara. Closest thing to a mineral deposit around here is the caliche on Salt Creek."

"Well, who does own the mineral rights, Ned?"

"The Northern Ute Tribal Council. They own all the rights to this tract. Mineral, riparian, timber—you name it." He gestured at the waist-high sagebrush. "Not that there's a whole lot in the way of timber around here."

An opening. "Not like Lodestone Canyon, eh?"

"You can say that again."

Well, well, so Billy had discussed the canyon with Ned. How far did that discussion go? Might as well ask.

"Why did you boys propose this land for a Section 206?"

Apologetic smile. "You're talking to the wrong man, Sara."

"You mean it was all Bill's idea?"

"You bet." He leaned against my car fender. "Bill gave me a call back in June. It was all pretty hush-hush. He wanted to know if this tract was still on the Section 206 reserve list."

"How did Bill know about that?"

"Hell, I told him. We were fishing for bluegill one time in Mantua, and I got to telling him about this tract. I told him it was the last place on our mother, the Earth, that anybody'd ever want to swap for."

"How did it get on the list, Ned?"

"The tribal council put it on back in 1976. They were hoping to trade up—get some better land. Weren't any takers, though."

"So what was Bill's idea?"

"He said we ought to write up a letter and mail it to the BLM. Ask them to move on the original tribal council request."

"Which was to—"

"Swap this here land for a tract with equivalent acreage."

"Did he say which tract he wanted to swap for?" I asked.

"Afraid not, Sara. Bill was downright secretive about that. He said there were gonna be a lot of happy faces when it was all over, though."

Mild fussbudget face. "Did he say anything else to you?"

Running his thumb along his jaw, Ned gave me a long, thoughtful look then he said, "Bill was very anxious about the rights. Particularly the timber

179

rights. He wanted to make sure the tribal council got them.''

Timber rights! A glorious tingle raced down my spine. All at once, I understood what Billy had been up to.

"Quick question, Ned. Suppose a logger wants to cut on land where the tribal council holds the timber rights . . . can he do it?''

"Sure, Sara. But for him to get the go-ahead, the council's vote has to be *unanimous*. Our logger would probably find it easier dealing with the Forest Service.''

I grinned, remembering my cousin's sudden interest in getting elected to the Northern Ute Tribal Council.

Billy, you sneaky boy. I never knew you had it in you.

Casually switching the topic to mineral rights, I quizzed Ned about the BIA policy on site surveys, then offered him a drink from my canteen. After that, he went to work on my car engine. As for me, I relaxed in the shade of my Spanish bayonet awning and reflected on my cousin's scheme.

By June, Bill must have realized that there was no way Alfred J. Longhurst was going to play it straight. My cousin's formal protest had been sidetracked, and Alfie was busily circumventing the entire review process. It was only a matter of weeks before Longhurst issued the permit to cut.

So Billy had come up with an alternative plan. Fishing buddy Ned Pahaka had told him about the long-stalled Section 206 request on this desert land. Billy knew that the desert tract was a rough match for the acreage in Lodestone Canyon. Best of all, had the transfer gone through, Lodestone's timber rights would have reverted to the Northern Ute Tribal Council. As the newly-elected council member, my cousin would have been able to veto any permit to cut in the canyon.

Sneaky, sneaky, William . . . using bureaucratic sleight-of-hand to transfer Lodestone out of Alfie's clutches and into the relative safety of the Bureau of Indian Affairs. You really did play this thing close to the vest, didn't you? You hid the planned transfer from everyone—even your guileless co-conspirator, Ned Pahaka.

But someone had seen through your scheme. Someone had understood what a threat it was to Cue and the boys. Someone with a detailed knowledge of the Land Policy and Management Act. But who? Had Alfie Longhurst realized how you were end-running him? Had Karl Eames been poking around in your Forest Service career, trying to get something on you?

Who tumbled to your scheme, Bill?

If I could find the answer to that, I just might have the name of Billy's killer.

By late afternoon, I was back in Clover Creek. I had thanked Ned for his roadside repairs and solemnly promised to have the offending carburetor looked at. There was just under an hour left in the business day. So I spent it at City Hall—at the Tax Assessor's office, to be precise.

· There I stood, at the formica-topped counter, thumbing through a hefty records book while the tax assessor herself rummaged in a filing drawer. From the rear, the assessor bore a spooky resemblance to an old acquaintance of mine, Carlotta Calder, the matron at the Disciplinary Unit in Billsburg, South Dakota. Same potato-shaped figure and fleshy Dutch chocolate forearms and meaty calves marbled with varicose veins. Many, many bad memories set my fingers to trembling.

When a woman commits a crime in South Dakota, she gets sent to the correctional facility at Springfield, commonly known as the Big Dollhouse. Occasionally, the officers there get an inmate—like moi—who won't put up with all their shit. An inmate who thinks she's coming out ahead by bouncing clever one-liners off the guards. And . . . well, those Springfield screws don't have to deal with it. Not when they've got Miss Carlotta majoring in attitude adjustment out there on the prairie.

There were plenty of nicknames for the Disciplinary Unit—*Heartbreak Hotel, Little Outhouse on the Prairie*, and, my personal favorite, *Miss Carlotta's School for Girls*. And her *graduates* all come back to Springfield the same way, too. Tearful, shrill, cowed, fifteen pounds underweight . . . and very, very anxious to please the guards.

I buried my consciousness in the financial records, seeking escape from a flood of bitter memories.

Found out something of interest. Cue's real name was Henry Taylor Broward. I wondered how he got the nickname *Cue*. Hanging around pool parlors, no doubt.

Even more interesting was the fact that Cue Broward was the majority shareholder in High Timber Associates, Inc. He held just over seventy percent of the common, which had been issued back in February. Karl Francis Eames was the second-largest shareholder with twenty percent.

So it looked as if Cue would benefit most from the Lodestone Canyon cut. He'd be taking seventy cents on every dollar the aspen brought in.

That made my immediate task much easier.

You see, on the way back to town, I had made up my mind to continue Billy's crusade. I was going to transfer Lodestone Canyon into the BIA, and I was going to pressure that greedy little weasel, Alfie Longhurst, into doing it for me.

Closing the records book, I thought of Toni Gee, my mentor at Springfield, and let out a hushed giggle. You'd be so proud of me, Toni. Your favorite student is about to invent a whole new scam—*the Section 206 game!*

To be perfectly truthful, it was really a variation on an old con game known as "The Goat Pasture." But nobody had ever done it with Uncle Sam's land before.

Like any successful con, it always works best with an audience of one. Your credibility declines in direct proportion to the number of people who've heard your clever tale. A competent grifter can completely control one mark. If she goes for two, she loses her focus—and control of the game.

Cue Broward was my focus. With him in my back pocket, I'd be able to force Longhurst to make the transfer. But first I had to con old Cue into wanting another piece of land. Daunting task, that!

As I carried the huge book back to the gray steel shelves, I glanced at the office bulletin board. And a list of names caught my gaze. A single listing jumped out at me. *Eames Lumber Company.*

How about that? Eames Lumber is one of several firms that have applied for a deferral of tax payments during this tough recession year.

I remembered Karl's anxiety at the barbecue. No doubt about it—Karl Eames desperately needed that Lodestone Canyon cut to stay in business. And if he had found out what Billy was up to . . .

Brushing the speculations aside, I returned the book to its proper shelf and thanked the assessor very kindly. Believe me, the lady was far more personable than Miss Carlotta. Then I danced down the granite front steps of City Hall three minutes before closing time.

"Over here, gal."

The voice was like thunder way back in the Wasatch—distant, deep and menacing. I glanced instantly in that direction. And there he was—Deputy Ty Braddock, back in his mirrored sunglasses mode, lounging against the passenger side of his green-and-white Pontiac Grand Am cruiser.

I flashed a sweet Angie smile. "Good afternoon, deputy."

Wham! Ty's huge fist nearly dented the car door. "Git that Injun ass over here!"

Disobedience was a luxury I couldn't afford. So chin up, fold the hands daintily, approach the brooding lawman.

Ty's hard mouth was a perfect upside-down U. *"Good afternoon, deputy."* His falsetto mimicry nearly made me laugh. "Wherever did you get those lovely manners, Miss Sara?"

Coy smile. "Miss Carlotta's School for Girls."

"Your daddy got money or somethin'? How come he's sendin' his daughter to some fancy-ass finishin' school?"

"It wasn't that fancy, Mr. Braddock."

"Fancy enough to give you airs, Miss Sara."

I didn't like his mocking tone one single bit. "Something I can do for you, deputy?"

Savoring every motion, Ty Braddock reached behind him and unhitched his nightstick. It was a bruiser, varnished oak, blunt and ugly, a miniaturized Louisville Slugger. Flicking his wrist suddenly, he brought its smooth wooden length against my face.

"Owww!" Blinking, I winced at the miniscule sting.

Ty's nightstick caressed my cheek. "I don't think I like them airs, Miss Sara." He leaned so close I could smell the hamburger onions on his breath. "No, I don't! Fact is, if there's one thing that truly pisses me off in this here world, it's some blankethead squaw thinkin' she's a lady." Grinning, he lowered the baton. "Now, listen up, gal. I don't give a rat's raggedy ass what kind of fancy finishin' school you went to. To me you're just another squaw. You got that? A sassy little grasshopper-eatin' *squaw* straight out of the old wickiup! And no way am I ever gonna let some smart-mouthed little squaw put on airs in front of Miss Gail!"

Glancing to the left, I saw my own expression—features rigid, eyes highly frightened—in the deputy's opaque sunglasses.

"You think I didn't hear you sass Miss Gail?" His lips turned upward in a feral smile. I heard every damned word, gal. Lucky for you ol' Cue came along when he did. You think you learned manners at that finishin' school? You'd have learned 'em a damned sight quicker in that parkin' lot!''

Ty's mammoth hand closed around my left bicep. Then his free hand levered open the cruiser's passenger door.

"If I had the time, I'd make you awful damned sorry for sassin' Miss Gail. But *he* wants to see you, so we're gonna have to settle for second best.''

"He?''

Ty's only response was a deep-throated chuckle. He slam-dunked me into the passenger sat, walloped the door shut, then glowered at me through the open window.

"Now, here's how you're gonna handle it, squaw. You're going to write Miss Gail a letter apologizin' for your . . . for your . . . damn, what's that big word Miss Gail used?''

"Insolence?'' I added helpfully.

"That's the one.'' Acerbic grunt. "You can word it any way you want. Just make sure there's plenty of *I'm sorry's* in it. Do it up nice and fancy like at finishin' school. She's gonna feel a whole lot better when she gets that letter from you. And when Miss Gail is happy, I'm happy. And when I'm happy, a little squaw's life can be so much more pleasant. You understand my meanin', Miss Sara?''

Watching him amble around the front of the cruiser, I asked, "What if I'm not in a writing mood?''

"Then you'd better get in the mood right fast, my gal!'' He pulled open the driver's door. "Because if Miss Gail don't get that letter, you 'n' me are gonna take a ride up to the Circle B. Cue's got an old woodshed on the premises. We'll see if that razor strop's still hangin' from the peg. And when we're all finished, and you're through bawlin', we'll go on up to the house, and you can apologize to Miss Gail in person.''

As he eased his bulk into the padded seat, the cruiser leaned noticeably to the left.

"Does Linda Beckworth have to write one, too?" I inquired.

"Never you mind what Miss Linda's about!" He groped along the cluttered dashboard for his carkeys. "You've got your own little chore to do."

"Would you mind telling me where we're going?"

Twisting the ignition key, he snorted. "Christ! If you ain't the nosiest little squaw I ever met!"

"In some states, deputy, this could be construed as kidnapping.''

"Not in Clover Creek." Stepping down hard on the gas pedal, Ty flashed me a sidelong grin. *"Construed?* Shit, you got to be a teacher, Miss Sara, the way you talk.''

"I take it, then, I'm not under arrest."

"Did I read you from *Miranda?* Sit back, gal, and button it. Mr. Sager wants to see you.''

So I fastened my seat harness and maintained a dignified ladylike silence, wondering all the while what Gail's daddy wanted with me. Surely Mrs. Broward hadn't run tattling to her father.

Sitting back, I let my gaze sweep the interior. I don't mind admitting I was more than a little nervous. After all, Ty had lied about his actions at Dynamite

Pass the day of Billy's murder. The bit about Mr. Sager could be another lie.

My anxiety quadrupled when I caught a glimpse of Ty's multiple weapons. For a second I thought I was in the Terminator's car. Hardware galore! One Benelli twelve-gauge autoloading shotgun strapped to the driver's door. Sawed-off Winchester Model 97 twelve-gauge tucked into a custom-made leather scabbard under the dash. And a nine-millimeter Firestar Model 43 automatic in a hideaway holster on the steering column.

Knowing Ty's predilection for throwing his weight around, I could readily understand why he'd turned his cruiser into a rolling arsenal.

As I looked around, I had the strangest feeling that I was a reluctant guest in Ty Braddock's home. That he had no other life apart from this cruiser. The interior had the flavor of an incorrigible old bachelor's living room. Old, stained cardboard coffee cups in the plastic drink caddy. Rolled-up gun magazines and dogeared comic books. Oh, Lord, don't tell me he's a *Punisher* fan! Piebald rabbit's foot dangling from the rearview mirror. Plastic-windowed bill envelopes lashed to the sun visor with sturdy rubber bands.

Then my gaze drifted down to the floormat and I let out a whispery gasp.

A small object sat midway between the firewall and my trail boots. A small, white object that sent a sudden shiver of horrified recognition through me.

A freshly-eaten applecore.

Chapter Ten

My gaze zeroed in on the applecore. Panic time!

Oh, shit! I thought, Ty's the one who followed me up to Dynamite Pass yesterday. Did he see me reading trail sign?

Hey, where is this guy *really* taking me?

Panicky thoughts rampaged through my mind. I fought down the adrenaline surge, willing myself to stay calm.

Dammit, Angie, use your head! The applecore belongs to the mystery man with the soft-soled shoes, remember? There's no way in hell Ty Braddock could have made those footprints. Our deputy friend tips the scales at close to three hundred. Even in stealth boots, Ty's footprints would have been a whole lot deeper.

Okay, so it was somebody else. Jack Sunawavi, maybe? That made sense. For people on opposite sides of the law, Jack and Ty were awfully good buddies.

Another chilling thought. Were we on our way to meet Jack?

Time for the direct approach. I unbuckled my safety

harness and plucked the applecore from the rubber mat. Stern glance of womanly disapproval. "You need a housekeeper, Mr. Braddock."

"I thought I told you to button it," he muttered, steering the cruiser past the storefronts of North Center Street.

"There is such a thing as spring cleaning, Ty."

Holding the core aloft, I spied a familiar male bite pattern, the very same configuration as the bite on the squirrel's applecore. So Ty had been entertaining, eh?

The deputy flashed me a ferocious look. "I know a little squaw who, if she don't keep that big yap shut, is gonna clean out this here police car with a toothbrush!"

Lobbing the core into the dashboard's dangling trash bag, I replied, "Just making conversation, deputy."

"You want some conversation?" The mirrored shades swiveled toward me once more. "Okay. Next time you run into that boyfriend of yours, tell him I want to see him. Got that?"

"Boyfriend? Which one?"

"I sure as hell ain't talkin' about Denny Simms."

I did a perfect imitation of Billy. "You'll have to be a little bit more specific there, deputy."

"Jack Sunawavi." Ty slowed the car as we approached an intersection. "Next time you see him, tell him this. 'Friday night, Jack. The usual place.' Tell him it's real important."

"Newsflash, Ty. Sunawavi isn't my boyfriend."

"Don't give me that horseshit. I seen you with him at the Patch." Clearly troubled, Ty faced forward again. "Simms said Jack was in town yesterday. I

190

dropped by his momma's in Cottonwood this mornin'. No sign of him there. Son of a bitch! I ain't got time to chase his Injun ass all over this here county."

I listened with interest. So old Jack knew Dennis Simms, as well. My nemesis was moving in rarefied circles, indeed. How many patrons of the Briar Patch could claim instant access to Cue Broward's lawyer?

"You make sure Jack gets that message, gal."

"It might help if I had a few more specifics."

"Miss Sara, you keep stickin' your cute little nose into Jack's private business, it's gonna get smacked!"

I let the subject drop.

Well, another theory for the trashcan. That wasn't Jack Sunawavi munching on an apple an hour ago. Deputy Braddock hadn't seen his Nuche buddy in days.

The radio's sudden static crackle dispelled my reverie. A woman's voice spattered out of the speaker. "One-adam-four, this is Dispatch. You there, Ty?"

He grabbed the microphone. "I copy, Shirley. Over."

"Ty, we got us a big rig overturned on 302 north of Scipio. Multiple car crash. We've got casualties. Sending all units. Over."

A fussbudget face on Ty Braddock was something to behold. "Dammit, Shirl, I'm on a job!"

I detected a teasing note in the dispatcher's voice. "Sheriff Mortensen says for you to get your fat ass right down there, Ty."

The big deputy scowled. "Tell that son of a bitch to take it up with Mr. Sager." And he tossed the mike at the radio.

When Shirley came on again, she sounded so respectful I thought she was addressing the Pope. "We copy, one-adam-four. Call in when you're finished. Dispatch out."

Needless to say, I was mightily impressed with the impact of the name *Mr. Sager*. And I felt a little bit better about being here with Ty Braddock. We must really be on our way to see the great man, I figured. Somehow I just couldn't see Ty putting his job at risk by taking the hallowed name in vain.

Mischievous smile. "Tell me, Mr. Deputy sir, do you get paid for these errands you run? Or is this a complimentary service for the county's First Family?"

At first, he looked as if he was going to explode. But then, despite his best intentions, a smile tugged at the cherubic mouth.

Rhino grunt. "Wouldn't you like to know!"

"Actually, I would. No, really, Ty, I'm curious. How did you get hooked up with the Sagers?"

His smile broadened at the onset of delightful memories. " 'Cause I recognized opportunity when she sashayed down the street."

I took a guess. "Opportunity being Miss Gail?"

He gave me a quick startled look. "Damn! You're a sharp one. How'd you hear about that?"

"Oh, just some idle talk at the barbecue."

"Ahhhhh, they don't know jack shit." Relaxing in the driver's seat, Ty put one thick-knuckled hand on the steering wheel. "Mr. Sager never sent me after that son of a bitch. I did it my own self. See, Miss Gail had it kinda rough when her momma passed on. She was the last of the litter and the only girl. She 'n' her daddy used to scrap somethin' fierce when she hit her teens. I guess Miss Gail went a little crazy when she got to Maughan High. Runnin' with bikers and trash. I used to see her out in front of the high school, stickin' out her chest whenever she wanted some biker to give her a ride. Then she went and stuck it out at the wrong biker—Nick Mallanney. Pure Grade A no-good trash.'' A surge of pride made him seem taller. "So one night I'm on patrol, and I see Miss Gail comin' down the street, cryin' and holdin' her face. Seems she 'n' Nick had a scrap, and that son of a bitch whomped on her some. Poor gal didn't want her daddy to see her like that. So I drove her out to my momma's place, and we put her up in the guest room. Then I went lookin' for Mallanney. Put on my sap gloves. You ever seen them things, Miss Sara? Shiny black leather gloves with lead plates reinforcin' the knuckles.'' Deep, rich, good-humored chuckle. "I walked up to that big ol' Harley of his, planted my boot on the saddle, and pushed it right into the arroyo. Told him it was too much bike for a faggot like him. So he come at me, and we played some Biker Bop.''

"Biker Bop?''

"Sure, Miss Sara. That's when you bop a biker in the face with a five-pound sap glove.'' He pantomimed a right jab at the windshield. "Biker goes down like a sack of old horseshoes. Then you pick him up and bop him again. And again. And again!'' Shaking his head fondly, he relished the memory of his rookie days. "Well, to make a long story short, 'bout a week later I got this envelope in the mail with six nice, crisp hundred-dollar bills in it. Plus an invitation to dinner with Mr. Sager. He told me I could pick up a few extra bucks lookin' after Miss Gail. Sort of an unofficial chaperone, you know? So I did that for a spell till Miss Gail went off to that fancy finishin' school in Brussels. We been friends a long time, me 'n' Miss Gail.''

"And did our high-spirited heiress keep you busy?"

"Not half as busy as Cue's little gal. Now *she* was a handful!" Rueful bass chuckle. "Miss Linda commenced to droppin' her drawers at fourteen. Couldn't ever get enough of it. She drove ol' Cue plumb loco. Once a month, sure as shit, I'd get a call on a runaway, and it'd be Miss Linda. I don't know how many times I saw ol' Cue grab that gal by the collar and haul her out to the woodshed. Didn't do a bit o' good, though. Miss Linda just kept shovin' it at every boy who took her fancy.'' He chuckled again. "She ain't hurtin' these days, though. Not for men and not for money. Since she divorced Jimmy Beckworth, ol' Cue's set her up with that record shop. So now she can play at bein' a businesswoman. Make no mistake 'bout it, though, she still gets that allowance every month." Ty's boot touched the brake lightly. "Well! Here we are, Miss Sara."

Peering out the windshield, I spied a neighborhood of venerable homes shaded by box elder and mountain juniper. Ty parked the cruiser in front of a grand old Queen Anne double-decker. A black wrought-iron picket fence encircled the lush front yard. A pathway of honeycomb-shaped cement blocks led up to the round, protruding, colonnaded front porch. The house itself was strangely angular, Gothic, subtly suggestive of century-old Mormon tabernacles. Distinctive slate-shingled gables and beveled glass windows and starburst porch corners and three tall, slim, Dickensian chimneys.

I undid the safety harness, then opened the passenger door. Ty's huge hand came to rest on my shoulder.

"It was a pleasure talkin' to you, Miss Sara. And I just know you're not gonna repeat a word of our conversation to anybody. Not even to Jack." A hard edge spoiled his jocular tone. "You don't want to spend the rest of August sleepin' on your front side, now do you?"

I wriggled out from under his distasteful grip. Refused to give him the satisfaction of a direct reply. "Thanks for the ride, deputy."

"Anytime, gal."

Once inside, Ty made me wait in the hallway while he called on the great man. I spent a few minutes admiring the woodwork. Believe me, people, you are never going to see carpentry like that again. The trimming was golden oak, hand-carved and lovingly polished with flaxseed soap. A stylized S dominated the arch over the newel post. That circular stairway would have been right at home in old Vienna.

A house fit for a reigning family, as indeed the Sagers were. Chandeliers with beehive frosted-glass shades. Panelled cedarwood doors. A plush antique carpet in Persian cloth-of-gold.

A few minutes later, Ty brought me into the Gun Room, all walnut and damask drapery and trophy animal heads roaring at nonexistent enemies. Out of the far shadows stepped my host, Truman Kimball Sager.

He was a slender, stoop-shouldered man in his

middle sixties, wearing a houndstooth jacket with leather elbow sleeves and dark brown slacks. Despite the heat, a firmly-knotted club tie dangled beneath his prominent Adam's apple. His face was narrow and angular, with thick eyebrows, a droopy white Clemenceau moustache, and a fringe of lank white hair reaching around the back of his head. He looked me over carefully, puckered dry lips, and drawled, "Thank you, Ty. That will be all."

Mr. Sager had a very soft and considerate voice. However, Ty reacted as if he'd been jabbed in the ass with a branding iron. He vacated the room at once, leaving the languid Mr. Sager to sip cranapple juice from a cocktail glass and to study me with steely, intelligent, bluish-gray eyes.

Gesturing at an empty armchair, Truman said, *"Ambe, indaanis. Bigoshkwaawaadabi."*

Wide-eyed blink of astonishment. *Guess what, Chief? You and I aren't the only people in Clover Creek fluent in Anishinabemowin.*

I declined the invitation. "No thanks, Mr. Sager. I'll stand."

The local monarch smiled as if he'd scored an important point. "You're Ojibway, aren't you?"

"That's one name for our people. Me, I prefer our true name . . . Anishinabe."

"I stand corrected, young Sara." He smiled at me over the rim of his glass. "Soyazhe is a Ute name, though. Are you married?"

I shook my head. "My mother was Anishinabe." No lie there! "Your pronunciation isn't bad, Mr. Sager. Where did you learn?"

"Willmar, Minnesota. I was an LDS missionary

196

there for two years. I made it a point to learn all the Lamanite languages. Although I must confess I'm more comfortable with Sioux.'' Slight apologetic smile. ''Excuse me . . . *Lakotiya!*'' His slate-blue eyes brightened with sudden enthusiasm. ''I have quite a collection of Lamanite artifacts. Would you like to see them?''

''Sure, Mr. Sager.''

''This way, please.''

Well, Gail's daddy was no liar. He'd turned the South Room into a veritable museum of Native American artifacts. Row after row of oak-trimmed display cases. Nuche dance drums. Twined Paiute basketry. Shoshoni buffalo lances. Pointing out the showpiece item in each case, he gave me a lecture worthy of an anthropology prof. I spotted a few choice items in his collection. Had they been known to the Heyes Museum in New York, the Sager telephone would have been ringing off the hook.

Like all Latter-Day Saints, Truman believed that Native Americans are descended from Laman, a noteworthy sinner in The Book of Mormon. I didn't bother to debate the issue. Way I see it, people's religious beliefs are their own business. And I've been called a lot worse things than a *Lamanite*—remind me to tell you about the spearfishing protests at Lac du Flambeau sometime.

The tour ended in the spacious parlor. Mr. Sager plucked a fragile porcelain figurine from the ornate mantelpiece. ''See this?'' He presented it with a showman's flourish. It was a lovely Dresden shepherdess, decked out in robin's-egg blue. ''My family brought it with them from Heidenau in Germany.

197

They nearly lost it when they fled Nauvoo. *Gross-mutter* sent my great-great-grandfather, Ernst Sager, after it. The Gentiles had already set their house on fire, but Ernst went in for it, anyway. He was a brave man." Flashing a proud smile, he set it back on the mantelpiece. "This little lady came across the plains in a pushcart. Just like my family."

"Did Ernst build this house?" I asked.

"Yes, but not until he was an old man."

"He was a carpenter, wasn't he?"

"As a matter of fact, yes. He worked on the Kirtland temple when he first came to America, then he worked for Truman O. Angell on the temple at Nauvoo." The old man beamed at me. "How did you know that?"

"It shows in the workmanship." I rested my fanny against the armrest of a plush sofa. "I'm thankful for the tour, Mr. Sager. But somehow I don't think that's the reason you asked me here."

"And it's not, young Sara." Frowning, he put down his empty glass. "I have been reliably informed that you have an interest in Lodestone Canyon."

"In the mineral rights, yes."

"*Just* the mineral rights?" Slate eyes gave me a shrewd look.

"What else would a geologist be interested in?"

"Money!" Crossing slender arms, he confronted me suddenly. "As you undoubtedly know, there's a potentially valuable stand of timber in the canyon. Are you interested in that? I would greatly appreciate an honest answer."

"Mr. Sager, I understand aspen isn't that valuable."

"And that's where you're wrong. Times change, Sara. Are you at all familiar with the construction industry?"

I waggled my palm. "Little bit."

"A firm in which I am a substantial investor has developed a new technology for manufacturing fiberboard. That's the material used in drywalls and floors. It's tough, lightweight, and wears like cast iron." He gave me a lofty look. "Aspen is a key ingredient in the manufacturing process."

"And Sager Lumber supplies the aspen."

"Not all of it. I have a purchase agreement with High Timber Associates for seventy percent of the boardfeet coming out of Lodestone Canyon."

"Which you'll resell to the construction industry for how much?"

"That's hardly a concern of yours, young Sara."

"Who's handling the remaining boardfeet?"

Gail's daddy paused, wondering if he should share that information. Then he answered, "Eames Lumber."

"So the *weed tree* is bringing in big money at last, eh?"

He nodded. "The profit margin on aspen has expanded considerably."

"That'll have Karl Eames kicking up his heels."

"I beg your pardon?"

"I hear Karl's having money troubles."

Mild sympathy flickered in the old man's eyes. "I'm afraid Karl doesn't quite understand that diversification of one's investments is a necessity in these latter days before the coming of our Lord Jesus Christ."

"Well, I guess that answers just about everything, Mr. Sager," I said, crossing my legs at the ankle. "Except for one last question. Why did you have me brought here?"

"I wished to discuss the Lodestone Canyon situation—in private. I'm prepared to buy out your interest, Sara." His eyes held a steely gleam. "Nothing must stand in the way of that cut."

"What cut? Longhurst says he's just updating the management plan."

The Clemenceau moustache bristled fiercely. "Let's not play games with each other, Sara. You and I both know the Forest Service will be issuing that permit. My informant is always quite accurate."

"And who might that be, Mr. Sager?"

Cold smile. "The same person who informed me of your presence at the Broward barbecue."

"Uh-huh. Did your daughter play tattletale, Mr. Sager?"

Bluish-gray eyes reflected unfeigned surprise. "You spoke to Gail at the barbecue?"

"You bet. She introduced me to your pet deputy."

So Gail hadn't told the old man, eh? That meant it had to be either Ty Braddock, Dennis Simms, or Cue himself.

Truman's soft voice developed a keener edge. "I'm not certain I enjoy your sense of humor, young woman."

"Then let's keep it serious, Mr. Sager." Solemn-eyed expression. "What if I were to swear to you on the Bible that I have absolutely no interest in taking an option on Lodestone's timber?"

Extending his right hand, Gail's daddy smiled.

"Then I would say, 'Welcome to Clover Creek, Sara, and I look forward to seeing you in church.' " Sinewy fingers brushed mine. "Please—let me show you out."

"You seem awfully certain that this cut will go through."

His chin rose stubbornly. "It will. Rest assured of that."

"There seems to be a lot of opposition," I added, keeping pace with him. "Those environmentalists from Salt Lake City—"

"The Tribe of DAN!" His narrow cheeks turned an angry crimson. "Drunkards, pagans and fornicators! Those blasphemers have no place in Zion."

"They say it's a one-of-a-kind ecosystem—"

"Now, you listen to me, young woman." He just wouldn't let me finish a sentence. "The Bible says we are to worship the Creator, not the creation. God *gave* us that timber. We're supposed to use it, not stand around staring in mute adoration." Slate blue eyes glistened in absolute fury. "Don't give me that look, young woman. Your Lamanite ancestors were no different. They made use of the land as well." His whispery shout made me flinch. "Those Salt Lake pagans! Who do they think they are? Are we supposed to change our way of life to suit *them?* Willow Valley is ours! We Saints dammed the canyons, built the roads, tamed the mountains. Who has a better right to the land than we?"

I was tempted to say, *"The Nuche!"* But I stifled my personal feelings in favor of extracting more information.

"They're not the only ones opposed, Mr. Sager. I

understand that Bill Shavano, the timber sales officer, was also against a cut.''

Gail's daddy stiffened at the mention of Billy's name. It took him a second or two to respond. ''He was and that is most regrettable. I spoke to William once or twice. He impressed me as an extremely level-headed young man. I'm disappointed he threw in with that—that *trash!*''

I was most impressed with Mr. Sager's reaction when he spoke the name *William*. His fists clenched so hard that the knuckles stood out. A lot of animosity there!

Realizing that he had an audience, Mr. Sager calmed himself at once. We resumed our march to the front foyer. Touching the knot of his club tie, he cleared his throat and said, ''I will not sin against the Lord by speaking ill of a man so recently dead. This way, Sara.''

''Did Gail ever speak to Bill Shavano?'' I asked.

Truman gave me a quick stern sidelong glance, but he chose not to respond. Instead, he offered a paternal smile. ''I do hope you'll come and visit again. I'd like us to be friends. And I do hope you'll confide in me should Mr. Broward attempt to persuade you to enter into any sort of business arrangement.''

I caught the teeth-gritting tension behind the name *Broward*, then remembered what Kate Thornley had told me about Gail's gaudy Las Vegas wedding.

Schoolgirl blink. ''Are you telling me ol' Cue's not to be trusted?''

''Spencer Phillips did and he lived to regret it.''

''Who's Spencer Phillips?'' I asked.

"A very dear old friend of mine. He used to own the Circle B."

Reaching the front door, I turned to face the Mormon patriarch. "You don't like him very much, do you?"

Drawing his shoulders back stiffly, he replied, "The man is Gail's lawful husband."

"I didn't see you at the barbecue, Mr. Sager."

"I'm a very private person, Sara." For an instant, the stern gaze softened. "I live only for the day when I shall rejoin my beloved wife in eternity."

"You won't come to his barbecues, yet you're partners with him in that construction company. Why is that, Mr. Sager?"

"True enough. Broward is a sinful man, and one day he will burn in that lake of unquenchable fire." An expression of furtive satisfaction flitted across Truman's face. "In the here and now, however, Broward has his uses. He builds expensive homes, and he earns me a substantial amount of money. Zion must grow, Sara. Though a sinner and a Gentile, Broward has his role to play."

"Why did your daughter marry him?"

As he pulled open the panelled door, the old man's slate-colored eyes reflected infinite sadness. "My dear, I have been asking myself that very same question for the past ten years."

We faced each other in sudden silence. I told myself that this devout old man might very well be responsible for my cousin's murder. That a word or a gesture from him may have triggered the events leading to Billy's death. But it didn't do any good. I

203

couldn't help feeling sorry for him. For all his wealth and all his power, Truman was just a lonely, soft-spoken old man whose beloved, strong-willed daughter was forever lost to him.

I touched his bony wrist. Sympathetic murmur. "It wasn't your fault, Mr. Sager."

Startled, he looked up at me. Judging from the expression, he must have thought I was reading his mind. The moustache quivered angrily as he stepped away from me.

"You are an impertinent young woman!" His slim forefinger pointed at the sidewalk. "And I will thank you to leave my house!"

The Queen Anne door slammed loudly in my wake.

Well, Ty Braddock had left me high and dry on North Third Street, the moneyed folks' neighborhood, a good mile and a half from my parked car. Good thing I was wearing my hiking boots. It would have been a blistering stroll in heels.

Since I was in the neighborhood anyway, I headed three blocks west, cut across Center Street, and dropped in at the Valley View Market. Picked up a few items for supper. While standing in the speedy checkout line, I ruffled through the *Enquirer* and giggled at the misadventures of a certain red-haired duchess. Speaking as a princess myself, you'll never find Anishinabe royalty behaving like that.

Just then, a male whisper hailed me in my native language. "Improving your mind, *Noozis?*" Glancing over my shoulder, I grinned at Chief. *"Watchiya,*

204

Nimishoo. How are things up in Cottonwood?"

"Interesting." He jutted his chin toward the wall-sized window. "I didn't see your car in the parking lot."

"Long story, *Nimishoo*. Walk with me downtown, and I'll fill you in."

So we walked down Center, my grandfather and I. Always the gentleman, Chief toted the grocery bags. As we strolled along, I brought him up to date on my recent doings.

". . . just about it, *Nimishoo*. When Billy realized that Longhurst was going to circumvent the hearing process, he knew he had to move fast. He remembered what Ned Pahaka had told him about that Section 206 land near Penrose, and he decided to fast-shuffle Lodestone into BIA jurisdiction."

"If aspen is as valuable as you say, that gives Eames one hell of a motive," Chief added.

Slow nod. "Eames was certainly desperate enough to have Billy killed."

"Or to have done it himself. You can forget about those two old boys from the cafe—Billy's sparring partners." Chief's smile was grim. "That Joe Nielsen's still got his arm in a cast. Compound fracture. And Ed Kearns lit out for Florida the day he got his first disability check. He was at some Tampa motel the morning Billy got killed."

"Sure about that, *Nimishoo?*"

"Made the long-distance call myself. Had a nice chat with the desk clerk. Ed's taken to wearing a neck brace all the time. He's a bit nervous about insurance

205

investigators. Other than that, he's alive and well and living in Margaritaville.''

"There's still Longhurst," I said, thinking of the stonewall he'd given me in his office that day.

"Afraid not, *Noozis.*" Chief let out a weary sigh. "Longhurst was nowhere near the Topanas that Tuesday. It was *Career Day* at Maughan High. Longhurst spent the whole morning there, trying to interest seniors in the Forest Service."

"Positive?"

He nodded. "I spoke to Longhurst's secretary, Arlene, and double-checked it with your friend, Jayne Clark. Triple-checked it with the receptionist at the high school. He was there, all right."

Fussbudget face. "He could have slipped out, *Nimishoo.*"

"Highly unlikely, child. He was sitting up there on the auditorium stage in front of just over a hundred teenagers." Slow shake of the head. "If Karl Eames bushwacked Billy, he did it all by himself."

"Same thing with Cue," I added. "But I think ruthlessness, not desperation, is the motive there. If Cue knew Billy had flimflammed Longhurst, he would have made an example of him. Shown everybody what happens when you mess with the meanest ol' hound in Clover Creek."

"Yeah, I've heard Broward's a prime son of a bitch."

"A pluperfect shit!" I added, folding my arms. "And he could have counted on the deputy's help. Our friend Ty has a habit of making himself indispensable to the big boys."

Glancing at me, Chief said, "I think we've taken

206

this as far as we can, *Noozis*. We've got the physical evidence back in Heber. You've proven Braddock a liar. Let's let Della take it to the feds. That deputy's the weak link. He knows damned well who was up at Dynamite Pass with Billy that day. If the FBI leans on him, he'll crack wide open. He'll point fingers. Bet on it."

I flashed my grandfather a sad smile. "What about the canyon?"

"Angie, when this mess breaks, Lodestone Canyon's going to be the last thing on Longhurst's mind," Chief replied, switching to English. "For years he's been letting Cue Broward nibble away at Uncle Sam's forest. He's going to have to talk long and hard to keep his ass out of Leavenworth."

"You know, Chief," I whispered. "If I can pull this off—if I can work a 'Goat Pasture' game on ol' Cue—the canyon will be safe. No one will ever threaten it again."

"Too dangerous!" he muttered, shaking his head. "We have enough. Let's get out of here."

I cast a fond smile at the Wasatch range. "You know, a pristine forest in Lodestone Canyon would make a fine memorial to Billy."

Exasperated look from Chief. "In case you haven't heard, fraud is a *felony* in this state, my girl. If you try to con Broward, and it goes wrong, you're going to be checking into the Utah version of the Big Dollhouse."

"Cue will never know what hit him, Chief."

Frustration tensed his aged features. "It ain't just the Sagers and the Browards you have to worry about,

Angie. There's that friend of yours, too. The one who knows you *aren't* really *Sara Soyazhe*."

"Jack Sunawavi." I stopped in my tracks. "What about him?"

"I've been dropping that name quite a bit in my travels. Jack sure leaves a lasting impression. Trouble is, he's harder to see than air."

"What do you mean?"

Chief let a plastic shopping bag dangle from each hand. "I mean, he ain't been home to Cottonwood since a week ago Saturday. Old Jack tends to roam a mite, I hear, but he's never stayed away this long before. He's got the home folks wondering."

A week ago Saturday. Thoughtful Angie frown. The night Jack tried to hustle me out of the Briar Patch.

"Wondering what?" I asked.

"Wondering if he's pulled a job in Wyoming or Idaho. Folks think maybe that's why he's on the dodge." Chief's quizzical gaze turned northward. "Something funny's going on up there, Angie. Doe Sunawavi—that's his mother—I hear she's a sociable type. But she ain't left that house in days."

"Where's the house located?"

"Out at the end of Dead Horse Road."

"Doe Sunawavi?" I repeated.

"Short for Dolores. You thinking of calling on the old lady?"

"Mmmmmm—the thought did cross my mind."

"I don't think she'll talk. Jack's an only child. She won't hear anything bad about him."

"Might be worth the trip anyway, Chief."

"It might." Chief tilted his broad head to one side.

208

"In the meantime, missy, would you mind explaining just what the hell a 'Goat Pasture' is?"

And so, eager to oblige my grandfather, I outlined my brilliant plan to save Lodestone Canyon.

You'd have loved it, Billy boy.

Chapter Eleven

At eight the following morning, I was standing in front of the trailer's dresser, clipping on a pair of silver pendant earrings, smiling with satisfaction at my wardrobe choice. Today I was Corporate Angie, smartly turned out in a classic powder blue suit. Trim polycotton blazer with notched lapels and a slim, fanny-hugging skirt. Trail boots had given way to polished Aigner dress pumps with three-inch heels.

My smile faded as I mulled over the conversation with Chief the previous evening. Questions, questions. Why was Jack Sunawavi on the dodge? Because of Billy's murder? Was Jack really hiding out? If so, why?

Cold clammy tickle at the back of the neck. The better to hunt yours truly, perhaps?

Disquieting questions pursued me out of the trailer. I set out for the Circle B, eager to keep my morning appointment with Cue Broward, but then I changed my mind and pulled into the parking lot of the Rimrock Cafe. I needed to use their pay phone.

Pop in the quarters. Hi, operator, got a long-distance call here. Patch me through to Millcreek, would you please? One ring and then Cindy Polenana's lovely voice came on line. "Hello?"

"Hi, Cin. It's Angie Biwaban. Got a minute?"

"Angie, hi! How's everything in Pierre?"

Good question, I thought, and one better left to Paul Holbrook. "Just fine," I replied, and then, after treating Cindy to an anecdote or two, I casually switched topics.

"So how's the new lock working out?" I asked. "Is it keeping out the riffraff? In particular, that creep in the fringed vest!"

"You mean *Jack!?*" Relief lightened Cindy's tone. "Lord, I haven't seen Jack Sunawavi in weeks. Not since the day you were here. I think you scared him off, Angie."

"He hasn't hassled you at all?"

"Not a bit." Pleasant laughter tickled my ear. "I'll never forget the look on his face when you raised that skillet. Priceless! That's one I owe you, Angie."

"Forget it, Cin. Nobody's keeping count."

"Enough talk about that bastard!" Cindy exhaled heavily. "Let's talk about something more pleasant, eh? Any new men in your life, dear?"

So Cindy and I had a cozy, gossipy chat. After we said our goodbyes, I popped in some more quarters, got hold of Information, and tracked down the number of that convenience store across the street from Cindy's house.

It's not that I don't trust you, Cin. It's just that, if Jack Sunawavi really is stalking you, chances are he's taking care to stay out of your line of sight.

211

An adenoidal voice came on line. "Morning. Seven-Eleven. May I help you?"

"Good morning." Brisk and efficient contralto. "My name is Lucretia Reyes, and I'm an investigator with the state Department of Public Safety. Are you the store manager?"

"Well, yes. Ah, who did you say you were with?"

"The Utah Department of Public Safety." Somewhere on high, golden trumpets flourished. "Motor Vehicle Investigation Division. Sir, may we count upon your cooperation?"

Anxiety came through loud and clear. "Uhm, of course, Miss Reyes. Is anything wrong?"

"Routine inquiry." Leaning against the cafe's redwood wall, I cleared my throat. "Tell me, are you familiar with the Victorian house directly across the street?"

"Yes, ma'am. I'm looking at it right now."

"Have you seen the following vehicle parked at that address? A Dodge Cummins Turbo Diesel pickup truck, midnight blue, Utah license plate SG7-498?"

"Gosh, I don't think I ever . . . no! No! Hot damn! Wait a minute!"

I heard a *bumpetty-thud* as he put the phone on the counter. His voice sounded a little further away.

"Hey, Darryl, you remember that big ol' pickup Todd was raving about? Was that a Dodge?"

"Sure was." Another distant masculine voice. "Big dark blue Dodge. Some Indian was drivin' it. Who's that on the phone there?"

"Police lady. When did Todd see that truck?"

"Shit, I don't know. Two or three weeks ago, maybe."

212

The store manager duly informed me that Jack's Dodge hadn't been seen in the neighborhood for at least two weeks. So I gave him another question for the helpful Darryl.

"You seen it since then?"

"Not me," he said. "And, hell, I reckon Todd woulda said somethin' if he'd seen it. You know how he gets about a brand-new pickup. What's that gal want to know for?"

"It's stolen," I told the manager. "Four guys used it to hold up the Farmers' Credit Union in Pocatello. If you see it again, contact the Utah Highway Patrol. Don't mess with those boys. They're armed and dangerous."

"Son of a bitch!" the manager gasped. I hung up.

Okay, Jack, I thought, strolling out of the cafe. So you haven't been to Millcreek since the day I was there. And it looks as if you haven't been home to Mama since the night we met at the Briar Patch. So what's going on, Sunawavi? Why are you avoiding your bosom buddy, Ty Braddock? Just why are you laying low?

Chief was right. Jack Sunawavi was a tough man to touch base with. During the past two weeks, he'd only been sighted twice. Once by Dennis Simms and once by me.

Unless that wasn't Jack Sunawavi in the Dodge.

But if it wasn't, then who was it?

Ty Braddock? No, I don't think so. Otherwise, Ty wouldn't have asked me to relay his message. The deputy is no actor. No way could he have successfully faked his irritation with Jack yesterday.

I opened my car door and tossed a worried glance

at the evergreen slopes of the Wasatch. He was out there somewhere. Jack Sunawavi was the wild card in this whole deal, and I couldn't quite shake the feeling that he was gunning for me.

Thirty minutes later, I stepped onto the spacious front porch of the Broward house and planted my index finger on the brass doorbell button. Chimes sounded behind the door, punctuated by the sound of a chair scraping the floor. A muffled baritone voice said, "I'll get it."

Shiny black patent leather purse tucked beneath my arms, I squared my shoulders and watched the front door swing open. Flashed a brilliant Angie smile at the familiar dark-haired man in the crisp heather blue suit and Western string tie. Hooded Easter Island eyes blinked at me.

"Sara! What are you doing here?"

"Hi, Dennis. Just dropped by to keep my appointment with the boss man. Is he in?"

"He is." Curt nod from the lawyer. "I wasn't aware you were coming, though. Cue and I are going over some titles for Willow Valley Realty."

The clumping of boot heels interrupted him. Cue's booming voice reverberated through the parlor. "Is that Sara Soyazhe I hear? Get your ass outta that doorway, Denny, and let the little gal in."

Dennis obediently backpedaled, and I swept past, chin high and beaming. Cue crossed the parlor like a runaway horse, his brawny hands outstretched in welcome, a broad countrified smile on his lips. Seizing me by the shoulders, he yanked me forward and planted a noisy smooch on my left cheek.

"Been wonderin' when you'd be comin' around,"

Cue said, holding me at arm's length. "Whether it's clothes or business, a woman just can't seem to make up her mind."

"I've been giving your offer a lot of thought," I replied, smoothing my blazer sleeves after Cue relinquished his grip. "And I've decided to take you up on it."

Cue winked at his lawyer. "Told you she was a smart little gal." And then, placing a comradely arm across my shoulders, he shepherded me through the parlor. In his blue rodeo stripe shirt and ranch jeans, with his wrangler's tan and thinning white hair, he looked strangely out of place in the midst of all this *House Beautiful* stylishness. "Come here, Sara. I want to show you something."

Yes, the decor was definitely Gail. Embroidered camelback sofa and matching Queen Anne wing chairs. Federal-style white doors and a plush Turkish rug. And an oval hand-tooled coffee table fashioned from durable Santa Fe oak. There was a scale model sitting on the coffee table, a miniaturized housing development showing curved tree-lined streets ending in cul-de-sacs.

"Yours?" I asked.

"Damned right. That is Willow Valley Realty's next big project." Beaming with pride, Cue placed both hands on his hips. "I just bought the Slash Bar C north of town. We're gonna put some mighty fine homes in there. Gonna call it Taylor Ridge, after my momma. She was a Taylor." He nodded at Dennis. "Still got the title search to do, though. Need it for the insurance."

Frowning mildly, Dennis glanced at the Swiss

cuckoo clock perched above the mantlepiece. "You know, Cue, you're supposed to be at the dairy for that eleven o'clock meeting."

"You'd better sit in for me, Denny. Me 'n' Sara here got us some mineral rights to discuss." He flashed me a greedy smile. "I tell you, Sara gal, if I ever get to do it again, to hell with cowpunchin'! I'm gettin' into insurance. Those sons of bitches—they're bettin' I'm gonna die, I'm bettin' I'm gonna live—and they're usin' my money to cover both bets! Go on, gal. Rest yourself."

Smoothing the back of my skirt, I occupied one of the wing chairs while Cue sprawled on the sofa. Standing beside its padded armrest was Dennis, his dark eyes watchful and curious.

"Now then, Sara . . ." Cue spread his hands in an expansive gesture. "Tell me how you're gonna make me rich offa them Lodestone mineral rights."

And there it was—the magic moment when the mark is most receptive. Feeling my nyloned knees tremble, I leaned forward and showed old Cue a beguiling grin.

"Let me ask you a personal question first. How much money are you going to pocket on that Lodestone Canyon timber cut?"

"Pretty close to a million, I guess."

"How would you like to *double* that, Cue?"

He sat up at once, his gaze thoughtful and intensely curious.

"And that's just the first quarter," I added. "By the end of the year, you'll be spilling money on your way to the bank."

"How?" He stared at me shrewdly. "Lodestone's

216

aspen won't fetch that much. Not even from old man Sager's fiberboard company.''

"I wasn't talking about timber.''

"Minerals?'' Dennis seated himself on the sofa armrest. He was equally attentive. "Sara, we've studied the geological survey. There's nothing of value in that canyon.''

"That's where you're wrong, Dennis. The canyon itself has value . . . as a *bargaining chip.* It can be swapped for more valuable federal land. To be specific, a tract which could make you the richest man in Utah.'' Displaying an impish smile, I tilted my head toward the lawyer. "Ask him what a Section 206 is, Cue.''

When I said *Section 206,* Dennis's eyes blinked twice, and Cue's face settled into an expression of stern amiability. The lawyer knew what I was talking about. But Cue himself had veiled his own reaction with the aplomb of a master poker player. I couldn't tell if he knew or not.

Without being asked, Dennis said, "Section 206 is part of the Federal Land Act, Cue. It allows Washington to swap federal land for private holdings and vice versa.''

"And it allows the BLM to swap its land for federal land held by other bureaus of the Department of the Interior,'' I added.

Nodding slowly, the rancher asked, "So what do you have in mind, Sara?''

"I'm talking about trading up, Cue. Swapping Lodestone for a tract under the Bureau of Indian Affairs. A very lucrative tract with its mineral rights still unassigned.'' Sitting back, I tugged at the hem of my

217

slim skirt. "One million for Lodestone's timber? That's small change compared to what you'll be making off this tract."

Thumbing his moustache, Cue scowled. "If it's so damned valuable, Sara, why don't you just buy some private land of your own and use it to swap?"

"It's not that easy, Cue. This is treaty land. The tribe won't let it go unless they get an equivalent tract of land in return."

I caught a glimmer of sudden comprehension in Cue's blue eyes.

"We talkin' about the Utes, gal?"

I nodded.

"Do your people know how valuable that BIA land is?"

"No! It's an old family secret."

Slow grin on the rancher. Turning to Dennis, he drawled, "Boy, you'd better hustle if you're going to make that eleven o'clock meeting."

Vivid disappointment strained the lawyer's expression. "I'd really like to sit in on this, Cue."

"No need, Denny. I'll brief you later." His tone hardened. "Go on!"

Glaring at me, Dennis stood, buttoned his suit jacket, and headed for the door. His anger was nearly palpable as he strode past me.

Following the lawyer's abrupt departure, I remarked, "You came down a little hard on him, Cue."

"Oh, Denny'll get over it. He's a big boy now. Fine hand with them law books, too. Every once in a while, though, he forgets he's hired help. Needs remindin'."

"Been with you long?"

218

"Ever since he got out of Stanford law school." Relaxing against the sofa cushions, Cue showed me a fond smile. "Alice—my first wife—she knew Denny's momma real well. His daddy was Doug Simms. Used to be Karl Eames's foreman at the mill."

"Did Eames help with the college education?"

"Not likely, Miss Sara. Karl Eames is the stingiest son of a bitch on God's green earth. Mean as an ol' diamondback, too. Denny's daddy come to work drunk one time, and Eames fired him. I guess Denny was 'bout twelve then. Family lost their ranch. Had to move into town. Reckon it turned Denny into a . . . shit, what's that word?"

"Overachiever?"

"Yeah, I guess you could call him that. He's sure put his ol' daddy in the shade, though. He was twenty-seven when Mordecai Hodge made him a full partner. Lot of drive in that boy. I like that. Too damned many ass-sitters in this here world." Cue's narrow-eyed gaze skewered me. "Now we've got us some privacy, Miss Sara, we can talk. Where's that BIA land of yours?"

Waggling an upright forefinger, I grinned. "Not so fast, Cue. We're not partners yet."

Blue eyes gleamed in amusement. "Partners!?"

"Throw in with me, Mr. Broward, and I'll do more than tell you. I'll *show* you. I'll take you there."

Cue considered my offer for several tense moments. And then, his features crinkling in a kindly smile, he placed both boots on the carpet and stood slowly. "All right. We'll do it first thing in the mornin', gal."

"You won't regret it, Cue."

"Rein up, sweetiepie. I ain't agreed to that partnership yet. I just want a look at this here tract." Nimbly he sidestepped the coffee table. "Why does it have to be swapped with Lodestone?"

"Because Lodestone, like the BIA tract, has unassigned mineral rights," I explained. "You have to have equivalent sites in a Section 206 transfer. You can't swap unassigned rights for assigned rights."

"Makes sense." Tongue in cheek, he gave me a long, thoughtful look. "Just one question, little gal. Why come to me with the offer?"

"I don't have clout with Interior. You do."

"And where'd you hear that, Miss Sara?"

Meeting his hard gaze, I smirked. "All around town, Mr. Broward. People say Alfie Longhurst is mighty eager to please you."

He let out a sudden good-humored chuckle. "That's understandable. He won't be workin' for Uncle Sam forever. Man's got to think about his future in this here county."

"The BIA tract is already listed for a possible Section 206 transfer," I added. "I can't move it on my own. I need a partner. Somebody who can prod the Department of the Interior into making the switch."

"Bottom line on the deal, Sara."

Saucy Angie smile. "I show you the tract. You see to it that Longhurst makes the transfer. After the 206 goes through, we take out the leases in partnership and split the profits fifty-fifty."

"*Leases?*" Sheer cupidity radiated out of him. "What kind of leases?"

My smile turned enigmatic. "You'll see."

"Damned right! And I'll see *you* at six-thirty tomorrow mornin'. Don't bother comin' out here, gal. I'll pick you up in Clover Creek.''

At that moment, I heard a soft footfall in the kitchen doorway. My first reaction was alarm. Had we been overheard? And then, whirling to the right, I saw a cheerful Gail Sager Broward come breezing through the doorway. *"Darling . . . ?"*

The rancher brightened instantly. "Right here, biscuit.''

I could well understand the reason for Cue's broad, lascivious smile. His Mormon bride looked quite fetching in her riding outfit. Skintight tan britches, a sleeveless black silk tank and polished knee-high equestrian boots. A silken kerchief bound her dark brown hair into a Grecian ponytail.

But I couldn't understand the expression of surprise on Gail's pretty face. Or the sudden trailing-off of her seductive, singsong greeting.

Gail gave her aging husband a timid peck. "I thought you had a meeting this morning, Cue."

"I did. But I sent Denny in my place. Ain't nothin' big on the agenda, anyway." Fond smile for the spouse. "What are you doin' home so early?"

Gail artfully avoided his casual touch. "I cut it short. That daughter of yours is out there shooting at anything that moves.''

"And hittin' it, too!" Brimming with fatherly pride, Cue flashed a broad smile. "My Linda was Utah junior women's sharpshootin' champ two years straight.''

Reaching behind her head, Gail untied the kerchief knot. Tension spoiled the lovely line of her mouth.

Fierce glance at me. "Would you mind telling me what *that woman* is doing in my house?"

"*Your* house!?" Crooked smile on the rancher. "You pencil in your name on the deed again?"

His humor failed to appease the lady. "What's she doing here, Cue?"

"We're just talkin' a little business, Sara 'n' me."

"Monkey business?"

I detected a shrill note in Gail's angry voice, a faint echo on insincerity. She seemed to be deliberately trying to provoke a quarrel.

Winking at me, Cue said, "A judge might call it that, eh, Sara?"

Dark eyes flashing, Gail confronted her husband. "If it's your freedom you're looking for, Henry Taylor Broward, that can be arranged."

Being a woman, I could see right through Gail's act. I'd done the same thing myself a time or two—provoked a shouting quarrel with Rory whenever I felt I was being neglected.

Being a man, of course, Cue was completely taken in. Worse than that, his own temper began to fray. Careful, Miss Gail. You don't want to make him *too* mad. If he storms out of here, you won't get to kiss and make up.

Cue's cheeks reddened. "Oh, you'd like *that*, wouldn't you?"

"As a matter of fact, I would!"

"Well, forget it, Gail honey." That hoarse pseudo-sweet tone of his gave me the goosebumps. "I'm too damned old to pull up stakes. I like the current arrangement just fine."

"Is that a *fact!*" Gail's tense face quivered two

inches from her husband's. "Then why do you spend Monday nights in Salt Lake!?"

"You know how it is with old punchers, gal." Cue's expression made me awfully damned glad I wasn't married to him. "When they come up on a dry waterhole, they go lookin' for the next one."

"You're *disgusting!*"

"Sorta changed your opinion, haven't you?"

Folding her arms tightly, Gail performed a pert about-face. "I have nothing further to say to you, Mr. Broward."

With an arrogant swing of those well-shaped buttocks, Miss Gail put her nose in the air and took her leave.

And they call *me* a spoiled princess!

"Good afternoon, Mrs. Broward!" Cue hollered, intent on having the final word. "Try not to split the doorjamb, okay? Oh, and make sure Daddy gets a full report!"

The upstairs slam sounded like an artillery burst. Seething in frustration, Cue planted one gnarled hand on the sofa's crest. "You still livin' at Thornley's trailer court?"

Brisk Angie nod.

"Fine! I'll pick you up there tomorrow." He hooked his thumb at the front door. "Saddle up and ride, gal."

"Cue, I'm sorry about what happened."

"Don't be! 'Tain't your fault." He headed for the stairwell. "Biscuit's got a hair up her ass, and I got to go pluck it."

Now, a careful con artist would have beat a hasty retreat from that house, but me . . . well, I just couldn't resist the opportunity to have a look around. Cue's casual mention of Kate Thornley had put me on my guard. I'd never told him my Clover Creek address, so it had to have been someone else. Dennis Simms, perhaps. I began wondering how thoroughly old Cue had checked out Sara Soyazhe.

Lift one leg at a time. Off with the spikes. Ouch shoes are much too noisy for skulking.

My stockinged feet glided noiselessly along the polished Spanish tiles of the main corridor. I heard muffled, angry voices overhead. The wily rancher and the young wife continuing their squabble.

Ah, and here's the study. It was a small, walnut-trimmed sewing room that had been converted into an office. Desktop computer, hard disk, laser printer and fax machine. Gunmetal gray filing cabinets surrounded the spacious desk. Always the puncher, Cue felt most at home in a corral.

Holding my shoes in my left hand, I gingerly slid open each file drawer and did some hasty rummaging. Kept an eye out for familiar names. But there was no mention of Billy or Sara or Lodestone.

Quick search of Cue's sprawling desktop. The blotter's thick rim held many pink telephone messages. No mention of my cousin or the canyon. Slide open the center drawer. My, what a surprisingly neat arrangement of pencils, pens, tacks, labels and bills. For all his laid-back cowpoke image, Cue Broward was a compulsive organizer.

Searching the bottom drawers, I listened to the clamor upstairs. Such language, Miss Gail. And from a Mormon princess, too. If Daddy ever heard that, he'd be reaching for the saddle soap.

The drawers offered nothing of value. Standing erect once more, I thumbed through Cue's desk calendar and found an interesting notation. Scribbled on the page for Monday, August third, were the initials R.C. and a seven-digit phone number. The first three digits were five-three-three. Which put Mr. R.C. in downtown Salt Lake.

Even more interesting was the page for Tuesday, August fourth, the day Billy was murdered. That page was blank.

I jotted R.C.'s phone number on a pink slip, then padded swiftly out of there.

Judging from his personal telephone log, Cue Broward was a very busy man. Nearly every moment of his working day was accounted for. Cue appeared to schedule his time well in advance, and that led to an interesting question—namely, why did Cue leave Tuesday the fourth wide open?

I began wondering if Cue himself had set up the ambush. He could have put the squeeze on Longhurst—had his boy Alfie send my cousin up to Dynamite Pass on a fool's errand. In the meantime, Cue could have phoned his pal R.C. in Salt Lake and set himself up for an overnight alibi.

The rest would have been so simple. Purchase a McCulloch chainsaw at any hardware store along the Wasatch Front. Have dinner with R.C. Turn in early at the Holiday Inn. Rise and shine at 3 a.m., leaving a good five or six hours to drive directly to Dynamite Pass. Lug the chainsaw into the woods. Sit down, have a smoke, and wait for the unsuspecting forest ranger to arrive.

I visualized the pass and its lodgepoles and those

faint soft-soled footprints made by a slender man six feet tall. Cue Broward fit that description to a T. And yet, thinking of Dynamite Pass, I experienced once again that sensation of unfocused anxiety. I couldn't quite shake the feeling that I'd missed something back there. Some important little clue.

Maybe it was time for a return visit to the murder scene.

Pausing at the front door, I slipped on my high-heeled pumps one at a time. Grimaced at the marital clamor drifting down the stairs. Definitely no kiss-and-make-up after *this* spat.

Normally, I would've recommended a good divorce lawyer, but those two would soon be facing a hassle that would make their domestic troubles seem trivial, indeed. Uncle Sam doesn't like people who chew up his forests for private gain.

As I exited the house, a chilling sound halted me on the top porch step. The metallic *click-chock* of a lever-action rifle. My eyes shifted to the left, and there she was. Linda Beckworth, Cue's rambunctious daughter. Fun-loving divorcee and one-time sharp-shooting champion. She was standing at the corner of the house, her fine blond hair windblown, casually clad in a white cotton blouse with a laced-up front and shoulder-puffed sleeves and a pair of taut stretch Levis. For accessories, she had a high-powered Winchester Model 94 XTR tucked beneath her arm in a grouse shooter's hold—rifle barrel parallel to the leg, muzzle pointed at the ground.

Linda's expression shifted from surprise to a naughty delight. Her Elvis lip-curl became more noticeable. "What were you doing in that house?"

226

"Talking to your father." Slowly I descended the stairs.

"Why don't I believe you?" she wondered aloud, heading straight for me. The Winchester barrel came up fast.

Of course, it was pretty risky, baiting a hot-tempered cattle princess who's holding a loaded rifle in her hands. But I had to discontinue Linda's current train of thought.

"How's your boyfriend, Miguel?" I asked.

Cracking a feral grin, Linda set the Winchester against the porch foundation. "His name's Arturo. Good thing for you that you got it wrong."

"Why is that?"

"You're new around here, Injun, so you don't know the score yet. Talk to a few gals. They'll tell you how it is. You wave that little ass at my man, and here's what happens."

Lifting her palm, Linda pummelled it three times in fast succession. *Smack, smack, smack!* Sadistic giggle. "He won't think you're so pretty no more!"

Lifting my chin, I became Mary, Queen of Scots. Much too serene and dignified to be hit . . . I hoped.

"I wouldn't advise that, Mrs. Beckworth."

She had the hearty chuckle of a schoolyard bully. "Want to know what you can do with that advice, little Injun gal?"

I took a defiant step forward, then restrained myself. *Cool it, Angie. This isn't the exercise yard at Miss Carlotta's. Maintain your cover. Sara the Geologist wouldn't come out swinging.*

So I flashed a ladylike scowl. "If you hit me, you're going to end up in a place you won't like very much."

227

"Yeah!? What place is that?"

"The bars tend to spoil the view from the window."

"Keep dreamin', little gal!" Linda's smile showed perfect teeth. "You file a complaint against me, and you watch how fast it gets lost in that courthouse. I've been kickin' ass for years. Ain't nobody done a damn thing about it." Another giggle. "And they ain't going to, either. Not so long as my daddy has his say 'round here."

Just then, I heard a yowl of feminine outrage coming from the upstairs window. The sound amused Linda, drawing her gaze upward. A broad, pleased smile crept across that arrogant mouth. "What are those two scrappin' about?"

"Biscuit has a hair up her ass," I reported nonchalantly.

Linda made a face. "Shit! What else is new?" Rapidly losing interest in bullying me, she retrieved her Winchester. "If that daddy of mine had a lick o' sense, he'd have unloaded that bitch years ago."

"I got the impression he cares for Gail."

"Then he's a damned fool." Cradling the rifle, Linda turned to me again. " 'Course, Daddy always was kind of stupid about women."

"I take it you don't approve of Miss Gail as your father's wife."

"Wife!" Harsh laugh from the sharpshooter. "Easy to see you're new around here. Miss Gail ain't his wife, dummy. She's more like a permanent houseguest. She put a damned lock on her bedroom door four years ago."

"Why doesn't he divorce her?" I asked.

"Pure mean cussedness, that's why." Linda's smile turned frosty. "Way Daddy sees it, Gail's got to hold up her end of the deal. Nobody twisted her arm. She said 'I do' of her own free will." Her sidelong glance found the upstairs window. "When Gail asked for that divorce, my Daddy said nobody had ever welshed on him, and it wasn't going to start now and certainly with no damned Sager!" She cackled merrily, taking a perverse delight in discussing her stepmother's love life. "Gail figured Daddy was gonna be a little gentleman and move on out and let her hunt up a new man. Didn't happen quite the way she figured. Daddy stayed right where he was. And Miss Gail . . ." Prolonged burst of delighted laughter. "Well, she doesn't like doin' without, that's for damned sure. She takes that big black stallion o' hers out for a ride every chance she can." More laughter. "Practically wearin' out the seat of them fancy ridin' britches."

"I don't suppose it's any fun for your dad, either."

She shrugged. "Reckon he figures on waitin' her out. He's a hard man, my Daddy." A sudden pained expression tensed her pretty face. "But he's a damned fool about women."

. "Most men are."

She glanced resentfully at the window. "I wish he'd smarten up and run her off." Clenched teeth. "Or, better yet, let *me* do it!"

"Miss Gail seems to be pretty steamed up about your father's visits to Salt Lake."

Linda flew to her daddy's defense. "Well, if she don't want him goin' to the Rimfire Club, she knows how to keep him around."

"Rimfire Club?" I echoed.

"Yeah. Down in Salt Lake. Private place on North Temple. Got to run a mighty big herd to get in there. That's where Daddy goes when he gets to feelin' the urge to play some shotgun poker with Jim Ayers and Ralph Parley and the governor."

"Your Mormon stepmother doesn't approve of poker?"

Contemptuous smirk. "You are one dumb Injun, you know that? Ain't the poker that's got her frettin'. It's Daddy gettin' all liquored up and crawlin' up to the second floor—when all she's got is Maharajah's saddle." Linda started to laugh, but she didn't quite make it. Unpleasant memories transformed the smile into a forced skeletal rictus. "He did that a lot after Mama died. Sometimes he'd bring one of 'em home. Those trashy women of his. Bitches thought they were gonna move right on in. But they didn't stay. I saw to that!"

By now, Cue's sugarplum was really beginning to frighten me. Her long, well-manicured fingers caressed the Winchester. Glazed aquamarine eyes hinted at a deteriorating contact with reality. She began looking at me as if I were one of those trashy women from the Rimfire Club.

I had to change the subject before that over-the-hill tomboy realized how much fun it'd be to shoot the high heels off my Aigner pumps.

Aiming my chin at the Winchester, I remarked, "Cue tells me you're pretty good with that."

"Dog's nuts!" A smile of genuine pleasure tugged at her lush lips. "Best in the state of Utah!"

"Best female shot, you mean."

Laughing in derision, Linda lifted her rifle and took

aim at a distant pasture. "You see that gate back there?"

I did. She was referring to an old whitewashed cattle gate on the back fence, a good two hundred yards from where we stood. Beside the gate, perched on a flat-topped fence post, sat an empty long-necked beer bottle.

"See the bottle?" she added, lifting the stock to her shoulder.

"Just barely."

Cheek pressed to the stock, Linda peered through the butterfly sight. "Keep watching it."

The rifle blast stung my ears. The bottle exploded into a fine spray of scintillating shards.

Mightily impressed, I turned to the heiress. I didn't like the thoughtless, casual way she had levelled that rifle—as if squeezing a trigger were the most commonplace happening in the world. She hadn't even bothered to shout a warning first, to keep any bystanders out of her line of fire.

Linda flashed me a teeth-gritting, lopsided smirk. "Point out the man who can do that!"

"If I find one, I'll let you know." I took a nonchalant step away from Cue's tigerish offspring. "Tell me, what's the secret of your success?"

"What do you mean?"

"How do you hit the target every time?"

"Very easy, little gal." Linda's proud smile turned utterly brittle. Again I caught a glimpse of the deep-seated hurt in that woman's eyes. "I just pretend the bullseye is my Daddy."

Dead silence. As I inched away, the charming Mrs. Beckworth lapsed once more into brooding. I decided

231

not to push my luck any further. Giving her a polite nod, I made a hasty retreat to my waiting car.

All at once, my ears detected the hellish *click-chock* of that Winchester. My shoulder blades turned to ice as I heard the fresh bullet slide into the chamber. I halted, whirling instantly, my dark eyes wide and wary.

And there stood Linda, rifle stock at rest on her canted hip, the barrel pointing skyward, smirking like an incorrigible brat.

The smirk widened. "Or *anyone else* I don't particularly like!"

Her sick, reverberant laughter chased me all the way back to the car.

On the way back to Clover Creek, I thought about Cue's hell-raising daughter and wondered if my stomach butterflies would ever go away.

Damn you, Broward—your daughter needs help. Your darling Linda isn't the harmless, fun-loving, good-old-girl who wins shooting contests and who'll settle down just as soon as she meets the right man. She's an emotionally disturbed young woman with a pronounced sadistic streak, and if you don't get her into some kind of therapy, chances are she's going to use that rifle on a target a little more lively than an empty bottle.

Couldn't Broward see that?

Letting out a ragged sigh, I stepped on the brake and slowed the Accord. The city limits sign whizzed by me on the right.

Of course he couldn't see it. None of us can. Cue

Broward could no more be objective about Linda than I could be about Chief or Aunt Della or Grandma Biwaban. Or Billy.

We are each experts on everyone else's family.

Time would eventually solve the Linda problem. Daddy's protection would end with his eventual death. Policemen have notoriously long memories, and Miss Linda had been thumbing her nose at them for years. They'd come down hard. Her old chaperone, Ty Braddock, will probably be the one to slap on the handcuffs. If she was very lucky perhaps she wouldn't be sent to the state prison in Draper. Perhaps Sheriff Mortensen would have her carted off to Provo for psychiatric observation. Maybe then she'd get the professional help she so desperately needed.

So, Angie, on with the mission. Cue wants to see the valuable BIA land, eh? Let's make it well worth his while. I took a quick glance at the dashboard clock. It was just after one o'clock. With luck, I could be in Penrose by sundown.

Driving down Center Street, I spotted a Dodge dealership on the other side of the white line, remembered Jack Sunawavi's brand-new pickup, and thought of a way to kill two buffalo with a single, well-aimed arrow. Flipping the signal lever, I cut my speed and swung into their spacious driveway.

The place was called Remuda Dodge, and the name was spelled out in raised aluminum letters on the side of the building. I parked beside a line of shiny new Dynasty LEs. As I emerged from my car, I spied an earnest-looking salesman behind the huge showroom window. He was straightening his tie out on the lot before I even slammed the car door.

"Hi! Can I help you?" He was in his mid-forties, sparse blond hair, banker's moustache and an outdoorsman's tan. A very hearty baritone voice, hinting at Willow Valley roots.

"Hi!" Neighborly smile from Angie. "Do you have any used oil? Say, forty-weight oil?"

"Well, I guess we could spare a gallon. What do you need it for?"

Inspired alibi. "I just bought a used lawnmower. The blade shaft is pretty rusty. I figured to loosen it with the oil."

The salesman walked me into the air-conditioned showroom. The blast of chilled air turned my blouse damp. Glancing back at my Accord, he registered an expression of mild confusion. "Say, that's a rental, isn't it?"

"That's right. And that's the other reason I'm here." Rueful Angie smile. "My Escort finally bit the dust. I was hoping to make an appointment. Maybe come in and look at a Dynasty."

Tanned features brightened at once. "Have you got a minute? I can show you—"

"Hey, I'd love to, but I'm on my lunch hour. That's why I wanted to make the appointment."

"No problem. Here, take this." He handed me a white business card, and I learned I was talking to Duane Teller, the sales manager.

"What's your name?" he asked.

"Sara Soyazhe."

"New in Clover Creek?"

"Reasonably." I noticed that he was keeping his left hand out of my line of sight. He was probably planning to yank off the ring the minute my back was turned.

"How'd you hear about us?" Duane asked.

"A friend of mine bought a Dodge Cummins Turbo Diesel here. He gave you people a glowing recommendation."

"Really?" The salesman perked right up. "What's his name?"

"Jack Sunawavi."

"Oh, yeah . . . Jack." Duane's smile lost some of its glow. He brought the wedding band into view. No way was he messing with one of Jack Sunawavi's lady friends. "How does he like it?"

"He loves it. He had a little trouble with the cab light, though. It burned out."

"Well, tell Jack to bring it in. We'll replace it. The thirty-day warranty is still good."

"You haven't seen him?" I leaned against the polished fender of a brand-new Dodge Shadow. "I thought Jack brought it in last week."

"Oh, no, Jack hasn't been back here since he bought it."

"And when was that, Mr. Teller?"

"Oh, a couple of weeks ago. Saturday, I think."

"August the eighth?"

"That's right."

Four days after Billy died, I thought. And added, "Jack told me he bought it straight out of the showroom."

"Indeed he did!" Duane chuckled, shaking his head at an amusing memory. "That was the fastest auto loan that ever went through our finance office."

"What do you mean?" I asked.

235

"I mean, that ol' boy walked in here, pointed at the truck, and told me he wanted to buy it. I said the financing would take a few days. And that Jack—he reaches for his wallet and pulls out a wad that'd choke a horse. He slaps it down on the table and says, 'How's that for a down payment?' So we sat down and counted it. There was six thousand dollars on that table. Sixty one-hundred dollar bills. Cold green cash!" He let out a polite laugh. "I told my finance director to get right out here. I'll bet he was dreaming about Ben Franklin's face that night!"

"Jack put down six kay in cash?"

"You bet! He just laughed and said, 'There's more where that came from.' I didn't argue with the man. I handed him the title, the purchase agreement and a pen."

I fired a nervous glance at the stand-up digital clock on Duane's cluttered desk. "Ah . . . about the oil, Mr. Teller—"

"Oh! Oh, sure. Let me talk to our repairs manager, eh?" Broad, eager-to-please smile. "Then you can make that appointment."

Watching Duane Teller head for the repair shop, I felt more uneasy than ever. Jack Sunawavi had never struck me as the steadily-employed type. Yet he had walked into Remuda Dodge four days after Billy's death and plunked down six thousand in cash for a brand-new Dodge pickup.

According to Chief, the Nuche people in Cottonwood believed that Jack had pulled some sort of robbery up in Idaho. They must have seen him flashing those hundred dollar bills, too.

So how did you come by your new-found wealth, Jack? Who paid you that six thousand dollars? And, more importantly, *Why?*

Chapter Twelve

Cue let out a chuckle. "What's the matter, Sara? Don't you care for my little playtoy?"

Responding with a fussbudget face, I smeared sunblock on my upraised leg. My trail boot was resting on the rear bumper of Cue's favorite plaything, a classic white 1957 Cadillac convertible, complete with soaring tailfins, checkerboard chrome grille and spiffy whitewalled tires. A long-dead Texas longhorn had donated his headgear for the hood ornament.

"Kind of conspicuous, isn't it?" I replied. Lowering my leg, I poured some thick cream on my palm, then put my left boot on the bumper and continued the process.

"That's the whole idea, gal." Cue stood beside the tailfin, looking like any working Utah hand in cotton twill Brushpopper shirt and rivet-studded blue jeans. Judging from the grin beneath his sunglasses, he thoroughly enjoyed watching me lather my legs.

Giving the tailfin an affectionate pat, he added, "Got the idea from an ol' boy I worked for down in Texas. 'Broward,' he told me, 'when I drive down the streets of Uvalde, I want ever' damn son of a bitch to know who it is!' God, I surely loved that big ol' car of his. Told myself if I ever made it big, I was gonna buy me one just like it.'' Lovingly he stroked the chrome stripping. "Took me six years to find her, Sara. Cost me fifty-five thousand to have her restored. But she's worth every penny.''

I recapped my plastic bottle. "Fifty-five thousand? That's a lot.''

"Chickenshit money.''

I pushed the trunk lid a little higher. Cue saw me reaching for my backpack and surged forward. "Oh, no, you don't!" We had a brief tug of war. "Give it here, gal. Come on.''

"Hey! It's *my* backpack!''

"Ain't no woman gonna play pack mule when I'm around.'' He wrestled himself into the harness. "I'll do the luggin'. You just lead me there.''

Shouldering my canteen, I said, "Look, Cue, you're not a young man any more. Sitting in an air-conditioned office is no way to train for a desert hike.''

Moustache bristling, he took me by the shoulders and spun me around. "Don't you worry 'bout *me,* little gal! I could cross that saltpan with this here pack over one shoulder and *you* over the other.'' He slammed the trunk loudly. "Move out!''

So we left the Cuemobile parked on the shoulder of the road beside a rusting wire fence, and passed through the BIA gate on our way inland. It was just after eight-thirty, and I felt the sun's keen bite through the cotton of my oversized yellow T-shirt, though there were enough lengthy shadows beneath the sagebrush to allow for cool walking. And enough leftover morning dew to dampen my bike pants. Rimming the far horizon were the sandy beige Promontories, wreathed by a stark cerulean sky.

On and on we walked, Desert Angie and the intended victim of her "Goat Pasture" game. I was getting downright familiar with this turf. This was my third traverse in as many days.

I'd made the previous crossing last night, lugging my red one-gallon can full of used motor oil. I don't mind admitting that I had some misgivings about this plan. For one thing, the Sierra Club would never approve of what I was about to do. It would be pollution, pure and simple. But I was willing to sacrifice three square feet of desert arroyo to save the aspens of Lodestone Canyon.

For those of you who have never been fleeced by Toni Gee and her fellow grifters, a "Goat Pasture" game is one of the oldest cons around. The idea is to get the mark to buy a worthless piece of land in the mistaken belief that it would make him rich. My Section 206 game was a variation on this theme. I wanted to convince Cue Broward of the necessity of swapping this land for Lodestone Canyon.

As we walked along, my eyes swept the terrain ahead, seeking the trail marks I'd made the previous night. And . . . sure enough, there's the broken spire of that lonely Spanish bayonet. Angle off to the right a bit. Can't be more than three miles to that dry wash leading down to Salt Creek.

Cue kept up the pace without complaint. Tough old

buzzard. I could feel the weight of his blatant masculine stare on my calves and derrière, and wondered if he was getting ideas. Hmmmmm, maybe I should have put him out front.

I decided to engage him in conversation. Hopefully that would keep him from entertaining any naughty notions. Just one problem, though. What do you say to a man you suspect of killing your cousin?

"So how'd you get the name *Cue,* Mr. Broward?"

"Ohhhh, picked it up at a bar in Winnemucca."

"Pool player?"

"Not exactly." Wry chuckle. "One time I borrowed money from this ol' boy and bought some fancy-ass stock certificates. Turned out the slick that sold 'em to me was printin' 'em up in his garage. So the ol' boy I owed the money to—he showed up at that bar with his brother and a couple of in-laws. They sure do grow 'em big in Winnemucca." Memories drew another chuckle. "Well, Sara, they was almighty riled. I told 'em I was good for it, but they was of a mind to do somethin' hurtful. They come at me, all four at once, so I picked up that cuestick and we had at it!" Sidelong grin at me. "Alice come down to the jailhouse and bailed me out. The fine took every last dollar in egg money she had squirrelled away. Weren't the first time we were flat-busted broke, Alice 'n' me. Weren't the last, either."

"Did you ever pay him back?"

"Every last cent, Sara gal. Took me a few years, but I paid him off. Nowadays, every Christmas, I send that ol' boy a bottle of Jack Daniel's, just to show there's no hard feelin's." Cue's voice turned wistful.

"I got the money now, so I can afford to be generous, but I'll tell you somethin', Miss Sara. If I lost it all tomorrow, I wouldn't cry none. I'd do some cussin' and climb into that saddle and go string wire again. Ain't what I'd want to do, not by a long shot! But if'n I had to, I would. That's just the way I am. I'd tough it out. Sorta runs in my family."

Glancing over my shoulder, I added, "Including the girls?"

"Meanin'?"

"I've met Linda."

For a moment, Cue seemed to wilt under the pack's weight. Pale blue eyes became infinitely sad. "It would'a been a lot different if Alice had lived, you know." Lengthy sigh. "I tried to make a lady of that gal. Weren't no hand at it, I guess."

"The problem's a little more serious than that, Cue."

" 'Tain't no problem, Sara. She's just a tad on the wild side, that's all. She ain't done nothin' I didn't do when I was her age."

"You mean, at the age of twenty-five you were running around Winnemucca, punching out all the single guys?"

Cue's thick eyebrows lowered. His lower lip jutted angrily.

"We'd get there a whole lot faster, Miss Sara Soyazhe, if you paid a little more attention to that trail and a little less to my family!"

So I shut up. We passed through fields of waist-high greasewood, our boots kicking up gritty sand and loose pebbles. A large brown grasshopper landed on my boot, rode my instep buckaroo-style for a while, and then bounded off into a clump of june-grass. As we came out of the dry meadow, the slope tilted downward, angling off into a sandy gully and some broken rocks. Waggling my left hand, I led Cue into the defile. The waterless streambed gradually deepened and widened, meandering past clumps of small sandstone boulders and beds of powdery silt.

Of course, I knew exactly where we were going, but I took my own sweet time getting there. The scam would look better if Cue thought I hadn't been here in a while. Down the arroyo I marched, taking a hasty sip from my canteen, eager to make the sting. Behind me trudged the rancher, his breathing just a tad louder than before.

"Don't see too many ore-bearin' rocks 'round here, Sara," he remarked, opening his own canteen. "What in hell are you takin' out them leases on?"

"There!"

I pointed out a shady spot on the arroyo's sandstone wall, clearly identified by its proximity to a pale red buttress. It looked as if it belonged on Chartres cathedral. You couldn't miss it, not even in moonlight.

Together we dashed across the arroyo. Cue capped his canteen on the run. Standing on the soft loose sand, I gestured at the dark stain at the base of the crumbly wall. Cue said nothing, but his eyes widened in surprise.

"Smell it," I murmured.

After ditching the backpack, Cue flattened out like a commando and put his nose to the spot. Nostrils quivered. He blinked in amazement. Then, wetting his forefinger, he rubbed off a bit of the blackened sandstone and touched his tongue.

Almost at once, he spit into the sand. Rising to his knees, he shot me an eager inquisitive glance. "It *is*, isn't it?"

Grinning, I said nothing.

Blue eyes gleaming with avarice, Cue stood and hammered the spot with his boot heel. He broke off a fist-sized chunk and picked it up. Then, with trembling fingers, he produced a book of matches and struck one.

The tiny flame tickled Cue's sample. I heard a hissing sound and a muffled pop. And a blue flame flickered upward from the stone.

Cue let it drop. *"Oil!"*

Yes, indeedy, Mr. Broward. Oil. Black gold. Texas tea. The fluid that can bring whole continents to their knees. Trouble is, this batch has already been to the refinery.

"How!" Gritty hands seized my shoulders. He flashed a bright-eyed lunatic grin. "How'd you know it was there?"

"My great-grandmother told me."

"How'd *she* know?"

"Because her grandmother told her. Long story, Cue."

"Sit down, dammit! I want to hear it all."

I found a shady spot pillowed by cool, damp sand. I sat with my back to the sandstone. Scheherezade was weaving her tale, and never was there a more eager listener.

"My family once lived down near Utah Lake. Then all those white settlers started coming in after Appomattox. A few of our villages got raided, and Chief Black Hawk went on the warpath. Most of my people fled into the Wasatch—"

"But your great-grandma's grandaddy—he thought different, right?" Cue interrupted, sitting cross-legged before me. "He lit out for the desert, didn't he?"

Nodding, I smiled, "This land wouldn't feed a whole village. But a single family—that's a whole different story." I scratched my upraised knee. "My family lived ten years around here. Nobody knew they were here. Then that crooked old bastard N.C. Meeker, the Indian agent, he rounded them up and sent them to Towaoc. Great-grandmother was born there. When she was a little girl, her relatives told her all the stories about this place. And when I was a toddler, she repeated them to me."

I paused to catch my breath. Cue was staring in rapt attention. On with the tale, princess.

"Well, it got pretty cold during the winter, Great-grandmother said, and they burned greasewood to heat their lodge. Then they found something else. Great-grandmother called it a black rock that burns. The family always thought she meant some kind of coal." Pause for dramatic effect. "When I majored in geology, though, I learned that there isn't any coal in northern Utah. And that got me thinking." I gestured at the stained sandstone. "This is what you call a petroleum seep, Cue. There's a whole lake of oil down there. Natural gas, too. The gas puts pressure on the petroleum, forcing it up to the surface."

Licking parched lips, Cue rasped, "How much oil, Sara?"

"Rough guess? Oh, a reservoir as big as Lake Superior. Enough oil to fuel every automobile in Utah until the Twenty-sixth century." I patted the rough sandstone behind me. "I think it's an offshoot of that oil-rich Green River formation in Wyoming."

"And you *knew* it was here?"

"Let's just say I had my suspicions. I've been looking for this spot, every year now, for the past three summers. I didn't know exactly where it was. Great-grandmother said it was somewhere southwest of Penrose."

Trembling with excitement, Cue rose slowly to his feet. "The oil rights . . . you said they're *unassigned?*"

Pert Angie smile, followed by a vigorous nod.

Blue eyes goggled at me. "And no one's *ever* taken out a lease?"

Ladylike shake of the head.

Letting out an earsplitting whoop, Cue lifted both fists and did a quirky war dance in the sand. Round and round he whirled, like a demented flamenco dancer. Intoxicated with the thought of limitless wealth, he cut loose with a prolonged burst of exuberant laughter.

And then he remembered me. His gaze feverish, he reached down, grabbed my wrists, and hauled me to my feet.

"Not a word to anyone! You hear me, woman? You don't tell *anyone!* This is our secret. Understand?"

I winced at the harshness of his grip. "Does this mean we're partners?"

246

"Damned right! Your schoolteachin' days are over, little gal. You're workin' for me now." Hugging me close, he shouted, "Professor Soyazhe? Horseshit! Couple of years, Sara, I'll buy the whole goddamned college and make you *president!*"

After letting me go, Cue scampered around the arroyo like a panicky chimpanzee, gathering up our hiking gear, kicking dirt over the footprints leading to the oil stain. He took the lead on the way back, chuckling to himself, moving along with a bouncy, skipping stride.

"Goddammit, Sara, quit draggin' your feet!" he roared.

Sweat dampened the T-shirt between my shoulder blades. The canteen slapped my right hip. "Cue! You don't have to run."

"We got to get home. I got to put Denny to work on them leases. Got to talk to Longhurst, too. Shit! What do you call that thing again?"

"Section 206," I replied, trying to keep pace with him. "Tell Longhurst there's already a request-for-transfer on file with the BLM. All he has to do is approve it."

"You sure them Indians are willin' to give it up?"

"Positive! The tribal council put this tract on the Section 206 transfer list back in the Seventies," I told him, remembering what Ned Pahaka had said. "There were no takers."

Cue uttered a hoarse chuckle. "Sure woulda been if them ol' boys down in Houston had talked to that great-grandmomma of yours!" He cast me an impatient glance. "When do I get the permit to drill?"

"One thing at a time, Cue. First, we have to get this tract out of the BIA, and that won't be too hard. My people will jump at the chance to swap this land for Lodestone Canyon." For once, I was being absolutely sincere. "Places like Lodestone are sacred to us."

"So all Longhurst has to do is sign some papers."

"Right. The minute this tract comes under the Bureau of Land Management, you can file your application for the mineral rights." I displayed a glorious Angie smile. "And the oil is yours!"

For a moment there, I thought old Cue was going to kick up his heels. But instead he let out another tremolo of triumphant laughter and rubbed his hands eagerly.

"All *right!* Sara, we're meetin' at my place tomorrow mornin'. Ten o'clock sharp. You, me and Denny." Shrewd-eyed squint. "Maybe I'll have Eames and the boys over in the afternoon. Give 'em the bad news first hand. If they still want to cut timber, they're gonna have to deal with Dan Kaniache."

"I don't think Karl Eames will be too pleased to hear that."

"Them's the breaks, my gal." Vulpine smile. "Man's got to look out for his own best interests, right? I can't see shittin' 'round with Lodestone when I've got all that oil a-bubblin' up back there."

My, my, how quickly Cue had switched to the singular!

Stifling a wry grin, I asked, "You really wanted to cut that aspen, didn't you?"

"I ain't one to turn down a dollar, Sara. 'Sides, it's kind of a game I play with Gail's daddy."

"I'm not sure I follow."

"Oh, that ol' Mormon son of a bitch is always tryin' to squeeze me out." Cue shifted the backpack slightly. "When I heard he'd bought into that fiberboard company, I knew what he was up to. He was gonna jack up the price on everythin' they sold to Sager-Broward Construction. Once we were hurtin', he'd offer to buy me out." He gave a self-satisfied chuckle. "So I went him one better. Went after the aspen his fiberboard company needs."

Seeing a sudden opening, I remarked, "Of course, having Longhurst in your pocket didn't exactly hurt."

"Not a bit, gal. Lumber's a real competitive industry." He gave me a jolly wink. "It's mighty nice havin' a peek at all them Forest Service RFPs before they go out."

My heartbeat quickened. "Did Longhurst tell you about Shavano?"

"Hell, no. One o' them damned kids did."

I frowned in confusion. "Kids?"

"Yeah. One o' them college kids Ty busted. He said he'd been up to the canyon with Bill Shavano." Scratching his sunburned nose, Cue added, "I went right downtown to see Longhurst, asked him what the hell's goin' on. Why his boy was showin' them pointy-heads around. That was the first Al'd heard about it, and that's when I found out about that goddamned memo Shavano wrote." Ferocious grin. "When I got done with Al Longhurst, that ol' boy was fetchin' 'round pretty desperate for toilet paper. 'If there's a problem in this office,' I told him, 'you damned well let me know!' "

"Why did Ty Braddock go after those kids?" I asked.

"Oh, I ran into Ty downtown that Saturday. Then Gail come along, all bent out o' shape 'cause them pointy-heads were passin' out leaflets in front of the tabernacle. Save the Canyon—that kind of shit. Ty said he'd take care of it." Cue shot me a canny sidelong look. "Next thing I know, there's a story in the *Herald* 'bout the big dope bust at the junior high school. Paper said ol' Ty found ten pounds of marijuana in that trunk."

"Any idea how it got there, Cue?"

The rancher burst into laughter. "Maybe them pointy-heads put it there and clean forgot all about it. I hear that locoweed affects the memory."

I kept right on probing. "So that's how you found out that Bill Shavano was disloyal to the brand."

"More or less."

"Did Shavano try anything else to stop you? Call Washington? Anything like that?"

"Not that I'm aware of." Suspicious glance. "Why are *you* so damned interested?"

Backpedaling away from that hot topic, I replied, "There can't be any problems with Lodestone, Cue, or the deal's off. To do a 206, we must have an equivalent tract. Lodestone's the only one that fills the bill."

"Don't worry 'bout it, Sara. Longhurst'll take care of everythin'."

Lapsing into silence, I reflected on Cue's words. Of course, he could very well be lying. He might know all about Billy's land-transfer scheme.

Ahhhhh . . . but if he *knew,* then why did he fall so hard for my Goat Pasture game?

And, no mistake, gang—ol' Cue went for it. That kind of enthusiasm is hard to fake. The lord of the Circle B actually believed there was a vast petroleum reservoir beneath the sands of that nameless arroyo.

Doubts simmered at the back of my mind. If Cue hadn't known about my cousin's plan, then where was his motive to kill Billy?

Sure, Billy was a threat to the proposed timber cut. But he was a low-key threat, not that much different from the Tribe of DAN. It didn't make sense. Why would Cue murder Billy and not take action against those three valiant environmentalists?

Cue lied about the kids? Suggested the frame-up himself?

No, Angie, that doesn't quite cut it. Cue's offhanded description of Ty Braddock and wife Gail has the ring of truth. I could definitely see Ty trying to win favor with Miss Gail by hanging a frame on those three college kids.

Besides, Cue had left me with the impression that Lodestone's aspen really wasn't that important to him. The proposed timber cut was just another gambit in the never-ending chess game between Cue and his Mormon father-in-law. Had Cue truly needed the timber, he wouldn't have been so willing to swap for it— not even for the promised riches of Oil Dorado!

Hmmmmm, let's sidetrack the impressions for the moment and concentrate on the facts. Fact Number One—Broward was nowhere near the Circle B or his many business concerns the Tuesday morning Billy

251

got killed. Well, I had the number. Why not call the mysterious Mr. R.C. down in Salt Lake and have a chat? Find out which hotel Cue checked into and then get the exact time he checked out.

I did some quick mental mileage calculation. If it was anytime after six a.m., there was no way Cue could have made it to Dynamite Pass. Not in a car, anyway.

So I hustled along, four steps behind the rancher, my ballcap brim low on my forehead and the sun-kissed sage tickling my hips. Up ahead, smothered in heat haze, was that motorized mirage from the Age of Elvis, the Cuemobile, behind the rusty fence.

Cue spoke up. "Well, now! Looks like we got some company."

Looking up, I saw two Nuche men step off the caretaker's porch. Ned Pahaka I recognized at once. The other man was a quarter-century older, thick-bellied, bull-necked, big-shouldered and with a face like a Colorado cliffside. Baggy jeans and a short-sleeved madras shirt covered his huge belly like a maternity smock. The sight of that face stirred vague feelings of recognition. I knew I'd seen him somewhere before—and recently, too—but I couldn't quite remember where.

Welcoming smile from Ned. "Hi, Sara! Don't tell me you're back again."

"Hi, Ned." *And thank you very much for the corroborating statement. You've just raised my credibility in Cue Broward's eyes.*

The older Nuche man shook his head wryly. "What the hell are you doin' out here, Cue?"

"Doctor says I need the exercise, Dan." Cue ushered me forward. "Sara, this here's my good friend and elk-huntin' partner, Dan Kaniache. Dan, meet Sara Soyazhe." He reached for Ned's hand. "Don't believe I know your name, young fella."

While the men got introduced, I stood there with a frozen smile on my face. And a deer-in-the-headlights expression in my eyes.

Dan Kaniache!?

I wanted to slide down the nearest badger burrow. Of all the people to run into in this godforsaken salt-pan—Dan Kaniache, the chairman of the Northern Ute Tribal Council! Despite the midday desert heat, I experienced a sudden clammy chill. Dan couldn't stop looking at me. His dark eyes narrowed. "What did you say your name was?"

"Sara Soyazhe."

His hard mouth tensed thoughtfully as he struggled to remember. "Do I know you?"

Indeed you do, Mr. Kaniache. You're the tribal elder who watched me do the Hoop Dance at the Cascade Springs powwow. You also saw me talking to Billy. *And if you mention that to Cue Broward, I'm sunk!*

Hastily I manufactured a schoolgirl expression. "I don't think so, Mr. Kaniache."

Quizzical gaze from the Nuche elder. "Where are you from?"

"Rock Springs, Wyoming."

"Wyoming?"

He wasn't buying it.

"Actually, I was born in Towaoc." I struggled to keep the shrill note of panic out of my voice. "We left the reservation when I was a baby. Daddy went to work for the oil industry.''

My inspired prevarication gave him pause. Stroking his blunt chin, Dan asked, ''How long have you been in Utah?''

''Since June. I just moved to Ogden.''

I could have put Dan's mind at ease by mentioning the powwow, but I didn't dare. I couldn't risk him mentioning Billy—that would blow the scam for sure. So I stood there, clutching my canteen with shaking hands, watching desperately as Dan Kaniache struggled to remember where he'd seen me before, and hoping against hope that the memory would elude him.

Just then, Ned Pahaka inadvertently came to my rescue. Tilting his thumb toward the sagebrush, he remarked, ''Find anything interesting back there, Sara?''

Cue stiffened at once. Alarm flickered in those blue eyes. Undoing the clasp, he wriggled out of the harness and chucked my backpack into the back seat of his Cadillac.

Flashing a regretful smile, he drawled, ''You know, boys, I'd love to stick 'round and chew the fat. But it's gettin' awful hot, and I promised the little dolly a tall, cool drink.'' He gave a nod at the caretaker. ''Nice makin' your acquaintance, Pahaka.''

With that, the anxious rancher seized my elbow and hustled me into the Caddy's passenger seat. In less than three minutes, we were underway and I watched Ned and Dan vanish into a billowing cloud of dust. Judging from the expression on the Nuche elder's face, he thought Cue and I were having an affair.

I touched my forehead with the back of my wrist and let out a long, shallow exhalation. Now that's what I call a *narrow* escape!

Cue kept his Stetson brim low to ward off the slipstream. His pistolero moustache arched in stern disapproval. "Sara gal, if'n you want my signature on any kind o' contract, you better learn to keep your mouth shut!"

"I didn't tell him anything!" I protested hotly.

"Oh, no!? Then how come that fella knew you've been out there a-lookin'?"

"I ran into Ned in the desert last week, that's all," I lied, raising my hands haplessly. "I told him I was studying formations. I never told him what I was looking for."

"You told him pretty damned near *enough!*" Thoroughly agitated, Cue stepped down hard on the accelerator. I watched the needle creep past seventy-five. *"Formations?* Shit! Why didn't you put up a neon sign while you were at it!?"

"Cue—!"

His sinewy fingers tightened on the steering wheel. "From now on, woman, you don't go near that damned arroyo less'n I'm with you. Got that?"

Folding my arms, I slumped in the plush Caddy seat, momentarily content to yield to my new partner's wishes. Anything to advance the sting. Still, I made sure Cue Broward got a good look at my fussbudget face. "Whatever you say, Mr. Broward."

* * *

Well, Cue did mix me that tall, cool drink at his private bar in the Circle B rumpus room. Together we sketched out the rough details of our new joint venture, tentatively entitled *South Promontory Development Enterprises, Inc.* Cue promised to have Dennis Simms draw up a draft contract agreement for my review. Then he dismissed me with a noisy cheek kiss and went out to have a look at the herd.

By the time I got to Cottonwood, it was just after four-thirty. I dropped in at the Raspberry Ridge Motel, eager to compare notes with my grandfather, but Chief didn't answer the buzz. So I left him a note—in Anishinabemowin—and wandered into the motel's cocktail lounge in search of the public telephone.

I found one about ten feet away from the big Steinway piano. Very strange decor in there—an odd blend of the Old West and Art Deco Manhattan. Hopalong Cassidy meets the Fabulous Baker Boys. Instead of being sprawled on the piano, the blond chanteuse was belly-up at the bar, screeching with soprano laughter at the off-color jokes of a trio of diligent drinkers. Maybe that's why they call it Happy Hour.

I dialed Mr. R.C.'s number in Salt Lake and caught a busy signal. I went for a brief stroll on the shady side of the motel, then tried again. Still busy.

Well, I could have found a comfortable chaise lounge in the motel's air-conditioned lobby and waited for Chief's return, but the entrance to the Topanas National Forest was right on the outskirts of town, and I was dressed for the outdoors, anyway. I was still a little bit uneasy about the murder scene. I still had that nagging feeling that I'd overlooked something.

So it was back into the Accord and north on 302. About three miles past the big brown Forest Service sign, I picked up a two-laned blacktop angling off into rugged Alpine terrain. The metal sign, peppered with rifle slugs, read "County Road 10—Dynamite Pass." A very steep uphill road, that—the kind Utah closes for the winter every Columbus Day. A low, forested ridgeline paced me on the right, the gentle side of Lodestone's high, vertical cliffs.

Ten minutes later, I drove into the familiar upland meadow. Slowing the car to a crawl, I inched along until I spotted the telltale lodgepole pine with the gashed trunk, then I hit the brake, taking care to keep all four wheels on the asphalt. I was leaving no tire tracks for possible identification. After switching off the ignition I put on my ballcap and sauntered over there for a second look.

Odd feeling of *déjà vu*. The tracks had hardly weathered at all during the intervening week. I spied Billy's logger treads and Ty Braddock's deep, pointy-toed imprints and the shallow, lopsided traces of the unknown visitor. Who had come up here with the McCulloch chainsaw? Cue Broward, fresh from Salt Lake City? Karl Eames, intent on removing the biggest obstacle to the Lodestone Canyon cut? Or Jack Sunawavi, obligingly toting a chainsaw for his best buddy, the real murderer, Deputy Ty Braddock?

Frowning glances at the slim lodgepoles and the blue camas and the ripe alpine grass. Detailed scrutiny of the footprint chaos at the foot of the disfigured lodgepole. More feelings of irritation. *Dammit, Billy, what did I miss? What did I overlook on my first trip up here?*

I glanced at the marked lodgepole. The chainsaw gash resembled an eerie smile. I had the spooky feeling Dynamite Pass itself was laughing at me.

I formulated a checklist. Billy, Ty, the visitor and the paramedics. All footprints accounted for? *Right.*

Ty tracks leading to the moraine? *None.*

Short stump high on the wounded lodgepole, marking the spot where the hefty bough broke off? *There it is—straight overhead.*

Jumble of confused footprints where Bill's body lay? *Right there.*

Gritting my teeth, I cast another frustrated look around. Damn! What was missing?

Memory dredged up the Ty Braddock story that had appeared in the *Saguache County Herald.* I could hear the deputy's voice booming in a far corner of my mind.

". . . I saw Shavano's truck parked by the side of the road. I stopped to investigate. I climbed a steep ridge and saw the injured Shavano some distance away, covered by a lodgepole limb."

I felt a sudden transcendent shimmer of excitement. My wide-eyed gaze pingponged back and forth across the pass, zipping from the pine-needle carpet at the foot of the lodgepoles to the rows of fragile blue camas to the grass stalks rustling in the slight breeze.

Where's the lodgepole limb?

My gaze climbed the tall trunk, zeroing in on the blunt stump forty-five feet away. I ran to the tree and touched its bark. My fingers came away sticky with pine sap.

So you didn't lie about that part, Ty. There *was* a

heavy bough covering Billy's body. You saw it and reported it. But what happened to it?

I felt the fine hairs prickling on the back of my neck. I knew the paramedics hadn't disposed of the limb—they were far too busy trying to save my cousin. They would have simply tossed it aside and gone on with their work.

And Ty Braddock couldn't have done it. After all, why would he have gone to the trouble of disposing of a huge lodgepole limb and then *mentioned its presence* in his official report?

No, only the killer would have had a compelling reason to remove the limb from the murder scene.

I had a pretty good idea why, but I needed some confirmation, and in particular, a closer look at that stump.

It was easier said than done. At five foot four, not only was I too short for the Rockettes, I was way too small to reach the lodgepole's lowermost branch. It hovered tantalizingly five feet beyond my reach, and the nearest stepladder was back in Cottonwood.

Fervently I wished for a logger's arrival, preferably one equipped with climbing spikes. As I examined the gray, thin-scaled bark more closely, I realized that a logger had already been here. My thumb encountered a small circular hole on the right. I found its mate on the left. Someone had gone up this tree wearing spikes. The killer, perhaps?

Smiling with satisfaction, I walked through the forest, picking up dead, windblown branches, and broke off thumb-sized pieces eight inches long. Returning to the tree, I stuck one of these crude pitons in the lowermost hole. *Voila!* Instant stepladder!

Up the trunk I went, mouth firmly set, with the arches of my bare feet wedged into the junction of lodgepole trunk and wooden piton. My trail boots waited far below. On such delicate underpinnings, I needed the sure sensitivity of bare skin to feel for solid footing.

If the killer had made these spike holes, then he had certainly come to Dynamite Pass well-prepared. A chainsaw and climbing spikes. Sounded as if he had carefully thought it all through.

The stump loomed just overhead. I climbed a little further, then deposited my derrière on a sap-stained bough. I caught a dizzying glimpse of the meadow forty feet below. It was like being perched on the flagpole of a four-story building. Heart thumping, I hugged the lodgepole trunk with my left arm.

My free hand gingerly prodded the stump's smooth leading edge. Fresh sap enmeshed my fingertips. Flecks of sawdust clung to the stunted limb's sticky underside.

Well, I thought, here's more proof—if proof were needed—that cousin Bill was murdered. Whoever had climbed up here had cleaved the weighty bough very nicely with that McCulloch chainsaw. Just one question, though. How did he persuade my cousin to stand down there, meek and motionless, while the bough came plummeting down?

The answer is, he didn't. He smashed Billy's skull with the real murder weapon and carried him to the foot of this tree, then he donned his spikes and, with the chainsaw hitched to his safety harness, started climbing.

The fallen limb had been camouflage, pure and

simple. Stage dressing to convince the onlookers that my cousin's death had been accidental.

Wait a minute—if that's the case, though, then why did he remove the severed limb *after* Ty Braddock and the paramedics had departed? And why had he let Ty Braddock, a trained lawman, see that chainsaw-smooth break on the lodgepole limb?

My lips tensed in confusion. None if it made any sense.

I came up with two possibilities. One, Ty was an accomplice, and he knew the scene was a set-up the moment he called it in.

Two, the killer had *wanted* Ty to see it.

That option seemed to be sheer fantasy. Yet, the more I thought about it, the more likely it seemed that the scene had been staged especially for the deputy's benefit.

But why? Why show Miss Gail's favorite deputy concrete evidence of foul play?

And why had Braddock covered it up?

What if Ty himself was the killer? Then the bough's disappearance made perfect sense. He would have let the paramedics get a real good look at it, and then he would have hung around after the helicopter's departure and reduced the incriminating limb to kindling.

Frowning, I looked to the towering cumulus clouds for further inspiration. My reverie shattered when something exploded the tree trunk three inches above my head.

KAAAAAROWWWWW! The rifle shot reverberated across Dynamite Pass like a prolonged peal of thunder. Toothpick splinters and shards of lodgepole bark peppered my ballcap.

Sniper! I thought frantically, *and he's got the range!*

And there I was, perched on that high limb like a sleeping owl—the perfect target.

Chapter Thirteen

I reacted instinctively, hurling myself face down on the narrow limb. An angry hornet, emitting a thin supersonic shriek, zoomed through my outflung hair. In its wake came another thunderous *KAAAAA-ROWWWWW* from that distant high-powered rifle.

Yeah, he had the range, all right. For all I knew, a third steel-jacketed bullet was blazing down the fire-track, intent on blowing a great big hole in Charlie Blackbear's favorite granddaughter. I had to get out of the line of fire—*fast*.

So I rolled off the limb, letting gravity handle my getaway, hoping that another sizable limb blocked my path of descent. Hoping, too, that I wouldn't hit it hard enough to break ribs.

Paws of bristly lodgepole needles raked my bare arms and legs. I cried out as my shoulder snapped a small branch. Suddenly, I was clear of the tangle, dropping toward another hefty bough.

Grunting, I caught it at the juncture of stomach and hip, slapped my palms on it, and performed a graceful Olympic spin. Spying another solid branch off to my right, I shoved off with both hands and let myself plummet.

Thirty feet above ground is no place for an Olympic routine, but I really had no choice. I had to stay on the move. If I hesitated, even for a moment, he'd put the crosshairs right on me.

I arched my spine and tagged the springy branch with my lumbar curve. My cap went spinning into space. Twigs slashed at my swirling hair. Knifing my legs forward, I rolled off that branch and hurtled toward the lowermost tier.

Perfect catch! Round and round the limb I twirled, losing speed with every rotation. Had this been a high school meet back home in Duluth, no doubt Coach Hansen would have been leading the cheers. *Bravo, Angie!* But I wasn't patting myself on the back, not just yet. I still had a dozen feet to go before I hit ground. And rarely do lady gymnasts attempt a dismount from a second-story window.

I released my grip, and dropped like a ripe acorn, then forward-rolled in midair in order to get my feet under me. No good, though. I was running out of airspace, and I knew I was coming down all wrong. So I crumpled into a fetal ball, forced my muscles to go slack, and waited for the fearful impact.

The crash was rough; I screamed like a cat. Fortunately the undisturbed pine needles offered a meager cushion. The jolt took my breath but not my consciousness. Bright stars danced in my field of vision. Ignoring the throbbing pain in my left shoulder and sick with vertigo, I forced myself to crawl forward, seeking cover behind the lodgepole's roots.

My face felt like a hot balloon. I shook my head

vigorously, trying to clear it, but that only made the nausea worse.

A small dust geyser erupted three feet from my toes, punctuated by the rifle's deep-throated roar. I scrambled behind a hefty taproot, wondering who was squeezing the trigger up there. An image of a giggly Miss Linda suddenly sprang to mind. I shuddered at the thought of those sick aquamarine eyes peering through a rifle scope.

KAAAAAROWWWWW! My ears tingled in recognition. I'd heard that sound plenty of times on the Gunflint Trail. A Magnum, unless I missed my guess. A little too throaty a roar for Linda's Winchester. And judging from the interval between those treetop shots, it was probably a bolt-action model.

So maybe it wasn't Linda. Then again, that Winchester might not be the only long gun in the Broward family arsenal.

Another dusty plume, this one a good distance to the right. I relaxed a little. Whoever it was, he wasn't shooting for effect. He was trying to flush me from the cover of this lovely thick trunk.

No thanks, pal. I like it just fine where I am.

The interval between the bullet strike and the sound of the gunshot meant he was firing from a good distance away. Four or five hundred yards, perhaps. Hmmmmm, that put him up on the high aspen-covered ridge. An ideal perch for a sniper, offering a panoramic view of Dynamite Pass.

When no further rifle bullets came calling, I sneaked a peek over the taproot and let my gaze roam the wooded slope. Tense seconds passed, and then I saw a flock of spooked nighthawks cartwheeling out of the trees. Found you, bastard!

I elevated my gaze past the treeline, up into the scree at the crest of the ridge. Sure enough, the sniper burst into the open, running like hell for the summit. From my vantage point, he was a tiny dark-haired figure toting a rifle. My mouth fell open at the sight of his open black fringed vest flapping in the skyline breeze.

"Sunawavi!" I gasped.

Why was I not surprised?

Hello, Jack. So that's what you've been up to all week, eh? He'd been trailing me at a distance, just itching for a chance to use the bolt-action .340 Weatherby Magnum cradled so lovingly in his pickup truck.

Graveyard humor brought a sassy smile to my lips. *That's three times you didn't score . . . asshole!*

You know, had I been Tim Holt or Chito Rafferty or any of those other TV cowboys Billy and I used to laugh at on Saturday afternoons, no doubt I would have limped over to old Paint, crawled into the saddle, and galloped after the varmint. But no, not me. With no gun and no transportation, I was very much content to lie there and tally up the bruises. Swollen hip. Throbbing shoulder. Headache like a sorority hangover.

So I stayed there, and heard myself sigh and moan. And took a fierce and transcendent joy in the fact that I was still alive.

* * *

"This has got to be the dumbest thing you have ever done," said Chief. We were sitting in the Accord's front seat, my grandfather and I, parked out at the end of Dead Horse Road. Just beyond the windshield, flanked by a generous box elder, stood Number Twelve, a.k.a. the Sunawavi residence, a moldering, rickety bungalow sharply outlined in the bright moonlight. There were patched screens on the windows, and the porch's peeling rail was missing several teeth. Obviously, the word *handyman* did not appear on Jack's resume.

"Don't try to talk me out of it, Chief."

I clambered out of the passenger seat, still clad in T-shirt, bike shorts and trail boots. Behind me, I heard the driver's door slam shut.

"Are you sure you didn't land on your head when you came out of that tree?"

"I know what I'm doing."

"What if she ain't alone in there? What if *he* came home while we were at the motel?"

Heading up the broken cement walk, I glared at my grandfather. "Thanks, Chief. Build up my confidence, why don't you?"

"Dammit, Angie, the man just took a shot at you! Are you gonna stand on his welcome mat and let him try again?"

"He won't try anything with you here."

"Really? You got that in writing, huh?" Shaking his head, Chief tagged along at my side. "You're running off half-cocked again."

"Don't worry. This'll work," I said, hoping Jack's mother would be suitably impressed by my wild hair and leg scratches. "Besides, I don't think he's home.

He's been avoiding this place all week. You told me that. Why would he come back now?''

"To get some more ammo, maybe?''

I climbed the wobbly steps with my heart in my mouth. Floorboards creaked beneath my trail boots. Nearly three hours had passed since my encounter with Jack Sunawavi up at Dynamite Pass. During that time, I'd driven to the Raspberry Ridge Motel, knocked on Chief's door, and asked to borrow his bathroom. A cold, damp facecloth felt good on all those scrapes and bruises, and while pampering myself, I had brought my grandfather up to date.

Chief was right, of course. This was a wild-ass gambit and one with a very slim chance of success. But if I could con Jack's mother into revealing his whereabouts, I could resolve the Sunawavi problem before he popped up again with a blazing Weatherby.

My knuckles rattled the screen frame. For a long moment, all I heard was the triphammer beating of my own heart, and then the shuffle of slippered feet disturbed the darkness. A small lamp went on, revealing a plump, pillow-backed sofa, a hooked throw rug, a portable color TV and a pair of Navaho sand paintings. A large, broad-hipped Nuche woman in a floral cotton bathrobe loomed in the doorway.

Dolores Sunawavi looked surprisingly like her son. Same taut lips and narrow nose and shrewd, slitted, pebbly eyes. But her face was rounder, softer, nearly cherubic. Her gray hair hung loosely in twin braids and was fastened with rawhide thread. She kept her arms folded tightly, holding the robe closed, containing her hefty bosom. I doubted if a tape measure could reach all the way around those hips. Stocky brown legs descended from the robe's hem, flowing into worn, torn leather slippers.

Her speculative gaze drifted from me to Chief. Clearing his throat, my grandfather said, "Mrs. Sunawavi?"

A nod was her only reply.

"We'd like to speak to your son."

Dolores's shoulders sagged wearily, and I knew she'd heard that particular phrase before. "He ain't here, mister."

So I went into my act. Wild-eyed Angie.

"I don't believe you!" Cupping my hand against the screen mesh, I hollered, "Sunawavi! Damn you! Get your ass out here! Right now, dammit!"

Coming in on cue, Chief grabbed my shoulders. "Take it easy, Miss Soyazhe. Look, his truck's not even in the driveway."

Jack's mother's eyes glimmered with interest. If ever you set a trap for a woman, always be sure to bait it with curiosity.

"What do you want with Jack?" she asked.

"There's been an accident . . ." Chief began.

"*Accident*, my ass!" I shouted, channelling both my fear and my anger into the performance. "He ran me off the road on *purpose,* the son of a bitch! Brand-new Dodge diesel pickup truck. Ran me right off the goddamned road! He thought I didn't get the license number, but I did!"

Dolores's dark eyes widened in maternal concern. My act had been a little too convincing. "Where is he?" she asked.

"That's what we'd like to know!" I shouted.

Pushing open the screen door, Dolores grabbed my

wrist. Plump features tensed with worry. "Where did this happen? Was he hurt?"

"Hurt?" I echoed, pulling my wrist free. "Last I saw of him, he was riding down County Road 10, laughing his fool head off. Big joke! My car's down in the gulch with a great big dent in the door. We'll see if it's so goddamned funny when he gets done talking to my lawyer!"

She looked as if she wanted to slap me. "When did this happen?"

"This afternoon—just around five o'clock," I replied, lowering my tone of voice just a tad. "This Dodge truck came barrelling around the bend, doing about seventy. I pulled away from the center line, but he crossed right over and clipped me on the door. Did it on purpose, too! Asshole! If I hadn't been wearing my harness . . . ." Conjuring up memories of those bullet strikes, I vented all those suppressed emotions. *"That son of yours nearly killed me!"*

"Take it easy, Sara." Chief massaged my shoulders, then turned to Jack's mother. "I'm afraid I witnessed it, ma'am. Your son's truck hit the Chevy. I gave Miss Soyazhe, here, a ride into town."

The woman seemed strangely relieved. "You saw him, too, then."

"Yes, ma'am. Up near Dynamite Pass." Chief showed her a solemn look. "We don't want any trouble, Mrs. Sunawavi. We just want to talk to Jack, that's all. Sara needs to know the name of his insurance company."

"Have you reported the accident yet?" she asked.

"I will! Don't worry!" Fierce Angie face. "And I sure won't forget to mention that he left the scene!"

270

Dolores turned to my grandfather. She preferred not to deal with the distraught young woman. "Look, mister, I ain't seen my boy in days. I don't know when he'll be back."

"Bullshit!" I cried.

Flashing me a taut-lipped glare, Dolores added, "God's honest truth! Jack walked out of here a week ago Saturday. He said he was goin' over to the Briar Patch."

A week ago Saturday. That was the night Jack accosted me at the bar. He hadn't been home since *then?*

I remembered Jack's animated conversation with Ty Braddock in the club parking lot that night, and I wondered if the deputy had advised Jack to lie low. Then I mentally kicked myself. Couldn't be! Ty doesn't know where Jack is. He proved that yesterday.

So what did Ty tell his Nuche buddy? Why did it send Jack fleeing into the night? And why had Jack, snug and safe in his hideout, suddenly decided to go gunning for me?

Chief spoke up. "Is the truck insured, Mrs. Sunawavi?"

"Sure is. Jack's got the certificate 'round here somewhere."

"Could you get it for us? We need the name of the company."

"I don't know." Horizontal wrinkles appeared on her broad forehead. "Jack sure hates it when I go through his stuff."

"This is a waste of time," I said, tapping my thumb against my collarbone. "Let's call *my* insurance company. They'll take care of Mr. Sunawavi."

The woman's mouth gaped in apprehension. Instantly she clutched Chief's wrist. "Please, mister! You've got to give me a little time. I'll find that certificate for you." A wheedling tone altered the pitch of her voice. "Please don't call the girl's insurance company!"

"Why not?" asked Chief.

" 'Cause they'll register a complaint with the sheriff. Reckless drivin' or somethin'." Her fearful tone was quite genuine. "Sheriff Mortensen hates my boy. He always has. He'll put Jack on the road gang, sure as shit!"

"It's not my car, ma'am."

Desperation shining in those dark eyes, Dolores turned to me. "You come back tomorrow, Miss Soyazhe, and I'll have that certificate for you. I promise. Jack's insurance will pay for your repairs. And if'n they don't, my boy's good for it. He's got some money now. I seen it." Gently she squeezed my hand. "Please don't turn him in. He's got a job now, and he's makin' good money. He's just startin' to get it all back together."

My features tensed with disgust. Not for poor Dolores, mind you, but for Jack Sunawavi, who had reduced his mother's life to one long series of apologies. How many years had she been making excuses for him? Fifteen? Twenty?

"He came right over the center line," I replied, my voice low.

Chief shot me a disapproving look. He didn't savor deceit. He disliked upsetting that poor woman with so flagrant a prevarication. I showed him an apologetic glance. All right, *Nimishoo,* I promise not to be quite so hardnosed.

272

Dabbing at the tear trails, Dolores sniffled. "J-Jack w-wasn't always like that, you know. He was a good boy. He never complained when I sent him to the store." Hastily she wiped her upper cheek. "It—it was high school changed him. He got in with trash—"

"Like Ty Braddock?" I interjected.

Nodding, she added tearfully, "That Ty, he wears the badge, but he's just trash. When Jack broke into that hardware store, it was Ty what put him up to it. Jack told me so himself. Judge Hillstrom, he gave my boy six months on the road gang. He wouldn't have done it to a white boy, but he done it to mine." Her anxious gaze flitted from me to Chief. "Jack's been in trouble plenty, I know, but he was turnin' his life around. If only she hadn't left him. That's what turned him so mean. When Cindy left, it tore him up inside."

"Cindy Polenana?" I remarked.

Puzzled look from Dolores. "You know her?"

"Vaguely," I replied, struggling to keep my tone conversational. Bad habit I've got, thinking out loud. "Way I heard it, though, Jack drove her off."

"That's a *damned lie!*" Mother rising to the beloved offspring's defense. But there was an edge in Dolores's voice that only jealousy could have sharpened. "That snotty bitch! She thought she was too damned good for my boy. Jack treated her just fine. She ran out on my boy and took up with that forest ranger."

"Forest ranger?" Angie the Echo.

"Bill Shavano!" Balling her fists, Dolores shook her head in misery. "Everything woulda been fine if

273

he hadn't come along." She seemed to blame my cousin for Jack's fall from grace. "He had his own woman. What did he want with *her?*" Snuffling gasp. "I wish he'd never met Cindy. I wish he'd stuck with that white gal of his—that one from the Circle B."

Cloaking my own growing irritation, I wondered how my grandfather was reacting to this posthumous abuse of Billy. To my astonishment Chief stepped forward and patted the woman's shoulder. "It's going to be all right, Mrs. Sunawavi. It'll work out somehow."

And then, with his palm against my spine, he ushered me toward the porch steps. "We'll be back tomorrow."

Features set in a warpath scowl, Chief propelled me down the walkway.

"Sometimes your patience astounds me," I whispered, switching to our people's language. "What gives, *Nimishoo?* You didn't give me a chance to learn the location of Jack's hideout."

"Hush, *Noozis.* We weren't going to learn anything more. She has no idea where her son is." Chief opened the car door for me. "She's worried about him, though. She fears something has happened to him. Something very bad."

"How could you tell that?"

"Easy. I have children—you don't." Flicking on the headlights, he added, "About Billy . . . are you thinking what I'm thinking?"

Solemn nod. "Miss Fancy Gal. Billy's old girl friend. You heard what the lady said. 'White woman from the Circle B.' "

274

"That narrows it down, *Noozis*. It's either the wife or the daughter."

"I think it may be the wife."

"Why do you say that?"

As we drove back to the motel, I explained about the long-term estrangement between Miss Gail and her elderly husband.

"Know something? All along, I've thought Bill's death was tied to Lodestone Canyon," I said, smoothing my hair. "Now I'm not so sure. Cue said he despised Billy because our boy was 'disloyal to the brand.' But maybe he lied. Maybe he found out that his precious Gail had taken a lover. Cue can't stand being upstaged by anybody. If he knew he was being cuckolded by an Indian . . ."

Just thinking about old man Broward's reaction made me shiver.

Tensing his eyebrows, Chief replied, "The connections are still there, then. Any of the suspects could have done it. Their motives are simply different, that's all."

"Right! They were all reacting to Gail's affair, not to Billy's opposition to the logging project."

The Raspberry Ridge Motel's huge neon sign beckoned to us from the left-hand side of the road. Chief slowed my car, hit the blinker light, and turned into the spacious driveway.

"There's just one problem, *Noozis*. Where does Jack Sunawavi fit into all this?"

I slapped the padded armrest. "Wish I knew! It's crazy, isn't it? It's as if we'd taken the pieces and put the puzzle all together. Now it forms a perfect picture. But there's still a great big piece in my hand named Jack Sunawavi.''

"Who is linked to Mr. Sager through Ty Braddock and to Mr. Broward through Dennis Simms.'' Chief pulled into an empty parking space. "We can't ignore Sunawavi, *Noozis*. I have a feeling he's the key.''

"How so?'' I asked, unbuckling my harness.

"Well, for one thing, he knows *you're* linked to Bill Shavano. He also knows your name isn't Sara, and that bothers me.''

"What do you mean, *Nimishoo?*''

"I mean, if Sunawavi knows your secret, then why hasn't he sold you out to Cue Broward?''

"How do you know he hasn't?'' I challenged.

"Would your Goat Pasture scam have gone so far if he had?''

"Good point.''

"Nothing Jack does makes any sense, *Noozis*. He knows you're a fake, but he doesn't mention it to anyone, not even to Braddock. He could easily expose you, and make a good deal of money out of it, but instead he goes into hiding.''

"Right! And if he's safely tucked away, then why would he put himself in jeopardy by shooting at me?'' I levered the passenger door open. "Suggestions, *Nimishoo?*''

"Find out some more about Jack Sunawavi. Exactly what does he know about the Sagers, the Browards and Billy. Where'd he get the cash money for that brand-new pickup truck? Who paid him off? Why?''

"That'll have to wait a bit. I'm meeting with Cue first thing tomorrow morning.'' I rounded the front of the Accord. *"Nimishoo,* did you mean it when you told Jack's mother we'd be back?"

"Surely did. It'll give us a chance to ask a few more questions about Jack." He surrendered the driver's seat to me. "Drop by the motel when you finish up, okay?"

"I'll be here."

At ten the following morning, I was seated on the divan in Cue's study, diligently studying the draft contract. Across from me, with his cowboy boots perched on a corner of the big oaken desk, sat my new oil partner, Mr. Broward, father of sharpshooting Linda. His lawyer, Mr. Simms, occupied a foldout steel chair beside the filing cabinets.

It was another August scorcher, and dress casual was the fashion order of the day. Cue and Dennis got by with open-necked madras shirts and trail jeans. Me, I was wearing a flowery, scoop-necked silk shell and a bright blue slim skirt. And mighty glad the household air conditioner was operational.

Dennis Simms bit his left thumbnail, unable to take his eyes off me. His expression was troubled, and no wonder. Had he submitted this draft contract to my old business prof at USU, he would have gotten a C minus for the course.

I showed him a delighted Angie smile, anyway. "Looks fine to me, gentlemen. You don't mind if I bounce it off my own attorney back in Ogden, do you?"

Dennis shook his head. "The draft document is yours to keep."

Lowering his bandy legs, Cue snapped, "You have that shyster o' yours scribble on it some and then bring it on back." Yellowing teeth appeared beneath his moustache. "Then you 'n' me'll get down to some real horse-swappin', Sara."

Still smiling, I stood up. "This could be the shortest partnership on record."

"Not if'n you want that oil pumped out o' the ground." Cue slid his chair back on squeaky bearings. "Why don't you stick around, little gal? I got Karl Eames and a few o' the boys comin' over at two. Might as well be here when I give 'em the bad news."

Collecting scattered photocopies, Dennis showed his boss a disapproving frown. "There's no need to scuttle the cut just yet, Cue. We could still pull it off."

"I ain't scuttlin' *anythin'*, boy." The softer Cue's voice, the keener it's edge. "I'm just pullin' out, is all. If Karl still wants to cut in Lodestone, he's just gonna have to work somethin' out with ol' Dan Kaniache. And I wish him luck. I never seen a man drive a harder bargain than that damn Indian." Sly wink at me. "You sure you ain't related to ol' Dan, Miss Sara?"

Angie giggle. "You'll find out when we get down to swappin'."

"Well, I hate to leave such a charmin' young lady to fend for herself," he said, rising from the chair. He cast a sharp glance at the desktop digital clock. "But I got me a previous engagement." Touching the small of my back, he shepherded me into the main hallway. "Them boys from the USDA are droppin'

278

by the meat plant. I got to be there to show 'em around.''

As Cue lifted his Stetson from the hatrack, I spied a petite Mexican maid with a generous figure and a wedge-shaped hairstyle bustling about at the kitchen counter. Cue spotted her, too, and let out a piercing, monotoned whistle. The maid responded at once, glancing over her shoulder, lush lips puckering inquisitively.

"Carmelita!" he bellowed, jabbing his thumb at me. "Fix-ay el luncho *para la señorita. Comprende?*"

Dignified nod. *"Si, señor."*

Dennis trailed me to the front door. The moment Cue boarded his Cherokee, the lawyer whispered, "I notice you didn't laugh this time."

"Your boss is beginning to rub off on me."

"He does have that effect on people, Miss Sara."

Dennis closed the front door behind us, and we passed from air-conditioned comfort into the dessicating heat of the Broward front porch. Putting my back to the pillar, I remarked, "You've been with him a long time, haven't you?"

"Ten years." He put on his own sand-colored Stetson. "Ever since I got out of law school."

Seeing an opening, I worked my way around to it. "Was your specialty corporate law?"

"Real estate. That's how I met Cue."

"Have you ever done any criminal law?"

"Some." All at once, Dennis was on his guard. "Why do you ask?"

"I ran into an old client of yours . . . Jack Sunawavi."

279

Emitting a gust of hearty laughter, Dennis shook his head ruefully. "Oh, yeah . . . *Jack!*"

"How many times did you represent him in court?" I asked.

"Once or twice."

"Ty Braddock tells me you talked to Jack last week."

"That's right," Dennis said smoothly. "I ran into him at S & S Hardware. He was buying mud flaps for that brand-new truck of his." Dark eyes gleamed with curiosity. "How do you happen to know Jack Sunawavi?"

"He introduced himself at the Briar Patch."

"Yeah?" The lawyer's voice turned flirtatious. "Don't tell me he got lucky?"

Tart fussbudget face. "He's not my type, Mr. Simms."

On came the ladykiller smile. "And what is your type, Sara?"

Sultry smile. "Well, I can be partial to tall, good-looking, dark-haired men in sand-colored Stetsons."

His smile broadening, Dennis leaned closer and brushed his thumb along my chin. "Why don't we continue this conversation over dinner?"

"I *do* hate to leave a conversation unfinished."

"What do you say, Sara? They grill a mighty fine sirloin at the Lean 'n' Mean."

Before I could reply, a frosty female voice rang out. "Cue's liable to grill your ass, Dennis J. Simms, if he catches you hanging around out here."

I peered over Dennis's shoulder and saw Miss Gail striding our way. Her long tanned legs disturbed the folds of her tea rose halter-top sundress. She kept her expression aloof and bland, but there was no mistaking the angry tension of that lovely mouth.

Nearly as surprising as Gail's profanity was the reaction of Dennis Simms. Dark eyes narrowed, then zipped to the right. His thin lips tightened in aggravation. For a split second, I thought he was going to turn and hit Gail.

But then he sighed, straightened, and calmly faced his employer's wife. "Just being sociable, Miss Gail."

"Is it my imagination, Mr. Simms, or did you come here to do some work?" she asked. She had the peculiar poise of Old Money, the fervent belief that the world would always sort itself out in accordance with her wishes. "Don't you have some zoning permit applications to finish?"

"Yes, ma'am."

Doing a crisp about-face under Miss Gail's watchful eye, the lawyer meekly headed for the front door. As soon as the latch clicked shut, she relaxed, rubbed one bare arm, and flashed a smile that would have gotten her elected state chairwoman of the Daughters of the Utah Pioneers.

"I understand you're having lunch with us this afternoon."

"True enough. And I don't have a written invitation, either."

Gail flinched a little at my needle but managed a brief trickle of ladylike laughter. "Don't be silly, Sara. You're not going to need one. Not anymore." Daintily she touched her lush brown hair. "Tell me, have you anything planned for the rest of the morning?"

"Not particularly. Why do you ask?"

"I'm taking Maharajah for his morning gallop. I'd like you to join me."

"Gail . . ." I smoothed the sides of my narrow skirt. "I'd love to, but I'm afraid I'm not exactly dressed for the saddle."

"No problem, Sara. I've learned to keep the guest closet well-stocked with blue jeans. I'll have Carmelita select a pair." Flawless teeth showcased a smile of triumph. "Size six, am I right?"

Sixty minutes later we were out on the trail cantering across a winter pasture bordered by the tawny foothills of the Wasatch range. A hot breeze stirred the long stalks of dessicated junegrass.

Off to my right, straddling the magnificent coal-black Maharajah, was that fanatic equestrienne, my hostess, Gail Sager Broward. Give the lady a blue ribbon for style. She rode like a jockey, knees properly flexed, outthrust fanny poised over the cantle, flushed and lovely in her smart riding outfit. Sleeveless tank in Kashmir green and matching silken throat scarf. Snug tan riding britches and glossy brown leather boots that would have been the envy of General Patton.

My mount was a spirited bay named Desperado. Gail's groom told me he had a nasty rodeo reputation, but he was a perfect gentleman, keeping pace with the lordly Maharajah, tearing up the dry earth with his hooves. I truly enjoyed that ride, the rocking rhythm of Desperado's rippling spine muscles, the stretch-and-kick of those powerful legs, the decisive nodding of his well-sculpted head.

A mile short of the back fence, Gail abruptly reined up and patted the stallion's head. Turning to me, she said, "Let's walk them in, shall we? I don't want my baby getting overheated."

"All right." Swinging my left leg over the pommel, I slid off the saddle. "You shouldn't spoil him like that, Gail. He's going to think he's a pet."

"He *is* a pet." Holding the bridle, Gail stood on tiptoe and made an exaggerated kissy-face at the wide-eyed thoroughbred. "Ooooooh, you're Mummy's darling, aren't you? Ooooooh, pucker up, babykins."

From the way she kissed Maharajah, you would have thought he was Kevin Costner. I almost laughed at the sight of that lipstick smudge on the stallion's upper lip. Instead, I gathered up Desperado's long rein and began walking. The black stallion trudged along obediently behind Gail. Her free hand smoothed the seat of her britches.

"Saddlesore?" I remarked, smiling in sympathy.

"A little—I'm out of practice. I haven't done enough riding this summer."

"You shouldn't try to do it all in one day."

"True enough." The rein dangled from Gail's right hand. "I don't mind walking, though." She shot me a knowing glance. "It gives the two of us a chance to talk."

"What would you like to talk about, Gail?"

Cool-eyed look. "The precise nature of your business with my husband."

"Why don't you ask your husband?"

"Because he'd only lie to me." Gail's cool smile

turned brittle. "The way he's been doing since the day we married."

I hoped she would keep right on talking. If she was the *Miss Fancy Gal* Donna Antero had mentioned, sooner or later she'd let something slip about Billy.

"Why did you marry him?" I asked.

"Because I was young . . . I was just home from Europe . . . I mistakenly thought I was smart and sophisticated . . . and he *blindsided* me!" Her voice tightened in indignation. "Cue has a tremendous *joie de vivre*. I'm afraid I became caught up in it. He convinced me that I was special—cherished—the only woman he could ever love. He knew exactly what would appeal to a sensitive young woman. And, like a complete fool, I fell for it. Cue gave me one year of newlywed happiness, and then he put me on the shelf with the rest of his trophies. He went right back to living the way he'd always lived." She flashed a tart smile. "So consider yourself warned, dear."

"Why would I need a warning?"

"Let's not play games with each other, Sara. I've seen the way he looks at you."

"I'm not interested in your husband, Gail."

"Aren't you?" She took an unhealthy pleasure in toying with me. "Do you know what I think? I think you cooked up this business deal just so you could meet him, and I'm not the *only* one who thinks that."

I wondered who else thought I was a gold-digger, but I knew better than to interrupt Gail when she was on a roll.

"That's it, isn't it?" she prodded. "You'll be seeing a lot of each other while you're putting together this deal, won't you?"

"That's a distinct possibility."

With a silvery laugh, Gail lightly slapped the trailing rein against the side of her boot. "Patience, Sara. He'll be yours soon enough. And you're welcome to him!" Calculating smile. "Of course, he won't be worth quite so much once he's free to marry you."

"Why is that, Gail?"

"Four years ago, I asked that son of a bitch for my freedom. I told him we'd both made a ghastly mistake. And he turned me down flat! He said he'd never let a damned Sager welsh on him!" Feminine knuckles tightened and turned white. "He's going to pay for that! Four years out of my life—ohhhh, he's going to *pay!*" She flashed me a heated glare. *"Broward vs. Broward* is going to have the biggest damned alimony in the history of Utah!"

"That's assuming the case ever gets to court."

"It'll get there—don't you worry about that." Smug smile of satisfaction. "There's at least one lawyer in this state who isn't scared of Mr. Henry Taylor Broward."

"Look, Gail, I'm sorry the marriage didn't work out, but I honestly don't know how I can help you. I think you'd be better off talking to a counselor."

"A counselor can't help me get rid of Cue. You can." Brown eyes shone with an eager light. "We can help each other, Sara."

"How so?"

"You help me get that divorce, and I'll help you land him. It's as simple as that, dear."

I was beginning to understand the motivation behind Gail's scheming. Flicking the rein absentmindedly, I gave voice to my thoughts.

"I don't understand it, Gail. For the past four years, you've been content to wait him out. Now, all of a sudden, you're determined to dump him. How come?"

Gail recoiled at once, her gaze evasive. "Is it really that important? You'd like to become the third Mrs. Broward. I'm quite prepared to hand you that title on a silver platter. All you have to do is play hard to get, Sara. Surely I don't have to advise *you* on how to handle a man."

I halted in my tracks and gave the heiress a searching look. "Actually, Gail, it is important . . . to me." Grim expression. "You see, if we're going to team up, we really ought to be open with each other. So . . . what's his name?"

"Whose name?"

"Your boyfriend's."

Bullseye! Gail stiffened instantly. She didn't even flinch, not even when Maharajah's nose bumped her between the shoulder blades. "I don't know what you're talking about."

"Oh, yes, you do. I'm talking about the man you plan to marry as soon as your divorce goes through."

Slightly pale, she tried to run a bluff. "You have a strange imagination, Miss Sara Soyazhe."

"Could be." I stroked the blaze on Desperado's nose. "Then again, it's kind of hard to understand why so enthusiastic a horsewoman as yourself would have neglected such a fine stallion as Maharajah." Sassy Angie smile. "Unless, of course, you had something else to occupy your time. Know what I think, Gail? I think you've done a lot of riding this summer . . . but not on Maharajah!"

286

Brown eyes flared in indignation.

"So what's the rush, Gail? Is your lover getting interested in someone else? Or do you just want that divorce decree in hand *before* Cue finds out you've been cheating on him?"

Taut-lipped, Gail did not respond.

So I kept up the needling. "If you want the divorce that bad, then why don't you just let Cue know about the boyfriend?" Pained grimace. "Then again, there's no guarantee Cue would be civilized about it, is there?"

"Cue wouldn't *dare* lay a hand on me!" she cried. "Daddy would—!"

I decided to go for broke. "Maybe it isn't Cue you're worried about. Maybe it's Daddy. Maybe you want to be back in Europe with a nice big chunk of alimony before your Mormon elder father finds out about your boyfriend." Another needle. "Or is that *plural?*"

"Ohhhh! You little—!"

"There's plenty of names on your dance card, honey. Mr. X, Ty Braddock, Bill Shavano—"

"What!?" Gail blinked twice in utter astonishment. Then on came her sorority president face—placid, stern and dignified. I frowned mightily. That wasn't the reaction I'd been looking for when I dropped Billy's name.

"Where did you hear *that?*" she snapped.

"It's common talk around the Briar Patch."

"Then I shall thank you *not* to repeat it!" Gathering the reins, Gail approached her stallion from the left, grabbed the pommel, and put her boot in the stirrup. In an eyeblink, she was back in the saddle.

"Women have been *jailed* in Utah for slander." Wheeling her mount around, she cast me a savage glance. "And it's really not that difficult to convict an *Indian!*"

Head high, Gail galloped towards the distant barn, leaving me and Desperado in the swirling dust.

Mounting up again, I wondered if the lady's not-so-vague threat was for real. And then I remembered the acid in her tone when she said the word *Indian.*

Obviously, Miss Gail, you don't share your father's interest in and respect for our people, which makes it highly unlikely that you had that affair with Billy.

In my mind, I was back at the Patch, listening to Donna Antero tell me about Miss Fancy Gal. I could hear Donna's tipsy voice saying, *"I'm not mentioning names, you understand."*

Why not, Donna?

I suddenly realized that I'd made the same mistake as Chief. I'd assumed that Sager influence had ensured that silence. But Miss Linda came from a prominent family, too. Perhaps Donna had been more worried about Linda's penchant for fisticuffs than Sager disapproval.

So Linda had been Billy's girl when he first moved to Clover Creek. I could understand the attraction. Linda had a raw physical sensuality coupled with a wild unpredictability—just the kind of filly my relentlessly masculine cousin would have wanted to tame.

But you can't build a relationship on that. Love can blossom on a mattress, but it can't grow there. As time went on, Billy would have been confronted with more and more evidence of Linda's emotional instability. The pranks that had seemed so amusing at first would now seem childish, vengeful and cruel. Her violence would have begun to alarm him. Being Billy, he would have tried to help her. In the end, though, he would have realized it was hopeless, and he would have let the affair die.

Another interesting thought. How had *Linda* reacted to the split? Did she shrug and go chase another one of those cowpokes Donna had told me about? Or did she ambush my cousin up at Dynamite Pass?

For now, though, we take Gail Sager Broward out of the running. She's cheating on Cue, all right. But my cousin wasn't the other man. Remember the time Gail breezed into the parlor? That musical greeting of hers—*"Darling!"* The lady had been awfully surprised to find me and Cue standing there. Who did you expect to find, Miss Gail?

On the way back to the barn, I let Desperado set his own pace. My mind roamed back a couple of weeks, re-examining all the facts, seeking something I might have overlooked, no matter how trivial or how small.

And, speaking of small, there's still the matter of Billy's missing tobacco pouch. It wasn't at the murder scene, and it was nowhere in Billy's trailer. I thought back to the scratched trailer door lock. I knew someone had broken in shortly after the killing. At first, I'd thought he was just after that map. But what if he'd been looking for something else, as well?

Okay, suppose the intruder made off with Billy's tobacco pouch. If that's the case, then he must realize its significance. He must have known that Billy didn't have the pouch on him when he was killed.

But *why?* That's the question. Why would somebody steal Billy's tobacco pouch?

Further cogitation produced no answers.

Hearing Maharajah whinny, I looked up and saw Gail ride him into the stable. Tall in the saddle she sat, the crownless queen of Willow Valley. And in that moment I gave a thought to poor old Ernst Sager, youthful German carpenter afire with religious zeal, pushing his heavily-laden cart across the windswept prairie.

What would Ernst have made of his three-times-great-granddaughter, I wondered. That spoiled and self-centered heiress, as arrogant as any of the Junker nobility the Sager clan had left behind in the Fatherland.

Ernst was probably better off not knowing.

Rest well, pioneer, wherever you are. Think well of your progeny and keep dreaming of Zion.

Chapter Fourteen

Following Desperado's rubdown, I made my way to the house. As I set foot on the porch, the front door opened, and out stepped an amiable Carmelita. She greeted me with a toothy smile.

"Señorita," she trilled, breathless with exhaustion. *"Señor* Broward has been delayed at the meat plant. He will be here for your two o'clock meeting, however. And the *señora* . . ." Mild look of apology. "She won't be able to join you for lunch. She suddenly remembered a previous engagement."

Pert Angie smile. "Yeah, I'll bet!"

Stepping to one side, Carmelita made a quick gesture of invitation. *"Por favor!* You may use the guest room shower if you wish to freshen up."

Well! Who could resist an offer like that?

When I emerged from the frosted-glass stall, I found three fluffy violet bath towels draped over the bar and my clothes missing from the bed. I mean *everything!* Floral shell, blue skirt, indigo jeans, even my pantyhose. Oh, Carmelita!

"I put them in the wash," the maid informed me,

laying fresh satin lingerie on the bedspread. "They won't take too long. You want to look your best for this afternoon's meeting, *verdad?*" Sliding open the closet's louvered door, she reached inside and withdrew a fuchsia jacquard chemise. "I put one of the hands to work shining your shoes. Lunch is waiting for you in the conservatory. Enjoy, *señorita.*"

And out the door she flew—Cue's hyperkinetic maid. How I wished I could have brought her back to Pierre with me. Dream on, Angie. You know parolees are not allowed personal servants at the Department's halfway house.

I found the conservatory on the first floor, at the rear of the house. Bay windows overlooked the patio. My lunch occupied a two-person wickerwork table, complete with a sego lily centerpiece. On the plate lay a bulky BLT sandwich, wreathed with potato chips. Standing sentinel by its side was a sweating can of Coors Lite.

I finished lunch in short order, dabbed my lips with the linen napkin, and listened for Carmelita. I heard her busy footsteps directly overhead, then remembered the telephone in Cue's office. And decided to try my luck again with the long-distance operator.

Off with the beach sandals, princess. Securely tie the belt of the fuchsia robe. Then, down the main corridor, bare soles slapping the tiles. Tread softly, Angie. You don't really want to be the first woman in Utah ever arrested for committing burglary while clad in a chemise.

Once inside, I eased the door shut. Taking a seat on the desk, I grabbed a pencil and rechecked Mr.

R.C.'s telephone number, then I tapped out the numerals with the eraser tip. Five-three-three . . .

Ringing sounded at the other end. How about that? My luck was definitely changing.

Suddenly, a clipped tenor voice came on line. "Good afternoon. Rimfire Club. This is Walter Traxler speaking. May I help you?"

My chin sagged in surprise. R.C.—Rimfire Club. So that's where Cue had gone the night before Billy's murder.

"Hello?" said Mr. Traxler.

Oh, well! While I had him on the phone, I might as well try for corroboration. Clearing my throat, I threw out a rough imitation of the maid's singsong voice. *"Buenas tardes,* Meester Traxler. Thees ees Carmelita at the Circle B."

"Carmelita, hello! How are things in Clover Creek?" He had the jovial yet supercilious tone of the professional majordomo. "You sound like you have a cold."

"My nose ees all stuffed up, *señor."* I let out a phony sniffle. "I'm calling for Meester Broward. We got a bill in the mail, and now he ees ver' angry. He say you charge him for two nights."

"Wait a minute, Carmelita. Let me check that." Papers rustled close to the telephone. Then the desk man came on again. "That's right, I'm afraid. Mr. Broward didn't check out until after noontime. We had to charge him for the extra night."

"So he was there all night on the sixth?"

The majordomo sounded slightly embarrassed. "Well, yes."

"But that was not his intention, *verdad?"*

"Well, you know the rules, Carmelita. We don't want our members driving in that condition. I suggested that he remain the night, and he agreed."

I let out a giggle. "Bourbon always makes Meester Broward most eager to please."

Traxler uttered a mild harrumph, clearly uncomfortable with the notion of gossiping with a servant. "You needn't worry, Carmelita. We took excellent care of Mr. Broward."

"Bueno! I'm glad you put him up. The *señora* gets so upset when he comes home drunk." I flipped the calendar pages back to the proper date. "Wha' time did Meester Broward leave the Rimfire Club?"

"Just after two. The time should be listed on the bottom left-hand corner of the bill."

"Ah, here eet ees," I said, holding up an imaginary piece of paper.

"Sorry, Carmelita, but it is the policy of the club." Slight anxiety crept into Traxler's voice. "If you like, I could speak to Mr. Broward personally."

"Ahhhh . . . that won't be necessary, Meester Traxler. I'll take care of eet." I hopped off Cue's desk. *"Muchas gracias."*

"Glad we could be of service, Carmelita. Please be sure to give my personal regards to Mr. Broward."

"I'll do that, Meester Traxler. *Adios!"*

Tenderly I placed the receiver in its plastic cradle, smoothed the wrinkles out of my robe, and dropped the pencil back in its ceramic jar. I tiptoed back into the main hallway, closing the study door behind me, shifting my gaze this way and that, staying alert for sudden newcomers.

Well, I could deduct the name of Henry Taylor Broward from the list of suspects. Cue was still in Salt Lake City at 2 p.m., recuperating no doubt from the previous night's excesses. If Miss Linda's description of her father's drinking was accurate, and I had every reason to believe it was, then Cue was probably face down on the bed in the Rimfire Club's guest suite, emitting loud alcoholic snores, at the moment Billy was being killed.

Looks as if you have an ironclad alibi, Mr. Broward. Which means you're simply guilty of violating federal timber laws. So I don't feel quite so bad about pulling off my Goat Pasture scam and keeping that one-of-a-kind aspen ecosystem out of your greedy clutches.

Let's suppose for a moment that Lodestone's valuable timber is indeed the motive. If that's the case, then Karl Eames now moves to the top of the suspect list. Eames's company is teetering on the brink of bankruptcy. He desperately needs that Lodestone cut to pull himself out of the hole. It'll be interesting to see how Eames reacts this afternoon when Cue announces he's pulling out of High Timber Associates.

There was one avenue of conspiracy I had yet to explore. My grandfather had proven that those two loggers, Ed Kearns and Joe Nielsen, hadn't tried to kill Billy. But what if Eames had worked with somebody else? Say, Deputy Braddock . . . or Jack Sunawavi.

Better hurry up with my clothes, Carmelita. The gentlemen will be here in another hour.

* * *

Two o'clock found us in the Broward rumpus room. Somehow Cue had resisted the blandishments of his wife's interior decorators and had given this room his own personal masculine ambience. It reminded me of a small-town Masonic lodge. High-ceilinged walls panelled in choice hardwood. Plush, well-upholstered sofas and armchairs in earth-toned hues. Brushed Stetsons abloom on the old-fashioned hatstand. A cozy corner bar.

A cheerful Cue played bartender for the boys. Dennis Simms, considerably less jovial than his employer, stood near the bookcase. As for me, I was back in my floral shell and blue skirt, which had so recently been laundered by the redoubtable Carmelita, and half-buried in the cottony upholstery of an armchair. I had my legs demurely crossed, proudly displaying my newly shined shoes.

Once there was a glass in everyone's hand, Cue led a white-haired old timer over to my chair, and that's how I made the acquaintance of High Timber's favorite subcontractor, Pop Larkin. Pop couldn't quite understand what I was doing there, and Cue didn't bother to enlighten him. Instead, he left the soft-spoken old gent with the impression that I was one of Linda's friends.

I was more interested in another major logger. Off to my right, Karl Eames sat on the sofa, stolid, quiet, watchful, wearing a blue denim shirt with the sleeves rolled back to the elbow, burgundy dress slacks, and a traditional black cowhide vest. He did a lot of frowning, especially when he looked my way.

"Boys . . . ," Cue drawled, lifting both hands for silence. "You know me. I ain't one to stand on cer-

emony. When I got somethin' to say, I tell it straight.''
Expectant male faces turned his way. I watched Karl
Eames's mouth crinkle in puzzlement. '' 'Fraid I got
some bad news 'bout High Timber Associates, boys.
I'm pullin' out.''

Numerous bellows of surprise and dismay. I kept
my gaze on Eames. I expected him to jump to his
feet like Pop Larkin and the others. But there were
no shouts of dismay from the big lumberman. Karl
sat perfectly still for a long moment, and then he
suddenly lurched forward, as if he'd been shot in the
stomach. That blunt face registered a kaleidoscope of
emotions. Disbelief, then surprise, then alarm. Finally, his features settled into a sickish expression of
bleak acceptance. He lowered his head and said nothing.

Pop Larkin, on the other hand, did enough talking
for ten. ''God damn it all straight to hell, Cue Broward! You can't pull out now!''

Spreading his hands helplessly, Cue replied, ''Been
a rough year, Pop, even for me. Somethin's come up,
and I need the cash. I got no choice. It's got to come
out o' High Timber.''

''What about the cut?'' Pop shouted.

''It'll go through. Don't you fret none. The Forest
Service'll post that notice soon enough.'' Cue
sounded so sincere and so convincing that he almost
had *me* believing him. ''If you boys can get the financin', you can still go through with it.''

''What are we supposed to use for collateral,
Cue?'' another logger barked.

''Now, I wouldn't leave you boys high 'n' dry . . .
you know that.'' Cue Broward, sincerity personified.

Now I understood how he'd cheated that old Mormon family out of the Circle B. "Here's what I'm gonna do. I got controllin' interest in High Timber, right? I'm gonna divvy up them shares five ways 'n' sign 'em over to you boys. You show them bloc-shares to old man Sager, and you'll git that collateral."

Pop wasn't buying it. "Them shares ain't worth jack shit if'n there's no cut."

Cue's smile vanished. "There'll be a cut. You boys'll have to do all the upfront work, that's all."

"What about that twenty thousand you give me for the performance bond?" Pop snapped. "If there ain't no cut, how'm I supposed to pay you back?"

"Shit, Pop, you don't have to pay me back right away. You sell a few o' them prize ewes next spring, and I'll gladly consider it a down payment."

"What about *my* financin'? If I walk into First National Bank twenty thou in the hole, I'll be sailin' right back out again with Mr. Sager's bootprint on my ass!"

Smiling like a stock inspector, Cue put a gregarious arm across the old man's shoulders and said, "Come on, Pop. If we're gonna sort this out right now, we might as well get our noses wet." He steered the sheep rancher toward the corner bar. "You boys, too. Got me a bottle o' Jack Daniel's that needs emptyin'."

The party broke up. Most of the High Timber crowd followed Cue. A couple of ranchers hung behind, firing anxious questions at an antsy Dennis Simms. Rising from my seat, I spotted Karl Eames lifting his Stetson from the rack.

High heels tapping, I pursued him down the main hallway. "Mr. Eames? Aren't you staying?"

Casting a small sad smile over his shoulder, the logger replied, "No reason for me to stay, Sara."

"What about the timber cut?"

Broad shoulders shrugged. "That really isn't my concern any more."

Puzzled Angie frown. "At the barbecue, you said—"

"At the barbecue, there was still a chance we could pull it off," Karl interrupted, turning the hat in his weathered hands. "No chance of that now. Without Cue's backing, it's all over. The deal's off."

I trailed him to the front door. "But you need the money from that timber sale to get out of the red."

Eames stopped short. Turning, he flashed me a suspicious look. "Who told you that?"

I tried some name-dropping. "Ty Braddock."

Letting out a harsh chuckle, the logger said, "So he still keeps tabs, does he?"

"I guess." Tucking my hands behind me, I added, "Any particular reason why?"

"Ty'd love to see me fall on my face." Bitter memories soured Karl's expression. "I guess a lot of people would. Son of a bitch used to work for me way back when, before he joined the Army. He didn't last, though. Had to tell him four or five times to do somethin'." His stern eyes found mine. "I ain't an easy man to work for, Sara. Maybe I expect too much from people—I don't know. I've always tried to be fair." I watched his grip tighten on the Stetson. "That Ty—he's a mean one, young lady, and he has a long memory."

"What do you mean?" I asked.

"Ty used to be married. Did you know that?"

I shook my head, no.

"They got divorced 'bout two or three years back. The wife worked for me, too. Front office at the mill. She 'n' Ty used to scrap somethin' fierce. I don't know exactly what happened. Maybe she and Ty were spattin', and she chucked Pete Landers's name at him." Catching my puzzled expression, he added, "Pete—he works for me at the mill. Anyway, next thing I know, that big son of a bitch shows up in my lumberyard in full uniform, no warrant, no nothin', he proceeds to take that riot baton off'n his belt and crack Pete's skull with it. I mean, he beat that poor ol' boy right down into the sawdust. I yelled at him to stop. And that Ty—he looked at me like he wanted to *kill* me. He shook that damned baton and said, 'C'mon, you motherfucker! You want a piece o' this?' He kept tauntin' me . . . darin' me to come at him."

"I'm surprised he's still in uniform."

"Don't be! Mr. Sager is mighty grateful to Ty for past favors." Karl exhaled in disgust. "Sheriff should-d've thrown his fat ass right off the force. He didn't even have a goddamned *warrant!* Instead, they gave him one week's suspension without pay." His eyes gleamed with remembered humiliation. "You know, Ty didn't come there lookin' for Pete. That was just an excuse. He came there for me, 'cause I fired him all those years ago. He walked onto my property just to show he could get away with it. Son of a bitch shamed me in front of all my men!"

Eames seemed on the verge of a breakdown. Raw emotion clotted his vocal cords. He kept on talking, sifting through a long-sealed archive of rancid memories, inching his way toward the one that had really rattled him, wanting to confide in someone—anyone.

"Ain't right! It ain't! Live long enough, and it all comes back to haunt you. You do somethin', you think it's right, you don't think twice about it. And then, years later . . ." He glanced at me suddenly, his eyes filling with tears. "How old are you, gal?"

Little white lie. "Twenty-three."

"So young . . ." Hand quaking, he reached for the doorknob. "I hope it's different for you, Sara. I hope it never happens to you."

"What do you mean?"

"I hope you never get to be my age and see everything you ever wanted—everything you ever worked for—slide right down the goddamned tubes!" A teardrop twinkled at the corner of his eye. "And all because you . . . because you . . ."

He just couldn't get it out. He turned savagely, still clutching his hat, and stumbled down the porch steps to his car.

With one shoulder against the wooden pillar, I watched Eames's Cutlass Ciera drive away. Puzzled Angie whisper. "Now what was *that* all about?"

Cue had just told Karl Eames that the deal was off. Karl had to have the proceeds of that timber sale to save his company. His reaction should have been outrage, fury, anger—not a weary and forlorn acceptance.

Why was Eames acting as if he'd lost everything? He was still the sole owner and proprietor of the lumber company, right?

And then I heard Eames's parting words in the instant replay of my memory. *". . . see everything you ever wanted—everything you ever worked for—slide right down the goddamned tubes . . .*

Realization was like a skyrocket bursting into a shower of sparkles. Of course! It was so obvious. Karl Eames didn't own the lumber company any more!

My memory zipped back to the tax records I'd seen posted at City Hall. Eames Lumber had been listed as a tax delinquent. I felt my heartbeat quicken with excitement. What if Karl had hit crunch point *earlier* this year? What if he'd mortgaged the assets of Eames Lumber to resolve the tax mess? The lumber company would have a new owner, right? And that new owner would be far more concerned with pushing the Lodestone Canyon cut than Karl Eames.

Sudden chill. If this unidentified new owner had known of Billy's plan to spirit the canyon into the BIA, then he would have a powerful motive to murder my cousin.

Just then, I heard the shuffle of heavy footfalls and the baritone rumble of masculine laughter. Displaying a pleasant smile, I said farewell to each logger as he came out. Plenty of return smiles and "Nice meetin' you, Sara." Not much of a smile on poor old Pop Larkin's face, though. He'd have to sell a lot of sheep to raise that twenty thousand.

As I watched the last pickup roll beneath the Circle B's arch, I heard the drumroll of running feet behind me, followed by Gail's dismayed shout. "No! Don't!"

Curious, I turned idly to see what was going on. And then—

Whap! A fireburst of pain exploded across my cheek, corkscrewing my face to the right. Instinctively I shrank from the assault, then realized too late that the porch steps were right behind me. My high heel came down on empty air.

I managed the fall quite a bit better this time around. Going limp all over, I hit the turf on my side, rolled with the impact, and wound up facedown on the Browards' flagstoned walk.

I heard frantic breathing overhead. Sensation of fingers plunging through my raven hair. Linda Beckworth's angry voice hollered, "Up! Get up, you poison-tongued little bitch!"

A forest fire erupted all over my scalp. Linda had two good handfuls of Anishinabe hair. Clenching my teeth against the pain, I struggled to my knees. Sandpapery stone tore my nylons. Somehow I got both my hands on her wrists. She had forearms as firm as a young boy's. Probably spent an hour a day on the Soloflex machine.

With a shrill scream, I soared erect and broke her grip, then kicked blindly. My pump's pointed toe bashed something soft yet solid. Satisfaction welled within as I heard Linda's pained shout.

I retreated several steps, kicked off my shoes, and got my first coherent look at the situation. Three feet in front of me stood Linda, her fists clenched and upraised. The lady's attire was ranch casual—white sleeveless lace-trimmed V-neck top and stonewashed Wrangler jeans. But the expression beneath that elegant swirl of ash-blond hair would have gone much better with a combat comouflage suit. Her eyes glittered with fury.

Up on the porch stood Gail, wringing her hands

and showing the phoniest expression I've seen in years. "I tried to stop her, Sara."

Obviously, you didn't try hard enough, Miss Gail. And I wonder what you told Linda to get her so fired up in the first place.

Linda's forefinger swiveled toward the porch. "Biggest mistake you ever made, Miss Sara Soyazhe, talkin' to her! That bitch couldn't wait to throw it in my face!"

I cast a heated glance at the stepmother. "What did we talk about, Miss Gail?"

"Linda, don't! Please!" The lady Gail couldn't quite mimic the correct tone for sincerity. "If you hurt Sara, your father's going to be furious."

"Oh, I won't hurt her—*much!*" Linda was stalking me, fists at the ready, intent on doing some real damage. "Get somethin' straight right now, little Injun gal. Bill Shavano didn't walk out on me. I dumped *him!*" Saliva glistened at the corner of her mouth. "When I go steppin' out, I want to have fun! Get it? Fun! I don't want my man tellin' me what I can't do. Don't want him askin' questions 'bout me 'n' my daddy. Shit! Might as well be datin' some minister."

"This isn't necessary, Linda." I put out a conciliatory hand. "I don't want to fight you."

"You ain't got a choice, Sara," she spat. "You were badmouthin' my man. You bitches got to learn you can't go talkin' 'bout me behind my back." She shook her right fist eagerly. "You're gettin' a first-class whuppin', Injun gal. I'm gonna give you a nice, big, juicy black eye! And you get to pick which eye!"

Anywhere else, I might have laughed at this over-aged tomboy and her junior-high braggadocio. But not on the Circle B, and definitely not today. I was facing a violent and emotionally disturbed woman, two inches taller than me, with a body hardened by Soloflex. And the worst thing about the crazy ones— they never know when to stop hitting.

With a yowl like a wounded cougar, Linda hurled herself at me. I just managed to duck beneath her expert left-right combination. My outflung hair caressed her speeding fists. Then I drove my shoulder into Linda's ribcage and looped my arms around her thighs. My ankle shot behind her low-heeled boot, and down we went.

Linda's spine slammed the brown grass, eliciting a startled grunt. I dismounted at once, rolling beyond her reach. We came to our knees at the same instant, flush-faced and breathing hard. I brought my hand up from the ground and connected with a resounding slap. The impact turned my palm numb. Ignoring the pins-and-needles sensation, I gritted my teeth and clipped her backhand, as well.

The twin slaps were designed to enrage Linda—to make her take foolish risks, and the plan succeeded all too well. She came at me like a hurricane, punching every which way. Rocky Balboa on LSD.

Hedgehog defense, Angie! Lower the head and bend slightly at the waist. Cover the stinging face with the forearms. Let that crazed cowgirl dance around, thumping away with her frenzied fists. I gave her no openings. Her knuckles hammered away at my forearms, biceps, shoulders and skull. It was not unlike being outdoors in a Kansas hailstorm.

Soon Linda got wise to what I was doing. Wheezing and grunting, she grabbed me in a cockeyed half-nelson. Her kneecap tried to smash my face. I twisted my head at the last second, feeling the denimed knee scrape my face.

Linda was poised directly overhead. Flagging punches hinted at a growing fatigue, and I knew I'd never have a better chance.

I shot straight up, yelping as my head smacked the underside of Linda's chin. With a gargling scream, she stumbled away from me, unveiling her soft and supple tummy. The perfect target!

I drove straight in. I learned a lot about fisticuffs in the Big Dollhouse. Right foot forward, two over-hand jabs with the right. Left foot forward, jab with the left. Just like jazzercise, ladies. Left-left, right-right, cha-cha-cha!

Linda folded with surprising speed. She just wasn't used to female opponents who could fight back. Clutching her bruised belly with both arms, she sat down abruptly on the dry grass. Her ash blond head waggled from side to side. Anguished features struggled to shape the words *No more!*

Hitching up my bedraggled skirt, I snapped, "If you're smart, you'll sit there and behave yourself like a good girl!"

Linda's sulfurous reply would have peeled the paint right off her daddy's prize Cadillac.

"I mean it, Linda!" Schoolteacher Angie.

Cue's daughter burst into furious tears. I gathered that this was the first fight she had ever lost. "Shit! Shit!" She spat furiously. Pressing her fists to her temples, she screeched, *"Shit!"*

However, Linda did stay put, and that allowed me to have a brief chat with the stepmom. At first Miss

Gail looked like she was going to bolt. But she stood her ground with the brass of a French headwaiter.

"Where did you learn to fight like that?" she asked.

"Miss Carlotta's School for Girls."

Coy demi-smile. "I'm so glad Linda didn't hurt you."

Flashing an identical smirk, I aimed my thumb at the open doorway. "Time to head home to Daddy, Miss Gail."

"I beg your pardon?"

"If you hang around here, you may be needing a steak for *your* eye."

"Are you *threatening* me?"

"Wouldn't dream of it, dear." Brittle Angie smile. "Just a friendly warning, that's all. Your darling stepdaughter doesn't like the whipping she just got. Bet she's just itching to take it out on someone. She knows she can't whip me, so I guess she'll probably go after whoever put her up to this."

The color suddenly drained from Gail's lovely face. I blinked, and then I was all alone on the porch. I caught a glimpse of Mrs. Broward's trim backside fleeing up the stairwell.

Impish Angie smile. Poor Gail. She's going to spend the next six months looking over her shoulder. A marked woman, indeed!

And she wasn't the only one. Gingerly I touched the bruise on my left cheek. Ouch! Sure going to have a hard time explaining it to Chief.

* * *

307

"Hold still," my grandfather advised.

His thumb smeared a moist, greasy substance down my cheek. Bruised flesh began to sizzle.

"Owwwww! *Chief!*"

He continued the Anishinabe first aid. "Quit squirming, Angie."

"But it *stings!*"

Scowling, he kept up the ministrations. "Getting in a scrap—at *your* age! Dammit, missy, are you *ever* going to grow up?"

"Hey, I didn't start it, Chief. Linda swung first." I clenched my teeth. "Ouch! What are you using?"

"Mother Earth's favorite antiseptic. Yarrow leaves crushed in cold water." He took out a handkerchief and wiped the white petal fibers from his fingertips. "You still want to go through with this? Jack's mother might get suspicious if she sees that bruise."

"I don't think so. It was dark on the porch. She probably didn't get that good a look at me. But if she asks, I'll say I got it in the crash."

Up the walk we went, Chief and I. The Sunawavi house looked even more dilapidated in the fading daylight. The mountain breeze tickled my bare legs as I climbed the stairs. I'd left my shredded pantyhose in a dumpster back at Chief's motel.

Creaking porch boards announced our arrival. Jack's mother suddenly appeared behind the well-patched screen door. She wore a shapeless lilac housedress *sans* belt. And her nighttime braids had given way to a simple, part-on-the-right hairstyle. Other than that, it was the same Dolores. Same taut lips and narrow nose and pebbly dark eyes. She cast us a suspicious look, then blinked in sudden recognition.

"Oh, it's you folks."

Chief politely doffed his Stetson. "We won't take up that much of your time, ma'am."

"No . . . no, I'm glad you came," Dolores's voice seemed oddly strained. "I found the insurance policy. He—" Her husky voice nearly broke. "H-He kept it in the cupboard over the fridge."

She led us both into the small, cozy parlor. I studied her from behind and frowned at the sight of that graying hair. Newly cut ends caressed the collar of her housedress. My frown deepened. She'd shorn her hair since last night. But why?

Dolores flicked on the overhead light. As she turned to face us, I suddenly had my answer to that question.

A small black spot marked the middle of her forehead. Jack's mother was in mourning.

Sympathy filled my grandfather's expression. Like me, he had seen the Nuche death face before. "You have suffered a great loss."

Unable to speak, Dolores merely nodded.

"We did not mean to disturb you." He gave me an elbow nudge. "We'll come back another time."

"It . . . It's all right. You need the name of Jack's insurance company." Taking a prolonged deep breath, she tried to gather her composure. "I'll get it for you. I . . . I came across it a little while ago." Taut lips trembled. "Wh-while I was getting his things." She gestured at the tall-legged lamp table beside the small, pudgy sofa.

My gaze instantly scanned the tabletop, and my heart began to pound. Deck of cards. Hunting knife. Loose change.

These were *Jack's* things!

309

Then I spotted the small deerhide bag near the table's edge. The beige pocket sack with the beaded red thunderbird on the front.

My breath escaped in a startled gasp.

Billy's tobacco pouch!

Chief caught my inadvertent outburst. Glancing my way, he asked, "What is it—ah, Sara?"

Keeping silent, I pointed with my chin. My grandfather's obsidian eyes opened wide. Curious, Dolores approached me. Plucking the pouch from the table, I showed it to her. "Mmmmmm, very nice. Did you make this?"

"No, that's Jack's." Her eyes misted over. "He called it his lucky pouch. Said it was going to make him rich." She showed me a rueful, feeble smile. "I guess the luck was working, too. Right after he found it, he won that lottery up in Idaho and bought the truck."

"When was this?" asked Chief.

"Little over two weeks ago. A friend gave it to him."

"What friend?" I asked.

"Jack didn't say, but I think maybe it was Ty Braddock."

"Why do you think that, Mrs. Sunawavi?"

"Because Ty came around here looking for it a few days ago."

"Did he tell you why he wanted it?"

Dolores shook her head slowly.

Facing the sad-eyed woman, I murmured, "You didn't give it to him, though."

A single teardrop meandered down her brown cheek. "N-No." Her mouth trembled uncontrollably.

"J-Jack t-told me not to. He told me to hide it. He . . . he s-said we'd never lack for money again—"

And then she burst into anguished tears.

Without a word, Chief and I guided Jack's mother over to the worn sofa. Sitting down, she clutched her shorn hair and let out a wail of grief. I felt the skin prickle on the back of my neck. It was the same Nuche death song Aunt Della had sung for Billy.

I sat beside her on the sofa, taking her in my arms, gently rocking her back and forth. She kept up that doleful wailing chant. Excusing himself, Chief headed for the kitchen. When he returned, a minute or two later, he held a small box of tissues, and offered it to Dolores.

Sympathy softened Chief's voice. "Jack's dead, isn't he?"

Nodding, Dolores dabbed at her tear-stained cheeks.

"But he hasn't been home at all," I said, holding her trembling hand in mine. "How can you be so sure?"

"L-Last n-night . . ." Tear-filled eyes blinked rapidly beneath the Nuche death mark. "My son . . . he came to me in a dream."

My grandfather nodded gravely. "His *ini'putc.*"

Dolores warmed visibly at his mention of the Nuche word. Looking up at Chief, she added, "Yes, yes! His *ini'putc*—his spirit. It was Jack. He told me he was dead. He had come to say goodbye."

I glanced sharply at the tabletop. "You were collecting Jack's things for burial."

Nodding, she began weeping again.

Holding up the tobacco pouch, I said, "What do you plan to do with this?"

Fingertips whapped me on the back of the head. Turning abruptly, I saw my grandfather scowling at me. Whisper of disapproval. "Where are your manners, *Noozis?*"

Mild Angie grimace. *You're right, Chief. I stand corrected. Guess I've been hanging around white people too long.*

Tenderly I placed the pouch in Dolores's agitated hands.

After that, we did it properly. First Chief formally expressed his condolences to the grieving mother. Then I gave her a hug and did the same. At this point, Nuche custom dictated that we exchange gifts with the bereaved. But my grandfather and I had nothing to give.

Sudden inspiration! I peeled off my earrings, one at a time. And then, turning the woman's right hand upward, I deposited them in Dolores's palm. In fluent Nuche, I said, "Take these, please. And may your sorrow pass swiftly."

Jack's mother nodded, her mouth grim. She looked around for a few moments, seeking a small present to give me, and her gaze fell upon the beige tobacco pouch in her other hand.

Grieving maternal eyes looked at me solemnly. "Does this pouch find favor in your eyes, Sara?"

"It is very lovely."

"It is yours, then." And she handed me Billy's tobacco pouch.

* * *

Fifteen minutes later we were on our way back to the Raspberry Ridge Motel. Chief did the driving. I occupied the passenger seat up front, hefting the pouch in my hand. The little red thunderbird seemed to wink at me.

"Well, now we know who broke into Billy's trailer before I moved in," I remarked. "Jack Sunawavi."

"He was looking for that pouch," Chief observed aloud. "He knew it would be in the trailer. How come?"

I sighed. "Jack's been ahead of us all along, Chief. He must have heard about Billy's death from Ty Braddock. Jack went up to Dynamite Pass and looked things over for himself. He's a Nuche, and he was nobody's fool. He knew what it meant when he didn't find an offering at the foot of that lodgepole. My guess is he decided to cash in."

"Blackmail?"

"Right. As soon as he found out there was no tobacco pouch on Billy's person, Jack headed for the trailer. He's the one who stole the pouch. He must have grabbed those maps while he was at it, too. Once he had the evidence, he put the squeeze on the killer. Pay up, guy, or I'll send the pouch to Mortensen with a note about Native American customs. You heard the mother. Jack told her they'd never have to worry about money again."

"That means your second intruder was the killer, Angie. He was checking out the trailer for himself—making sure Sunawavi wasn't running a bluff." Chief flashed a thoughtful glance. "So that's how Sunawavi paid for the Dodge."

"That was just the first installment, Chief. Jack

was planning to mine that mother lode for years to come."

"The killer must have caught up with him right after Jack took that shot at you."

"You're right." Fussbudget face. "Billy's killer must have trailed me up to Dynamite Pass again. He saw Jack shooting at me, then took off after him." My frown deepened. "I don't get it, though. If Jack isn't the killer, then why was he shooting at me?"

"You were threatening his meal ticket, Angie. Blackmail don't work if the whole blamed world knows about the victim's wrongdoing."

"I don't know, Chief. Jack wasn't just trying to scare me off. He was shooting for real!"

"Are you certain it was Sunawavi?"

"Positive!" I tucked the tobacco pouch in my shoulder bag. "I saw the gunman. I'd know that black leather vest anywhere."

Eyes slitting thoughtfully, Chief murmured, "I keep rolling the dice, and it keeps coming up the same name every time—Ty Braddock."

"You think Ty did it?"

"Look at the evidence, Angie. Ty was on the scene. He lied about his actions there. You saw for yourself how anxious he was to find Sunawavi. He even asked you to pass on a message, remember? And then he turns up in Cottonwood, asking Jack's mother about the tobacco pouch."

My gaze turned doubtful. "I don't know. Jack and Ty seemed pretty chummy at the Briar Patch."

"Maybe Jack hadn't told him about the pouch yet."

"Jack wouldn't get rich blackmailing a deputy sheriff."

314

"You don't know how much Braddock has made off the Sagers over the years," Chief replied. "And do you know of anybody else out there looking for Jack Sunawavi?"

"No one! In fact, there's only two people who've even *seen* him—me and Dennis," I said, thinking out loud. "Let's see. Dennis saw him in Clover Creek last Wednesday. I saw him at the pass yesterday. So, if you're right, and it is Braddock, then he killed Jack last night—"

"And if he questioned Jack *before* he killed him, then he knows damned well where that tobacco pouch is," my grandfather interrupted. "Sooner or later, Braddock's going to show up back there, and when Dolores tells him about *us* . . ." Sudden alarm tightened his voice. "That's it! We're out of here!"

"Chief! What about the scam?"

"It's too risky, Angie." He tilted his chin at the windshield. "Idaho's just up the road. I say we slip over the line and let Uncle Sam's boys take it from here."

"But Cue's expecting me at the ranch. Longhurst is going to make the transfer. Once he does that, I can tip off the Tribe of DAN." I touched his muscular forearm. "I can wrap it all up in a couple of hours, Chief."

"They'll be wrapping you in a *shroud*, missy! Ty's wearing the badge—we ain't! He could shoot us both, then cook up some story and sell it to Mr. Sager." Chief's blunt head swiveled back and forth decisively. "The answer is *no!*"

"Chief—"

"No, dammit! How many times do I have to repeat myself?"

"It's the only way to save the canyon."

"N-O . . . No!"

"Two hours, Chief. That's all I'm asking."

"It's too damned *dangerous!* Can't you get that through—"

"Billy would want us to try."

The magic word—*Billy*. My grandfather's eyelids fluttered shut for a second, and he let out a long and weary exhalation.

"Two hours, you said?"

"That's all I need." I wet nervous lips. "Let's do it for Billy, Chief."

"Damn! How do I let myself get talked into these boneheaded . . ." he muttered, making the turn into the motel's parking lot. "All right. Here's how we'll do it. You're staying here tonight. Chances are Braddock doesn't know where I sack out. I'll follow you to the Circle B tomorrow then head back here. Soon as you're finished, Angie, you hightail it straight back to the motel."

"And then we take the scenic route back to Heber?"

"That's about it, girl."

"Sounds good to me." I smoothed the front of my shell. "Say, do you think we could drop by the trailer first thing tomorrow morning?"

"Why? Did you leave anything there linking you to Billy?"

"No way, Chief!" I had no qualms about leaving my trailer wardrobe behind. Even if the law confiscated them, the trail would lead to a dead end at *Sara*

Soyazhe's place in Ogden. "But I could do with a change of clothes."

Chief shook his blunt head vigorously. "It's better not to risk it. That bastard Braddock might have your trailer staked out. You can buy something here at the gift shop."

Startled blink! My tightwad grandfather was actually encouraging me to go out and buy some clothes? Well, well! Chief must be getting pretty desperate, indeed!

At that moment, of course, I had no inkling of how desperate my own personal situation was about to become.

Chapter Fifteen

"Took your sweet time gettin' here, didn't you?"

Cue held the front door open for me. He wore a striped, short-sleeved yoke shirt and his customary trail Levis. His pistolero moustache bristled with impatience.

"Sorry. I lost track of the time." Offering a sheepish smile, I stepped into the air-conditioned hallway. "Am I the last one here?"

Nodding, he pushed the door shut. " 'Fraid so. Longhurst beat you by 'bout ten minutes. Denny's been here since eight."

"Have you told either one of them why you want that desert land?"

"I told Denny yesterday . . . right after Biscuit lit out." He shot me an exasperated look. "You are turnin' my happy home life upside down, Miss Sara."

The house seemed unnaturally quiet. Looking around, I remarked, "Gail isn't here?"

"Nawwww, she's in town. Holed up at her daddy's. Scared shitless of Linda or some damn thing."

"Where's Linda?"

"Out in the stable. She's got a feed sack hangin' from the rafters, and she's out there whompin' away at it. Hollerin' *"Sara!"* ever' time she swings." Shaking his head sadly, he added, "That daughter o' mine is one sore loser. Don't know where she gets it from. Surely 'tain't from me. I told that gal—if you're gonna scrap like a man, you got to learn to take a whuppin'."

"That was a very comforting thing to say, Mr. Broward, considering the circumstances."

Sarcasm was lost on him. He led the way into the rumpus room while I gave every shadowy doorway a nervous scrutiny. I hoped to complete my business and be out of there before the heiress showed up for Round Two. The last thing I needed was another grudge fight. Lord knows I had enough of those in Springfield.

Dennis Simms and Alfred J. Longhurst both stood as we entered the room. It was definitely Summer Casual Day at the Circle B. Dennis resembled a working hand in his light blue shirt, open denim jacket and tight blue jeans. Longhurst wore knockabout chinos and a pastel green short-sleeved knit shirt that unfortunately called attention to the bureaucratic bulge at his waistline.

As for me, I was stunningly attired in the summer togs I'd purchased that morning at the Raspberry Ridge Motel gift shop. Dark brown slip-on moccasins. Cotton crewneck sweater tank in a lively shade of apple red. And a pair of roll-cuff denim slouch shorts in French frost.

Longhurst dug into his brushed leather briefcase.

He cast me a troubled look. He didn't quite understand what I was doing there.

Flashing him a disarming smile, I said, "Hi, Mr. Longhurst. Is Washington keeping you busy?"

Before he could reply, Cue stepped forward and snatched the heft sheaf of documents out of his hand. Peeling off the rubber band, Cue snorted and muttered, "This it?"

Nervous nod from Alfie. "Those are all the conveyance documents."

"Sit!" Cue's sharp gesture took in all the furniture. "I want a look-see at this first."

So the three of us quietly seated ourselves while Cue Broward, his bifocal reading glasses low on his battered nose, lounged in his favorite leather chair and skimmed over every single page in the transfer application. I grinned at the fellas. Dennis refused to smile back. He sulked on the sofa, long legs crossed at the ankle, plainly antagonistic to the whole proceeding. Emissions from the window-mounted air conditioner stirred his black hair. Longhurst sat on the edge of his chair, rubbing sweaty palms on his knees, desperate to say something.

Finally, Cue removed his glasses, rewrapped the weighty document, and tossed it in Alfie's lap. "Looks right fine to me. Three copies, right?"

Nodding, Longhurst stammered, "One for Washington, one for S-salt Lake, and one for my office."

Cue crooked his index finger. "Give the man a pen, Denny."

That's when the district supervisor's nerve broke.

"Dammit, Cue! I can't just—look, I haven't even posted the Intent to Transfer yet."

The rancher's gaze was pitiless. "Do it when you get back to the office."

"We haven't even had a public hearing." The pen trembled in Longhurst's grasp. "Cue, listen to me. This isn't a routine transfer we're talkin' about here. This is an interdepartmental transfer, and it involves a tract measured in square miles."

My heart began pounding. *Come on, Alfie. Don't be difficult. Sign the transfer order.*

"Sign it, boy." Steely gaze from Cue. "If I want to hear bellyachin', I can always phone the Sager place and talk to Biscuit."

Longhurst's unhappy face gleamed with sweat. "It's not just my office, you know. I—I need secondary approval from Salt Lake. Somebody's bound to ask questions."

I had much trouble maintaining my expression of pleased anticipation. I clenched my fists. *Sign it, you bastard!*

Cue's voice became dangerously soft. "Seems to me I've been payin' you good cash money to answer them questions."

"You don't *understand.* A transfer tract this big, and we're handing it over to the BIA. Nobody over there even knows it's coming!" Alfie's bureaucratic aplomb had vanished, unveiling the frightened little man who'd been there all along. "What if this gets back to the Inspector General? I'm screwed! Cue, my ass is sticking out there a mile!"

I wanted to kick him.

Damn you, Alfie—sign!

Cue Broward was off that chair in a twinkling, striding across the room, his craggy face terrible to

321

behold. Grabbing Alfie's shirt collar, he bellowed, "Now, you listen to me, you weasely son of a bitch! Ten years after the weddin' night is no damn time to start actin' like a virgin! Or maybe you've forgotten who paid for that shiny new house up on Juniper Ridge?" Twisting at the waist, he slammed the quaking supervisor against the chair. "I'm *done* askin' nice, mister! I need that desert land. I need it right now. And this Section 206 shit is the only way I can get my hands on it."

Then he picked up the document and dropped it on the coffee table in front of Longhurst. "You've had plenty of good years takin' my money, boy. And now, if you've got to sweat a little bit to earn it . . . well, that's just too damned bad—ain't it?" I flinched at his sudden roar. *"Sign!"*

Looking as if he wanted to weep, Longhurst signed all three copies. His pen wobbled back and forth across the dotted line. Tension flowed out of me like meadowlarks taking wing. I let out a long exhalation of gratitude and relief.

We're in the home stretch, Billy.

After that, I did my bit to cheer everybody up. I told Cue and Dennis my Ogden lawyer had looked over the South Promontory contract. He had no objections, and neither did I. Beaming with pleasure, Cue had Dennis fetch a final-draft copy of the contract. And then I borrowed Alfie's pen and gleefully scribbled the name of *Sara Soyazhe*. Both Cue and Dennis laughed when I joked about signing my life away. Poor Longhurst, though, was inconsolable.

As Dennis notarized the conveyance documents, Billy's old boss voiced the question that had been nagging him all morning. "Why do you want that desert land, Cue?"

"You'll find out, Al. Soon enough." Cue was making no happy announcements until his oil leases were properly filed with the BLM. "Right now, though, I got another little job for you."

The district supervisor looked up attentively.

"I want you to cook up an application for a federal oil lease," Cue said, hooking his thumbs in his cowhide belt. "The name of the company is South Promontory Development Enterprises, Inc." And then, walking over to the walnut bookcase, he plucked a white business envelope from the top shelf and, to my utter surprise, handed it to me. "Got a little job for you, too, Sara. Take that down to the First National Bank and open a checkin' account in South Promontory's name."

I peeled open the envelope. My eyebrows lifted at the sight of all those zeros. "Seventy-five thousand!?"

"That's what you call *initial capitalization*," Cue added, with a sly grin. "Gonna need us a little upfront money when we get them oil leases. Legal fees, reclamation bond, you know."

Curious gaze. "But it's made out to me."

"Tax reasons," he purred. "I want everythin' in your name, little gal, leastways for now." Cue's expression suddenly hardened. "Just make damned sure you bring that South Promontory checkbook straight back here."

Stepping forward, Dennis said, "Maybe I ought to go with her."

Oh, dear! That *would* be inconvenient!

323

Showing the lawyer a puckish smile, I tucked the envelope in my shoulder bag. "What's the matter, Dennis? Afraid I might get sidetracked down to Logan and the mall?"

Dennis chuckled. "Just trying to be helpful, Sara. The bank president is a friend of mine."

Slapping the lawyer's broad shoulder, Cue said, "Forget it, Denny. I need you for somethin' else. Get over to Dan Kaniache's place. Tell him he's just become the proud owner of Lodestone Canyon." He brought his hands together in a booming clap. "Saddle up, folks! There's work to be done!" A final crisp glance at me. "And, Sara, straight to the bank and straight back here, *comprende?*"

"No stopping at Hannah's Hope Chest, huh?"

His smile was only half-jovial. "If'n you ain't back here by lunch, I'm sendin' Stead Mortensen after that pretty ass."

Coy Angie smile. "You're the senior partner."

On my way out to the Accord, I glanced at the business envelope and wondered why he'd put *Sara* at the head of the company. I had the feeling something bad was about to happen to South Promontory. Something that would necessitate the sale of its assets, including the oil leases. He was probably planning to leave Sara with a pile of corporate debt while he took over the leases and did the drilling himself.

Just then, I spotted Cue's gleaming Caddy parked beside the ranch house. As white and as virginal as a wedding dress. It seemed almost a shame to spoil the waxed finish on that hood. But I couldn't say goodbye to the Circle B without leaving my own personal calling card.

I snapped open by bag, withdrew my lipstick tube, and then drew a large stylized tomahawk right behind those Texan longhorns.

The Sign of Angie! Evildoers, beware!

Giggling to myself, I hurried to my car. Forty minutes later, I was standing at the public telephone right outside Curt's Corner Conoco in downtown Cottonwood. A quarter tinkled down the phone's metallic throat. Smiling to myself, I tapped out the Tribe of DAN's number in Salt Lake City.

I was in luck.

Mickey Grantz hadn't left for the courthouse yet.

"Angela!" I detected a romantic undertone in Mick's voice. "How nice to hear from you. Are you in Salt Lake?"

"Not quite, Mick. On the state line." Toying with the flexible wire, I grinned. "Saguache County."

"What are you doing up *there?*"

"I've been busy the past couple of weeks. I thought you might be interested in what I've learned about Lodestone Canyon."

"Wait a sec. Let me grab a pad."

So I laid it all out for him, explaining Billy's Section 206 transfer scheme, Longhurst's collaboration with Cue Broward, and Jack Sunawavi's attempt to blackmail Billy's killer. Mick interrupted a few times to ask some very pointed questions. When I finished, he let out a low-pitched whistle.

"Enough for the FBI?" I inquired.

"It's a good running start. So the killer did away with Sunawavi after the first blackmail attempt, eh? Any idea who it is?"

"Right now, the front runner is the deputy. Ty Braddock, the one who framed your kids."

Concern flavored his tone. "I have four words of advice, Angie. *Get out of there!*"

"On my way, Mick. But I thought you ought to know . . ." Glorious Angie smile. "Shortly after nine-thirty this morning, Mr. Alfred J. Longhurst formally transferred Lodestone Canyon into the Bureau of Indian Affairs. The notice will be posted in the *Federal Register* in a couple of days."

"He did *what!?*" Mickey shouted.

Mischievous giggle. "Longhurst just carried out a perfectly legal Section 206 transfer. Lodestone is now under BIA jurisdiction, and there it will remain until he transfers it out again." Crooked grin. "Seems to me, though, that a competent environmental lawyer could run down to federal court and obtain an injunction preventing him from doing just that."

"I'll get right on it, Angie," he promised. "One more question—why?"

"I believe Cue Broward talked him into it."

"Sure! And did you have anything to do with that?"

"Now, now, Mick, I can't answer that. Not unless you're formally representing me."

Following a hearty laugh, he replied, "Send me a retainer, then. I'm dying to hear the whole thing." His voice turned serious. "And get out of there, Angie—now!"

"Till we meet again, counselor."

I hung up. It was time to fold the show.

Well, I still had Cue's check for seventy-five thousand burning a hole in my shoulder bag. So, crossing the street, I strolled into the branch office of the First National Bank of Saguache County.

With the kind assistance of the head teller, I divvied the check into four money orders. The remaining five thousand went into South Promontory's brand new checking account. Sort of a consolation prize for Cue.

Seven doors down the street was the Cottonwood branch of the Saguache County Public Library. Unable to resist a chance to play Robin Hood, I ambled through the open doorway, exchanged neighborly smiles with with the white-haired librarian at the old-fashioned circular desk, and talked her into letting me use the electric typewriter in the Resource Room.

The resulting letter warmed my heart.

Gentlemen:
Please accept this as my personal contribution to your legal defense fund. I hope this will assist in securing the acquittal of the three college students recently arrested here in Clover Creek.

Gail Sager Broward

This letter, plus a money order for thirty thousand dollars, I mailed to the Tribe of DAN in Salt Lake City.

Following a brief peek at the Saguache County phone book, I addressed the second letter to a certain luckless sheep rancher down in Scipio. It read:

Dear Pop Larkin:
Heard you was having money troubles. Please use this to settle your debts.

A Friend

Twenty thousand ought to cover your losses on that performance bond. Right, Pop?

The third letter I addressed to Mrs. Dolores Sunawavi, 12 Dead Horse Road, Cottonwood, Utah. Somehow I felt that Dolores deserved something more than a pair of loop earrings for her time of mourning.

Mother—
I may not make it home. If I don't, then this is for you. Remember, you are in my heart always.

Love, Jack

Into that envelope I slipped a money order for fifteen thousand dollars.

The final check—five grand—I wrapped in two blank sheets of typing paper and tucked into an envelope addressed to Ms. Angela Biwaban, General Delivery, Pierre, South Dakota, 57501.

Now, that name sounds vaguely familiar.

Hey, don't look at me like that. Robin Hood doesn't work for *nothing,* you know.

After that, it was straight over to the Cottonwood post office. I smiled radiantly at the counter clerk, purchased my stamps, did some licking and pressing, and pushed them one by one through the wall slot.

Then, clutching the strap of my shoulder bag, I headed for the glass doors. Within five minutes I'd be meeting Chief at the motel, and then it was off to Idaho. Lodestone Canyon was saved. Mission accomplished.

As my fingertips touched the glass, I spied a familiar green and white police cruiser parked at curbside. My smile vanished. A dreadful shiver ran through me. Heart pounding like a dance drum, I took a hesitant step backward.

A bass voice chuckled behind me. "Writin' home, Miss Sara?"

Panicky glance over my shoulder. Ty Braddock came lurching out of the shadowy alcove that housed the rental mailboxes, his massive hands upraised, his Stetson hat pulled low. His nasty cherubic smile brimmed with delighted anticipation.

Reacting instantly, I feigned a kick at his knee, then pivoted gracefully and streaked toward the exit. Jackrabbit Angie.

"Oh, no, you don't!"

Two steel clamps shaped like mammoth hands siezed me under the armpits and lifted me away from the door. The post office lobby spun sickeningly in my field of vision. Emitting a mild grunt, Ty hurled me away from him as easily as he might discard a basketball.

The marbled wall rushed at me. No time to go limp. Stunning impact! I bounced off the Smokey the Bear poster and dropped for what seemed like an impossibly long distance.

Wham! Multicolored starbursts obscured everything. The second impact deadened most of my senses. All except the monstrous headache rampaging through my skull. Eyes shut, I let out a hushed groan.

"Miss Gail's compliments, squaw!"

Ty's size fifteen boot wormed its way under my ribcage, then shot upward, flipping me over onto my stomach. My cheek slapped the cold linoleum floor. Soprano moan of protest.

And then one of those big clamps fastened itself around the belt of my slouch shorts, hauling my fanny skyward.

Ty let out a basso profundo laugh. "Upsy-daisy!"

Next thing I knew, the deputy had me loose-limbed and upright, headachey and dazed. My chin felt as if it were caught in a nutcracker. Opening bleary eyes, I discovered my face firmly wedged into the web of Ty's huge hand.

"Shit! This is no fun at all." The deputy's smirking mouth hovered an inch from mine. "Damned shame you ain't a man, Miss Sara. Then I could really enjoy myself."

My only reply was a piteous moan.

"Ohhhhh, does it hurt, little gal?" The hateful smirk widened. "Want ol' Ty to kiss it better?"

I struggled to make my lips work. "M-M-Mother-f-f-fuck—!"

"That what they taught you in finishin' school, Miss Sara? Shit, if I was your daddy, I'd want my money back." Grabbing a fistful of long raven hair, Ty spun me around and hustled me out the door. "Let's go, squaw. Time to pay the piper."

Down the post office steps we went, double-quick time. The sudden rush of fresh air revived me. Grunting, I aimed a shaky backward kick at his crotch. He blocked with that meaty thigh of his. The impact numbed my foot.

"Ooooooh, ain't you the frisky little miss!" Ty slammed me facedown on the cruiser's hood. The hard fender left me stunned and breathless. I felt myself sliding helplessly down the waxed surface and

330

groped feebly for a handhold. Like a watchful mother, the deputy took both my wrists and put them behind my back. I heard two brisk metallic clicks, then winced at the sensation of steel handcuffs biting into my skin.

"Let . . . Let me go, you son of a bitch!"

"Listen up, squaw. You got the right to remain silent—"

"There are laws against false arrest, Braddock!"

"Anything you say may be held against you—"

"Where's your warrant, motherfucker!?"

"And even a little Injun bitch like you can talk to some candy-ass lawyer. And . . . damn! What else?" His big features tensed in pouty frustration. Opening the cruiser's rear door, he shouted, "Fuck it! I ain't got time for that *Miranda* shit. Inside!"

"No!"

The deputy and I were drawing a crowd. Twenty onlookers, all of them Nuche. Sympathetic brown faces encircled the cruiser. One or two shot hateful glances at Ty as he grabbed the scruff of my neck.

Sucking in my breath, I let out a shrill Nuche holler. "Help me! Please! He's going to kill me!"

"Utes!" Ty's grim chuckle made my blood freeze. "Always resistin' arrest—!"

I didn't hear the rest. Something as large and as durable as Cheney Peak came plummeting out of the sky, smashing me on the peak of the skull.

Everything went black.

For a very long time, there was no light and no sensation in my personal universe. And then I gradually became aware of a vague feeling of forward motion. Swift motion. I felt a new surface beneath my cheek. Dull thoughts tried in vain to identify it. Linoleum? Nope. Pontiac hood? No. It was soft and cushiony, smelling of dust and vinyl.

The cushiony sensation ran the length of my front side. My moccasin insteps rested against a padded bar. Bit by bit, my sense of touch flickered back to life. Numbing ache at the wrists. Bruised ribs. And a headache on the same magnitude as an eruption of Mount Vesuvius.

Soft moan of anguish. I could feel the goose egg welling beneath my scalp. Gritting my teeth, I reached upward to hold my throbbing head. My wrists skrieked in agony.

The blinding pain brought me back to full consciousness. I remembered that I was handcuffed and facedown on the cruiser's back seat. Shaking the black hair out of my eyes, I peered at the chainlink barrier separating me from the driver's compartment. Ty's white Stetson and mammoth shoulders loomed behind the wire.

Turning to the right, I saw tall lodgepoles whizzing past the car window. A variety of smells assaulted me—stale coffee, dried vomit, reek of gasoline. I heard the transmission thump, then sensed a sluggishness as the Pontiac changed gears. Gravity tugged me back toward the cushion, and I knew we were headed into the Wasatch.

Brisk headache pain elicited a truly piteous moan. Warm chuckle from Ty. "How's your head?"

"Still intact . . . no thanks to you!"

"You'll live." Another basso profundo chuckle.

"Once Miss Gail gets her hands on you, though, you may wish you hadn't."

I grimaced in confusion. Ty was taking me into the mountains to kill me, right? So why the lighthearted cheer? And what did Gail have to do with it?

"What are you talking about?" I murmured.

"I hear you really got Miss Gail mad this time," the deputy replied, his tone jovial. "That, squaw, was definitely your big mistake."

"You've talked to Gail?"

Knowledgeable chuckle. "Next best thing, Miss Sara. The next best thing."

Ty lapsed into silence. Minutes later, the cruiser slowed to a crawl, then veered to the right. I heard the crunch of sand under the tires, then the engine's sudden silence and the sharp slam of the driver's door.

All at once, the rear door swung open, revealing the massive deputy and the sunlit meadow of Dynamite Pass. Reaching inside, Ty got a good grip on my belt. Out I slid, cursing and kicking. Ty paid me no mind. Grabbing me as if I were a suitcase, he yanked me out of the car and dropped me on the ground.

Without a word, the deputy put me back on my feet. I wobbled a bit at first, my ankles tingling with a pins and needles sensation. In no time at all, though, I was able to stand upright, breathing in shallow gasps, a bit wobbly, with thick raven bangs draping my forehead. Prodding my spine with his blunt fingertips, he herded me up a narrow woodland trail. "Let's go, Miss Sara."

It was a rough, rock-strewn trail, and it meandered uphill into the aspen forest overlooking Lodestone Canyon. Thirty-foot limestone bluffs hemmed us in on either side. Ty's forefinger gave me a no-nonsense poke whenever he thought I was lagging.

Perspiration stained the back of my sweater tank. My wrists wriggled helplessly in those handcuffs. I had this recurring mental image of the deputy stopping suddenly in his tracks, drawing the Colt Python from its holster, and taking careful aim at the back of my neck.

Calm down, Angie! If Ty was going to shoot you, he'd have done it long before now. We've passed three likely spots. At any one of them, he could have shot me and sent my cooling corpse sliding down into the ravine with little or no chance of it ever being found. But he didn't.

And that had me wondering why.

Just then, the deputy spoke up. "Hey! Did you ever give him my message?"

"Message?" I echoed.

"The one I gave you the last time, squaw. The one for Jack." Ty's tone turned petulant. "Son of a bitch didn't show."

A weird tingle ran up backbone. Wait a minute! I thought. He sounds as if he doesn't know Jack's dead.

Lie a little, princess.

"Look, Braddock, I haven't seen Jack in days. I never got the chance to give him your message."

"Shit!" Punting a fist-sized rock out of his path, he muttered, "What's that son of a bitch tryin' to pull? We need to talk, dammit!"

I blinked in amazement. He *really* didn't know.

But that's crazy, I thought. Chief and I talked to Jack's mother. Ty killed Jack after he came to the house, searching for the tobacco pouch.

Ty's hard knuckle rapped my spine. "You better be tellin' me the truth, Miss Sara."

"I am!" Honest Angie. "Last time I saw Jack was that Saturday night at the Briar Patch. You remember. You took him outside for a private talk."

"Good memory, gal."

"Well, I haven't seen him since. He hasn't dropped by or called me or anything."

"Ain't been home, either," Ty muttered. Frustration gave his bass voice a slight rasp. "Son of a bitch! We had a deal—"

"What kind of deal, Ty?"

"Never you mind 'bout that, squaw."

"So the last time you spoke to him was in the parking lot."

"That's right, little gal."

Walking along, I struggled to ignore my raging headache and did some hard thinking. So Braddock didn't kill his boyhood buddy. We were wrong, Chief. Jack Sunawavi wasn't blackmailing the deputy. He put the squeeze on someone else.

Someone with enough money to make the effort worth it.

The new owner of Eames Lumber, perhaps? The man who stood to benefit most from that Lodestone Canyon cut. The man who had found out about Billy's land-transfer scheme and killed him.

How interesting, too, that no one has seen Jack since that night at the Briar Patch. Not his mother. Not Ty Braddock, who's been combing the length and breadth of Saguache County. No one . . .

Whoops! Amend that, Angie. Two people have seen Jack—me and Dennis Simms. Dennis talked to

Jack at S & S Hardware on Wednesday. He told me so himself. And I've seen Jack twice . . .

Sudden fussbudget face. *Or have I? What did you see, Angela?*

On my first trip to Dynamite Pass, when I found the telltale applecore, I saw Jack's midnight blue Dodge truck speeding around a bend.

But I never got a look at the driver.

And the second trip, when I dodged the sniper, I saw a man emerging from the trees, with a telescoped rifle in hand, heading for the top of the ridge. A tall, slender, black-haired man, with his back to me. He was wearing Jack's black leather fringed vest.

Sudden realization felt like a carbonated soft drink fizzling away in my brain.

You realize, of course, that this means Dennis Simms is the only person who's seen Jack in the past two weeks. Or who claims he has.

Dennis is a tall, slender, black-haired man!

At a distance of five hundred yards, and wearing Jack's vest, Dennis Simms would have been a perfect match.

Ty's palm gave me a gentle shove. "Quit pokin' along!"

"I'm curious," I said, glancing over my shoulder. "What were you doing at the Briar Patch that night?"

Deep-throated chuckle. "Deliverin' a personal message."

"To Jack?"

"That's right, gal."

Time to test the theory, Angela.

Taking a deep breath, I asked, "Why did Dennis Simms want to see Jack?"

"Damned if I know." Chuckle of admiration. "That's right. You were standin' at the window, weren't you? I thought sure we were out of earshot. Miss Sara, you must have ears like an ol' bobcat."

We reached the summit at that moment. I found myself in a crescent-shaped meadow at the foot of a titanic cliff. Bluestem rippled in the slight breeze. The meadow sloped downhill, filtering into groves of lodgepole pine. A small green mountain loomed just beyond the groves, and behind that was the rugged rampart of the Wasatch.

As we crossed the meadow, I cast a nervous glance at that cliff. Thousands of cracks and fissures marred the gray granite. Solitary aspens had taken root in there. The cathedral-high balcony looked about as durable as Waterford crystal.

Several boulders littered the field at the cliff's base. Dennis sat on one of them, still in his denim jacket and jeans. He didn't react to our approach.

He was too busy munching on an apple.

"Here she is, Simms."

As he stood, Dennis swallowed and tossed the half-eaten apple away. He showed me a chilly smile. "I had an interesting talk with Dan Kaniache this morning. Ol' Dan finally remembered where he'd seen you before."

My heartbeat thundered in my ears.

"Dan thinks you're one hell of a dancer, Sara. He even asked about you at the powwow. Somebody told him you were Bill Shavano's cousin."

Ty's head swiveled sharply. "No shit!"

Beneath the shelf of brow, Dennis's cold eyes glittered. "So what kind of scam were you and your cousin trying to pull on the Browards?"

"You already know the answer to that one!" I snapped. "You saw the Section 206 request letter from Billy and Ned, didn't you? What did you do, Simms? Drop by the BLM office and turn the masculine charm on Jayne Clark?"

Vain sliver of a smile. "I don't know what you're talking about."

"Excuse me, but aren't you the lawyer who explained Section 206 to Cue Broward?" I shifted my gaze to Ty. The deputy watched the exchange with ill-concealed amusement. "Why don't you ask Dennis where your pal Jack is?"

"No need for that." Lowering his hatbrim, the lawyer managed to keep his voice calm and level. "Jack'll turn up. You were all in it together, weren't you, Sara? You, your cousin, Jack—all of you planning to take Miss Gail and her husband. It's all over, Sara. You're going to jail. And so is Jack, just as soon as the sheriff gets a line on him."

His delivery was so smooth, so plausible, that it frightened me. He must have contacted Gail's pet watchdog the minute he learned I was Billy's cousin. Shooting a panicky glance at the deputy, I blurted, "He's lying, dammit!"

"Mr. Broward gave her a check for seventy-five grand this morning. It'll be interesting to see if she still has it." Dennis grew closer, beckoning with one hand. "That her bag, Ty? There ought to be a brand new checkbook in it. Let me see."

The deputy tossed it to him. With an icy shudder,

I watched Dennis zip it open. Mouth dry, I suddenly remembered what else was in there.

"Jesus!" Dennis's quivering hand withdrew my cousin's tobacco pouch. His dark eyes swiveled toward me, narrowing in a murderous glance.

"What is it?" asked Ty.

Dennis recovered perfectly. Looking the deputy in the eye, he palmed the tobacco pouch into his pocket, then feigned a thoughtful scowl. "We seem to be a few checks short of the total, Ty."

The deputy's grip numbed my shoulder. "Maybe we ought to find out where that double-dealin' Jack is, eh?"

"All in good time, Ty." Smooth and confident, Cue's lawyer backed away from us. "Make sure she stays right here, will you? There's a phone in my car. I want to talk to Miss Gail before we do anything else."

"Don't worry! This little squaw ain't goin' anywhere." Ty plunked me down on a sofa-sized boulder. "You set!"

The moment Dennis disappeared in the trees, I turned to the scowling deputy. "He isn't calling Gail. She doesn't even know we're up here."

"Button it, Sara."

"Don't you *see?* You're armed. He's not. He's gone to get a gun. He's going to kill us."

Ty uttered a raucous laugh. "Sounds like you've been into Jack's home-rolled cigarette stash."

"Listen to me! Simms killed Bill Shavano. Your pal Jack figured out the truth and tried to blackmail him."

"What?"

339

"That night at the Briar Patch, Simms used you to set Jack up. And then he killed him." Jumping to my feet, I turned and displayed the handcuffs. "You think I conned the Browards? You're right! I did it! Take me back to Clover Creek and book me." Fearful glance at the empty trail. "Do it right now—*before* he comes back!"

The deputy burst into laughter.

"Use your head, Braddock. Why did Simms tell you to bring me here, eh? All the way out here!" Perspiration streamed down my face. "Don't you realize how stupid his story sounds? Why would Miss Gail confide in *him?*"

Sly knowledgeable grin. "She has her reasons, gal."

And then I understood perfectly. There's nothing like standing around in the hot midday sun, with your wrists in handcuffs, waiting for the killer to return, to get your brain cells operating at peak capacity.

Why hadn't I seen it earlier? When Gail breezed through the doorway with that mellifluous "Darling!" on her lips, she had expected to find Dennis, and I also understood the motivation behind Gail's tart tone the time she found him putting the moves on me. Jealousy, pure and simple.

Remembering Dennis's dinner invitation, I gave way to a shudder. I was suddenly very glad that the lady had shown up when she did.

"I could almost believe you, Miss Sara, 'ceptin' for one itty-bitty detail," Ty drawled, crossing those muscular forearms. "See, I already know who killed that Injun, Shavano."

"And you didn't make an arrest?"

340

"Some folks are just too damned big to touch, squaw. You oughta know that." An avaricious smile appeared beneath his mirrored sunglasses. Tap of the forefinger against his temple. "That bit o' knowledge is gonna do me a whole lot o' good. Miss Gail, too!"

Ahhhhh, now the light dawns!

"By helping Miss Gail get that divorce?" I prodded.

The deputy's mouth hardened with hatred. "That ol' Gentile fucker's done ruined her life!"

"I see. You tell Gail, and then she blackmails Cue into letting her go." I shook my head in disbelief. "You stupid bastard! Cue Broward didn't kill Billy. It was *Simms!*"

"Cue wasn't around that day. I checked."

"You didn't check hard enough, Ty. Cue was in Salt Lake. And he has eyewitnesses, too."

Facial muscles twitched with uncertainty. "You— you're lyin'."

Grim chuckle from Angie. "Boy, you really thought you were going to cash in, didn't you? This was ten times better than punching out Gail's old biker boyfriend. You thought you'd caught the hated husband on a murder rap." I babbled on, feeling it all come together. "You told Jack, didn't you? Or maybe you two got drunk together, and you said a little more than you should have. You got Jack interested in the Shavano killing."

"We had a deal—!"

"Yeah, but Jack doublecrossed you," I interrupted. "He did some investigating on his own. He found out who really killed Billy. Better than that, Jack found proof, and he used that proof to blackmail

341

Simms. And that's why nobody has seen Jack Suna-wavi for the past two weeks, Ty. He's *dead!*''

Fuming, Ty whipped off his sunglasses. ''No, he ain't! He's just hidin' out—''

''Where?'' I shouted. ''You've looked all over this county, Braddock. Face it—when you gave him that message from Dennis Simms, you sent Jack Sunawavi to his death!''

Swinish blue eyes glared at me.

Now I understand why Dennis had let the deputy get a look at the smooth, chainsaw-trimmed edge of that tree limb. Casting a terrified look at the trail, I lashed out again. ''Simms suckered you, Ty. He set you up. He's the one who sent you to Dynamite Pass the morning of the murder. Isn't he? What did he tell you? That Cue left the ranch in a rage? That it had something to do with Linda?''

Ty's thick underlip dropped in astonishment. ''How the hell did you know *that!?*''

Now that I had him reeling, it was time to switch tactics. Another wide-eyed glance at the trail. I had to convince the deputy—and *right now!* Dennis would be back any minute.

''Simms sent you to Jack's house, didn't he? He told you to bring back a small beige pouch, right? A pouch with a red beaded thunderbird on the front. Dolores told you she didn't have it.''

''How long you been followin' me!?'' he bellowed.

''What did Simms say when he told you to fetch that pouch?''

Ty's skepticism was steadily wilting. His tone

turned thoughtful. "He told me Jack had been to the ranch. Said he swiped somethin' of Miss Gail's."

"You didn't talk to Gail about it, did you?"

The big deputy shook his head.

In my most persuasive voice, I added, "Ty, you've known Miss Gail for years. Have you ever known her to collect Indian handicrafts?"

All at once, he stood erect, his gaze cautious and wary.

"Simms lied to you. That pouch is evidence. Jack used it to blackmail him."

One hand on his pistol, the deputy glared at the empty trail.

"Did you talk to Miss Gail today?" I added softly. "Or was it *Dennis Simms* who told you she wanted me brought here?"

For long, agonizing moments, he stood there, thinking it over. Then those porcine eyes narrowed in deep suspicion, and he let out a rhino grunt. "Walk ahead of me, Miss Sara. I'm takin' you in." Hitching his gunbelt, he added, "On the way back, you can tell me how come you know so damned much about Jack."

Thoroughly relieved, I started for the meadow's edge. The sooner we were off this mountainside, the better. And then a jarring sound drew me up short. The clatter of falling rocks.

Ty heard it, too. Shoving me to the ground, he drew his service revolver. "That you, Simms?"

"Yeah, Ty."

I looked around anxiously. The lawyer's voice sounded strangely muted, as if he were a good distance down the trail. But I knew those rocks had fallen nearby.

Holding the Colt Python in a two-handed stance, the big deputy took careful aim at the trail.

"Come on up, Simms. Let's you 'n' me talk."

My frantic gaze zigzagged back and forth across the cliff's face. And then I saw it—a trickle of pebbles just above and behind a stack of boulders. "Ty, no! He's—"

KAAAAAROWWWWW!

An invisible sledgehammer walloped Ty in mid-spine, hurling him forward on tiptoe. Three-hundred-pound ballerina in the opening scene of *Swan Lake.* A scarlet volcano erupted from his chest, sending a billowing cascade of blood and fabric and lung tissue skyward. The momentum of the Grand Slam bullet slapped him along like an oversized beach ball. Over and over he rolled, coming to rest at last against a half-buried boulder, face down in a slowly spreading pool of blood.

I heard the dreadful *click-chock* of the Weatherby's bolt. My spine trembled, anticipating the explosive bullet strike, and I let out a shrill yelping gasp.

"Stay right where you are, Sara."

Wriggling in the handcuffs, I managed to struggle to my knees. The rifle butt bopped me behind the neck. With a cry of dismay, I flattened out on the turf. Dennis's knee came down hard on my lower spine, pinning me to the spot. Stunned, I made no resistance as he hauled my legs upright. I felt nylon twine twirling round and round my ankles, then yipped as he pulled the cord tight.

"You ain't running out on me *this* time, little gal."

The pressure disappeared from my spine. "Got some questions for you. Did Jack give you that pouch?"

I clenched my teeth. Stoic Angie.

Then the Weatherby's warm muzzle came to rest just behind my jawbone. I whimpered in sudden terror.

"I'm not a patient man, Sara."

"I-I-I found out where Jack hid it."

"What about Shavano?" he asked, wandering into my field of vision. Tall, grim-faced, black-haired man clad in blue denim. The muzzle of that high-powered rifle never wavered. "You two in it together?"

Hoping to protect my grandfather, I fielded another white lie. "S-sure! Billy told me all about the canyon."

Flashing an amused grin, Dennis walked over to a nearby boulder, squatted on his haunches, and retrieved a dusty canvas sack. Shaking the dirt off, he carried it back. "Cute, Sara. Tricking ol' Cue into putting that canyon under the Bureau of Indian Affairs. I'm betting you're the one who thought that up."

Craning my neck to keep him in view, I said, "We didn't know you needed Lodestone's timber to salvage Eames's company, though."

Zipping open the gunny sack, Dennis let out a muted chuckle. "Eames dug himself into quite a hole. He was in tears, you know, when I finally foreclosed on him. Begged me not to do it. But I'd been waiting for that moment for a long, long time."

"Ever since Eames fired your father?"

He stared in amazement. "How'd you know that?"

"Cue told me."

Features tensing in indignation, the lawyer shouted,

"That bastard Eames ruined my family! We lost it all—the house, the ranch! Son of a bitch cut the heart right out of my daddy. Turned him into a damned drunk!" Those fierce idol eyes glared at me. "When I was thirteen, I'd have to go in there—go in the Patch—and fetch him home. I promised myself then and there—no matter how long it took, I'd get that son of a bitch Karl Eames! And I'd do the same damn thing to him he did to my daddy!"

"I'm surprised you didn't kill him."

"The thought did enter my mind." Superior smile. "But Eames had money, and I needed it."

I did some hasty guessing. "Miss Gail wouldn't leave her wealthy husband for a small-town lawyer."

"Something like that." Pulling a spool of white cord out of the sack, Dennis shot me an eager look. "I've done better than kill him, Sara. I've turned the great Karl Eames into a nobody. All those years he spent throwing his weight around, and now he's flat busted broke! He's going to spend the rest of his misbegotten life that way. And whenever he sees me, he's going to know why."

"What does Miss Gail think about all this?"

"She doesn't know—and there's no need for her to." Grim chuckle. "I have my pride, you know. I'm not going to live off my wife's money. In time, I will come to Gail as an equal. I'm going to claim that woman as my own. And then, when her father dies . . ." He left the rest unsaid, cherishing his vision of the future. Dennis Simms, the lord of Willow Valley. I wondered how long he'd wait before planning an *accident* for the old man. His dreamy gaze riveted onto me. "This is the way it should have been—the way it *would* have been—if it hadn't been for that bastard Eames!''

Rolling onto my left side, I said, ''That's very nice, Dennis. But what did Bill Shavano and Jack Sunawavi have to do with it!?''

''They shouldn't have gotten in my way.''

''You just kill the innocent bystanders, is that it?''

No response. With the spool under his left arm, Dennis lifted the rifle, levelled it at me, and peered through the Tasco scope. Icewater seemed to cascade through my veins. *Oh, terrific! Now you've really pushed his button. You should have kept your trap shut, Princess Big Mouth!*

His index finger stretched toward the trigger

I tensed all over, waiting for the gunshot.

Behind the scope, Dennis's mouth twisted in a savage grin. ''You know, I had you dead to rights up in that tree. I must have spent five whole minutes admiring that pretty face through the scope.'' With a dry chuckle, he lowered the Weatherby. ''I was too eager. I should have remembered I was shooting into the wind. Too many gusts down there in the pass. Spoiled my shot.'' Shouldering the rifle, he added, ''I swear, Miss Sara, you must be part squirrel. Once you began moving, I just couldn't put those crosshairs back on you.''

My stomach felt as if it were in freefall. At a range of five feet, that would not be a problem.

I sneaked a hasty glance at the dead deputy. Bile tickled the back of my throat. If the Weatherby had done that to Ty at point-blank range, what would it do to little me?

With that, Dennis turned his back on me, leaving

me trussed and handcuffed in the dry grass. He marched briskly upslope, heading straight for the granite cliff.

Rolling onto my middle, I grunted and thrust my feet toward my head. Calf muscles stood out in sharp relief. Putting my face to the ground, I clenched my teeth and strained to reach upward with manacled hands.

If I could get my ankles untied, I could run for it. And the Caucasian hasn't been born who can track *this* Anishinabe princess through a forest.

Shoulder tendons stretched and quivered. My body curled like a shrimp, my trussed ankles straining to reach my spine.

Dennis's hearty laugh put an abrupt end to my torture aerobics. "Forget it, Sara. You'd need a pocketknife to loosen that knot." I heard a heavy weight dragging on the ground behind me. "Here! I've brought you some company."

A putrid and ghastly smell assaulted my nose. Something loose and heavy thumped the turf. Gagging at the noxious stench, I peered over my shoulder.

And there, lying at Dennis's feet, was the corpse of a tall, hatchet-faced Nuche male, pretty well advanced in the process of decomposition. Bloated tissues softened his angular profile. Blowflies buzzed the dried pink hollows that had once been his eyes.

Choking on the thick smell, I averted my gaze.

Hello, Jack. Long time, no see. Fifteen days, to be exact. And you're not looking too good after two weeks wedged into a cliffside fissure. Still wearing the jeans and T-shirt I saw you in at the Briar Patch. No sign of the black vest, though. Dennis must have left it in your truck.

I heard a metallic clank as the gunny sack hit the ground. Kneeling beside it, Dennis said, "At the barbecue, you asked me what I did in the Army. I don't believe I ever got around to telling you."

I watched him rummage in the gunny sack.

"I was a Green Beret." Rueful smile. "I learned a lot at Fort Benning. Learned how to kill a man with one blow. That's how I did Shavano. One quick flick of the wrist. I followed him from the trailer park all the way up here. I came up on him while he was bending over to unlock the flatbed's gate. Slipped that blackjack out of my pocket and let him have it."

I thought of the strange lopsided footprints I'd found at the pass. So Dennis had carried both my cousin *and* the chainsaw across the meadow to set the phony scene. Billy's weight had been responsible for the deepening tilt on one side.

"Your cousin was still alive, Sara. But I knew he wouldn't live long. Not with that fracture. Yeah, I learned a lot at Benning. Combat sniping. Boobytraps." His smile turned blissful. "Demolitions."

He lifted a dynamite stick out of his sack.

Dennis went about his deadly work with a most disconcerting efficiency. Heart in my mouth, I watched as he counted out fifteen sticks of dynamite and carefully laid them side by side like an overgrown toddler playing with Lincoln Logs.

"You've got to plant the charges correctly, Sara, or all you wind up with is an earsplitting bang." Reaching into the sack, Dennis withdrew a black roll of electrician's tape. "You've got to know just where to put it to create the maximum shock. It's the vibration that knocks down the target.'' He cast a smiling upward glance at the fraying cliff. ''It shouldn't take too much to bring that a-tumbling down.''

''A dead deputy's kind of hard to explain, Dennis.''

''Sara, in about ten minutes, all this is going to be a field of boulders.'' With the utmost care, he tucked the white primacord into a thumb-sized blasting cap. ''The landslide should cover you all. But if it doesn't . . .'' Philosophical shrug. ''Well, Jack left a shovel in the truck.''

''The sheriff will never buy it. He's going to wonder what happened to Ty.''

''I've got it covered, gal.'' Lifting a small pair of pliers, he crimped shut the blasting cap's copper mouth, sealing its grip on the fuse. ''Few days from now, I'll tell Cue all about your scam. I'll make it look as if Braddock was onto you. Cue's not too bright. He'll figure you and Jack killed Braddock, and that's just how the sheriff will handle it.''

Standing up slowly, Dennis bounced the hefty dynamite charge in his hand. He flashed me a wolfish smile. ''Goodbye, Sara.''

He walked over to Ty, stooped at the waist, scooped up the dead deputy's pistol, and then tucked it in his waistband. Whistling to himself, he headed for the lofty cliff.

I didn't doubt his Green Beret expertise—not for a moment! Fifteen sticks of dynamite. A charge that big, tucked into just the right vertical fissure, would have that five-story cliff literally jumping away from the mountainside. Ty and Jack—*and Angie!*—would vanish beneath a shower of house-sized slabs.

Straining against Ty's handcuffs, I watched the lawyer artfully climb the talus slope at the base of the cliff. With a silent and disturbing competence, he studied a series of lofty fissures and then leaned into the last one on the right.

My ankles felt as if they were glued together. My desperate gaze travelled from my nylon bonds to that pitted granite cliff face.

Dennis was backing down the pebbly slope, unwinding his spool of white primacord. He halted a good fifty yards from the rock chimney, cut the fuse with a pocketknife, then drew a silvery cigarette lighter from his jacket pocket.

The flint ignited on his first try. He touched the tiny flame to the fuse. *Pssssst!* Like a Fourth of July sparkler, the blaze slithered along the line.

Dennis let it drop, and fled down the trail.

An arctic chill swept through me as I watched that fuse flame sputter along the ground.

Chapter Sixteen

Sweat poured down my face. I tore my gaze away from the fuse and I tried the torture aerobics again.

Arch my back. Ignore the shoulder spasms and reach upward. Try to touch my shoulder blades with my toes.

Straining fingertips brushed unyielding nylon.

Sobbing in despair, I gave up. No use! I couldn't reach the knot. I may have been limber enough for the Hoop Dance, but I was no contortionist.

Quick glance at the smoldering fuse. A plume of smoke marked its passage through the grass.

Tugging vainly at the handcuffs, I gave way to furious tears. If only I had a knife, I could free my ankles and run for it . . .

Almost at once, my tearful gaze zeroed in on Ty Braddock.

Idiot! The handcuffs! Ty has the key!

Fixing the deputy's position in my mind, I twisted violently to the left. Chin tucked in, elbows pressed to my side, I hurled myself downslope, rolling through the grass. Angie the Steamroller. Fist-sized stones bruised my legs. Browning meadow and blue sky twirled sickeningly in my field of vision. I squeezed my eyes shut, resisting the sudden surge of vertigo. I couldn't afford to lose control. Not now! If I rolled past Ty, I was finished.

Brushed leather slapped my face, halting my spinning journey. My nose wrinkled at the coppery stench of blood. Opening my eyes, I found my face at rest against a Tony Lama boot. Close call. Ten inches to the right and I would have missed him completely.

Struggling to my knees, I tossed an anxious glance back upslope. The smoke plume meandered toward the cliff's talus pile. My thudding heartbeat drowned out its fiery hiss. Only minutes left . . .

I was just about to try the pockets when I spied the small black leather pouch on his belt, right next to the walkie-talkie. Grunting with effort, I rolled between his lifeless legs. Ty made a ghastly squishy noise as the weight of my hundred-and-five pounds forced another gory pint out of that frontal gunshot wound. Trying to ignore the dreadful smell, I placed the back of my head against the deputy's meaty thighs, dug in my moccasin heels, and pushed.

Up and over Ty's buttocks I slid, gasping at the effort. Sucked in another long breath. Tried again. Calf muscles knotted and flexed. My sliding shoulder blades cut grooves in Ty's flaccid flesh. I dug in my heels and pushed again.

My fanny came to rest on his. Shaking the hair out of my face, I struggled to remain still. Not so easy when you're perched on a dead deputy's ass and your every motion causes his cooling flesh to wobble. My pinioned hands groped for the belt pouch.

I thumbed the flap open. Searching fingers circled the dark felt-lined interior. Damn you, Ty Braddock, if you put that bloody key in your pocket—!

Corkscrewing my face to the left, I watched in horror as the fuse sparkle emerged from the grass.

Suddenly, my fingers made contact with warm metal. With a crazed laugh of delight, I gripped the tiny handcuff key between thumb and forefinger. Slowly, carefully, I coaxed it out of the pouch. Then my fist closed around it.

Rolling off the deputy, I landed face down on the ground. Breathing in short gasps, I winkled the key into the lock. Metal wriggled in my numb and sweaty fingertips. Ohhhhh, don't drop it now, Angie, whatever you do!

Gritting my teeth, I squeezed the brass key and gave it a sharp, decisive turn.

The muted click sounded like a gunshot to me. Steel sprang away from my wrists. Success! I dropped the key and peeled off the handcuffs. And then, ignoring my chafed, stinging wrists, I planted both palms on the ground and swung my trussed ankles in front of me. Anguished gasp! Sitting bolt upright, I reached forward and clawed at Dennis's skilled knots.

My left thumbnail splintered. The taut nylon resisted my frantic assault. Lifting my gaze, I saw the fuse's fiery sputter winding its way up the talus pile.

"Oh, shit!"

Dennis was quite right. Only a blade could free me, and, unfortunately, my survival knife was locked away in the Accord's trunk back in Cottonwood.

That left me with only one option: *stop the detonation.*

And that wasn't so easy to do, not with my ankles trussed like a pot roast and twenty yards of grassy upslope between me and that sputtering fuse.

But I gave it a try, anyway. Pushing with both hands, I rose shakily to my feet. I thrust my arms out for better balance. And then, whoofing and grunting, I set off, hopping through the meadow. With a shrill, hysterical giggle, I thought of all those potato sack races back at Girl Scout camp.

The flame neared the top of the pile.

Hippity-hop, hippity-hop! *Come on, princess. You have a great sense of balance, right? Your Hoop Dance brought the crowd to their feet at the powwow. Another ten yards. You can do it.*

A dull, warm ache worked its way up from my ankles. Tilting my rigid arms, I swiveled my hips this way and that, fighting to hold that delicate balance. *Lose this sack race, Angie, and you won't be hearing the girlish laughter of fellow campers—just the deafening roar of a dynamite explosion!*

The fuse blazed merrily on.

I covered the remaining distance to the talus slope in a series of great galloping hops. And then I flung myself against that pile of loose stones. My right hand lashed out at the burning primacord.

Missed! The fuse sparkle danced beyond my reach.

Pushing with my elbows, I crawled up the slope. With a choking sob, I lunged at it again. Both hands, this time.

My flailing fingers clawed limestone. Leaving the ground, the blaze left the ground, eating its way up the dangling cord. Peering upward, I saw the red dynamite bundle tucked away on a jagged shelf well within the rock chimney.

Gasping in terror, I braced myself with my fingertips, pushed the stony pile with my knees, and resumed the pursuit. My torn thumbnail throbbed mercilessly, and an avalanche of pebbles threatened to drag me away from the fissure.

Agonizing moments whizzed past. I struggled to climb into the rock chimney. Less than three feet of primacord remained. The flare illuminated the shadowy cracks beneath the explosive charge.

With a cry of triumph, I planted my feet and lunged erect. My grasping hand strained for the dynamite.

The fiery sparkle inched its way toward the blasting cap.

Quivering fingertips brushed red plastic. The TNT smell wrinkled my nostrils. I yowled with frustration. I couldn't quite grab it. The bundle lay just beyond my reach.

I burst into tears of fury. Six inches to detonation! And there was absolutely no way for me to escape in time. That charge was going to blow in my face.

Desperation inspired one last frenzied effort. Grabbing a rectangular chunk of granite, I slammed it against the flinty shelf supporting the dynamite. Fragments trickled down the chimney wall. Mightily encouraged, I hammered away like a demented carpenter. The adrenaline rush soothed the ache in both arms. *Hit it again, Angie. Harder! Pretend it's that bastard Simms. Again—again—again!*

All at once, the ledge gave way in a shower of pebbly shrapnel. The dynamite landed at my feet.

356

Frantically I scooped it up, then gaped in horror at that last burning inch of primacord.

I bit down hard, catching the smoldering fuse between my molars. Heard the soft hiss as it encountered saliva. Yowled as the blaze seared my gums. Grimacing at the burn, I twisted my head to the right and extracted the blasting cap.

I wasn't out of the woods yet, though. That fuse was still burning. Even by itself, the average blasting cap has the explosive kick of a hand grenade. I let the dynamite drop and I spat the blasting cap into my hands, hurled myself to the ground, and stubbed out the fuse in the gritty sand.

A faint wisp curled upward from the blackened tip. A half-inch of white cord peeped out of the cap. Groaning in sheer relief, I rested my face against my forearm, then collapsed.

I came very close to fainting, indeed I did, but an insistent inner voice reminded me that he was still out there—Dennis Simms—and that he was still armed with that Weatherby rifle and Ty's .357 Magnum. He would be listening for the explosion. And when he didn't hear it . . .

Still groaning, I crawled into an upright sitting position, Then I groped for one of the sharp flint fragments I'd knocked from the ledge. Okay, so it wasn't exactly a knife. But my Anishinabe ancestors got along quite well for thousands of years using stones just like it.

And so, using my ancestors' favorite cutting tool, I sawed away at that miracle of twentieth century chemistry—nylon. I cursed Dupont under my breath. Damn! I ran the flint's keen edge back and forth. My pantyhose pops a run after one or two days. And I couldn't even cleave a strand on this cord!

At any second, I expected to feel the Weatherby's muzzle on the back of my neck, punctuated by Dennis's amused whisper, *"Don't bother, Sara."*

But perhaps my luck was beginning to turn. I sawed away diligently, grinning as those synthetic strands parted one at a time. I heard no footsteps on the trail, no rustling of aspen branches, no squawk and wing-flutter of disturbed birds. Just my own labored breathing and the soft whisper of flint scraping nylon.

Dropping the stone, I grabbed the fraying line with both hands and pulled. It gave way with an audible pop. Hurriedly I unbound my ankles. The blood rush warmed my numb feet.

With the first step I took, I let out an agonized gasp and wound up on my hands and knees. Returning circulation made my ankles feel like barbecued steak. After a few minutes, I tried again, slowly hobbling downslope.

I remembered the hand radio I'd seen on Ty's gun-belt. A quick call for help, and then I'd be on my way to the nearest bolt-hole. Let the Utah Highway Patrol handle Dennis.

As I reached the slain deputy, I looked down in dismay at the radio's smashed plastic casing. That half-buried boulder had made short work of it. I heard a crow guffaw at the end of the meadow. Keeping my head down, I padded over to some upright boulders and peered around the stony flank of one.

Grim-featured Dennis Simms moved stealthily up the trail, travelling in the approved Benning style. Leaning forward, head low, eyes level, his rifle poised to shoot from the hip. He had the alarming habit of pausing every few moments to look and listen. He checked out every hiding place, no matter how small or trivial. No wonder the Army had made him an officer.

I saw Dennis stop short, then realized—much too late—that he had sensed me staring at him. His Stetson swiveled in my direction, and a tiny flame-wink appeared at the rifle's mouth.

Bweeeeowww! The stone beside my face exploded, peppering my skin with mica chips. Instantly I dropped behind cover, my heart pounding, wondering what to do next.

Terrific! I thought, crawling over to the deputy. Dennis knows I'm loose, and he knows I'm still up here. There's no cover uphill in the scree. And if I start downslope, he can easily pick me off. I'd never get out of rifle range in time.

An image of the blasting cap suddenly loomed in my mind.

Too bad Ty's not a smoker. With a cigarette lighter or a matchbook, I could ignite the fuse again and use the blasting cap as a makeshift hand grenade.

Sudden chuckle of inspiration. Since when does an Anishinabe princess need matches to make fire?

Kneeling, I grabbed Ty's steel handcuffs.

Dennis's voice drifted up the trail. "What happened, Sara?"

No time for repartee. Dashing across the meadow, I halted before an aging aspen and found a sliver of dry split bark and broke it off.

"Did the fuse go out? Well, I'll just have to string

another one, won't I?'' His voice sounded closer. ''How'd you get loose, honey?''

Ignoring his taunts, I ran to a venerable cedar tree. Its bark is the ideal kindling. I tucked the handcuffs in my waistband and gripped the aspen sliver with my teeth then plucked another sharp stone from the ground. Scraping the stone up and down, I shaved strips of bark from the cedar. Catching them in my free hand, I mentally apologized to both trees. *I owe you both some tobacco, my friends.*

''Not talking, eh? Smart girl! I think I'll do it a little different this time.'' Ominous *click-chock* of the Weatherby's bolt. ''I'm going to shut you up for good *before* I lay that fuse!''

Running at top speed, I headed for the cliff. Stop Number Four on Angie's impromptu scavenger hunt. Within seconds I had found my cozy niche, a dry mudhole surrounded on three sides by crumbling limestone boulders. Like a nervous squirrel, I cached my booty there, then went to retrieve the dynamite bundle.

''Don't make me come looking for you, gal.''

Sorry, Dennis, but that's exactly what you're going to have to do. I ripped dessicated stalks of grass from the turf.

Mocking laughter from Dennis. ''Come out, come out, wherever you are!''

Huddled in my hideaway, I poured my cedar shavings on a patch of dry earth. Then I painstakingly built a miniature teepee with the brittle stalks, ensuring good ventilation. A fire needs to breathe, you know.

''You're pissing me off, Miss Sara.''

Really? Gosh, Dennis, perhaps I ought to run back to town, grab a violin, and play some old sad songs. Just wait right here for me . . .

Gripping the handcuffs, I peered around the edge of the boulder. Dennis was advancing along the base of the cliff, hatbrim back, cradling the Weatherby in both hands. His index finger rested lightly on the trigger.

I ducked out of sight and reached for a chunk of flint. *Do it now, Angie. Now! Before he comes close enough to hear the clink of flint against steel.*

"You are really asking for it, Soyazhe." Deadly chuckle. "I think I'm going to have a little fun with you *first.*"

My left hand held the cuffs side by side. Taking a deep breath, I lifted the flint high.

"Going to show you what you've been missing, little gal."

Snick! A shower of sparks pelted my grass teepee. Every one of them fizzled out.

Smug laughter. "Miss Gail never had any complaints."

I struck again. Sparks cascaded downward.

Nothing!

And again. More sparks. Like fireflies, they all winked out.

The lawyer's voice sounded awfully close. "Are you waiting for someone to save you, Sara?" Tigerish laughter. "You little fool! Nobody even knows you're up here."

Again and again. The kindling refused to catch.

"There's no white knight riding to the rescue this time, Sara."

Hand shaking, I raised the stone. Dennis was so close now he was bound to hear it. But I had no other choice.

I struck hard.

Clink! Most of the sparks bounced off the teepee. But a few got in, and one of them began to smolder.

I heard the sudden sharp intake of Simms's breath. He was less than eight feet away, looking up into the rocks. He'd heard the strike.

I froze instantly, not even daring to breathe.

But Dennis was playing it cautious. "You up there, Sara?"

Actually, I was on my hands and knees, softly blowing into the teepee. A faint wisp of smoke spiralled upward from the shavings. A tiny orange flame appeared.

"Dammit, answer me!"

Flames rapidly consumed the stalks. No problem, though. I had no need of a long-lasting fire. Just one hot enough to ignite my sliver of aspen bark.

KAAAAAROWWWWW!

I flinched all over at the gunshot, but I realized that Dennis was only trying to spook me. He thought I was further up in the jumble of rocks and boulders. Heat bathed my face as I leaned over the fire. My fingers stuck the aspen in the flame.

"Bitch!" His footsteps came through loud and clear as he passed by my hideout. "Where the hell are you?"

I pulled the bark sliver away from my dying fire. A bluish-white flame sputtered to life. I turned the sliver over and over, letting it catch fire on both sides. Fierce grin of satisfaction. Perfect!

Groping for the blasting cap, I thought back to all those childhood weekends up at Tettegouche. I had learned a lot from my grandfather. Such as the fact that the aspen—like its cousin, the birch—secretes an oil, a flammable fluid that turns any piece of bark into a ready-made candle.

I figured on five minutes of burn time before it sputtered out. Staring at the blasting cap, I hesitated.

Sure, Angie, it'll go off like a small grenade. But what if you miss? What if the blast doesn't disable him? This is the only weapon you have. And Dennis has two guns.

My gaze zeroed in on the dynamite bundle.

So maybe I throw just one stick. That ought to do it, right?

The blasting cap seemed to glower at me. *You know how to prime a single stick for detonation?*

No! I thought, picking up the taped charge. I wasn't even sure I could set this batch off. All I can do is mimic Dennis, put this cap exactly where I found it, relight the fuse, and hope for the best.

Trembling all over, I stuffed the blasting cap back into the dynamite bundle.

If this doesn't work, I'm dead!

Flaming aspen in one hand, dynamite charge in the other, I squatted behind my boulder. Easing upward a few inches, I peeped over the rim.

And there was Dennis, showing me the broad back of his denim jacket. His keen dark eyes scanned the cliff's fissured face. The Weatherby's barrel moved back and forth, ready to fire.

Decision time! If I threw it, I would most certainly kill him. If I hesitated any longer Dennis would soon walk out of throwing range. I might not be able to elude him when he came this way again.

Features grim, I waved the flaming aspen sliver beneath the blackened fuse. Primacord sizzled and sputtered. I nearly dropped the bundle when I heard that hideously familiar hiss. Knees quaking, I reared upward, holding the charge aloft. Quarterback Angie going for a long one.

Dennis's peripheral vision was astounding. He saw me pop up and reacted instantaneously, twisting violently to his left, levelling the rifle, squeezing off a shot.

KAAAAAROWWWWW!

A furious hornet tore through my hair, the heat of its passage scorching my scalp. Even as I hurled the dynamite, I was reacting to the shot, leaping backward, badly startled by the near miss. Panic added oomph to my throw. The explosive charge spiralled through the air.

Then my moccasin sole slipped on a patch of moist mud, and down I went. Even as I toppled, I heard it thump the ground, followed by Dennis's horrified shout. "Oh, no—*no!*"

BAH-ROOOOOM!

Before I even hit the ground, a searing wind came pouring over the boulders and carried me off into oblivion.

Long, long time in utter darkness. Deep, velvety, impenetrable darkness. I mean, the really *opaque* kind! No thoughts at all. Another glacier could have started down Lodestone Canyon again, and I wouldn't have known about it. Or cared.

And then, in some strange and inexplicable way, I gradually became aware of my immediate environment. It wasn't exactly knowledge. It was more like a jumble of momentary impressions. The clean, crisp feel of newly-laundered percale. The low humming of an air conditioner. The subtle scent of medication.

My head felt as though it were stuffed with wet cotton. Thoroughly enmeshed in darkness, I struggled to pull cogent thoughts together. And then a vaguely familiar masculine voice whispered, *"Noozis?"*

The voice conjured up a flurry of vivid scenes. Sturdy hand-built Alpine cabin on a forested ridge. Gray seas crashing on a rugged rhyolite shore. Kindly, blunt-featured man pushing the ferns aside, revealing the decaying maple log and the wing-beating ruffed grouse.

"Noozis, can you hear me?"

A warm, broad palm touched my forehead. Uttering a feeble groan, I struggled to pry my eyes open. The lids went up like Broadway curtains, slowly and majestically. Took a few seconds for my vision to swim into focus. My grandfather's anxious face peered down at me.

"N-N-Nimishoo?" I murmured.

Then a feminine voice said something in a strange language. Took me a second before I recognized it as English. Shifting my gaze to the right, I saw a brunette, middle-aged nurse standing in front of a night-darkened window. "She's awake," she told my grandfather. "I'd better find Doctor McCracken."

My glance roamed the pastel blue room, taking note of the overhead TV, the computerized monitors, the night table, the I.V. stand and the call button. I felt a tickle on my right wrist. Lifting that hand, I read the plastic identification tag.

It was most reassuring to see the name *Sara Soyazhe* and my address in Clover Creek.

In our language, Chief asked, "How do you feel, *Noozis?*"

"Awful!" I pursed my lips painfully. "Wh-Where am I?"

"Logan. The Highway Patrol flew you in by helicopter."

My throat felt parched. "When?"

"Twelve hours ago. It's three a.m." Chief's anxious expression gave way to one of intense curiosity. "What happened up there?"

"Long story, *Nimishoo.*"

"You better give me the Reader's Digest version then, 'cause that nurse won't be gone for long."

So I told him. And, believe me, that grandfather of mine had much difficulty maintaining his composure.

"Of all the *stupid—!*" he snapped, keeping his voice down. "Fifteen sticks of dynamite! Pick it up and *throw* it!?" His face tensed in exasperation. *"Noozis,* don't you *ever* use your head? Why do you think Simms played out such a long fuse?"

"Look, what do I know about explosives!?"

"It's a damned good thing you fell down. Those rocks shielded you from the brunt of the blast. Otherwise, you'd look just like—"

366

Chief cut himself short, displaying a sickish expression.

"Simms?" I murmured. "How bad . . . ?"

He sat beside me on the bed. Gentle sigh. "I saw worse on Okinawa."

Showing a feeble smile, I reached for his hand. "How'd you find me?"

Modest shrug. "Nuche people came to the motel and told me about you and Braddock. I figured he took you up to Dynamite Pass. You know, scene of the crime and all that."

Surprised Angie blink. "And you tracked us up that mountain?"

"Are you kidding?" For the first time that night, my grandfather cracked a smile. "That fat-assed deputy left a trail Ray Charles could have followed."

Chief explained how he'd heard the explosion and rushed to the scene and found me half-buried in blast debris. He'd dug me out, checked for major injuries, and then carried me fifty yards downslope. Hearing the approach of the helicopter, he'd taken to the woods and emerged a short time later, as if he were just arriving. My grandfather, the interested civilian. He's the one who identified me as *Sara Soyazhe*.

"Three men dead up there." Chief's face turned somber. "The law's going to want to talk to you, missy."

"Oh, let them!" Fatigued sigh. "No sense both of us hanging around to face the music." I gave him Mickey Grantz's telephone number in Salt Lake. "Give him an anonymous tipoff, *Nimishoo*. Tell him where he can find Simms's chainsaw. Then take off."

"And you, *Noozis?*"

Brave but rueful smile. "I'll think of something."

Just then, the brunette nurse returned with a lanky, red-haired physician. He seemed quite surprised to see me awake.

Turning my way, Chief whispered, "I'll be in Heber for a day or two. Join me . . . if you can."

"You could head straight for Duluth."

"I could." He stood slowly. "But there are photos of you and me at the house. I'd better remove them *before* the law pays that call on Matt and Della."

Good old Chief. Always thinking of my best interests. What a grandfather! Honestly, I wish every woman had one.

Doctor McCracken looked me over thoroughly, ran me through that silly routine with the penlight and the moving fingertip, and then confidently announced that I had suffered a major contusion on the back of my head.

I could have told him that!

Well, I wanted to sleep, but the doctor wasn't quite sure if I'd sustained a concussion or not. So, just to be on the safe side, he advised me to remain awake, and ordered Nurse Edith Spangler to sit up with me.

Turned out for the best, too. Chatting with Edith, I was able to concoct a plausible explanation for my presence on the mountain. I did some minor editing after she left for her 5 a.m. rounds. And when the Logan sheriff arrived three hours later, I had it all down pat.

Well, you see, sheriff, it's like this . . . there I was, hiking up by Dynamite Pass, when I heard these two men arguing. Deputy Braddock and Dennis Simms. Braddock said he'd been investigating the disappearance of his good friend, Jack Sunawavi. He knew Simms had been the last person to see Jack alive . . .

I made Ty Braddock sound like the greatest detective since Sherlock Holmes. I had him finding the tobacco pouch, visiting Jack's mother, unearthing Billy's scheme, figuring out how it would have ruined Simms. I told how I'd seen the deputy accuse Simms of both murders—how Dennis had grabbed the rifle and fired point-blank. Plainly distraught, I described my own unsuccessful attempt to slip away after the shooting. Explained how Dennis had caught me and slugged me with the rifle butt.

Explosion? What explosion, sheriff? Simms told me I knew too much. Then something cracked me on the head, and I woke up here.

As those grim-faced lawmen filed out, I listened to their muttered comments.

". . . that explains what Braddock was doing there."

". . . coroner says Sunawavi's been up there for days."

"Simms must have crimped the charge all wrong."

"Right! The charge blew up in his hands."

They'd be back, of course. But in the meantime I'd given them plenty of testimony to weigh. Much of it was supported by the evidence, too—by the tobacco pouch in Dennis's pocket and the chainsaw and Jack's black leather vest.

369

There was one gaping loose end, however. And *he* turned up at the hospital that afternoon, waving a copy of the *Logan Herald-Journal*.

"What the hell is goin' on, Sara?" They probably heard Cue down in Salt Lake. "I got newspapermen parked on my porch. Ever'body wants a damned comment. Denny's dead, and so's that there deputy." He tossed the newspaper on my coverlet. "You got a heap of explainin' to do, little gal!"

Wry Angie smile. "Hello, Mr. Broward. Yes, I'm coming along just fine, thank you."

"I want answers, Sara! Just what are you 'n' that shyster son of a bitch tryin' to pull?"

"Whatever do you mean?"

"I mean . . ." Cue's blue eyes sizzled, ". . . I had me a little talk with the bank president. He tells me there's only five thousand dollars in the South Promontory account. Where's the rest of it, Sara!?"

I looked away. Not out of shame or remorse, mind you, but because I had just about had it with this braying ex-cowpuncher, this small-town power broker whose boundless appetite for corruption had contributed in part to my cousin's death.

"Well?" he thundered.

Facing him once more, I displayed a pleasant grin. "Basically, it's what's known as a Goat Pasture, Cue. The idea is to get the mark to invest his money in a worthless piece of land. Our deal was a variation on the theme—exchange good land for worthless land."

He blinked at me as if he couldn't quite believe what I was saying. "Worthless? But the *oil—!*"

"There's no oil in that arroyo, Cue. Ooops, let me

amend that—no oil except the gallon I poured on the ground. But don't tell the EPA."

"My *money!*" Cue's face turned the color of a Wasatch mountaintop in January. "Seventy *thousand—!*"

"Are you familiar with the word . . . *gonzo!?*"

The rancher made inarticulate sounds of rage.

"Thanks to you, Mr. Broward, Lodestone Canyon is now under the Bureau of Indian Affairs. Which means that one-of-a-kind aspen forest is going to die a natural death centuries from now. The tribal council will take good care of that canyon. Bet on it!"

Reddening in fury, he sputtered, "Is *that* what this is all about!?"

"You've got it, pard." Brilliant Angie smile. "Lodestone Canyon . . . you just gave it back to the Indians."

Seeing his enraged expression, I slid over to the far side of the mattress. "Look, Broward, we stole it fair and square . . . just like you white men."

"Get out of that bed!" Cue bellowed, clutching his belt buckle. "I'm taking that seventy thousand right offa your Injun hide!"

I didn't even have to hit the call button. Cue's yelling brought hospital security on the run. Two burly men in evergreen smocks pulled him away from my bed. As the nurse stepped between us, I faked out Cue and made a mad dash to the bathroom.

Turning the lock, I heard his fists pummelling the door.

"Dammit, Soyazhe, I'll hang that Ute hide o' yours on a fence!"

371

Leaning against the porcelain sink, I prayed that the door would hold.

"You're goin' to jail!" he shouted. "You hear me, gal!?"

"So are you and Alfie!" I teased. "Hey, maybe the three of us could start a club. Prison Pen Pals. I'll be down in Draper, and you'll be . . . say, where do you suppose Uncle Sam will send you, Cue? Leavenworth, I hope!"

The bathroom door rocked on its hinges. "Little Injun bitch!"

"You're a sore loser, Broward. Just like your daughter. I knew it all along."

Masculine voices sounded on the other side of the door, followed by the clamor of a brief tussle. Cue's bellowing receded into the distance. The nurse knocked on the door and advised me that it was safe to come out.

So I did, and I spent a highly enjoyable fifteen minutes at the window sill, peering down into the hospital parking lot and watching a maniacal Cue Broward harangue the staff. He jumped up and down, kicked a Buick's fender, and then shook his fist at my window.

Flashing a sweet Angie smile, I waved right back.

Enjoy the laughs while you can, princess. There'll be precious few of them at the state penitentiary. The state of Utah does not look lightly upon grand larceny—even when it's for such a noble cause.

The smile faded from my face, and I went back to bed. I snuggled against those two spongy pillows, and wondered what the state women's prison was like. Wondered what Paul Holbrook would say. I took a small measure of solace in the fact that my grandfather had gotten clean away.

I must have fallen asleep sometime in the late afternoon, because the next thing I knew, the hospital room was in darkness, and there was a bright light shining in my face. Shading my eyes with my left hand, I blinked rapidly and peered up at two slender females in nurse's caps. My mouth was sticky with the aftermath of sleep. Swallowing hard, I tried to speak. "Hmmmmm . . . wh-wha'?"

The nurses moved into the circle of light. Freshfaced blondes, both of them. Nineteen or twenty. Hair pinned back, peaked white caps, and halter-style aprons in alternating pink and white stripes. The one on the left held a stack of bath towels in front of her.

"Sara?" the other candystriper whispered. "Sara Soyazhe?"

"Mmmmm—yeah?" Still sleep-dazed, I fumbled to raise myself on one elbow.

"Come on, Sara. Time for your shower."

"I—I don't need a shower. Why don't you just let me go back to sleep?"

"Hospital rules," the towel-toter added. "And we've, uh, we have to change the bed. Right, Bets?"

"Right, Tracy."

I kicked off the coverlet and swung my legs over the side of the bed. The nurses hovered impatiently. Like a sleepy toddler, I trudged across the room. The air conditioner painted a chilly stripe across my bare backside that roused me in a hurry. Hospital jonnies are no protection against sudden gusts.

As I reached for the doorlatch, Betsy and Tracy

broke into a giggling fit, seized my arms, and hustled me into the bathroom.

"Hey!" I gasped. "What are you doing?"

"Sssssssh—quiet!" Tracy peered through the slender opening between door and jamb, then closed it all the way. Turning the lock, she whispered, "You want to get out of here?"

I blinked in amazement.

"Mick sent us. We're with the Tribe of DAN." Betsy presented her stack of towels. "There's a state trooper guarding the lobby. But we can leave with everyone else when the shift changes at eleven."

Brushing the front of my jonny, I said, "Thanks, hon, but I'm not exactly dressed—"

"Mick took care of it." Grinning, Betsy lifted the top towel, revealing a neatly folded nurse's uniform. "Size six, right?"

How very thoughtful of you, Mr. Grantz. And what an eye for a lady's figure, too!

Sunday, September sixth, found me back home in the Northland, huffing and puffing as I jogged down a moist forest trail in Tettegouche State Park. And a lovely day for running it was, too. Bright sunshine and horsetail clouds scudding high over Lake Superior. Birch and aspen rustling in the soft breeze. Nightly chills were transforming the maples, tinting the hillsides with scarlet and gold. My Reeboks pounded along the narrow pathway, past the nodding grass stalks and the ox-eyed daisies, still abloom. Smiling Anishinabe princess in her gray bike shorts and purple leotard and matching ballcap.

I'd been in Minnesota just about a week, ever since Tracy and Bets had given me that lift to Denver. From there, I caught a Northwest flight to Minneapolis and an air shuttle home.

I spied the DNR map box just ahead and knew I was nearing that familiar marsh just off Lax Lake Road. Veering to the right, I headed straight for Pikwakon Ridge. The steep roof of Chief's Alpine cabin loomed above the trees. The sight sent a fresh surge of energy into my weary legs. It's a long five miles to Shovel Point, you know, and the return trip is mostly uphill.

Jogging up our rutted driveway, I saw my grandfather emerging from his trusty Bronco pickup.

"Tayaa!" Chief shouted, lifting a bulky manila envelope. "What are you doing, Angie? Don't you have to pack?"

I bounded to a halt right in front of him. Breathless wheeze. "I'm packed." I stretched backward for a second or two, then took a thankful bow and planted my palms on my knees. Long, deep breaths. Sidelong grin. "Just saying goodbye to Tettegouche. Much as I hate to."

"Paul's going to be looking for you at the restaurant tomorrow."

"Please, Chief, don't remind me." Rotating my shoulders, I asked, "What's that?"

"Mail call. I took a peek at our post office box while I was down in Silver Bay." He handed me the package. "For you—it's from Della."

Intrigued, I tore it open, then extracted a folded newspaper. Snapping it open, I spied the masthead of the *Logan Herald-Journal*. A three-column headline captured my glance.

SAGUACHE COUNTY DEATHS RULED HOMICIDE

Clover Creek, Utah (AP) — The grand jury delivered a verdict of homicide yesterday in the recent deaths of two Saguache County men.

After reviewing the evidence, the jury announced that William M. Shavano, 29, of Clover Creek and John Sunawavi, 32, of Cottonwood had indeed been killed by attorney Dennis Simms.

Simms himself perished last week in an explosion near Dynamite Pass after slaying Deputy T.P. Braddock, who had been investigating the mysterious deaths.

Further down the page was a story of equal interest.

GOVERNMENT WILL SEEK INDICTMENTS

Salt Lake City (AP) — U.S. Attorney Thomas C. Hammond announced today that the Justice Department would seek indictments against private loggers involved in the Lodestone Canyon scandal.

Hammond said Karl F. Eames, a prominent Clover Creek lumberman, had agreed to turn state's evidence and testify for the prosecution.

Facing indictment are Henry T. Broward, the wealthy Saguache County rancher, and Alfred J. Longhurst, the Forest Service district supervisor.

At the bottom of the page was a paragraph circled in red ink.

Meanwhile, the search continues for Sara Soyazhe, the young Ogden woman alleged to have stolen $70,000 from Broward in a flimflam scheme.

Beside this paragraph, in my aunt's bold handwriting, was a brief personal message.

Young lady, we have to talk!!!

Reading it over my shoulder, Chief said, "Maybe you'd better give her a call when you get back to Pierre."

Showing a sickly smile, I refolded the newspaper. "On the other hand, maybe it'd be better if I gave her a few days to simmer down."

Chief cast me a severe look. "I warned you, miss. You should have told Della *everything* before we saw them off."

"Come *on*, Chief! My ears were ringing enough as it was."

"You've got to talk to her sometime."

"Listen, November will be here before we know it."

"She has the number of that halfway house in Pierre."

"She *does?*" My expression was a blend of alarm and indignation. "Well, who gave her *that?*"

"I did," he said calmly. "You know how Della worries about you. And she hates it whenever you lie to her."

"It wasn't a lie, Chief. It was an omission. There *is* a difference." I tossed the folded newspaper through the open window of his truck. "That woman's temper isn't exactly improving with age, you know."

"Neither is yours," he observed wryly. "What are you so testy about?"

Leaning against the truck door, I crossed my legs at the ankle. "I don't know." Heartfelt sigh. "Just wondering what we accomplished out there, I guess."

Chief touched my shoulder gently. "We found the man who stole Billy from us, and he has been justly punished. That's something."

"But Billy is still dead," I replied, meeting my grandfather's sympathetic gaze. "And he's going to be dead for a long, long time."

"As will we all, child. As will we all."

I spread my hands helplessly. "I . . . I can't help feeling it isn't enough. There's still this gaping hole in my life."

"In everybody's life. Della has lost her son. I, my grandson. You, a brother." His blunt fingertips lifted my chin. "It's sort of like the aspen tree, Angie. The tree doesn't live, die, and live again. It lives, dies, and is no more, leaving only the memory of its glistening leaves. Billy is gone from us. And all that's left for us—are the memories."

"I can't help it, Chief. I keep feeling there's more we could have done . . . more we could do. But what else is there?"

Chief tilted his head at the forest. "We can do what we haven't yet done. Say goodbye to him . . . our way."

Blinking away the tears, I showed him a poignant smile. "I'll get the tobacco."

And so, on a high, windswept granite ridge, overlooking the placid blue lozenge of Lax Lake and the evergreen slopes of the Sawtooth Mountains, we built Billy's memorial *waginogan,* my grandfather and I, and kindled the sacred fire.

And while I danced a solemn lament, my grandfather stood before the crackling fire and sang our people's age-old prayer song.

"K'neekaunissinaun, ani maudjauh.
K'neekaunissinaun, cheeby meekunnaung."

Our brother, he is leaving, I thought, kneeling before the fire. Tears ran down my face as I slowly lifted my hands. Our brother, on the Path of Souls.

I made a bowl of my upraised palms, and Chief circled the fire, loosening the thong on his tobacco pouch. With a solemn nod, he filled my cupped hands.

Voice breaking, I said, "We grieve that you cannot remain with us. But it is the will of *Kitchi Manitou.* Each man, each woman, is allotted a span of time and a quantity of good to fulfill. And although we may regard your span of life as all too brief, the good that you performed was more than that expected of any man."

I poured the shredded tobacco into the flames.

"Have a safe journey, my brother."

Bluish-gray smoke billowed upward from the fire. The breeze caught it, pushing it far beyond the cliff's edge. I watched it spiral through the skies above Lax

Lake, heading for the unbroken forest on the western
horizon.

Heading for Utah.

"MIND-BOGGLING . . . THE SUSPENSE IS UNBEARABLE . . .
DORIS MILES DISNEY WILL KEEP YOU
ON THE EDGE OF YOUR SEAT . . ."

THE MYSTERIES OF DORIS MILES DISNEY